ARCHANGEL

DAW novels by Margaret Fortune

The Spectre War:

NOVA
ARCHANGEL

PHASE ONE

Admiral. Together they formed the three cornerstones upon which the entire Celestial Expanse now rested. And not just the Expanse, but—

The human race.

The Chairman made an impatient noise, and with a deferent nod, the Admiral indicated the planet over her shoulder. "Gentlemen, this footage was taken just hours ago from deep within Tellurian territory. No doubt you recognize the site."

Both men nodded. As the other major power within the inhabited universe, the Tellurian Alliance had been both ally and enemy in turn throughout history, its vast array of colonies and planets united under the rule of this one world on the screen before them. Just a few short years ago, the Alliance had been as mighty as the Expanse, a rival to be reckoned with. But that was before.

"Strange," the Doctor murmured. "Even after the invasion, it still looks exactly the same. The ships are gone, of course, but the planet itself—"

"Yes, of course. We've all seen this before," the Chairman interrupted, his modulated tones like oily serpents twining around one another in an endless spiral. "That hardly explains why we're here, though. Perhaps you would care to elaborate?"

The Admiral shrugged a shoulder. "Watch."

With a flick of her chit hand, she forwarded the footage, speeding the feed so that hours passed within minutes, minutes within seconds. Together the three watched in perfect silence as the day faded away before them, the sun setting over the edge of the world to let night fall across in its place. The footage continued to run, everything still but for the moving image on the wall. At last the Chairman shook his head.

"It's so dark. Shouldn't we be seeing the city lights by now? We're over the western edge of the Pacific. That's Tokyo, Jakarta, Seoul—"

"That's what I'm trying to tell you, gentlemen," the Admiral said, pausing the feed on the planet below. She bowed her head—in prayer, in mourning, or perhaps simply in thought—eyes only for that dark expanse before them.

"All the lights have finally gone out . . . because there's no one left to turn them on."

Onboard the *CES Retribution*
Flagship of the First Admiral of the Celestial Fleet

THE PLANET FILLED THE VIEWSCREEN, *a spark of brilliance in swirls of blue and white. It shone like a jewel within its corona of light and air, its recorded beauty reflecting off the cold, hard metal of desk, chair, charts, and viewport. From her position beside the swirling feed, the First Intergalactic Admiral of the Celestial Fleet folded her arms as two images appeared on the digitized wall opposite her.*

"Admiral," the Chairman greeted from the first frame, his tall form materializing against the background of a sumptuous office, all leather and hardwood and wine-dark upholstery. A member of the Expanse's small oligarchy, the Board of Directors, and its true ruler in all but name, he had the commanding air of a man used to obedience. His high-collared suit, a tailored affair in the patriotic gold-trimmed black of the Expanse, bore the patterned half-star marking him a member of PsyCorp.

In another frame to his right, a second man emerged against the backdrop of an orbital laboratory, slender and white-haired. Another leader of men, though in a very different way. The Doctor nodded in greeting, his frost-blue eyes vaguely disapproving.

Though when were they ever not? *the Admiral thought acidly.*

She surveyed the group with an arched brow. Chairman. Doctor.

1

"GO, GO! C'MON, people! Let's move it!"

Footsteps pound against the hard metal decking, and I stop to wave a couple of scientists on. "Pick it up, everyone!" I exhort them once more. "The docking bay is still half a station away!"

At the back of the group, Madison shepherds the stragglers while ahead Tabs leads, aero-launcher at the ready as she keeps her nose alert for any scent of the enemy. Her pace, no more than a light jog for me, might as well be an out-and-out sprint for the civilian scientists cordoned between us. Already several are gasping, clearly out of breath though we've hardly covered half a klick, and I can see the pace starting to lag. Some of the greatest minds of the century they might be, but these people are no athletes. Nor are they exactly spring chickens.

We reach the end of the hallway, and Tabs pauses to unlock the door. I jog in place as she slaps the universal de-keyer on the lock. One of the squatters managed to trigger the station locks, securing every door in the place at once. Tabs can get through it with her device; it's just a question of how long it will take.

And who might catch up with us in the meantime.

I scan my eyes back over the hallway behind us, though I know it won't do any good. Our enemy can't be seen, can't be touched, can't be heard. Like terrible ghosts, the Spectres are incorporeal, aliens with the power to take any human being as a host. And once they bond with a human to become a squatter, there's no way to get them out.

Short of killing the host, that is. Talk about one hell of a cure.

"Corporal?" I ask through my helmet mic.

"*Working on it, Sorenson,*" Tabs answers. "*Madison, how are the civvies doing?*"

"*Holding up so far.*"

"*Good! Sorenson, keep an eye on the fences for me.*"

"On it."

I key the map display on my helmet, scanning the projection on the left side of my face shield as it enlarges. A miniature layout of the station appears before me, red dots indicating the positions of all the force fences in the habitat. Over half of them are blinking, a sign that they've been triggered by ghouls—Spectres that haven't bonded with a human yet. I count the number of intact fences between us and them.

"Four fences," I bark tersely into the mic, then take a deep breath. Four—that's good. We could still make it. As I watch, the farthest one begins blinking. *Slag.*

"Three fences, Corporal!"

"*I got it,*" she yells back as the door in front of us springs open. "*Take point, Sorenson. I'm going to clamp it in case any squatters are behind us.*"

I automatically shift to the head of the group as Tabs stays behind to secure the door. "Let's go, people! There're only three fences between you and infection. C'mon, move!"

I set an even tougher pace than Tabs did, but either the short rest or the threat of permanent enslavement did the trick, because everyone is up and running now. We sprint down the corridor, turn down another hallway, and come through an archway into the main courtyard.

Zipping around the tubs of trees and beds of flowers interspersing the room, I head for the exit at the far end. We're two-thirds of the way when several station security officers burst out of another entrance. They shine crimson in the setting light of the red dwarf star beaming through the high dome above us. *More escapees?* I wonder as I dodge a park bench on my line toward the exit.

A burst of light whizzes by my left ear as one of them shoots his pistol at me.

Nope.

Shoving my aero-launcher under my arm, I pull out my stun pistol and fire back. "Corporal, we've got squatters!"

"I see them!"

From over my shoulder, I see Tabs swing around from her position at the rear to cover us from the side while Madison covers us from the middle of the pack. Their pistols whine in short, sharp bursts as they exchange fire with our attackers. I see one squatter go down and can't help wincing. For all that this man is firing at us, he doesn't truly know what he's doing. No doubt the Spectre in his head has made him believe *we're* the infected ones. To shoot him is pitiable.

It doesn't make him—or his cronies—any less dangerous, though.

More shots ring out. A light starts blinking in the corner of my eye, but I ignore it, intent on herding my charges through the firefight to safety while Tabs and Madison lay down cover. A scientist just behind me lets out a cry as he's hit, clutching his shoulder as he starts to fall. Barely pausing, I heave him up against me, shielding him with my body as I pull him along.

Reaching the far archway, I usher him into the arms of two of his comrades on the other side. Then I'm running back out into the courtyard, waving the scientists on through the exit as I go back for the stragglers. A young woman is pinned behind a tree; she's more than happy to run for the door once a blast from my pistol takes down the shooter. A frightened lab tech is frozen behind a rose bush, unwilling to move until I haul him bodily out from his corner and drag him toward the archway. I only stop long enough to throw a shrieking blond doctor over my shoulder along the way.

Back inside the archway, I release my charges and lean back around the frame to lay cover fire for the final scientists. Madison's already here, doing emergency first aid on an injured civilian. As the final few crowd safely into the passageway, I use my helmet scan to take a quick headcount. Two, six, eleven, eighteen. Twenty-three.

Slag. We've lost one!

"Sorenson, Madison! Over there!"

I'm whirling around before Tabs finishes speaking. She's stationed about halfway across the courtyard, where she's taken refuge behind a park bench. Charring on her vest shows she's taken a couple of hits, but she's still in top form, picking off a squatter with an easy shot to the thigh. Her gaze meets mine as she throws a quick nod out across the floor. My eyes zero in on where she nodded, and I freeze. I've just found my missing scientist.

He must have gotten turned around in the confusion, for he's way past our side of the courtyard and into the squatters' area. Even from here, I can see the blood oozing through his smock as he lies unmoving on the floor.

"I see him, Tabs," I reply. "If I lay down cover, can you reach him?"

"Negative. There's too much open space between me and him."

She's right. There's not enough cover; with all the fire she's drawing, there's no way she'd be able to reach the injured man without getting gunned down herself. With Madison on first aid, that leaves me. Quickly, I assess the scene, then nod.

Jamming a fresh energy cartridge into my gun, I tell her, "I think I can get him. Just keep 'em busy, Tabs. Madison, cover these civvies at all cost."

"Will do."

"Affirmative."

A quick volley of bursts from my pistol sends the enemy ducking for cover, and then I'm running out into the courtyard. Darting from tree to bush to bench, I try to stay hidden as much as I can while my long strides eat up the floor. A couple of pistol blasts graze me, but I barely notice. I'm only about fifteen meters away when two squatters come down through the bushes just meters away from my target. Before I can take action, they move left, disappearing behind a stand of palms about halfway between me and them.

I swear softly. "Tabs, can you get those guys?"

A pause. *"Negative. They're using the gazebo as cover. I can't get the shot."*

I frown and blink my eyes four times fast. The infrared vision in my combat lenses snaps on, enabling me to pinpoint the squatters' locations through the small gaps in the tree trunks, but the palms themselves provide too much cover for me to get a shot in. Except for a small opening high up between the fronds, the tangle of trunks and foliage are like a wall. Between these new guys covering the left and a couple of snipers blocking the path toward the right, there's no way to reach the man without getting hit. I stare at the scene in consternation, unable to find a solution.

"*Sorenson, if you can't reach him, you can't reach him,*" Tabs's voice comes softly through the com after a minute. "*It's not like you can just fly through the trees.*"

Fly! Inspiration strikes me like a jolt of electricity as I remember my g-ball days. I grin. It's crazy. No, it's insane! But it might just work . . .

"Madison, can you access the station controls for the courtyard?" I ask through a private channel. At his affirmative, I explain my plan.

I can almost see him shaking his head through the mic. "*You're lunar, Sorenson, you know that?*"

"Yeah. Are you in?"

"*Just give me the word, man.*"

I grin crazily and switch back to the main channel. "Tabs, hang on to something!"

Before she can ask what I'm about, I grip my pistol tight and sprint straight for the palms. Shots fly out around me, but I'm moving fast and they don't even get close. Harder, faster . . . the trees are coming up now. I have to time it just right. Springing onto a park bench just in front of the trees, I yell, "Now, Madison!"

The artificial gravity goes off just as I push off the top edge of the bench. I fly up and over, the sudden weightlessness giving me the bounce I need to soar high. I spot the opening in the palm fronds, tuck into a ball, and somersault straight through the gap.

"*What the—!*"

My pistol is out and firing before the squatters, suddenly weightless and disoriented, even know what's hit them. They both go down, taken out at point-blank range with perfect shots to the torso and head. Untucking, I aim myself for the injured civilian. A half meter away, I yell, "Drop me, Madison!"

The gravity goes back on with a whir. My restored weight hits me like a ton of titanium rods, sending me to the floor. After years of playing grav-ball, the sensation doesn't even faze me. Instead I uncurl, landing in a crouch just in time to catch the civilian before he can hit the floor. The sudden impact almost knocks the wind out of me, but I manage to stay on my feet. Dragging him into the trees, I quickly slap cauterizing patches over his wounds. He's alive and breathing, at least. Madison could tell us more. I throw the man over my shoulder as carefully as I can.

"Tabs, I've got him!"

"Meet you by the fountain in thirty?"

"You got it."

Either Tabs and I managed to seriously thin down our attackers or they're all still disoriented by the gravity shifts, but no shots ring out as I run for the fountain. Tabs meets up with me, and together we make for the archway. As soon as we're through, I hand the injured man to Madison and make a jump for the overhead gate. All of my g-ball skills pay off as I catch the bottom edge in one leap. Tabs grabs the other side as it comes down, and together we slam the heavy gate to the floor. The latch engages with a click, and Tabs immediately pops a clamp onto it.

We grin, thumping our chests and knocking the sides of our fists in one quick movement.

Tabs nods. *"Pro libertate—"*

"*—pro vita,*" I finish.

For freedom, for life.

We knock fists again and jog to catch up with our charges, who have gathered at another locked door at the end of the hallway. Tabs immediately starts on the lock while I consult my map.

"Damn," I curse quietly. Almost three-quarters of the station's force fences are blinking now. The way to the West Shuttle Dock is still clear, but behind us is a different story.

"Corporal," I subvocalize into my mic. "We've only got one fence left."

Tabs's eyes flick to her own visor display, then to the gate we just shut. She lets out a frustrated curse, and I know she's thinking the same thing I am—that no door in the galaxy, no matter how thick, can stop a ghoul. Quickly, she turns back to the lock.

Nail-biting seconds pass before the door springs open. We're on the homestretch now; I can see the entrance to the docking bay just meters down the corridor. By unspoken agreement, we all pick up the pace, even the scientists. Though I know we're not out of the woods yet, I let out a sigh of relief as we pass through the last force fence into the shuttle bay.

"Hey, slowpokes. Where've you been?" a voice greets us as we enter the port.

Arlo, Cress, and Reyes are there, ushering a knot of civilians through the lock onto the transport. Between the three of them, they've managed to round up another thirty or so civilians.

Tabs winks at me and answers. "Oh, you know Sorenson. He insisted on taking the scenic route."

"Stopping to smell the genetically engineered flowers again, Mikey?" Arlo asks, flashing his trademark cheeky grin.

At one time, I might have responded in kind. Winked back, made a joke about our flight through the courtyard. Now I just acknowledge the comment with a gruff shake of my head and turn back to the bay entrance. Through the com, I can hear Tabs and Arlo quietly speaking.

"*What about Christo's triad?*"

"*Overrun.*" Arlo hesitates. "*They spaced themselves. Didn't want to end up hunting their own.*"

Or they didn't want to become tools of the ghouls. Though it's not unheard of for soldiers who have been infected to take their own lives, my chest still tightens at Arlo's report. Through the com, I hear Cress murmur something that sounds like a prayer, and I know she feels the same way.

"*What are your orders, Corporal?*" Arlo finally asks.

"*Just get those civvies loaded, Guardian,*" Tabs answers in a terse voice. With Christo gone, she's the ranking NCO in our squad.

A sudden *blink, blink, blink* on the side of my visor draws my attention back from the conversation. The second to last force fence, the one at the courtyard archway, is down. My hands tighten on the barrel of my aero-launcher at the realization that only the fence at the entrance to the bay remains between us and *them*. Not that the force fence is anything like a real fence, able to keep things in or out. It will provide a warning, nothing more.

Behind me all joking has ceased, everyone working frantically to get the civilians onto the transport in time. The last of Arlo's group is boarding now, their feet shuffling in time to shouts of "Move it!" and "Let's go!" I gauge the number of people left to board and shake my head. *We're not going to make it.*

Tabs is clearly thinking the same thing. *"Reyes, keep loading!"* she calls out on the group channel. *"Madison, you help him. Arlo and Cress, cover their six! Sorenson and I will take the door."*

Cress and Arlo immediately swing around to the back of the boarding civilians while Tabs and I creep up toward the bay entrance. We pause just inside, shoulder to shoulder, launchers at the ready. Sweat beads my forehead, and I resist the urge to shove up my visor and wipe it away. Flaring my nostrils, I take a deep breath. And that's when I smell it: a faint sour-and-sweet odor, like the scent of rotting lemon tinged with honey.

Tabs and I exchange a look. "They're coming."

Against my will, my eyes stray to the clock in the upper right corner of my visor. Sixty seconds. That's how long it will take the pilot to get the transport off this station once the shuttle door closes. Once we blast off, we can outrun the Spectres easily. But if the Specs catch up before we take off . . .

Like I said, no door in the galaxy can stop them.

The aroma is getting stronger. I can taste it now, a sour film lying over my tongue. Sweat is rolling into my eyes, drops beading and falling as quickly as they are created. I ignore it, fanning my nostrils as I use my nose—specially modified to smell out ghouls—to try and get a count. *Seven, possibly eight?*

"Eight or nine ghouls about two hundred meters out," Tabs is saying into her com. *"How long?"*

"Two minutes," Madison's voice snaps back.

"You and Reyes will board right behind the civilians, followed by Arlo and Cress. Sorenson and I will try to keep them out of the docking ring for as long as we can before bringing up the rear. Sorenson!"

"Ready!" I snap back. The smell is pulsing through my nose now, running furrows straight into my brain, though my eyes see nothing of our invisible enemy. Tabs was right—it's definitely nine. I can pick out their individual scents, they're so close. My shoulders tense. It won't be long now.

"*On my mark,*" Tabs says. "*Three.*"

I raise my launcher.

"*Two.*"

The stench is practically on top of us.

"*One . . .*"

My finger tightens around the trigger.

"*Mark!*"

Compressed air bursts from the end of my aero-launcher. The recoil rocks my shoulder back in its socket, and I immediately lock the next gas cartridge into place. I sniff frantically for the enemy. To my relief, my nose tells me they've retreated about fifteen meters. I allow myself a tight smile. The ghouls' sensitivity to air quality makes the mix of gases in these launchers one of the most potent weapons we have against them. One burst will repulse a ghoul for a full minute.

"*They're coming back for a second pass!*" Tabs yells.

Give or take thirty seconds.

"*Almost there!*" Reyes shouts through the com.

I raise my launcher to fire again, but just as I'm about to squeeze the trigger, the enemy scents suddenly disappear. My hands falter, head swinging wildly back and forth as I frantically smell for the enemy. *What the hell . . . ?*

Sour-and-sweet bursts in my nose as nine ghouls drop through the ceiling behind us. Sirens scream out as the ceiling fences trip, and I whirl around to face the new threat. *Frag!* They must have ducked into the maintenance level above to avoid the gas!

"Incoming!" I call as the Specs zoom through the bay straight toward the remaining civilians, but Arlo and Cress are already there, repelling the ghouls with simultaneous bursts from their launchers that send the enemy flying back into the center of the bay.

"*We need to keep them from jumping out of the bay and into that shuttle,*" Tabs orders. "*Madison, grenades!*"

Clouds of gas billow up around the airlock as Madison tosses down grenade after grenade, seeping up in a fledgling wall between the civilians and the enemy. Reyes adds his launcher to the mix, sweeping it across the lock, the ceiling, the entire back wall. Anywhere and everywhere the ghouls might think to go. Meanwhile, the rest of us fan out in a circle around the ghouls, sending off burst after burst over them, under them, around them, caging them into the center of the bay where they have no escape. It seems like we have the situation well in hand when, from the corridor behind me, a surge of sour wafts through the air, strong enough to bring tears to my eyes.

"*They've got reinforcements!*" Tab yells, clearly smelling the same thing. "*At least fifty, and they're coming in fast.*"

Slaggin' hell! Nine is manageable; fifty will overrun us.

"*The civilians are in!*" Reyes confirms, followed by Tabs's, "*Full retreat now!*"

Pumping another burst into our cage of air, I retreat back through the bay toward the transport, Tabs hot on my heels as we circle the knot of Specs trapped in the center. Arlo and Cress continue to shoot off burst after burst with their launchers, covering us as we make our way through the docking ring. The air is so thick with gas I can barely see two meters in front of me, but it seems to be working, keeping the ghouls back even as we sprint for the airlock doors. If we can just hold them off for one more minute, we might have a chance.

Reinforcements fly into the bay just as we catch up to the others where they stand guard at the entrance to the transport. At Tabs's signal, Madison and Reyes jog inside, followed closely by Cress and Arlo. She motions me in next, and I pause just inside, turning so that I can cover her with my launcher—

Just in time to see the hatch whisper shut.

My heart drops out of my chest. "Pilot!" I yell as I bang my fist on the door release. "You closed the door too soon! Tabs is still out there!" I hit the door control again, but nothing happens. "Pilot!"

"*It's okay, Michael.*" Tabs's voice glides through my headset over the sound of her aero-launcher.

No!

"*There's too many of them,*" she continues. "*We'll be overrun if someone doesn't stay behind to distract them. To keep 'em away from the shuttle. Sixty seconds, eh? I can buy us that.*"

No! No, no, no! Not again!

But it's too late. Just like another time and another place, *she's* on the other side of the door and I'm on this one. And just like then, *she's* going to die, and there's not a damn thing I can do about it.

Her sweetness, her smile; the scent of her hair, like the flowers that grew around the playground back on Aurora.

I hear a clang as the docking clamps release the shuttle, the hum as the engines begin firing up. Involuntarily, my eyes stray to the clock on my visor. Thirty-six seconds, thirty-five, thirty-four.

Was this what it was like for you at the end, Lia? I wonder as I watch the seconds slip away.

More bursts from Tabs's launcher sound, followed by a soft hiss. Her injector. The medicine inside will suppress the psionic powers of any ghoul that tries to bond with her—for about fifteen minutes, anyway. Just long enough to keep fighting. Just long enough to cover us while we get away.

Fourteen.

Thirteen.

Twelve.

I wait for Tabs to speak again, to put her last free words into the universe before she goes, but they never come. A fighter to the end, the last thing I hear is the whoosh of her launcher. Then with a roar, the transport takes off. I take one last good whiff.

Nothing. Tabs did her job.

Jogging to the observation port, I stare out at the hull that was once ScyLab 185g. Silvery metal embedded in a blanket of stars and pitch. A light in a world of darkness, where some five hundred people once lived and worked. People not much different from Tabs.

I can't smell the moment she becomes infected, way out here in space. I can't scent the second the odor of sixty ghouls suddenly becomes fifty-nine.

But I can imagine it.

2 WE DOCK WITH THE *CES TRIUMPHANT* only minutes later. Arlo and Cress search the crowd for any potential squatters we may have missed in the commotion while Madison, Reyes, and I prepare the civilians for debarking. Out of a station complement of 520, we managed to pull off fifty-three altogether. We can only hope the other squads did better.

My mind flashes to Evadne 6, now under quarantine. Half a dozen triads sent in, all lost within thirty minutes. No successful evacuees.

Fifty-three is better than zero.

I'm helping a small woman with a pistol graze stand when all the hairs on the back of my neck suddenly rise. I freeze, all senses on alert as I feel the unmistakable sensation of someone watching me. I take a couple of giant sniffs, immediately thinking of squatters. While the ghouls are easy to smell, the squatters are another matter. In the early days, we could smell them as easily as any ghoul, but over time they learned how to use their hosts' scents to mask their own. Now it's almost impossible to smell out a squatter. Over time, as the squatters slowly consume their hosts from the inside out in their quest to breed, the hosts will begin to show physical signs—weight loss, yellowing skin, sunken eyes—but that won't happen for months, maybe even a year or so down the line. Not exactly helpful with this batch of newly-made squatters. Until PsyCorp can clear each person individually with a psychic scan, we have to treat every person on board as a potential enemy waiting to strike. Any suspicious activity will be immediately noted, with the perpetrator marked out for further observation.

My nose scenting nothing, I ease my head to the left and then right, searching out of the corners of my eyes for the watcher. For some reason, my gaze falls on a man off to my left. He's standing perfectly still, dressed in a plain tunic and pants that are an exact match for his snowy hair. Though he isn't doing anything objectionable, isn't really doing anything at all other than waiting to debark, something about him makes me uneasy.

I activate my mic. "Potential squatter at three o'clock. An older man, all in white—" I search his clothes for a name badge or insignia. Spotting nothing, I finish quietly, "Medium height, slender build, white hair."

A pause, then—

"I see him," comes Cress's reply. *"I'll keep an eye on him."*

I nod. Squatters can be unpredictable when abruptly unmasked. Better to keep tabs on them until they can be pulled quietly aside for further examination. "Affirmative. Sorenson out."

Ushering the woman with the pistol graze to the front of the crowd, I continue separating out the injured. A lab tech in a gray coat bumps into me from behind, jostled in the crush, and I suddenly feel a hand stroking my butt. I jerk away, eyes wide and face burning as I realize I was just groped by a scientist three times my age. Trying to stay as professional as I possibly can, I quickly direct her to a spot along the wall before she can decide to get any friskier. And here I thought I'd seen everything there was to see in this job.

I move on to an engineer with an oozing cut on his head next, pausing long enough to slap a cauterizing patch on his forehead before sending him over to join the rest of the injured. Soon after, medical personnel arrive and take three people off on stretchers. I recognize one of the injured as the man I rescued in the courtyard. Is he even still alive at this point?

With a shrug, I push the question away. I don't know, and I don't care. I did my job. The rest is not my concern.

The ones with lesser injuries are taken off next. PsyCorp will scan them for squatters before sending them down to the medical bay. Once they're gone, it's time for the rest of us to disembark. My squad and I space ourselves out in the crowd, watching for any suspicious activity and keeping an eye on any we marked as potential squatters.

I come through the docking ring at the rear of the pack, giving an inward sigh as the continued silence of the force fence confirms what my nose already told me—no ghouls. Passing through a short corridor, I follow the civvies into a medium-sized cargo bay where everyone will wait until they can be taken to PsyCorp to be cleared. Soldiers line the walls, pistols gripped loosely in hand as they stand guard over the crowd.

One of the soldiers nods at me as I pass. "Sorenson."

I nod back. "Anders. How's it looking?"

"So far, so good." His hand tightens on his gun. It's a stun pistol only, completely nonlethal. After all, everyone knows what happens if you kill a squatter. Still, it's clear his nerves are getting to him.

"Easy does it, Anders," I tell him. "It'll be over soon."

He nods, but his grip doesn't relax. I shake my head slightly but don't say anything else. I was a rookie too, not so long ago. I know too well that the anticipation of waiting for something to happen is almost worse than it actually happening.

Pushing farther into the room, I take up a position near the white-haired man I marked earlier. His hand is by his cheek as he speaks quietly into the chit stapled into his palm. I lean closer, trying to catch what he's saying, but I'm too far away. I wonder who he could possibly be linking at a time like this. Is he a squatter, secretly trying to communicate with his buddies in a last ditch effort before he's caught?

Great, now I'm coming up with conspiracy theories! I roll my eyes at my own paranoia. Well, whatever he is or isn't, something about him doesn't feel right to me. His furtive manner, maybe, or perhaps it's the uniform, devoid of any insignia or badge or anything else to mark him out. All I know is I'll feel a lot better once he's been taken to PsyCorp.

I stay attentive as the guards continue to take people away one by one for testing. Forty civilians, thirty-nine, thirty-eight.

My fingers twitch as the number drops further, and before I know it we're down to twenty-five. If any squatters are going to make a move, they'll have to do it soon. I keep my eyes on the room, looking for any suspicious movement, while a couple meters to my right, two officers speak in low voices about the evacuation.

"—without the official numbers yet, it's already clear the evacuation rate for this station is far below our usual percentage."

"That's hardly our fault, though," the second one objects. "This ScyLab wasn't even on the long list of probable targets, let alone the short one. It's like the enemy skipped over a hundred more likely targets in order to hit this one. That we were able to mobilize quickly enough to evacuate even a small percentage of station personnel is a minor miracle."

"You and I may see it that way, but I doubt the top brass will," the first remarks.

"So what else is new?"

Their conversation ends as a small disturbance breaks out on the other side of the bay—one of the people Arlo marked out earlier. I tense, ready for action, but Cress is already taking care of it, putting the squatter in an armlock and handing him over to a guard, who marches the man away.

Seventeen, sixteen, fifteen.

It's almost a relief when it finally happens. The lab tech who bumped me earlier catches one of the soldiers unawares, bashing him in the solar plexus and grabbing his weapon. She spins around, pistol pointed at the crowd. I go for my own stunner, but before it's even halfway up, Anders is there. He takes aim, pistol poised for a perfect face shot.

"No, Anders! Not the fa—"

The pistol flashes . . .

. . . and takes the squatter straight through the eye.

She drops like a stone, taken out instantly by the only shot from these guns that can actually kill. A sharp sour-and-sweet reek rips through my nose as the Spectre, now released from its host, takes to the air. I track it with my nose as it zooms up, then makes a direct arc toward a scientist in a gold lab coat.

I throw myself in front of him, dropping my pistol and grabbing for the aero-launcher on my back. "Everybody down!"

Even as I fumble for the weapon, I know it's futile. At most, I can hold it off. But with no way to kill it, it's not a matter of *if* the ghoul will take a host, only *who*. With the ghoul plunging straight at my face, I pump my launcher and squeeze the trigger.

The click of the empty chamber echoes through the entire bay. I let out a dark laugh. So this is how it's going to end, with infection, quarantine, and a slow death. It's a horrifying fate. But then, do I really deserve anything le—

Phthoooom!

The ghoul is only centimeters from my face when the burst from Madison's launcher blows it away. It flies back over the heads of the flattened crowd straight at Anders.

The odor abruptly disappears.

Arlo hits him with a quick stun shot to the chest, and then it's over. Now that the Spec's taken a host, only Anders's death can release it now. No one speaks as a couple of soldiers carry his limp body out.

As the final few wait to be processed, I once again feel eyes watching me. But not like before, not like on the shuttle. This time, it's everyone staring at me.

The man in white is the last one to leave.

————

Mission finally complete, I follow my teammates into the armory where PsyEnsign Dwaller is waiting for us. Arlo undergoes the check first while the rest of us stash our gear on the racks. When it's my turn, I nod a short greeting to Dwaller and take his proffered hand. The PsyCorp specialist is in and out of my mind within a minute, checking for the telltale presence of a squatter and nodding when he finds none. He's so skilled, I don't even notice he's in there.

Afterwards, we troop down the hall for our mission debriefing with the platoon's ranking NCO. Luckily, Watch Sergeant Morgan keeps the meeting short. The number of evacuees taken off the station before it fell? Two hundred and twelve. Less than half of the station personnel. The final count is actually 199, though, once the squatters got weeded out. I don't envy them their fates. They'll be officially tagged as prisoners of war and shipped off to a quarantine colony until we can find a cure for the infection.

Or they die.

Three years. That's how long most squatters last before the Spectres in their heads finish them off, consuming them from the inside out as they breed ghoul after ghoul. Another ticking clock, counting down toward death.

I hate clocks.

The meeting finishes quickly, and before long we're dismissed for some grub and downtime. At least, most of us are.

"Hold up a minute, Sorenson," Morgan says as I'm heading toward the door.

I stop at the command. "Sarge?"

She holds up her left hand in a wait gesture while she listens to something from her chit on her right hand. At last she nods slightly. "Affirmative, Lieutenant. Morgan out." Dropping her hand, she gives me a curious look. "That was LT. You're to report to the Rose Room tomorrow afternoon at thirteen hundred. The company commander wants to see you."

My mouth drops open. What could I have possibly done that would get the attention of the company commander? Involuntarily, I blurt out, "Captain Jessup wants to see me?"

"Do you know of any other company commander currently aboard this ship, Guardian?"

"No, Watch Sergeant!"

Morgan snorts. "Then I guess you better haul your butt down to the Rose Room tomorrow to see what Captain Jessup wants." A slight smile cracks her face. "Don't look so worried, Sorenson. LT and I will be there, too. You're a good soldier. Whatever's going on, I'm sure it can't be that bad. Tomorrow, thirteen hundred. Dismissed."

Still puzzling over the strange summons, I find Arlo and Cress waiting for me in the corridor. "What was that about?" Cress asks as we head back to the barracks.

"I'm not sure." Disbelief colors my voice as I tell them about the order.

"The company commander? Whoo! You've done it this time, haven't you, Mikey?" Arlo whoops, looping an arm around my shoulders.

Irritated, I shove him off. "I haven't *done* anything, Arlo."

"Still, there must be some reason Jessup wants to see you," Arlo persists. "What happened? You fart in the admiral's breakfast room or something?"

"Don't be deficient, Arlo." Cress turns to me. "You think it's about Anders?"

"I don't know. Maybe."

Probably.

Cress studies me for a moment, then shakes her head in a tacit change of conversation. "Mike, a bunch of us are going to raise a glass to Tabs and Christo and the rest tonight at nineteen hundred in the cantina. You in?"

My chest immediately tightens. Not that the invitation is unexpected; I've been to these informal memorials enough times before. Usually they involve either getting drunk or getting a slash. Or both. Still, the thought of going to this one makes my chest ache with an old pain I can't ever seem to shake.

Her vibrancy, her voice; the way her eyes would light up whenever I'd walk into the room, like I was the person she wanted most in the universe to see.

"Of course he's coming," Arlo says. "It's Tabs."

I swallow. Arlo's right. It's Tabs; it would look odd if I didn't show. I manage a nod. "Yeah, sure. I'll be there."

Whether I want to or not.

————

". . . and so there I was, soaking wet and completely naked, without even my launcher to cover my junk, and Sarge was like, 'Guardian, you have five seconds to give me one good reason why I shouldn't report you to LT right now.' So I said the first thing that popped into my head."

"Which was?" Evans asks curiously. A fresh slash encircles his arm halfway up his wrist, the thin laser tattoo joining another dozen of varying widths already there. A bracelet for each fallen comrade, black for infected and crimson for dead.

Arlo waggles his eyebrows and shouts, "Because I'm well hung, Sarge!"

Everyone bursts out laughing. "You didn't seriously say that," Cress says.

"God's truth!" Arlo claims. "So just as Villas was about to link LT, Tabs was like, 'Well, there you have it, Sarge. He's clearly delusional and can't be held responsible for his actions.'"

Roars of laughter follow, and even I can't help smiling a little. That sounds exactly like something Tabs would say.

"And Sarge let you off?"

"Sarge let me off. At least, he didn't report me. I still got a major jaw-down and a slagload of extra scut, though," Arlo confirms. "Well, that was Tabs for ya. Brains, courage, and a killer sense of humor. We won't see her like again soon."

"To Tabs!" someone yells, and everyone lifts their glasses and repeats, "To Tabs!"

I silently mouth the words and take a sip of my drink. Though the bubbles slice into my palate, hard and sharp, the soda itself tastes pale and flat, like it's been sitting out for a week instead of twenty minutes. Drumming my fingers on the bar, I stare at the clock and wonder how long before I can sneak away. At least another half hour, I decide reluctantly. Long enough for everyone to get good and drunk, anyway.

"Okay, it's someone else's turn now. Let's see, uh, Mikey! You're up. A funny story about Tabs."

Well, there was the time Tabs put cream cheese in Alvarez's vest, or that time she told Harrington he had a face like a dung beetle . . .

That day she blew herself up to save the human race.

A lump forms in my throat. This is why I didn't want to come to this memorial. Not because I don't respect Tabs, but because I knew it would remind me of *her*. Lia, the human bomb who sacrificed herself for the human race. Lia, whom I can't forget no matter how far I go or how hard I try.

My toes twitch inside my boot, and I quickly shake my head. "Nah, I don't have any good ones. Someone else go."

"You don't have any good ones? Seriously? Come on, you've gotta have something."

"I said no, okay?" My whole foot is jittering now, and I can't seem to stop it. "And quit calling me Mikey already. You know I hate that."

"Geez, Sorenson. Who put the bunch in your tighty whiti—"

Like a spring tightened one time too many, something inside me snaps. I have Arlo pinned against the bar before I even realize I'm moving. Drinks spill and glasses shatter. A couple of patrons scream. "You want to hear something about Tabs? She never took any bullslag from you, that's what I remember about Tabs!"

"Oh, yeah?!"

Madison and Evans are on me then, yanking me back by the arms. I angrily wrench out of their hold. "Ice down, everyone! Just ice down!" Cress yells.

"Hey, he's the one who started it," Arlo insists. I lunge at him again, but this time it's Cress jumping between us, giving me a hard enough shove that I would have fallen if not for Madison grabbing my arm.

"Seal it, both of you," Cress snaps, "before we all get thrown out."

My hands are shaking, but I stay where I am this time as Cress neatly calms down the bartender, promising to pay for the broken glasses and buying people new drinks. Everything sorted out in a matter of minutes, she takes my arm and tows me over to the bank of windows. ScyLab 185g is out there, a small orb shining in the distance.

"What the hell is your problem, Sorenson?" Concern is written over her face, and somehow the question doesn't feel offensive coming from Cress.

I shrug and focus my gaze out the window. Lights blink around the ScyLab, and even though I'm not nearly close enough to see, I know what they are. They're the welding ships, carefully sealing up every docking ring, portal, and emergency exit. ScyLab 185g is now officially under quarantine. No one gets in; no one gets out.

Cress shakes her head. "We all know you can be a little hotheaded, but that was a bit much even for you."

Hotheaded? I want to laugh. If only they knew—I didn't used to be like this. I was born an Arlo, telling funny stories and cracking jokes and never taking anything too seriously. But that was *before*. Now the anger rages inside, and I can't seem to put it out. Because the truth is, I'm pissed. I'm pissed that Lia's dead, and I'm pissed that I couldn't save her, and I'm pissed that everyone else is alive and she's not. But most of all, I'm pissed that the one person in the universe who could have saved her—who *knew* how much Lia meant to me and who *should've* had my back—didn't.

"It wasn't like that. It was Lia who made the final choice, Lia who chose to go N—"

"Don't! Don't you dare try to blame this on Lia."

"Why not? It's true. Admit it, Michael! It's not me you're really mad at, it's her."

"You're completely lunar! Why would I possibly be mad at Lia?"

"Because she chose everyone else in the universe over you!"

Even now, the words are still a sucker punch to the gut, the ring of truth in them undeniable no matter how much I might protest otherwise. Lia chose everyone else in the universe over me. And even though my head understands her choice, my heart can't get over it.

Cress's slap on the shoulder brings me back to the present. "I miss her too, Michael," she says, fingering the thick black slash around her forearm, "but she went out doing what she believed in. Can any of us ask for more?"

It takes a second for me to realize she's talking about Tabs, and by then Cress is gone. I stay by the windows and watch the welders. ScyLab 185g is a self-contained habitat. Food, air, water, energy—it can continue running on its own for some time. More than three years, that's for sure. Yes, those people will all die, but it won't be lack of necessities that kills them.

Which is worse, I suddenly wonder. Dying fast in one glorious blaze of light or slowly perishing over three long years of infestation?

I honestly don't know.

I'm so caught up in my own thoughts, it's several minutes before I notice that hair-raising sensation on the back of my neck, like some-one's watching me. My back stiffens slightly. With the squatters iden-tified and imprisoned, the watcher can only be friend, not foe. Cress, maybe, or Madison? Still, of its own volition, my hand creeps down to the nonexistent pistol on my hip. Quick as a cat, I spin around.

The memorial party is still going full swing, and the cantina is packed with various off-duty personnel. But if anyone was watching, they've already melted away into the crowd by the time I turn around.

3 THE NEWS HITS during a short break mid-training the next day. After running fitness drills for half the morning, we're given ten to get a drink or hit the hygiene units. I come out of the units to find everyone crowded around Madison. He's got his hand out, palm up, a news holo being projected from his chit.

"What's going on?" I ask the nearest guardian.

"Shh! Watch," Evans hisses with a nod to the holo.

Frowning, I turn my eyes to the program. My jaw goes slack as I read the caption at the bottom.

Everest Prime has gone down.

I can hardly believe it. Everest Prime—one of the largest, most central, most heavily guarded planets in the Celestial Expanse—has just been infiltrated by ghouls en masse.

I watch the footage with sinking horror. The closest areas to the infiltration have already been cordoned off, barricades trapping people within entire towns, even cities. Terrified mobs throw themselves up against the steel walls, crying to get out, only to be fended off by the Planetary Guard shooting stun guns and other nonlethal weapons to cover their retreat. Even outside the walls isn't quiet, with those separated from loved ones wanting back in, only to be arrested and evacuated.

The scene changes as the station flips to footage of areas farther afield. There the population is being evacuated off-planet as quickly as possible. Naval transport carriers wait in orbit as ship after ship ferries up the newly created refugees, while soldiers on the ground usher people to the ships and do everything in their power to keep the peace.

In other parts of the planet, rioting has already broken out among the frightened populace. News of the infiltration has reached them, and they're panicking, seeing ghouls where there are none and pointing the finger at anyone and everyone in their fear of the unseen. Martial law has been declared, and it's all military personnel can do to keep the situation under control.

I shake my head as murmurs break out around me from the rest of the platoon.

"Holy slag, a whole 8-class planet gone. If Ev Prime can go down, what'll be next?"

"You think they're gonna send us in to help with the evac?"

"Don't you know any spatial geography, dumb-bot?" someone else responds. "By the time we get there, it'll be all over but the dying."

"Oh my God! My family! My family is there!"

"Ice down, Guerrero. I'm sure they'll get them off in time."

I don't say anything, too shocked by the news to speak. It's been four and half years since we first encountered the Specs. That was when scouts from the Celestial Expanse and our chief rival, the Tellurian Alliance, discovered a new planet so earthlike everyone started calling it New Earth. Both powers immediately knew they wanted the planet. In fact, the TA and the CE went to war over it while New Earth sat green and empty, waiting for the eventual victor to come claim it. No one could figure out why such a paradise was completely uninhabited.

Turned out, it wasn't.

While the CE and the TA were busy fighting it out for the right to colonize New Earth, Spectres snuck off the planet with a small scout team from the Tellurian Alliance. Little did those scientists know the horror they were bringing home with them inside their heads. With their presence yet unknown, the squatters settled down to do what they do best.

Breed.

And breed, and breed, and breed.

Though incorporeal and invisible, the Specs still need host bodies in order to reproduce, and humans turned out to be the perfect carriers. With most people unable to even sense the presence of a Spec inside them, the ghouls took hosts and bred without anyone the wiser, spreading through the Tellurian Alliance like a deadly plague. Only the psychics were able to sense their presence, but by the time they put all the pieces together and formed a resistance, it was too late. Too late for the Alliance, that is, but not for us. The last act of the Tellurian resistance was to warn us of the threat before it was too late. They blew up half a space station to do it.

Lia blew up half a space station to do it.

That was just over a year ago, and since then we've been fighting a losing battle against an enemy we can't see, can't hear, can't touch. Though we've managed to expand on the Tellurians' technology, we've made little headway in learning anything about our alien foe. No one can agree on what they are—spirits, a form of energy, some other material completely beyond our ken? Besides their desire for hosts, we have no idea what they want, any more than we can answer questions like: How do they live? How long do they survive? Are they even sentient? They're remarkably impervious to our technology and are wily hunters. We have yet to create a human decoy that can fool them. In fact, their only weakness seems to be air— certain mixtures repulse them, and if given a choice, they avoid the vacuum, though as far as we can tell it doesn't actually seem to harm them. The one thing we know for sure is that they're *relentless*. Once they get a foothold into a new station or planet, they will sweep across the place until every last human being is theirs. Our only defense is to keep them out altogether, by quarantining squatters and preventing the enemy's spread via commercial and military transports, and so far we've been mostly successful, with the ghouls only taking down space stations and small, 4-class colonies and below.

But Everest Prime? That's a game changer. If they can get there, they can get anywhere.

"All right, Guardians! Enough gawping!" I jump at Watch Sergeant Morgan's roar. "As you've seen, the Specs can hit us any time, any place, which is why we've got to be ready. Shooting range, now! Anyone not there in two minutes gets extra laps. Move it out!"

Madison's holo disappears, and everyone immediately hotfoots it out the door toward the shooting range. Whether your grandmother died or you just found out one of the biggest planets in the galaxy has fallen, when Sarge says move it, you move it.

Though it's only training and we're light-years away from Everest Prime, somehow knowing about it lights something inside of me, propelling me through the halls as though this were a real op and not just a training run. Even the usual slackers like Arlo and Reece seem to feel the same, keeping up with the pack instead of lagging behind. It's amazing what you can do when the enemy is on your tail. Or in your head.

We cover the ground in a minute forty flat.

———

We spend the rest of the morning at the shooting range, practicing with various weaponry. Morgan gives us all a special reminder about why you have to avoid eye shots with your stun gun. Everyone knows why.

No one mentions Anders.

As the practice wears on, I start getting restless and twitchy. Again, I get that odd sense, like someone's watching me. Which is completely deficient, because everyone's focusing on their shooting. It's probably just the news about Ev Prime, I decide, putting me on edge.

We take a break for lunch, and then afternoon finds me outside the Rose Room for my meeting with the company commander. I shift nervously from one foot to the other. Though I'm sure my little standoff with the released ghoul in the cargo bay—along with Anders's subsequent infection—is the reason for my summons, I still feel uneasy. While the event was regrettable, it hardly seems worth the company commander's time. Infection is a fact of war, and after all, it was Anders himself who fired the fatal shot, not me. Some might even say that what happened to him was poetic justice. Not me, though. That would require actually believing there *is* some sort of justice in this twisted universe.

My palms are sweating, and I wipe them quickly on my pants before rapping crisply on the door.

"Enter," a voice bids.

My heart starts doing double-time as I stride into the room to find myself facing the company commander, Captain Jessup; my platoon leader, Lieutenant Penrose; and Watch Sergeant Morgan. I salute sharply, holding the position as my salute is returned, until at last the sergeant barks, "At ease, Guardian Sorenson."

I drop into position, hands laced behind my back as I take in the place. The room is spare but elegant, the dark wood of the conference table polished to a high shine and the walls digitized to present paneled walls, a few pieces of framed art, and even a bank of windows.

Though I keep my gaze straight ahead, I can't help observing the captain from the corner of my eye. Jessup looks strangely uneasy as he perches on a chair in the back corner of the room, hands laced together loosely across his lap. There's a distracted air about him, almost as though his main attention is not on me but on something else altogether. My gut clenches. Something isn't right. I have no idea what; all I know is that my gut is rarely wrong.

With a wave of his hand, the captain signals the platoon leader to begin.

"Guardian Sorenson," Lieutenant Penrose says, "we're here to review the events of yesterday during the evacuation of ScyLab 185g. Specifically, the events that occurred in the courtyard when your evac team engaged in a firefight with a group of squatters."

Surprise fills me, followed by unease. With Tabs's loss and Anders's infection, it hadn't even occurred to me that they'd be interested in the fight.

"I'm going to play back the footage," LT continues, "while you walk us through the events as they occur."

Penrose hits a control on the wall, and the middle section blanks out, to be replaced with a familiar scene. It's the feed from my helmet, I realize. While I knew our helmets had an automatic recording function, it never occurred to me that anyone ever took the time to download the feeds or—vacuum forbid!—actually *watch* them.

The feed plays, hectic and shaky from the action, as it focuses on a couple of civilians. The archway looms up, and then the view swings around and suddenly I see myself. So it's not my helmet feed at all, but someone else's. Madison's, I guess. Audio fills the room.

"Sorenson, Madison! Over there!"

"I see him, Tabs," comes my voice. *"If I lay down cover, can you reach him?"*

Oh. Now I know what this is about. This is about my rescue maneuver in the courtyard yesterday. My very risky, unapproved, and very non-regulation maneuver.

Slag.

At LT's urging, I narrate the events as they unfold on the wall. My decision to go after the man, my movements through the courtyard, and especially the maneuver itself. He stops the feed several times to ask me questions about how I came up with the idea, what made me think I could do it, and specifics about how I did it. When Tabs and I meet up at the fountain, Penrose shuts off the feed. He glances over at the captain.

Jessup slowly stands, eyes straying to the back corner of the room for a split second before coming up to stand before me.

"That was quite the maneuver," he says. "In fact, some might even call it impressive."

"Uh, thank you, sir."

"Why did you go after that man?" he suddenly asks, eyes narrowing in on me with laser-like precision. "Not only was he way outside of your area and covered by a bunch of squatters, but you already had a shiver of ghouls on your tail. By going after one man, you could have lost everyone."

I shift uncomfortably at the observation. I hadn't really thought about it at the time, just acted. Finally, I shrug. "In our mission briefing, we were told that ScyLab 185g was a critical base filled with scientists working directly to combat the Spectre threat. Our orders were to evacuate as many inhabitants as possible."

"And what if I told you the man you spent so much time and energy saving was a line cook from the cafeteria?"

I'd say: Good! We could use some decent grub around here.

The quip pops effortlessly into my mind, but I quash it before it can slip out. I meet the captain's eyes. "Doesn't everyone deserve a chance, sir?"

The captain raises an eyebrow but doesn't answer my question, instead responding, "You lost a valuable team member yesterday, Guardian. The ghouls caught up with you, and Corporal Tabitha Loren had to stay behind to cover your escape. Did it occur to you that if you had just left the man, she might have come back safe?"

Understanding bursts through me. I freeze, barely able to breathe as I contemplate that one terrible idea. That if not for me, Tabs might have survived.

My chin dips briefly, and I start to answer, then stop. Jessup is watching me intently. Too intently. *He's testing me.*

I word my answer carefully. "Chain of life, sir. The civilians are more important. They come first."

"One final question, Guardian. If you had to do it all over again, now that you've had time to consider it, would you?"

I pause, keenly aware of the weight of three stares focused straight at me. Is the right answer yes? Is it no? I have no idea, so I finally go with the truth. "The only thing I would have changed about yesterday is that I would have stayed behind while Tabs left."

Sarge and LT exchange a look.

"Do you have a death wish, Guardian Sorenson?" Penrose asks bluntly.

"I'm not purposely trying to get killed or infected, if that's what you're asking." That's true enough, at least.

His mouth quirks slightly. "It wasn't, but I suppose the answer is close enough."

Silence falls over the room. Neither the captain nor LT seems to have any more questions, but neither do they dismiss me. Jessup turns toward the wall behind him, shrugging his shoulder slightly in a questioning gesture.

It's a one-way wall, I realize. Opaqued on our side to look like a perfectly ordinary wall, but completely transparent to whomever occupies the other side. The question is: Who's been watching this little interview? Who does even the company commander defer to?

A door in the back corner of the room suddenly opens, and in walks Planetary Admiral Evayne Rosen, the commander of Gamma Fleet. It's all I can do to keep my mouth from falling open.

Admiral Rosen nods at the commander. "Thank you, Captain Jessup. Lieutenant, Watch Sergeant, your services are greatly appreciated. I'll take it from here."

Clearly dismissed, the three salute and head for the door. But I catch the quick look that passes between them before they exit.

They have no more idea what's going on than I do! My heart flips suddenly in my chest. Whatever it is, it must be seriously classified if the company commander is being kept in the dark.

I expect the admiral to start asking me questions now that the others are gone. Instead, she says, "He's all yours, Doctor."

Five seconds later, the white-haired man from the shuttle walks in.

4 WE FACE EACH OTHER across the table, the white-haired doctor and I. He speaks without preamble.

"You recognize me." Not a question.

"Yes."

"In fact, you singled me out as a potential squatter on the evacuation shuttle yesterday."

I shift uncomfortably under his direct gaze. Is he angry I mistook him for the enemy? His tone and face hold no expression, nothing to indicate what he's thinking. I shrug. "I did."

"Why?"

I hesitate, studying him for some sign of who he is or what he wants. This man's unceremonious arrival brought no name, no introduction, nothing but a chair and these pointed questions. If not for the silent presence of the admiral in the back corner of the room, I would wonder if his questioning was even sanctioned.

Involuntarily, my eyes dart to Rosen. She inclines her head slightly, a tacit order to answer. "A gut feeling," I finally say. "I sensed someone watching me and thought it might have been you. There was something . . . off about you."

"Off?"

"A plain white outfit, like a uniform but not. No name tag, no insignia. Nothing to mark who you are. Which would be normal enough on a regular space station, but we were on a ScyLab—a scientific research facility doing classified work. Hardly the sort of place where they let just anyone walk around unidentified."

A slight smile cracks his lips. "Very astute. In fact, you were right. I *was* watching you."

"Why?"

He leans back in his chair and steeples his hands, gaze considering. "Because I was trying to decide whether to offer you a job."

"A *job?*" My eyebrows leap halfway up my forehead. Is this guy for real? I sneak a surreptitious glance at the admiral. She waves her hand slightly, as if to say, *It's his show.*

The doctor catches the exchange and snorts. "Perhaps I should start at the beginning. My name is Dr. Daedalus Angelou, and I'm the current head of Division 7."

"Division 7?" I frown, not recognizing the designation. "Is that an Intelligence section?"

"Not exactly. Let's just say that Division 7 is a special sector made up of both military and civilian personnel working to further the war effort."

Further the war effort? I snort. *Yeah,* that's *helpful.*

"One of my responsibilities as head of Division 7 is to recruit new talent. In fact, it's the reason I was on ScyLab 185g." The corner of Angelou's mouth twitches ever so slightly, and it suddenly occurs to me that whomever he went there to recruit didn't make it off. "Usually, I focus my efforts on our civilian personnel and leave others to recruit our military people. However, when I saw your impressive rescue in the courtyard during the evacuation, I took a special interest in you."

"I—it was nothing any other guardian in my place wouldn't have done," I stutter, unsure how else to answer. I'd thought the meeting with the company commander surreal, but it's nothing compared to this.

"On the contrary, it was a highly non-regulation maneuver that took quick thinking, a resourceful solution, physical acuity, and considerable daring. I think very few people in your situation would have dreamed it up, and of those, even fewer would have been able or willing to execute it. As soon as I witnessed it, I pegged you as a possible recruit for my division. The real question is: Was the rescue a simple fluke or the real thing? I watched you during the evacuation and in the shuttle to try and determine which. Your later actions in the cargo bay made me think the latter."

"You mean after that squatter died, when I tried to fight off the released ghoul?"

"No, that was something any guardian might have done. Before that, with Anders. Two dozen soldiers in that room, and every single one of them was watching the squatter. Only you saw the true threat."

"Anders's kill shot," I say slowly.

"Anders's kill shot," Angelou confirms with a nod. "Just like in the courtyard, you sized up the situation in a heartbeat and acted. We need people like that in Division 7. People who can think on their feet and outside the box, who can not only dream up unorthodox tactics, but actually pull them off.

"After watching you in the bay, I asked the admiral to arrange the meeting between you and your superiors today. I also covertly watched you off-duty and during your training sessions. I wanted a chance to get a feel for your character, to observe you not just in action, but as a person, so I could determine if you would be right for our section."

"That's what the third degree from the company commander was all about?" I ask incredulously. "I thought my career was on the line, and the whole time it was just a *job interview*?"

It's all making sense now. My feeling of being watched on the shuttle and at the shooting range, my strange meeting with the company commander. The way none of the officers seemed to know what was going on despite giving the interview. Slag, he was probably the one watching me in the bar as well! I wonder what he thought of that little dustup with Arlo. Apparently not much if he's still offering me a job. That is . . .

"Then you *are* offering me a job?" I confirm.

"Oh, yes. I wouldn't have joined you today if I wasn't. I would have simply slipped away, a nameless ghost you'd never known was watching, and left the officers to decide if you should get a slap on the wrist for pulling such a risky maneuver, or a commendation. So, are you interested?"

Interested? That's one way of putting it. I lean back in my chair and consider this Dr. Daedalus Angelou. He struts around a classified ScyLab without even a name badge, commands interviews from a planetary admiral, and his whole purpose and identity are kept secret even from the Guard captain. He's neither military nor Intelligence, but something else altogether. I have no idea what, but whoever he is, he's powerful.

And for whatever reason, he wants me.

"What's the job?" I ask cautiously.

"Division 7 is officially classified as a Military Support Unit. It's made up of a core group of civilians, a small unit of PsyCorp agents, and a military section made up of members from all branches—Navy, Ground Forces, Celestial Guard," he adds with a nod at me.

I frown. Military Support? But that's made up of mostly scut units—garbage hauling, ship detailing, waste disposal, that sort of thing. Why on earth would they go to so much trouble to recruit me for something like that?

"Upon joining, you'll get an immediate promotion and a pay raise." Angelou pushes a tip-pad at me. "Here are the basic details."

I scan the pad. My eyes practically fall out of my head when I see what my raise would be. They open even wider when I see the section on hazardous duty pay. One thing's for sure—this is some pretty high-priced support work. At least it would be if it is, in fact, support work. I eye the doctor warily. "What exactly would I be expected to do?"

"You'd still be doing much of what you already do, using the skill set you've acquired as a guardian. However, let's just say your missions would be a bit more *unorthodox* than you're used to."

Unorthodox? That could mean practically anything. This guy is the king of vague, that's for sure.

As if reading my mind, Angelou adds, "Unfortunately, there's little more I can tell you unless you opt to join us, but I can say this: In a month with us, you'll do more for the war effort than you would in twenty years as a guardian. Stay a guardian, and you'll be doing riot control and station evacuation until we win the war—or lose it. Join Division 7, and you'll be one of the few who helps determine *if* we win this war."

I nod. It's a tempting sales pitch. Still, I'm not completely oxygen-deprived. The selective recruitment process, the vague job description, the unimpressive unit classification, the high pay? This has all the earmarks of something highly classified, highly secretive, and highly *dangerous*.

"So just how long a life expectancy can I expect to have in this 'Military Support' job? I mean, compared to being a guardian?"

Angelou shrugs. "I'm not going to lie to you. If you join this unit, chances are when you leave, it'll either be under quarantine or in a body bag." He leans in over the table and lowers his voice. "But then, the way this war is going, chances are that may be everyone's fate, military or not."

Shivers run over me at his bass rumble. Like the rest of the population, I'd thought we were doing a good job containing the enemy threat. Even after a year and half, the majority of the Expanse is still free and untouched by the war. Squatters are imprisoned with ruthless efficiency, while infected areas are quickly evacuated and quarantined. But something in Angelou's piercing gaze and intense voice suddenly has me questioning everything I've been told. My mind flashes to Everest Prime, and I recall my earlier thought: *If the enemy can take down Ev Prime, they can get anywhere.*

I run the decision through my mind. Stay a guardian and do the expected, or take a dangerous leap into the unknown?

I don't even need to think about it. I lean in and meet Angelou's gaze. "I'm in."

Angelou smiles, a sly twist of the mouth that puts me in mind of a boa constrictor grinning at a rat. "I thought you'd be. There's just one more thing."

"Which is?"

"Since you were only sixteen when you joined up, you had to get permission from your legal guardian before you could enlist. Normally this would be sufficient for all military duty. However, as you're still a minor and you're being transferred to an entirely different division, you'll need additional signed consent."

I blink as his words sink in. So in order to transfer to this highly classified, extremely dangerous "Military Support" unit, I first have to get my *grandma's* permission?

Perfect.

———

"Michael!" The holo is grainy and pale, the reception poor, but I can still see Gran's eyes positively light up at the sight of me.

"Hey, Gran."

"Where are you? *How* are you? Michael, you don't hmail enough."

I grin as her expression morphs from joy to curiosity to annoyance at my lack of communication skills. "It's good to see you too, Gran."

Her face softens. "I worry about you."

"Yeah, I know."

For a moment, I drink in her face. Gran is more than just my grandmother. She raised my sister and me for a good three years or so, after the war for New Earth started and our parents were reassigned. Warships—no children allowed. It's funny. At the time, I was less than thrilled to be packed off to live with a grandma I barely knew, but now that those years are over, I find myself missing that short time on New Sol Station.

Before Lia came back and signaled the beginning of the end.

My breath catches slightly, and I quickly push the thought away, asking Gran, "So how's the new station? Have you gotten to move back into your apartment yet?"

She nods. "Two weeks ago. They got the new hub built and fitted into the station a few months earlier, but they wanted to do a bunch of tests before they let anyone back on. Plus, they needed to outfit the habitat rings with all the new tech—force fences and such. Luckily, with my job as an air specialist for the rings, I was one of the first people they let back on." Gran laughs. "You know, the hub has that 'new station smell' now? All I have to do is close my eyes and I feel like a little girl again, coming onto the station for the first time."

I smile slightly at her reminisces. Apparently, I'm not the only one missing better days. She chats a bit more about the new station, then suddenly says, "I ran into PsyLieutenant Rowan the other day. He asked about you."

My shoulders tense at the name. It was Rowan who'd let me out of the holding cell they threw me in when I refused to leave the Slip-Stream station. Rowan who'd tried to calm me when what I already knew in my heart was confirmed: that the station hub full of Specs had been blown to kingdom come.

With Lia on it.

I howled like a banshee when I found out; Rowan must have thought I was out of my fragging mind. I let out a bitter snort. No wonder he asked about me.

"I told him you'd joined the service," Gran continues. "That you were a guardian now and doing well. He said good for you."

Yeah, I'll bet he did.

Gran pauses. "He also asked about Teal."

My fists clench, nostrils flaring at the sound of my little sister's name. I level Gran with my coldest stare. "Gran, *don't*."

Gran, being Gran, completely ignores the warning. "Michael, this is ridiculous! It's been over a year. Don't you think it's time you got ov—"

"Teal *knew*. Teal *knew* what Lia was, what she was going to do, and she let her get off that SlipStream anyway. She *lied* to me! If she had only told me—"

"But she didn't, Michael," Gran interrupts, "and whether she was right or wrong, what's done is done. There's nothing you or I or Teal can do to change it now. All we can do is move forward. Lia cared about you and Teal both. The last thing she would have wanted was to come between you."

"Lia. Is. Dead."

We stare at each other, gazes deadlocked, until finally Gran looks away. It's not the first time we've had this argument, and I doubt it'll be the last. She's determined to fix things between Teal and me, while I know that'll never happen. It's one of the reasons I don't call or hmail her much. I wouldn't have called her now, but Mom is on a warship who-knows-where, and Dad is on another ship who-knows-where-else, and they'll only get to their hmail the-hell-if-I-know-when. With Angelou leaving tomorrow, Gran is the only one in range who can grant permission in time for me to shove off with him.

If only I'd been born a month earlier.

I sigh. "Listen, Gran. There's another reason I'm calling you. I've been offered a promotion, but I need signed consent to accept it."

"A promotion? Already?" Gran brightens up slightly at the news. "Michael, I'm so proud of you!"

"I linked you the form, if you could sign it. The division head wants me to leave tomorrow."

I wait patiently while she pulls up her hmail and finds the form. My stomach clenches as she starts reading the document. I try to hurry her along.

"You don't have to read it all, Gran. It's just a lot of boring military red tape."

"Nonsense! My grandson's been promoted. I want to read all about it."

"Really, I don't have a lot of time for this call."

Gran gives me a *look*. "Michael, I'm not signing something I haven't read. If you have to go, I can link it to you later."

Damn! I was afraid she'd say that. "Just try to hurry," I finally mutter.

My fingers twitch as I watch her read through the form. I've seen it already. It's amazingly vague—much like Angelou himself—but to someone with a late husband, daughter, son-in-law, and grandson in the military, it's clear enough. As soon as she lifts her gaze, I can tell Gran has read between every line of that consent form.

"Michael, what exactly have you gotten yourself into?"

"Like it says, it's a Military Support Unit," I reply evenly.

"The unusually high raise, the hazardous duty pay, the fact that this form takes seven pages to tell me basically nothing . . . whatever this is, it's not Military Support. At least, not any Military Support I know of. Michael, I can't sign this without talking to your parents first. Even then, I'm not sure I'd want to sign it."

"I don't have time to wait for them," I tell her. "They made you my legal guardian when they took off five years ago. You don't have to tell them *anything*."

"Michael!"

"Gran, you're the one who talked them into letting me enlist in the first place. You remember that?"

She reluctantly nods. "Even after two months, you were still distraught over Lia's death. When you said you wanted to join up, I thought it was a good sign. I hoped the discipline would do you good."

"And it has, Gran. You were right to let me come. Now you need to let me keep going. You need to trust that I know what I'm doing. Besides, I'll be eighteen soon. All you'll do by refusing to sign is delaying the inevitable, because no matter what you do, *I'm going.*"

Gran stares at me for a long moment. "Why do you want this so badly? Is it the pay? The promotion?" When I don't answer, she adds softly, "You can't keep running away from her memory forever, Michael. One day you're going to have to stand fast and face it."

I look away. "I don't know what you're talking about."

"No?"

Just that one word, hanging in the air. I dare a glance back at her. Like a bolt out of the black, it suddenly occurs to me that in the eleven months since I've been gone, Gran has aged. The lines in her face are more pronounced, the threads of white in her hair more numerous. Her eyes look tired. While the rest of us have scattered to the winds, she alone has stayed behind. She alone has stood guard over the memories no one else can bear. I wonder how she has the strength to do it.

She shakes her head. "Your parents—"

"You can explain it to them, I know you can," I say, seizing the change of subject like a drifting man a space line. "Tell them I want to advance up the ranks—that'll make them happy. Tell them I'm doing my *duty.*"

My lips twist slightly on the word. It was what Dad told me when he sent me off to live with Gran after being reassigned four years ago. That it was his *duty* to go. From the expression on her face, Gran apparently remembers, too.

She snorts derisively, expression grim and set. Finally, she sighs. "It's your life. It's not my job to make your decisions for you, much as I may want to. All right, I'll sign on one condition."

I frown. "What?"

"Promise me you'll call your sister."

Call Teal? "Like hell I will!"

The words are out before I can stop them, but I refuse to take them back.

Gran shrugs. "Okay. Then you can explain to your CO why you can't accept."

Sorry, Angelou. I'd love to join your super-secret, ultra-dangerous

Military Support Unit, but my granny refused to sign because I wouldn't call my traitorous baby sister. Yeah, that'll go over *real* well.

I scowl. Gran has me over a barrel, and she knows it. Now it's my turn to sigh. "Fine."

"Fine what?"

I glare at her. "Fine, I promise to link Teal."

"During daytime hours on Iolanthe, and not in the middle of the night when she's sleeping."

Damn! Gran knows me too well.

"Fine. I promise to call Teal during daytime hours. Happy?"

She signs.

Just before she links off, Gran leaves me with one last parting shot. "Michael, whatever happens when you call . . ." She hesitates, as though suddenly unable to find the words to say what she wants to say, and finally shakes her head. "Just don't forget who the real enemy is."

And then she's gone.

The next morning, 0800 on the dot, I meet Angelou at Docking Ring 3A and board the *Arandora*, a Colt Crawler bound for parts unknown. I don't bother to tell anyone goodbye.

Onboard the *CES Arandora*
Colt Crawler Ship En Route to Classified Destination

THIRTY-SIX BILLION DEAD.

Ninety-eight percent infected.

Three point three years left until the total annihilation of the Tellurian population.

The Doctor shook his head. Even the knowledge that they were simply estimates gleaned from imperfect data collection methods failed to render the numbers any less terrible. The enemy was burning through the Tellurian Alliance even faster than anyone had predicted, though whether that was because they'd miscalculated the rate of spread, the required breeding time, the original number of Spectres, or some other factor altogether, no one really knew. It was hard to study an enemy you couldn't actually see but could only examine through the swath of destruction left in its wake.

The stats for the Celestial Expanse were both better and worse. Better because they were so much less dire; worse because they weren't numbers for a rival empire across the universe, but home.

Two hundred and fifteen thousand dead.

Four percent infected.

Nine point eight years left until the total annihilation of the Celestian population, and with it, the human race.

And with the recent fall of Everest Prime, those stats were only going to get worse.

The Doctor leaned back in his seat and listened as the Admiral briefed them on the latest invasion, her feed in the wall panel on the left while the Chairman's resided on the right.

"Seo Pak City. Location: Seo Pak Province on the eastern continent of Everest Prime. Total area: 698.3 square kilometers. Population: 4,006,083. The first force fence tripped at precisely 0720 local time. The city was quarantined by 0753, and the fence data shows we had full saturation within a matter of hours."

"Two hours and seventeen minutes, to be precise."

The Admiral acknowledged the Doctor's addendum with a haughty twist of her chin that made his teeth grind. Between her superior intellect and cunning ambition, her eventual advancement through the ranks had always been inevitable, but even he'd been shocked by how swiftly she'd risen. It was the kind of meteoric rise made possible only in wartime, as the climate of fear grew and your rivals fell. The kind of rise built upon the bodies of the dead, just so long as you didn't mind climbing over them.

Something she'd long since proven, to his deep-abiding sorrow, that she had no problem with.

"Everest Prime," the Chairman stated, his words a perfectly enunciated clip. "They had every security measure we have available— force fences, Sniffers, OPs, a sizeable contingent of PsyCorp officers—"

"But not secrecy," the Doctor countered. "Not isolation. It's a Class 8 planet with a population to match and three jump path connections. It's a simple numbers game. More incoming and outgoing traffic means more chances for them to get past our security."

The Chairman's lips thinned, and he frowned, clearly not liking that answer. "You sound like you expected Ev Prime to get hit."

"It was inevitable that something big would get hit eventually," the Admiral pointed out. "The issue at hand isn't that Ev Prime got hit, but *how* it got hit."

She waved her chit hand, and a miniature city sprang up from her desk, holographic streets, avenues, and highways crisscrossing around buildings to create a glowing maze across the glass.

"*This is Marceau, the last city hit before Everest Prime, enhanced to show the force fence network.*"

The Admiral flicked her thumb, and they watched as the first light lit up on the north edge of the city. Within seconds, the entire northern perimeter was glowing crimson. The lights continued down, sweeping south into the city while fanning out on either side of the main thrust until the entire grid was the color of blood.

The Admiral waved her hand, and the city melted away to be replaced by another. "*And Okenedo, hit two weeks before Marceau.*"

They came from all sides this time, every single perimeter fence lighting up in a matter of seconds until the whole city was ringed with fire. The Mandela Monument, at the very center of the city, was the last place to light.

Another gesture, and Okenedo disappeared. The Admiral brought up a final grid. "*Now here's Seo Pak City the morning of the invasion.*"

She crooked her thumb, and a tiny red light sprang up toward the center of the city. A second later, another light began glowing several klicks to the east while a third lit right on its heels down in the southern district. Four more activated almost simultaneously, all within the inner city, and then pinpoints of light exploded in all parts of the grid. Within a few minutes, a neat pattern of lights covered the entire city from end to end.

Stunned silence.

"They were already in the city," the Doctor finally stated, lips twitching as he stared hard at the holographic map sprawled across the desk.

"Impossible! Not only does Seo Pak have one of the most advanced force fence networks in the Expanse, they have a whole team of Sniffers dedicated to patrolling the city at regular intervals to smell for ghouls. Or at least, they did." The Chairman shook his head. "No, the data must be wrong."

"It's not wrong," the Admiral denied. "They checked and doubled-checked the data. Not a single Sniffer reported smelling anything prior to the invasion, nor did a single fence trip outside of regular tests."

The Doctor's eyes narrowed, nostrils flaring and mouth pressing into a hard line. "How in the universe did four million ghouls manage to sneak into that city without anyone noticing?"

The Admiral met his gaze, eyes hard as frosted glass. "That's exactly what we have to figure out."

5 I PACE RESTLESSLY BACK AND FORTH in the small cubicle allotted as my room. One, two, three, four. Turn, one, two, three, four . . .

It's no good. The angry energy burns me up from within, the twitching of my fingers and fisting of my hands inadequate to still the storm inside. With a huff, I drop to the floor and start doing push-ups.

In the past couple of weeks since boarding the crawler, I've done a *lot* of push-ups.

Our journey to the base is slated to take approximately three weeks. Assuming we *are* going to a base of some sort. When I asked the crew exactly where we're going, they referred me to the captain. When I asked the captain, she referred me to Angelou. And when I asked Angelou, he said—and I quote—"You'll see."

Which is pretty much the same answer I get from him whether I'm asking about my new position or making small talk by wondering what's for dinner. Because who knows what horrible thing I might do with *that* information, stuck out here in the middle of space.

Yeah. Paranoid much?

My biceps burn, the muscles in my chest and arms flexing as I press my body down to the floor and back up again. *Seventy-three, seventy-four, seventy-five.* Tired of push-ups, I roll over onto my back, shove my feet under the bunk, and start doing sit-ups.

There isn't much to do on the crawler. Aside from being Angelou's occasional gofer, I have no official duties. Most soldiers in my position would be glad of a little R&R. A chance to record hmails home, play some HoloGames or catch up on reading, even study. Not me. I like a tight schedule. I like it when they push us from dawn to dusk, until you're so tired your eyes close the minute you hit your bunk, only to wake up and do it all again the next day. Hard training, life-and-death missions. I'm like a shark; I have to keep moving. When I'm moving, I'm okay. It's only when I stop that I start sinking under the weight of it all—the anger, the pain, the betrayal.

The loneliness.

I finish the sit-ups and move to the portable chin-up bar stuck in the door frame. Sweat is beading over my skin, gluing my undershirt to my back. I concentrate on the simple motion of pulling my body up and down, refusing to let my thoughts stray to anything else . . . or anyone.

Her sassiness, her spark; that little dimple, left cheek only, when she smiled.

As usual, I fail.

Exhausted at last, I drop from the bar and grab my canteen. As I guzzle some water, a low *screee* thrums through the deck, signaling our entrance into a jump path. I throw a hand on the wall to steady myself against the sudden kick in propulsion, gasping as a fist of pressure squeezes around my torso. Heart, lungs, muscle and bone; it's as though my insides are being infinitesimally compressed, forced inward from every angle as the path closes in around us. I swallow against the internal claustrophobia and try to block it out. According to the experts, the sensation is both completely normal and completely groundless at the same time. My innards are not being crushed; my organs are not getting slowly liquefied into oblivion. So they say, anyway.

In an effort to distract myself, I glance at the time: 1005. Good. The day's lists will be up by now.

Dropping gingerly onto my bunk, I activate my chit and log into the CIpN—the Celestial Interplanetary Net. I drum my fingers impatiently on my knee as I wait for the lists to load. As soon as they come up, I access the Recent Additions list. To my relief, Everest Prime is still the most recent entry. Neither of my parents' ships is on the lists, nor is New Sol Space Station. Iolanthe isn't listed either.

Not that I care about Iolanthe, one way or another.

Going back to the main page, I scroll through the various lists. Quarantine lists, denoting the space stations, colonies, and planets fallen to the ghouls. Evacuation lists, naming the lucky civilians who were safely evacked from hot spots and relocated; Squatter lists, designating the known infectees who have been sent to quarantine colonies to live out the rest of their short lives. Then of course there are the military lists—IIA and KIA lists, citing the military personnel infected or killed in action.

I click on the link for Everest Prime. Though the infection began over a week ago, the lists continue to be updated as more cities fall and evacuees get processed in. Seo Pak City, Neo York, St. Luis, the Triple Cities—every major population center on the planet. They all hit the list the very first day, taken by a strike so well coordinated we never even had a chance. But then, when your enemy is made up of invisible wraiths who can take any human in the universe as a host, it's inevitable they'll get spies in high places. We've tried to stop the spread of sensitive information between squatters, cutting off interstellar communications once a planet is quarantined, but it's believed the ghouls can still communicate telepathically. With an advantage like that, it's no wonder the enemy always seems to be one step ahead of us.

I continue to scroll through the infected sites. Now that ten days have passed since the initial invasion, the smaller cities are starting to hit the lists. Which doesn't mean everyone in them is infected, only that ghouls have been detected in those places. It will take time for the squatters to breed enough ghouls to infect everyone. The scientists have estimated it takes the average squatter anywhere from three to eight weeks to breed a ghoul. In the meantime, guardians like me will continue to evacuate people for as long as they can. Until we start losing more people than we're saving. Then, just like ScyLab 185g, we'll close up shop and pull out. Quarantine the planet and leave everyone to their fates.

I let out a low whistle. Quarantining such a massive planet is going to take one hell of a planetary net. Not that a planetary net can stop a ghoul any more than a regular fence can, but it'll keep any squatters from getting out to spread the infection further. Simple distance will keep the ghouls in. They could no more fly to the next planet than we could walk there. Even just a simple trip from a planet to its closest moon could take years; a trip across a single light-year would take them almost thirty-six million years. Not exactly a stroll in the park. That's why they have to catch a ride on human ships in order to spread through the Expanse.

Lists checked, I switch over to a popular comedy holo, watching with fixed determination until the low vibration signaling our exit from the path finally thrums through the deck. Relief courses through me as the pressure on my insides eases, that sense of inward claustrophobia quickly dissipating. I feel almost normal now. Maybe in a minute I'll do another round of push—

Thwump!

I slam into the wall as the shuttle reels, hit hard by . . . I don't know what! I grab onto the bunk just as we're buffeted again from the other direction. My muscles tense in an instinctive fight-or-flight response, my nostrils automatically flaring, though I know whatever's going on has nothing to do with ghouls. Incorporeal as they are, moving anything is outside their abilities. Now *squatters*, on the other hand . . .

I push away from the bed as a hail of smaller somethings smashes against the hull from all sides. Missiles, gun barrages, plasmashot? I have no idea, but I'm not going to sit around waiting to find out. I've got my gear on and launcher shouldered within sixty seconds. Pistol at the ready, I hit the door control. It hisses open to reveal an empty corridor. As I creep outside, I link Angelou on his private channel through the mic on my helmet.

No answer.

Slag. Is he just being cagey as usual, or is he in trouble? Moving through the corridor, I pull up a holo of the ship and check for warm bodies. Unlike the usual large-scale military vessels I've been living on, the crawler is a small shuttle crewed by a minor complement of fifteen. It's about stealth and speed, not brute strength. Including

Angelou and me, that's only seventeen of us altogether. Not very good odds if someone tries to board us. The holo shows seven life signatures on the bridge, including Angelou's. That's where I'll head.

More hits sound across the hull as I jog through the halls, and the shuttle slews a bit as the pilot maneuvers the ship to avoid the worst of the onslaught. I jerk to the side but manage to keep my footing and keep moving. I wonder why we haven't fired back yet. Surely we're not going down without a fight. Maybe we're gearing up to run?

The bridge is standing open when I arrive, and I charge in without a moment's hesitation, stun pistol at the ready. Angelou and the captain are both there, upright and apparently unharmed. Five other crew members sit at various consoles, also seemingly okay. My eyes move to the rest of the room, and that's when I catch sight of the forward wall, digitized to show the view outside. My mouth falls open. It wasn't missiles or cannon shot that hit us.

It was debris.

My arm drops as I realize what I'm looking at. This isn't minor debris, the wreckage of a shuttle that miscalculated coming out of jump or the remains of a scavenger ship lost in space. This isn't even a junkyard, one of the numerous heaps floating here and there in space until someone gets around to cleaning it up. No, this is a *battlefield*.

Great hulks drift as far as I can see, once-mighty cruisers now tritanium skeletons scorched with laser fire and blasted open to space. Entire corvettes have been cleaved in half while some of the smaller ships of the line have been blown into barely recognizable corpses. More debris floats among the larger refuse: cracked and bloodied fighter craft, maneuvering wings sheared off and blackened, cargo and other bric-a-brac loosed to space when their ships were blown to kingdom come. My eyes fasten on a hunk of jagged metal close up on the screen. *CES Nefarious*. It's Celestian.

God help us.

As if hearing my thoughts, Angelou suddenly turns. He looks me up and down, gaze lingering on my visor, launcher, and stun pistol. "Ooh rah, Sorenson," he says drily, unmistakable amusement touching his eyes and lips.

I feel a flush rise in my cheeks. So I overreacted. Leave it to Angelou to make me feel like a total dim-bot for simply doing my job! "I didn't get a response to my link," I answer stiffly as I remove my helmet. "I was afraid there might be trouble."

I half expect another mocking retort, but he only nods, amusement fading from his eyes into something grave and unreadable. Surprised at the seemingly civil response, I venture to ask, "Where are we?"

"The Yongsu System, just outside the Xanshi Jump Path."

I immediately recognize the name. Xanshi is part of one of the few direct jump lines between Alliance and Expanse space, the first of three consecutive paths leading from them to us. When the news about the Spectre invasion originally broke, Xanshi was one of the first places hit by the Spectre-controlled Tellurian Fleet. After all, there was no need to uphold the farce of a ceasefire once the truth was out. They came in force, ready to break down our borders and spread throughout the Expanse the same way they'd already done in the Alliance.

And it wasn't just the fleet that came. The footage of Lia going Nova made it all the way into Alliance space, and for the first time the Tellurian public learned what was happening. Hundreds of thousands of refugees made for the jump paths, desperate to escape an enemy most were already infected by without even knowing. Xanshi, along with a couple dozen other jump paths, was besieged with Alliance ships of any and all stamps looking for a way in.

My mouth goes dry as I stare out at the debris floating dead and lifeless before me. I remember seeing footage of the Battle of Xanshi on the feeds, decisive footage showing our ultimate victory. What the hell happened here?

Angelou snorts when I ask the question, the edge of mockery back in his voice. "You think that was the only battle we fought here? They just kept coming and coming, over weeks and months, until eventually they overwhelmed us. Our fleet fought as long as it could, then retreated back to the next jump path. That's war, Sorenson. Even if you eventually do win, it doesn't mean countless battles weren't lost along the way."

"But the news feeds, the footage."

"Do you believe everything you hear on the feeds?"

"No, of course not, but—" I stop abruptly, unwilling to admit the reason I'd believed the propaganda.

That I'd believed it because my *parents* had said it was true.

I let out a sour laugh, not even bothering to get angry at their deception, but skipping straight to bitter resignation. My parents, my sister, *Lia*. Is there anyone in my life who hasn't lied to me in the name of protecting me? The throbbing in my chest tells me no.

We continue picking our way through the battlefield, moving slowly but surely through the slag. Our pilot does his best to steer us around the wreckage, but still various fragments continue to bounce off us as we go, sometimes striking in random plinks and other times pattering steadily against the hull like rain on rooftops. Though I'm not exactly supposed to be on the bridge, neither does anyone throw me off, so I stay, perching at an empty console in the back and watching the remains drift by. It's better than being alone. Especially now, when the corpse of an empire waits just outside my window.

We're perhaps halfway through the field when I see it. Blinking out from across the field, then blocked by refuse, then suddenly there again.

A red light.

The pilot sees it at the same time. "Captain," he begins, but she's already cutting him off.

"I see it. Analysis?"

He shakes his head. "I'm getting nothing from the console; the field is interfering with our instruments. Offhand, I'd guess it's a stray targeting buoy running on reserve power, but I'd have to get closer to be sure. Do you want me to take us in for a look?"

The captain hesitates, eyes flicking to Angelou in question, only answering when he gives her the minutest nod of the head. "Yes, Lieutenant, but use stealth mode only for now."

"Acknowledged."

Running lights shut off, and the engines' hum abruptly cuts out as the stealth field drops over the shuttle, dampening signs of our presence. While it won't make us completely invisible, it will make us much harder to detect, at least until we get near. The pilot changes course, slowly easing us to port until we're wafting more or less in the direction of the light. Though no pilot myself, I can still admire the way he lets us sway this way and that, mimicking the look of a piece of debris stirred up from the cloud and now ricocheting gently off the various heaps of slag.

I grip the edge of the console as we continue to creep closer, eyes fastened on that far-off crimson blinking steadily through the black. No, not steadily, I suddenly realize as we pass through the worst of the debris fragments. Three fast blinks, three slow blinks, three fast blinks.

S.O.S.

By the sudden intake of the captain's breath, I can tell she sees it too.

"Lieutenant, magnify that image now."

The image on the viewscreen enlarges, then enlarges again, the light momentarily beaming bright on the screen before cutting out once again as we drift behind the bulk of a damaged cruiser. My fingers drum nervously on the console, and I find I'm holding my breath even as we sail under the cruiser and emerge from cover.

It's not a targeting buoy at all, but a *ship*.

"Life signs?" comes the captain's crisp query.

A pause, then the pilot's answer. "Sixteen."

My heart clenches. Sixteen people, stranded and slowly dying within a field of death, only to be found at the last minute. The odds are so impossible; maybe I was wrong. Maybe there is some small bit of justice left in this twisted 'verse.

The captain is querying her crew rapid-fire, asking in a terse voice about grappling fields and rescue equipment, and whether the corvette would hold up under a tow or simply break apart under the strain, and could they counter the latter if they could find a way to reinforce the hull—

"Is it Celestian or Tellurian?"

Everyone stops as Angelou speaks for the first time since we discovered the field, excitement over finding survivors abruptly doused as we all wonder the same question. *Are they actual survivors . . . or squatters?*

The pilot takes a deep breath. "I'll try to find out, sir." His hands dance over the console as he zeros in on the corvette and starts rotating the image, looking for some sort of insignia or identifier that can tell us whose it is. A parade of images slide by, one after another, but the corvette is so scorched and scarred from battle, any vestige of a name has clearly been long scored off.

We drift up, moving around the corvette for a better look at the rest of it, only to find that the opposite side has been completely destroyed, blasted into meaningless fragments that ping uselessly against our hull. Even the underbelly, which might hold some specialized features that could help us identify it, is too damaged to tell us anything.

For an hour, we scan and rescan the ship, looking for an answer that isn't there. At last the pilot sits back in his chair. "I'm sorry, sir," he finally says. "I can't tell. I can't tell if it's Celestian or Tellurian."

Silence.

"Maybe if we towed it to a station with a force hoop?" one crewman suggests.

"It'd never make it through a jump path," the pilot answers. "The only way would be to offload the survivors onto the crawler."

And we can't do that, remains unspoken. Not that it needs to be said, with no way to determine if they're Celestian or Tellurian. Human or squatter. As everyone knows, where there have been squatters for any significant period of time, there are almost *always* ghouls.

"Can we hail?"

"We could, but their communications array is completely burned off, so I doubt they'd receive the message."

"Morse code with the lights, like they're doing?"

"Even assuming they could both see the signal and answer, what would we transmit? 'Hello, do you have any ghouls on board?'"

The crew's debate abruptly peters out, all ideas exhausted as everyone is forced to face reality. Something twists up inside of me at this tacit recognition. Even though I understand the necessity, the idea of leaving sixteen people to die feels wrong in the most fundamental of ways. All I can think about is my parents, if it were them on that corvette, despair turning to hope at our sudden appearance only to disintegrate as we turned and flew away.

"Destroy it."

Angelou's order is absolute, his voice as cold as the vacuum that surrounds us. For a moment, no one speaks, but something in the air thickens, churns with unspoken emotion. They hold gazes for a moment, Angelou and the captain. His eyes are lit from within, brilliant and implacable, and even within the cabin's silver stealth lights, they glow with an intensity that makes me shiver. He looks like a madman.

The captain looks away first. "Lieutenant, you have your orders."

With a brief nod, the lieutenant queues up the weapons and brings us around to firing position. It's only when he finishes keying in the sequence, finger poised over the final button, that I flick my gaze back to Angelou. Though his expression hasn't changed, something in his demeanor seems to have softened just the slightest bit. As I watch, the doctor suddenly crosses his chest in a quick gesture, so swift I almost don't recognize it for what it is, lips moving in a silent prayer even I can recognize: *Kyrie eleison.*

Lord, have mercy.

Then, signaling to the lieutenant with a wave of his hand, he stands back and watches as a corvette with sixteen survivors is blasted straight to hell.

6 DEBRIS FLOATS PAST ME, a million shards of death cutting through space, bleeding the white void black with blood. It's as though we pierced the very fabric of the universe itself, made it bleed 'til it aches, until the pinprick of stars is the only part left not saturated by it.

We've left the remains of sixteen people long behind us, but still the battlefield stretches on, a tapestry of destruction that, like the conscience, does not quickly fall away. I watch it go by from the small lounge/galley, slumped in one of the big swivel chairs along the observation wall, digitized, as usual, to show the ever-changing view from outside the ship supplied by the main sensor feed. Not my first choice of locations, but it's better than being cooped up in my tiny room once again.

It's better than being on the bridge. With Angelou.

The door opens, followed by the sound of voices. I immediately tense, but it's only the pilot and another crewman—Veracruz, I think. I draw my shoulders in and hunch down in my chair, hoping they're simply here to grab a couple of mealpaks and go. The last thing I feel like doing right now is socializing.

No such luck. The rustlings and rippings of the paks are quickly followed by the sound of two butts hitting seats. I want to leave, but

I'll look like a total vac-wipe if I show myself now after ignoring their entry. I squeeze my eyes shut and hope they eat fast.

"That was some lunar slag this afternoon," Veracruz says after a minute, loud chewing followed by a swish and a gulp.

"Yeah, well, what could we have done? It's not like we had a force hoop to tow 'em through. Couldn't risk taking ghouls on board."

"I know, but destroying it?"

"They were dead men anyway," the pilot says practically. "We just made it quick and painless instead of slow and agonizing."

"I guess. Still, if only we'd been able to identify it."

The pilot laughs. "Probably better we didn't. You know what I think? I think even if we'd identified it positively as Celestian, he still would've given the order. Paranoid bastard. He's so afraid someone might track us, might find his precious facility, he'd blow up his own mother to keep his secrets."

"No kidding."

I recall the slightly crazed look in Angelou's eyes, that implacable ruthlessness, and I shiver, unwittingly sensing the truth in the pilot's words. What was it Gran said when I asked her to sign the transfer? *Michael, what exactly have you gotten yourself into?*

Yeah, she may have had a point there. Damn! I hate it when Gran is right. It usually means I'm wrong.

More chewing followed—finally!—by the rustling of plastic as they ball up their pak wrappers and toss them into the recycler.

"Well, maybe Angelou's right," the pilot concedes. "I mean, what do guys like us know about winning a war, anyway? Especially one as fragged up as this."

Footsteps make for the door, then Veracruz says, "You know what I wish we could do? Do it like New Sol. Stick all of the enemy in one place and *bam!* Take 'em all out at once."

My whole body freezes, stomach lurching at those careless words. The pilot's answer, caught up in the sliding of the door, flits past my ears, but neither sound really registers within the reverberation of Veracruz's suggestion.

Do it like New Sol.

I never saw the station blow. I was in a holding cell in the Upper Habitat Ring at the time, knowing only that something terrible was going to happen, but I was helpless to stop it. It was only after it was all over that I saw what Lia had done. That I looked out into space and saw the remains of the station hub, no more than a cloud of debris gleaming dully under the lights of the search ships. Inorganic debris only. Lia, of course, would have been vaporized in the blast.

Lia *was* the blast.

Not that I knew that at the time. All I'd known was that she was one of the last members of the Tellurian resistance, come to New Sol Station to stop the Spectres before they could spread into the Expanse and take us down just like they'd taken out most of Telluria. The plan had been to separate out the Specs and inform the authorities of the invasion. We had never intended for anything to blow up. We had never intended for anyone to die. Or so I'd thought. But then, I hadn't known Lia was a bomb. I hadn't known her mission was to die.

"All Lia thought about in the end was you. 'Tell Michael: If I could have stayed, I would have.' That's what she said."

Maybe Lia was thinking about me in the end, but it wasn't *me* she said goodbye to. It wasn't me she trusted or confided in or plotted with. It wasn't *me* she hugged goodbye before getting off that train. It was Teal. And even now, that one small thing still makes me bleed as black inside as that void outside.

Leaning back in my chair, I let the pale infinity of space wash over me and wonder if I'll ever be able to forgive her for that.

———

Three days later, we arrive at Kittridge Promenade, a space station situated at the entrance to five intersecting jump paths. Despite the stop being prearranged, it still takes ten hours to actually dock. Even after we fly through the force hoop twice, the station still withholds clearance to land. I'm not surprised. With the fall of Everest Prime, no one can be too careful. All it would take is one ship full of ghouls or squatters to destroy the place.

In the end, Angelou has to get on the line and transmit his official codes before they let us dock at the orbital platform, or OP. All stations and planets have them now—separate mini-stations anchored well away from the actual space station created specifically for docking and refueling. The OPs are held to the highest security standards. If a single force fence triggers, the whole platform will completely lock down—no one in or out—until a military unit can arrive to assess the situation. If a single tender launches without permission, it'll explode long before it ever reaches the station. Harsh but effective, at least in part. Though more than one station has been saved by their OPs, the Specs continue to make inroads into the Expanse no matter what we do.

Like most OPs, the Kittridge Platform is bristling with soldiers armed to the teeth with stun guns. After passing through the force fence, we're immediately taken to a holding room and scanned by two PsySpecialists, one of whom is eighty-five if she's a day. With the war on, any and all psychics are being pressed into service no matter what their age.

Finally released, I follow Angelou out of the holding area and into the OP proper. I heft my duffle higher on my shoulder, eyebrows rising as I take in the bustling concourse. Vendors of all kinds line the halls, hawking everything from spare parts and spacer rations to luxury jewels and exotic clothing. Corridors jut off from the concourse on either side, leading to docking rings and cargo bays, and digitized ads scroll over every spare inch of wall. Despite the noise of the crowd, I can still hear the sharp sizzle of meat, marinated and fried in large vats of oil and onions, echoing through the concourse. With so little traffic coming through the station itself, clearly a number of merchants have decided the extra risk inherent in the OPs is worth the additional commerce.

A tall spacer shoulder-bumps me as I walk, unable to avoid me in the crush, and my fingers involuntarily reach down to touch the pistol at my hip. At one time, this sort of general station chaos was second nature to me. Now, after a year immersed in the order and discipline of the service, the disarray makes me uneasy. When you're a guardian, chaos usually means one thing: Spectres. Even knowing everyone here has been cleared of being a squatter, I can't stop myself from constantly scanning the crowd, looking for signs of trouble.

"Something wrong?" Angelou asks dryly, apparently picking up on my edginess. He carries a slim metal case over his shoulder but nothing else. Between his instruction to bring my duffle and his own lack of luggage, I'm not quite sure what to make of this little layover.

"Just keeping an eye on things," I answer. "What's going on? Are we stopping over here?"

"Let's just say I've arranged for other transportation for the final leg."

Of course he has.

Angelou pauses by a holoscreen flashing ads for a station shop offering delivery to the OP. I tap my foot nervously as he subvocalizes into his chit. Lowering his hand, he takes off through the concourse. I elbow my way after him, both admiring and hating the way he seems untouched by the jostling of the crowd, his air of authority such that people unconsciously move out of his way no matter what path he chooses. As we shuffle through a narrow cross-corridor to emerge into a parallel concourse, I hear a man's voice, pitched to carry over the crowd.

". . . when the final day of reckoning comes, they shall rise up into the light, dissolving into the One True Way! And with them shall go their Faithful Servants, the Divine Believers who have worshipped them here on this plain, giving of their Minds, their Bodies, and their Souls that they may find the Path of Enlightenment so long denied us!"

Instant hatred suffuses me at the words. My gut clenches, fingers wrapping around the stun pistol at my hip even before we round the corner and the speaker comes into view. He's standing head and shoulders above the crowd on an old grav sled, his long cloak billowing down around him in an oil slick of color, like a dark rainbow shimmering in ever-changing waves of black and gold, purple and red. An iconic robe, recognizable anywhere in the Expanse and worn only by sworn members of one religious sect.

The Order of the Spectre.

My mouth twists in disgust. They first started appearing over a year ago, just shortly after the recording of New Sol exploding hit the nets. These so-called "Spectre Priests" with their new religious sect devoted not to destroying our invaders, but embracing them. They claimed to be infected, mouthpieces of the squatters sent to tell us the truth: that we should not be afraid of this new species, but welcome them. Of course it was all bullslag. Squatters can't even speak *to* their hosts, let alone through them! No, this was a purely human madness, built upon nothing more than lies and fear and willful blindness.

Luckily, the Order's day was short-lived. It rose in the early days of the war, catching on with just enough people to cause a whole hell of a lot of trouble. Riots broke out over their preaching; overly devout recruits tried to break quarantine lines; an offshoot sect even tried to petition the government with a new law against harming Specs. Then came the Atropos Incident. Ten thousand supplicants attempted to break through a planetary net, bound for the Spectre-ridden planet below, and got caught in the net. Three ships were destroyed, sliced apart by the net's roving energy bands. The footage was on all the feeds for weeks. After that, sentiment for the Order paled. The first big colonies fell to the ghouls, followed soon after by some very terrifying footage gathered from within the Alliance—footage of emaciated squatters dropping dead in the streets—and as quickly as the Order rose, they fell. Public opinion turned on them. Order meetings were bombed and Spectre Priests beaten in the streets. Recruits left in droves until only the most devout remained, and even they were quickly driven underground by the public backlash.

"Join with me, oh Brothers and Sisters! Lay down your fears and let yourself be guided to a new way of living!"

Well, *almost* all of them.

Bile oozes at the back of my throat, coating my esophagus in a layer of bitter rage. My fingers brush along the disappointingly nonlethal stunner at my hip once again, and all I can think is:

For people like this, Lia died?

The urge to beat the life out of this bastard thrums through my hands—an urge shared by several others judging from the mutterings in the crowd—but I force it down. Security is keeping a sharp eye on the situation, and I have no doubt that were I to get arrested, Angelou would have no compunction about leaving me here to rot. So I tuck my head down, close my ears, and hurry through the crowd behind Angelou as fast as I can. As I pass by the grav sled, I can't help catching sight of the tattoo on the priest's wrist—that of a dark rainbow twined about an eight-pointed star—and listening as his final words, some passage of scripture, echo in my ears.

"'*And like a crown of thorns, she'll carry the mark of the Savior upon her brow, though none who see will know it for what it is. She'll hold our fate in her hands, ignorant and unknowing, until the eleventh hour when her eyes are finally opened and the many coalesce to one. Only then, full knowing, will her fingers unclasp and—'"*

He pauses for just a moment, the echoes of his voice still reverberating through the hall in a silvery whisper that seems to linger in the air. Then—

"*'Ashes, ashes, we all fall down.'*"

Even though I know it's nothing more than meaningless drivel cooked up by some old kook, I can't help shuddering at the prediction. And the weight of those final six words still hangs off my shoulders long after his voice has faded away in the swirling crowd.

———

An hour later, we leave the station behind, taxiing out of the docking port with far less ceremony than when we arrived. Our pilot is a slender woman with inky hair whom Angelou introduces to me as Pilot Specialist Sarai Chen. Along with the standard pilot's wings on her collar, she also bears a patch denoting *Delta Team* on the left shoulder of her gold-trimmed flight suit. Ten pilot's chits, one stamped into the base of each finger, gleam from her palms. After returning my greeting with a somber nod, she takes us out with quiet efficiency, setting course for the jump nexus just off our port side.

I examine the cockpit with quiet awe. This ship is nothing like the crawler, but a state-of-the-art, high-tech piece of machinery, from the curving silver walls to the translucent holopanels. The cockpit where we strap in is small and curved, almost a flattened dome resting at the top of the ship. With the ceiling and walls digitized to show the view outside, it's enough to give the impression of sitting directly under the canopy of space itself. Not that the canopy of space is particularly interesting once you've stared at it for two hours. Before long, I'm dozing in my seat, eyes fluttering closed as my tired brain begins to drift . . .

I jerk awake to find that the whole universe has gone out while I slept. No stars, no station; just a flat, opaque darkness in the view beyond the screen.

All the hairs on the back of my neck rise as I feel that familiar sense of claustrophobia and realize we must be in jump. Feeling it is bad enough, but seeing it is worse. I've lived half my life in space and would never have considered myself afraid of the dark, but this starless space is enough to make my mouth go dry and my heart go numb. I'm forcing in yet another breath when the vise around my chest constricts, like a giant fist squeezing, hard and fast. Stars flash before my eyes, choking out my field of vision, and for a fleeting second everything falls away . . .

. . . and then it's back, the universe restored as though it never left. Only it's changed. Kittridge is gone, and in its place, painted across a canvas of stars, hangs a single planet. Two suns, three moons, glittering like a pastel jewel in the night.

I gape in awe, stunned by the utter beauty of the planet growing across the screen with each second we advance. We're headed directly for it, and somehow I know this is no way station, no stepping stone to yet another system. This is our final destination.

"What's it called?" I ask softly.

"Prism," Angelou answers, a strange gleam in his eye. "We call it Prism."

Compared to the Kittridge OP, the platform orbiting this part of the planet is silent and empty, all bare metal walls and echoing halls. Though the OP is more than big enough for planetary use, being at least three times the size of the Kittridge OP, there are so few ships docked here I can only assume it's been appropriated for base use only. No civilian traffic allowed.

We stop over just long enough to allow two stern-faced psychics to clear us. Then, reboarding the ship, we drift down toward that glowing aura below, to that razor-thin place where space kisses the sky. We hover in the breath between their lips for one tender instant . . .

And then we fall.

7 WE DROP INTO THE ATMOSPHERE like a meteor, streaking down through the upper layers with a speed I can feel all the way down in the pit of my stomach. Flares of gold blaze across the viewscreen, fireworks of heat and light that illuminate the cockpit from every angle, while just beyond, tendrils of cloud begin to materialize. In thin furls at first, billowing up in a nearly invisible counterpoint to our breakneck fall, then coming together in heavier drifts of white, pink, lavender, and teal. They close around us, cutting us off from the black of space to cocoon us within froths of pastel mist that gleam gold-edged and glowing under the suns' light.

I clutch the armrests of my seat, exhilaration gripping me as our acceleration only increases. The mists are blurring before my vision, the individual colors bleeding together as we slice through the atmosphere like a laser through ice. Our descent is so smooth that the rapid patter of my heart feels at odds with the ride, barely a tremor to mar our passage but for the soft roll of the mists rippling out from the ship like waves around a stone dropped in a pond. And like a stone, we continue to sink, pulled down and down by the strong arm of the mysterious planet below. A rhyme from my childhood suddenly flashes into my mind.

> *Desert, forest, ice, or sea—*
> *What new world waits for me?*

Before I have time to wonder, a faint whistling whips through the cockpit, and the ship jerks up without warning. My body lurches against the restraints, heart skipping a beat before I realize it's just Chen hitting the brakes. The ship is slowing down now, its speed checking noticeably though it doesn't feel like we've dropped nearly far enough to hit landing distance. Turbulence buffets us from either direction, pushing the ship this way and that, and then a thick bank of clouds whooshes up on all sides. Dense, heavy things that obscure the screens and blot out the sun. For an endless minute, we're shut within the cloudy void, walled in by condensing vapors that hover in the strange place between air and liquid, and then we're free. We tumble down out of the cloud line—

—and into the rain.

I hear it first, pattering across the cockpit light and steady, and then the visual comes, silvery drops sprinkling down around us even as translucent mists continually rise up in curling flumes from below. I marvel at the effect, unable to imagine what could cause weather patterns quite like this. "What is this place?" I dare to ask.

Angelou smiles, not one of his sly grins but something almost tender, a slight upturn of the lip that gravitates up his face to light his eyes. "Show him, Chen."

Our pilot flicks her hand, and the floor beneath my feet turns to mists. I gasp, my body reacting before my brain can reassure it the floor is still there, now merely digitized with the view below. I'm about to ask what this is all about when up through the thinning mists it appears like a crystal flower unfurling its petals toward the sun.

A sky station.

Sheer awe has me slipping my straps and stepping out across the cockpit for a better look. Directly below, the central habitat glitters like a cut diamond, its faceted edges catching the light and refracting it in heavenly beams through drifts of lilac and white. Gossamer spokes of all lengths spool out from the center in a dozen directions, each ending in its own crystalline habitat wing, while landing bays curl like vines between the walkways. The design is irregular, every habitat a different size and shape, but somehow the irregular petals only make the station more exquisite, like a wildflower blooming in a garden of rising clouds beneath a silver rain.

"This is where we're going?"

Angelou nods once, and I shake my head in disbelief, murmuring, "This isn't like any military base I've ever seen."

"That's because it isn't a military base." Angelou releases his straps and comes to stand beside me. His gaze never leaves the station, and it occurs to me that if there's a heart lurking beneath that sly exterior, it lives solely for that crystal world adrift in the mists.

He nods to the station below. "*This* is the most important place in the whole of the Expanse. It is the place where the war will truly be won or lost, the fulcrum upon which everything else rests. Success here means the survival of the human race; failure will bring only death. It is a place only few have the privilege of calling home, and now, you're one of them." Angelou extends his hand, eyes glowing with a cerulean fervor that seems to emanate from his very soul, and slowly smiles. "Welcome, Sorenson, to R&D."

———

Research and Development? Impossible! I'm no scientist. What could they possible want with a guy like me in R&D?

My head is spinning. That this place, this sky station hanging within the pastel mists of some far-flung planet, could even exist at all is mind-boggling. That *I* could somehow be a part of it is only more confounding. My thoughts are so scattered, I'm not even sure how to put my astonishment into words.

Apparently my consternation shows on my face. "Surprised, Sorenson?"

"I don't get how this place is even possible," I admit, "let alone what *I* would be doing here."

"Don't you?" Angelou raises an eyebrow, as if doubting I could really be so clueless. His eyes narrow. "Do you know why, after all this time, we're still fighting this war?"

I shrug. "We can't kill 'em. At least, not without killing ourselves in the process. The human bomb—" My throat chokes up, and I cough a couple of times to clear it. "The human bomb the Tellurians created is so destructive, it would completely destroy the territory we're trying to reclaim, along with any people living there. No point in killing the enemy if it destroys the very thing we're trying to save."

The strangest look flashes over Angelou's face, but before I can even attempt to decipher it, it's gone. "Exactly. We can't kill them. We can't capture them—not in ghoul form, anyway. We can't even communicate with them. All we can do is fight a defensive war. Quarantine infected areas, evacuate survivors, contain squatters; do everything possible to prevent them from spreading. But no matter how rigorous our protocols, eventually a few find a way through. The fact of the matter is that until we can do one of the three—kill, capture, or communicate—we've already lost this war."

I inwardly shiver. Though Angelou said nothing I didn't already know, I've never heard it phrased that way before: *We've already lost this war.*

"That's why R&D is so important," Angelou continues, gesturing at the crystalline station winking gold within the clouds at our feet. "While the Navy and Guard and Ground Forces are putting up a valiant fight on the front lines, ultimately our survival depends on whether the people in that station can find a way to neutralize the enemy, one way or another."

I slowly nod. It makes sense. What doesn't make sense is— "But why am *I* here? I can see why you'd need scientists and researchers, even support personnel, but why a guardian? You didn't really bring me just to be a janitor or waste scrubber, did you?"

Angelou shakes his head. "You disappoint me, Sorenson. You may not be a scientist, but I would think your resourceful mind could see your use. Think about it. What's the one thing you have to do once you create a prototype for a new technology?"

"Well, test it to make sure it works, I guess."

"But how do you test a prototype on a ghoul when you can't capture one?"

"I suppose you'd have to take it out into the field." The light flips on in my head at last, and I can't help flushing in embarrassment that it took me so long to see. "That's why I'm here. To take their technology out into ghoul territory to see if it works."

I don't need Angelou's affirmative to confirm my theory. It all fits together now. After all, a guardian like me—young, strong, trained to handle ghoul- and squatter-infected situations—would be far better equipped to brave enemy territory without dying or becoming infected than the typical science personnel. And even if I were to get taken, so what? Guardians like me are a dime a dozen. Not like these scientists, whose brilliant minds may be humanity's only hope of survival. To put someone like that at risk if there's someone else who can do the job would be lunacy.

I stare down at the floor once more. Even with our speed checked, we've dropped most of the way to the station in the last couple of minutes, and now the shining compound looms up beneath us, so close I can start to see small details. Lights, viewports, even the shadow of movement within one of those gossamer walkways. It's beyond beautiful, and yet the more I look at it, the more my awe turns to uneasiness. Something about this place, this station in the sky, isn't right. The shining compound, the rising mists, the silver rain. There's something *ugly* about this pastel paradise; I can feel it in my gut. Within the swirling mists and the golden light, something untenable is hidden, like a monster waiting to snap its teeth should we go too far.

I bite my lip, struggling to figure out what it is that's bothering me, but before I can pinpoint the source of my unease, Angelou speaks.

"Regret taking the job?"

I lift my head and meet the challenge in Angelou's gaze, strangely energized by the crackle of intensity in his eyes. "Not for a minute."

He laughs. "I knew you were the right choice. Now before we land, there's one more thing."

He pulls out his metal case and opens it on the seat he stashed it under. It takes everything in my power not to crane my neck to try and see what's inside. Angelou pulls out a short injector.

I eye the metal tube suspiciously. "What's in that?"

Angelou returns my gaze levelly. "A coma capsule."

My eyebrows shoot up. I've heard rumors of these, but I didn't think they were actually real. Supposedly they freeze your tissues into a form of living death, liquefying your brain stem and putting you in a permanent coma while still keeping you alive just enough to imprison the Spectre in your head. The squatter gets a useless host, and the human gets an ugly half-death. At least until they die from exposure or thirst, that is.

I shiver at the idea. As a guardian on the front lines, I'm prepared to face death, even infection and quarantine on a penal planet, but *this* . . .

My gaze involuntarily goes to Chen where she sits silently at the pilot's yoke. *Is he for real?* I can't ask the question aloud, but she seems to know what I'm asking anyway, lips twisting in reluctant empathy as she raises one arm to reveal the tiny bump on her wrist. I spy the same bump on Angelou's. Pushing up my sleeve, I stick out my arm. "Go ahead."

The injector is cold, but the capsule burns as he shoots it into my wrist. I listen with half an ear as Angelou explains how to trigger it. It's only after he puts away his injector and restows the case that I think to ask, "Can it be triggered remotely?"

"Yes."

His answer doesn't surprise me in the least.

My mind flashes back to our very first conversation in the Rose Room on the *CES Triumphant*, to Angelou's answer when I asked about the potential danger.

I'm not going to lie to you. If you join this unit, chances are when you leave, it'll either be under quarantine or in a body bag.

I finger the spot where the capsule was inserted. Only now do I understand—there *is* no chance about it.

———

Back in my seat, I watch as we make our final approach to the station, spiraling down through the misty rains like a leaf drifting down toward the ground. If anything, the place only grows more striking the farther we come, and yet for all its outward beauty, I still can't escape the feeling that something about this place isn't right.

My eyes scan the base once more—the habitats, the walkways, the mist. Though there's nothing outwardly wrong with any of it, my earlier sense of unease is back tenfold, and I can't help thinking: *I'm missing something.*

"Why a sky station?" I ask after a moment. "I thought the energy expenditure required to hold such a station aloft was too high to make it cost-effective. Why not just build a space station?"

Angelou shrugs a shoulder. "Simple. You can't start putting extra artifacts in orbit around a planet without someone noticing. When the enemy can be anyone, anywhere, secrecy is our best defense. That's one of the reasons we chose this planet: the atmosphere. The mix of gases plays havoc with standard scanning equipment, making it almost impossible to detect the station if you don't know it's here."

If you can't put it in space, why not just put it on the ground? Unless there's some reason you can't.

I stare down at the station again, but this time instead of looking at the base itself, I look around it. For a long minute, I see nothing. Just falling rain and rising vapors.

Falling rain and rising vapors.

Like something just below the station is heating the air abnormally hot, forcing it to rise up until at last it cools and condenses into thick clouds, raining back down in showers of gleaming silver, only to evaporate and repeat the cycle once again. A horrible suspicion takes shape in my mind. Blinking my eyes rapidly to magnify the view, I activate the infrared in my combat lenses, and gasp. Stretching as far as I can see in either direction is an ever-shifting latticework of red light nestled within the orange and yellow clouds. Horror fills me as I realize just what I'm looking at.

It's a planetary net!

But planetary nets are used for just one thing these days, which can only mean . . . Prism is infected.

R&D is hanging directly over a planet *full of Spectres.*

8 PURE SHOCK FREEZES ME IN PLACE as I finally realize just how warranted my earlier uneasiness was. *Spectres! We're hanging over a planet full of Spectres!* I'm not even aware I've spoken aloud until I hear Angelou's dry voice behind me.

"Ideal, isn't it?"

I lift my head at his words, eyes widening as I take his meaning. While I look at this planet and see an enemy stronghold, Angelou sees it as one giant laboratory! Its people, not tragic casualties to be mourned, but *lab rats.*

Every cell in my body revolts at the idea, though the logical side of my brain has to admit it makes a certain amount of sense. In a chilling, inhuman sort of way.

I'm still reeling as we continue our descent, angling down through the mists instead of straight toward the station. For the first time I catch sight of the four platforms hovering well away from the main station, like a compass rose with the station at its center. I raise an eyebrow. *More OPs?* Well, not Orbital Platforms, I suppose, but Atmospheric Platforms. Four APs seem overly paranoid, even for Angelou, until I see the sparkling energy sphere completely encompassing the station. Not simply APs, then, but part of the shield array, an army of small spherical generators that surround the station and project an energy shield blocking anything corporeal that might try to push its way in. Huge signal dishes deck the platforms, giving them yet a third purpose: data collection and communications. I silently nod, appreciating the efficiency.

After flying through one of the most complicated force hoops I've ever seen, we land in a hangar on the outside edge of the closest AP and disembark. Once the psychics clear us, we walk across the AP to the inner edge, where we board a small tender for the main station. Another smart design, allowing them to shunt everyone through the APs without ever taking the energy shields down.

As we close in on a landing bay affixed to the Central Habitat, I dare to broach the question that's been on my mind ever since I spotted the net. "Aren't you worried the ghouls might eventually make their way up here?" I tentatively venture. "Or that R&D might . . . fall on them?"

Angelou's laugh is like an old-fashioned gunshot, short and sharp. "It's true, the Spectres aren't confined to land the way we are. However, the odds of them actually finding this one station within the whole of Prism's atmosphere are astronomically low. It would be like finding a pebble in an asteroid field. Additionally, it's worth remembering that while the enemy can fly, they are still limited by distance and speed, even more so than we are. While we have technological ways in which to boost our capabilities, as far as we've been able to determine, they don't."

I blink, unraveling the explanation in my head until I reach the core response: *We're too far up and too well hidden.*

"As far as the station falling," Angelou continues, "not to worry, Sorenson. The systems keeping the station aloft have redundancies upon redundancies. Only an act of God could take this station down."

I raise an eyebrow. *An act of God or an act of Angelou?*

Clamping my lips together, I stifle a snort. Somehow I don't think the doctor would see much of a distinction between the two.

The shuttle alights in the landing bay with a soft clank. As Chen powers down the ship, I shoulder my duffle and follow Angelou across the pad. After weeks of travel, I'm eager to see the new base. While I've never been on a sky station, I've been on plenty of space stations. Some, like New Sol, were almost like living planetside, with orderly rows of streets and housing complete with green lawns and shady trees. Others were gray and artificial and austere, the workings within as cold as the vacuum without. I wonder which one R&D will be. We step out onto the station, and I immediately realize it's like no station I've ever been on.

We're standing within a wide, curving concourse circling the outer edge of the habitat. Sunlight beams down through the high ceiling, glinting along walls and floors all formed from some crystalline material ranging in color from cloudy pearl to glasslike purity. On the inner track lie various establishments—offices, shops, lounges, restaurants—while the outer wall might as well be one giant observation deck, the see-through surface providing a front row seat to the ever-shifting kaleidoscope of pastel mists and silver rains. Through the transparent surface, I can see the glimmer of another habitat way off in the distance, its gossamer walkway leading back to some point farther down the concourse.

Hefting my kit higher over my back, I continue to look around as I follow Angelou down the corridor. Green plants—flowering shrubs and lithe creepers—flourish within niches carved into the walls, their greenery tickling the arms of elegant benches placed sporadically along the corridor's outer edge. Miniature waterfalls trickle down the walls in soft rivulets, feeding the thirsty roots, and everywhere I look are tiny rainbows. They glow along walls and in corners and across benches, their colors arising naturally from the prismatic effects of sunlight through crystal. I glance down to see more mists swirling beneath my feet in drifts of lavender, gold, and pink and realize that despite my first impression, this habitat is actually more toric than spherical.

Angelou briefly points out various features as we go, his words sliding in and out of my ears in a running commentary.

". . . a native mineral, very strong, very durable. Not only more cost-effective than most alloys we might have used, but with tremendous capacity for absorbing and converting solar radiation."

". . . both traditional Terran plants as well as other more galactic varieties—all gengineered for maximum oxygen exchange, of course—and with plant fertilizers contained in the water, the whole system is largely self-sustaining."

". . . polarity of the energy shield allows it to repel energy-based weapons along with solid objects—as well as lightning strikes, of course. It's still completely permeable to gases and liquids, though."

There's a narrow, two-way slidewalk running down the center of the corridor. Angelou shows no inclination to step on, though we pass a couple of women in lab coats sliding in the opposite direction. I peer at the moving tiles and catch small glimpses of the inner workings through some of the more transparent bits of crystal. Despite that quick glance, I realize the station designer was actually very strategic in their use of the mineral, choosing nearly transparent pieces for storefronts and viewports while saving the cloudy, opaque pieces for where more privacy is generally desired.

After a few minutes, we end up in a small office perhaps a quarter of the way down the outer concourse, the words *Central Habitat Administration* digitized across the door in curling letters. Angelou nods to the receptionist on duty and leads me to a desk and console in the back.

"This is a secure facility, and much of the research done here is highly classified," Angelou explains as he scans in and punches some commands into the console. "Information is on a need-to-know basis. So is access to the various facilities on the base. At this point in time, I'm clearing you for Habitats 5 and 7. H5 holds the barracks for the Testing Division, and H7 houses our training facilities. Additionally, you along with everyone else on base have access to the Central Habitat, where we are now. Depending on your duties, temporary access may also be granted for other areas as the need arises."

"Yes, sir."

Angelou motions to the scanner, and I place my hand on it, palm down. The scanner glows for a moment, a tingle running through my fingers as my new clearance is programmed into my chit. I flex my fingers, almost fancying I can feel the biometal filaments from the chit lacing through my nerves.

Finishing up in the office, we return to the main concourse, continuing on until we reach a sliding hatch on the outer wall. Through the clear crystal, I can see a long walkway stretching out into the mist. The sign digitized on the hatch says *Habitat 7*.

"The main computer holds the bioscan for every individual on this station," Angelou explains as we scan our chits on the access panel and step into a small airlock. A soft hum buzzes through the chamber. "If the bioscans in the airlock don't match the chit scans, both doors will lock until security can arrive."

I nod, the translation perfectly clear: *Don't try to sneak into a habitat you're not cleared for.*

The hum quiets, and with a soft click, the opposing hatch slides open. Despite its spindly appearance from the outside, the narrow walkway is perfectly solid on the inside, though it sways slightly with the wind. It's also empty, only a slidewalk to mar the crystalline interior. We hop the walk and glide out into the swirling mists. Halfway down the tunnel, I happen to glance down. I couldn't see it before through the Habitat's thicker floors, but I can see the planetary net now, shifting in a continually-moving latticework so fast the individual lines are a mere blur—a bright blue blur, now that I don't have my infrared activated.

I shiver at the glowing reminder of the enemy so nearby. I can't see them, all those hundreds of klicks below—couldn't see them even if they were literally right on the other side of the crystal beneath my feet—but it doesn't matter, because *I* know they're down there, ghosting through dead cities and silent plains, sitting and watching and *waiting.*

And I suddenly realize I've never been more terrified in my entire life.

————

After another bioscan at the far airlock, we breeze into Habitat 7. While similar to the Central Habitat and made from the same crystalline mineral, H7 is more of a flattened oblong than a torus, with weight rooms, gyms, and a shooting range instead of general recreational areas.

Angelou leaves me in an office at the far end of the habitat with Emil Asriel, the Team Leader of Delta Team. The doctor stays only long enough to make a brusque introduction, and then he's gone, already subvocalizing into his chit before he's fully out the door. I find myself breathing a sigh of relief as he disappears. It's like

Angelou's very presence has been a constant weight on my shoulders that only now, once it's been removed, can I recognize.

Asriel turns out to be as straightforward as Angelou is cagey, his blunt manner accompanied by a colony-bred accent I can't quite place. Either age or the job has begun to take its toll, as crow's-feet frame his eyes and gray streaks drizzle through the hair at his temples, and his entire office has that lived-in look that suggests a guy who has no life outside the job. He reviews the dossier Angelou linked and asks me a few questions in his neatly clipped tones before filling me in on the basics.

"The Testing Division here on base is currently made up of four teams: Alpha, Beta, Gamma, and Delta. Each team is made up of anywhere from seven to ten members, called Tech Specialists, plus one Team Leader and one Assistant Team Leader, or ATL, whose job it is to assist the leader and take over in the event that they are unable to fulfill their job."

If the Team Leader is infected or killed, I mentally fill in.

"Depending on the mission parameters, we may combine two teams for a joint op if we need a larger force. At other times, we may split a single team in half, or even into triads, if smaller forces are called for."

I nod, and Asriel continues. "You'll start out as a Tech Specialist. However, if you distinguish yourself in service, you could eventually be promoted to ATL or even Team Leader as positions open up."

"Tech specialist?" I ask with a frown. "I don't recognize that rank."

"That's probably because it isn't a military rank. While we do have some military personnel on base, R&D is primarily a civilian operation and is run as such. This includes the Testing Division, which draws recruits from all branches of the military, both officers and enlisted, as well as civilians with special skills. Specialists are expected to obey their ATLs and Team Leaders regardless of what ranks they may have held before their transfers.

"However, keep in mind that while the base is run as a civilian operation, due to its classified nature, it's still technically designated as a Military Support base. As far as anyone outside of R&D is concerned, you're still a soldier with the CE military."

"So what becomes of me if I leave R&D? Do I just go back to my current guardian rank?"

Asriel hesitates. "That will be determined if and when such a situation occurs."

Somehow I get the feeling that "situation" never occurs. A frisson of anxiety tingles down my spine, but I nod and answer anyway, "Understood, sir."

"Normally, the Division Commander would assign you to a team, but since she's away on a recruiting mission, I'm temporarily handling her normal duties. I've decided to put you on my team for now. They're currently short a member, and they have a mission coming up tomorrow."

"Tomorrow?" I ask, surprised. "I don't need any training first?"

Asriel blinks. "Can you stand in a moving vehicle and shoot an aero-launcher?"

"Sir, yes, sir!"

"Then it sounds like you're ready." A wry smile cracks his mouth. "We're having a mission briefing in ten. If you still have concerns afterwards, we can speak again. Now, do you have any questions for me before we go?"

I'm about to say no when I catch sight of a small image digitized in the corner of his desk—the sole digital in an office with little in the way of personal effects. In it, a group of ten—four women and six men—cluster together in a familiar-looking hangar bay. Asriel is second from the left, his excited grin and crisp black uniform a match for the others beside him. I give a nod to the digital. "Is that Delta Team, sir?"

Startled, Asriel glances at the image. A strange look comes over his face, as though the picture has been here so long he's completely forgotten its presence. After a moment, he shakes his head. "That's Alpha Team, actually. Not just any Alpha Team, but the original— the first testing squad recruited for Dr. Angelou's base after the Spectre War began. This was taken the night before our first mission." He points to a stocky woman with a single utilitarian braid falling down her back, then to a tattooed man on her left. "Padma is our current DC, and Lake is running Gamma now."

I nod, appreciating the history. He doesn't identify any of the others in the digital, and it occurs to me that none of them are around anymore. Moved on to other assignments or casualties of war? Wisely, I don't ask.

We meet up with the rest of Delta Team in Briefing Room 3, a small lecture hall with an array of seats on shallow risers ascending up through the back of the room. Several people are already there when we arrive, chatting as they lounge in seats or lean against the chair backs. They turn as we enter, eyebrows rising at my appearance. A tall woman, her forearms rippling with muscle under all the black and red slashes lased on her skin, lets out a whoop.

"Ooh, fresh meat! Who's the new guy, TL?"

"In a second, Ty." Asriel motions for them to sit, waiting until all butts have hit seats before finally introducing me. "Team, this is Tech Specialist Michael Sorenson, lately of the Celestial Guard. He arrived today with Dr. Angelou and will be joining us on our mission tomorrow."

"Angelou recruited you himself?" Ty lets out a low whistle. "You must be something else. Angelou rarely bothers with us testing grunts."

I shrug, uncomfortable with the idea that I'm anything special. "Right place at the right time, I guess."

"Or the *wrong* place at the *wrong* time," Ty cracks.

I only shrug again in answer, though inwardly I can't help wondering if she didn't just hit the nail on the head with that one. Still, it's better than the truth, which is that I was merely a consolation prize after the scientists Angelou really wanted were lost on ScyLab 185g.

"Specialist," Asriel says with a telling look. Ty quiets down with a muttered apology, and Asriel gives me a brief rundown of my new teammates.

Like me, Ty also comes from the Guard, though a different division. In only a few short years, she's already been awarded a Celestial Star for valor in the field and a Level Six Marksmanship rating. She waggles her eyebrows and winks at me when she's introduced, and I find myself thankful that my dark skin covers the slight blush that blooms over my face.

Chen is next, her presence briefly startling me until I recall the Delta patch I saw on her upper arm when we first met. As well as ships, she's also skilled at piloting several types of ground vehicles.

When not running missions with Delta, she fills in as a pilot where needed, which explains why she was the one to pick up Angelou and me at Kittridge.

Backing up Chen on piloting duties is Herrera, also a fighter pilot from the CE Navy and an ace like Chen. Short and dark, he has the swagger of a guy who's overcompensating, though for what I have no idea. He gives me a classic "point and tongue click" when he's introduced, and I struggle not to roll my eyes.

Our Assistant Team Leader is Archer, who comes from Ground Forces on Zenith Major. With his buzz cut, barrel chest, and thick arms, I would have pegged him as a heavy gunner, but it turns out he originally trained as a medic. His greeting is short but cordial, and I find myself instantly liking him. He reminds me of a guy I knew in the Guard. Serious and dependable, he seems like the type you can always count on to have your back.

The slight Zephyr is downright tiny compared to Ty and Archer, but the wiry muscle beneath his uniform marks him as a former member of the ZG Corps, a special military division focused exclusively on performing dangerous and high-risk missions in zero-gravity environments. He's also a bit of a celebrity, I find out, having performed in a well-known company of ZG acrobats before being drafted. It certainly explains the silver-tipped eyelashes and gold-streaked hair. He sniffs when he's introduced, and I find myself suspecting he's one of those little guys with big attitude.

Though Angelou mentioned civilians when he recruited me, I'm still surprised to find out the final two team members are both civilian specialists. RC is our technical expert, an engineering grad student who was attending one of the most prestigious universities in the Expanse until the ghouls crashed it a year ago. Evacuation turned to recruitment, eventually landing him in R&D. Though his pale olive skin and brown hair are nondescript enough, his dark eyes spark with intelligence.

Zel is the other civilian, a lanky redhead with gold highlights in her long ponytail and the most iridescent green eyes I've ever seen. With her tall form and fit physique, I'm not surprised to find out she used to be a professional athlete, though oddly enough, no one actually states what sport she played. There's something naggingly familiar about her, but damned if I can figure out what it is. Probably saw her play once somewhere or other.

Intros over, we finish the meeting with a quick briefing for tomorrow's mission. The rest of the evening goes by in a whirlwind as I get assigned equipment, uniform, and bunk, as well as getting an informal tour of the dormitories and training facilities by Archer.

The next stop is the infirmary for a quick medscan and an injector full of standard Prism vaccines. While I'm there, the doctor on call inserts a Circadian Optimizer behind my left ear. The tiny biochip will induce hormone secretion at strategic times in order to help my body adjust its sleep-and-wake cycles to match this planet's unique patterns. At last, I end up in Asriel's office once again, where he fills me in on some basic procedures and protocols before officially clearing me for tomorrow's mission.

"Nervous, Sorenson?" Asriel asks.

"I'm just glad to be getting some action after weeks on a shuttle, sir."

Asriel nods. "Let's just hope you're still this enthusiastic after the mission, Specialist. Dismissed."

———

I lie on my bunk and listen to my roommates sleep. RC wheezes every other breath, and Zephyr snores like a gen-amped pig on steroids. Herrera is so still that for a split second I wonder if he died in his sleep and nobody noticed. I watch him for a couple of minutes until at last he barks an unintelligible sound and jerks over onto his side. He mutters a few words, then finally subsides back into sleep.

I sigh and turn over onto my back. In just a matter of hours, my first official mission at R&D begins. Infection, death—either outcome is a significant possibility. That's not what's worrying me, though. That's not what's keeping me up into the wee hours of the night while my roommates lie blissfully unconscious. Queuing up my chit, I check the hour for about the millionth time. 0130. That's 0930 on Iolanthe.

I have to make the call.

My teeth grit and my stomach clenches, muscles tightening up the way they always do when I think of her. Teal. My sister, my best friend. My Judas.

The thought of calling her after all this time—almost a year now—makes me feel sick with anger, but I made a promise. And even though Gran isn't here, even though she wrung that deffin' promise out of me under duress, I can't quite bring myself to break it. Not that I couldn't put it off. I've been putting it off for weeks, giving myself excuse after excuse not to call, and all this time that promise has hung over my head like some wretched axe waiting to fall. Only I can't put it off any longer; I have to cut the blade free and watch it come down.

With a sharp breath, I jerk up and swing my legs over the side of the bed. Padding into the adjoining hygiene unit, I shut myself into one of the cubes and link into the base's communication system. I follow the automated instructions carefully, grimacing slightly as the operator informs me my call will be monitored in real time for security purposes. Because this call won't be hard enough with*out* some stranger listening in. One more reason why I shouldn't have put it off so long. Still, I agree to the terms, then settle down to wait as the operator begins the complex process of connecting the call.

Within thirty seconds, I'm drumming my fingers on the side of the hygiene cube, unable to stay still despite the soothing hold music on the other end of the line. My chest tightens with each breath, and my mind involuntarily drifts to the last time I heard Teal's voice. To the messages she left on my hmail all those months ago.

She started calling almost immediately after I joined up and left. Once a week or more at first, leaving self-righteous messages in her snotty, know-it-all tone, telling me how everything had to be the way it was, how Lia had to die. How it was Lia's *choice* to go Nova and Teal'd had no right to stop her. All the same bullslag arguments she'd thrown at me back home before I finally stopped listening, finally stopped talking to her at all.

Self-righteous messages had eventually turned into frustrated, angry messages. Messages demanding that I pick up, that I call her back, that I hmail, asking if my brain was completely deprived of oxygen or if I still had an iota of intelligence left. Of course I'd never answered her. I shouldn't have even listened to her messages at all, but some deficient part of me couldn't seem to resist. I'd almost gotten thrown out of the Guard during that time, her fury only amping up my own. I was constantly itching for a fight, and only countless hours in the gym and combat training kept me from throwing a punch at people simply for asking what they were serving in the mess that night. But the weeks and then months passed, and finally the calls tailed off, until at last they stopped coming altogether. Until that day.

The anniversary of the day Lia died.

Her message, audio only, was less than a minute long.

"Hey, it's me. I was just calling to . . ." A long pause. *"I'm just calling to say I'm sorry. I'm so, so sorry."*

Even now, the backs of my eyelids prickle as her voice whispers in my head, and I brusquely blink the sensation back. Not that the tears are for Teal. No, only Lia. Always for Lia.

"Tech Specialist Sorenson?" The hold music disappears as the operator's voice comes back on the line. "Your call has been connected."

I hear a click on the other end of the line, then a soft chiming indicating that it's vibrating on her end. For a moment, I think she won't answer. Then suddenly, "Hello?"

It's like a punch to the gut, hearing her voice after all this time. Exactly the same as it's always been, as though only a day has passed and not months.

"Hello? Who is this?"

In spite of myself, my heart leaps at the sound of her voice, and I find myself remembering that old saying: *Blood is thicker than water.* For a moment, I'm tempted to open my mouth, to speak—

Her sincerity, her soul; she always seemed to know the right thing to say, even when I didn't.

—then the familiar rage burns every other emotion away until there's nothing left but pain. Pure, unadulterated, lacerating pain.

A wall slams down in my heart, so hard and unyielding not even the pain can stand up to it. I sever the link with a single gesture.

There. It's done. I promised I'd call Teal.

I never said I'd speak to her.

Onboard the Personal Space Station *Solaria*
Home of the Chairman of the Celestial Expanse

"*START AT THE BEGINNING; leave nothing out.*"

The prisoner flinched, jerking his head left and right as the disembodied voice echoed through the interrogation room. Fearful eyes darted in a futile cycle over table, chair, door, and window. Not that there was anything to see. The room had lain spare and unchanged for over a half hour, ever since the medtech had emptied the injector of drugs into the prisoner's veins and left.

From the padded leather chair in his office, the Chairman coldly smiled as he watched the digitized feed splayed across his wall. Even from uncountable light-years away, his voice still had the capacity to intimidate. It was only a pity he couldn't actually be there in person. The pathetic glitch was so scared he'd bet even his own modest psychic abilities would be able to sense this prisoner's fear.

Pity, indeed. There was such power to be found in fear, in allowing another's weakness to flow through you and become your strength. But then, he never left his personal station anymore. It was regrettable, but circumstances were what they were. Couldn't be helped.

On the wall, the prisoner was shaking his head. "I don't understand. I've already explained a dozen times. I was working dawn patrol in the Solace Quarter, as usual. The streets were quiet, only *the earliest risers up, and it was sunny." He paused, a quiet sorrow in his eyes, as though the fact that it was sunny only made everything that was to follow so much worse. "The air was crisp, cool. Pure, that faint scent of the city in the morning that's more memory than reality. I'd made my rounds twice through the quarter at that point, and I hadn't smelled anything. Until . . . I did."*

He started to raise his hands, only to be pulled up short by the metal cuffs chaining him to the table. Helplessly, he let them drop.

The Chairman opened his mouth to speak, abruptly stopping as an all-too-familiar tremor shuddered through his left hand. Quickly he shifted his hand out of the feed's range before anyone could see. His eyes fell on the ever-present injector in the corner of his desk, so close and yet impossibly far. Unable to use it without the others noticing, he instead concentrated on his hand, willing the tremors to cease, afraid to speak lest the telltale slur return to give him away.

From over the Chairman's shoulder came the Admiral's voice from another digitized panel along the back wall. "Move it along, Chairman. The Spectranol they gave him will last a week or more, but the Psi-lac will wear off within the hour."

Spectranol, to keep a squatter from breeding. Psi-lac, to suppress its psionic influence.

The Chairman's jaw clenched at the Admiral's rebuke even as the Doctor added his agreement from yet a third panel. As the head of TruCon, the largest corporation in the Expanse, the Chairman was in charge of the production and distribution of all Spectre drugs. He knew as well as they—better than they!—just how long these drugs would last.

His eyes went to his lower desk drawer with its veritable storehouse of pharmaceuticals. In point of fact, he knew the specific effects of a lot of drugs far better than he'd like.

To his great relief, the tremors suddenly eased, normality returning as quickly as it had fled. Conscious of the eyes over his shoulders, the Chairman refocused his attention on the prisoner, finally feeling safe enough to prompt him with a carefully enunciated, "Until you did?"

The Sniffer shook his head, tears leaking down his face. "I hadn't smelled anything—I swear to you!—and then suddenly they were just there. *Ghouls in every direction, so many I couldn't even smell their individual scents, just this thick, heavy stench, like one great sour-and-sweet blanket suddenly dropped over the world all at once. I went for my injector first, per procedure, then I called it in."*

A sob shook the man's shoulders, and the Chairman made a moue of disgust. He abhorred weakness of any kind, strove never to show his own myriad ills, and had zero patience for anyone who did.

He waved the last statement away. "I'm sure you followed procedure to the letter. What I want to know is where *they came from.* Surely you must have had some clue. A direction, a scent on the wind, something."

"Where did they come from?" the prisoner repeated dully. He let out a final sob, then pulled himself together with a visible will. He slowly raised his face to the camera, his stricken eyes as hard as diamonds.

"Nowhere," he answered. "It was like they appeared out of nowhere."

Every hair rose on the back of the Chairman's neck at the word, its harsh finality echoing through his office though it was spoken in another place a million light-years away. He abruptly cut off the feed, eradicating the witness from sight and sense as though nullifying the feed could also nullify the implications abounding through the room.

"Was that really necessary?" came the Admiral's dry voice from the panel behind him.

The Chairman slowly spun his chair around to face the woman behind him. God, how he hated her! Her smug demeanor, her sly condescension. Even the Doctor's cold intellectualism and rigid moralizing were preferable. He hated her, but he needed her—and the work she did.

The Chairman smiled coldly. "It was clear he had no more of use to say."

"He said enough," the Doctor interjected, hands folded behind his back and mouth pressed into a thin line. "The enemy has changed. Just as the squatters learned to mask their scent, just like with the Nova tech. They're adapting."

Adapting? The Chairman inwardly snorted. *Weaponizing, really, was what the Doctor meant. The Spectres didn't use weapons; they were weapons. Any significant adaptation on their end was tantamount to developing a new weapon in their conquest of the human race.*

"And just how is it you think they've adapted?" the Chairman asked. "They got into the city without notice, it's true, but the fences still went off, and the Sniffers smelled them during the invasion. If the ghouls had learned to evade the fences or mask their scent, why reveal themselves? Far better to take the city unaware so they could spread their numbers freely without our intervention. Nor have we received any other reports of this nature. Have we?"

"No, we haven't," the Doctor admitted. "That still doesn't explain how they got into the city in such numbers, though."

"It was a test."

Both men glanced over at the Admiral in surprise. A frosty smile touched her lips, a nod to the ingenuity of the enemy rather than any real expression of pleasure directed toward the two men before her.

"Adaptation, previously unknown skill, some other tactic altogether. We've been so busy focusing on 'how' when we should have been asking ourselves 'why.' Adjusting their strategy, trying a new MO—this isn't random behavior. They're testing us."

The Chairman raised an eyebrow. "Yes, but testing us for what?"

"What does any combatant test the enemy for?" she countered, lacing her fingers loosely together. She studied her hands, drawing out the silence until it stretched taut through the air like razor-sharp wire. Dropping her hands, she met his eyes and spoke.

"Weakness. They're looking for our Achilles heel."

PHASE TWO

9 WE WHEEL THROUGH THE SAVANNAH in a blaze of sound, roamers purring through the crisp morning air. Light streaks over the southern and eastern horizons, spreading across the straw-like grass in crosshatched shafts of white and yellow. Persephone, rising in the south, her rays briefly kissing Demeter's just before she sets in the east.

I drop my hand through the open framework of the roamer and let the coarse stalks ripple beneath my fingertips. The savannah stretches out in every direction, gold-tipped and draped with the gossamer glimmer of spider webs, while off in the distance the metallic walls of a city gleam dully in the morning light. Here and there, grayish-brown trees dot the plain, their thin trunks twisting in strange designs while draping branches blow in the wind. Everything about this land is like a shadow—a wan, washed-out version of something once bold and bright—but in the brief crossing of sun over sun, it becomes something more. It becomes brilliant.

Someone coughs, and I turn my mind back to the mission. We're on the southernmost continent of Javeyn, one of Prism's three terraformed moons, lost to the Specs and quarantined approximately a year ago. While the majority of the southern population was evacuated ahead of the invasion, large pockets of squatters still remain, mostly within the towns and cities. They're not the ones we're here for, though. No, we're here for the ghouls.

I lift my head and sniff the air. Nothing. At least nothing alien. Just the cold dry rustle of a winter mistral whispering across the plain.

From the opposite side of the roamer bed, Zel catches my motion. She lifts her own nose and takes a giant inhale. "I'm getting nothing, Sorenson. You?"

"Negative."

"That's because there aren't any ghouls around, dumb-bots," Ty's voice crackles through the com. She makes a face at us through the open framework of the other roamer.

"Hey, watch who you're callin' a dumb-bot, you null," Zel razzes back good-naturedly.

"Most ghouls like to hang around the inhabited areas, cities and towns." Zephyr glances up from his GPS. *"That's why we chose this field in the middle of nowhere as a landing zone. Less chance of getting ambushed by the enemy on the way down."*

Ty and Zel exchange a look. *"Thanks for the lesson, Professor Obvious,"* Ty snorts sarcastically, and the two women laugh.

I frown slightly at their antics and survey the others, unsure what to make of my new team. Chen is at the wheel of my roamer, Archer riding shotgun as ATL and Zel in the back with me; while Zephyr drives Asriel, RC, and Ty in the other roamer. Herrera is hovering somewhere up in the air, babysitting the ship while being ready to make a quick pickup should we need one. Despite the good-natured bitching, everyone looks capable, ready. Still, tension coils in my gut at the idea of going into a mission with so little knowledge of my team. Especially a mission like this one.

We're going ghoul hunting.

I heft the High Frequency Sound Amplifier in my hands and examine it once again. The metal cylinder is approximately a meter long, with retractable spikes on one end and a control interface on the other. Four thin blue lights run the length of the cylinder, separated in between by long speakers. The whole thing is enveloped by a protective cover made from a hard, transparent material. When the sound amplifier is activated, it can produce tones spanning a wide range of frequencies and decibel levels. Too high-pitched for human ears, but not for ghouls. Just as our launchers can repel ghouls using the right mix of gases, theoretically we can use this device to do the same, assuming we can find the right sound frequency. So the theory goes, anyway. Now it's our job to put the theory into practice. But before we can repel any ghouls, first we have to find some.

I crouch in the back of the roamer, one hand on the railing of the open framework for balance as we drive west through the tall grass directly toward that gleaming city on the horizon. There are no roads to the east of the city, no human development at all. Just endless savannah up until the coastal cities some five hundred klicks away. With the terraforming on Prism's satellites only completed within the last fifty years, humans' expansion across the land is yet unfinished, large blocks of land still virgin and undeveloped.

The roamers eat up the ground quickly, crushing through the savannah without effort, and before long we're coming up on the eastern edge of the city. The force fence, a huge bubble of energy, wraps around the city above, below, and on all sides, extending a good thousand meters past its walls. The bubble is further subdivided into grids by additional force fence posts dotting the plain at regular intervals. The fences will only trip when a ghoul moves through one of the energy bands projected between two posts. Though the energy bands are currently invisible, they're keyed to shimmer blue if ghouls are crossing through them toward the city, red if they're moving away. I uplink the grid to my helmet and program it to do the same.

A slight tingle dances across my skin as we roll through the outermost fence posts. I press closer to the rails of the roamer, nose alert as we move closer and closer to the city. A hard breeze cuts across us as we turn directly into the wind, rustling the grass around us in swirls of pale gold, and that's when it hits me. A faint sour-and-sweet reek I'd know anywhere.

Ghouls.

My hands tighten on my aero-launcher as we coast deeper into the field. The closest ghouls are a good five hundred meters out at this point, the very limit of my olfactory capabilities, but still my heart rate ratchets up a notch. Half a klick isn't much when the ghouls can cover it in a minute flat.

Another hundred meters in, Asriel calls us to a halt. "All right, team! You've got your assignments. Let's do it."

A spurt of adrenaline races through my veins as I pop up through the frame of the roamer, launcher at the ready, and I allow myself a hard grin. Now *this* is what I signed on to Division 7 for. In the front, Archer does the same; we'll be covering Zel for the duration of the test as she operates the sound amplifier. In the next roamer, RC will be taking constant readings from the grid as Zel runs the various frequencies, covered by Asriel and Ty.

I watch Zel as she sets up the amplifier, placing it upright on retractable legs that spring from one end, her nimble fingers dancing across the control interface. The long blue lights snap on next, making the cylinder glow brightly under the cloudy sky. A moment later she confirms, "High Frequency Sound Amplifier activated and ready for testing."

Asriel nods and activates the recorder on his chit. "High Frequency Sound Amplifier Test now commencing at 0953 SGT, Mission Leader Emil Asriel recording. First test: frequency setting one, volume setting one."

He nods to Zel, and she starts the first pulse. As promised, the sound is too high-pitched to actually hear. However, I immediately feel a strange buzzing sensation tickling at my ear, not even a noise so much as a vibration. Judging from the others' reactions, I'm not the only one sensing it.

"What is *that*?" Ty asks.

"Dr. Rahman said that might happen," Asriel confirms. "While the sounds themselves are past our range of hearing, he said we'd probably sense some of the vibrations. Carry on."

I keep my nostrils fanned and eyes on the grid, but as far as I can tell, nothing changes. The ghouls seem content to stay where they are, neither moving away nor coming closer. RC, who's carefully monitoring the grid with much more sophisticated equipment in the next roamer, confirms my thoughts with a shake of his head. "No change."

We continue the test, going through combination after combination of frequencies and volumes while Asriel keeps an audio log of the process and RC keeps an instrumental one. While a far-off gridline occasionally lights, it appears more random than test-related. It doesn't take long for my initial excitement to turn to boredom, arms tiring from holding my launcher up so long. That's when Chen starts taking us closer.

Slowly we begin driving forward, Zel continuing to flip through the settings one at a time as we push on inexorably toward the waiting enemy. Our four-hundred-meter cushion begins to drop, by ten meters, twenty, fifty, and still we press on. My palms are sweating now, my ears itching from the constant low-level buzzing of the device.

One hundred, one-twenty, one-fifty. We're only two hundred meters away now, and still we keep going. The wind has picked up considerably, blowing in hard gales from the north. My foot is fidgeting in my boot as our margin continues to collapse, my nose sniffing convulsively for any threatening reaction from the enemy. Instead of just scenting Specs directly ahead, I can smell them off to the sides as well now. The possibility of getting surrounded only makes my nose twitch and my feet fidget more.

"You'll observe that they haven't attacked or attempted to approach us yet," RC comments from the second roamer. "One possible hypothesis is that the amplifier *is*, in fact, working, but as a defensive weapon rather than an offensive one. In other words, the sound isn't acting as a repellent to force them away, but more like a shield to keep them from approaching."

"That's what we're here to find out," Asriel says.

We continue on, sidling ever closer to our waiting nemesis at Asriel's command. We're a hundred meters out from a body of ghouls at least fifty strong when it happens. The roamer hits a nasty bump, and the amplifier pitches over. Before Zel can grab it, the device hits the rails with a loud *thunk!* The protective covering over the amplifier cracks and falls off, and instantly a supercharged draft of sour-and-sweet comes rushing into my nose. A moment later, red lights shimmer in two dozen places across the fence grid as every ghoul within a klick radius suddenly sits up and takes notice. Then they all take off flying.

Straight for *us*.

Even as Asriel yells, "Retreat!" Chen is wheeling us around, Zephyr right on her heels in the next vehicle. Sour-and-sweet burns my nostrils, the fences lighting up like red fireworks on three sides as an entire shiver comes rushing at us. I fire off burst after burst with my launcher, moving from side to rear as the roamer completes its circle and begins hightailing it back through the savannah, while Archer throws gas grenades to cover our retreat. Not that either effort is doing much good with the wind dispersing everything we put out within seconds. Zel scrambles to turn the amplifier off, but it's too late. Even once the blue lights go out, the ghouls still come, our scent in their nostrils just as theirs is in ours. More ghouls descend from up above, diving down like invisible birds of prey, and for a split second I'm sure they're going to surround us. Trap us within an unbreakable circle we can't escape from . . .

We burst through the knot of ghouls just before it tightens, pedal to the metal as we zoom away from the city. The enemy falls back, unable to match the speed of the roamers despite the tall grass slowing us down, and our marginal lead opens up with every second. A hundred meters, two, three. We pass the outermost posts of the force fence grid, zooming out through the savannah in a rustle of grass, and before long they're so far back I can barely smell them. I keep my launcher up, though the others are already letting out whoops and sighs of relie—

"TREE!!!"

The fallen tree looms up ahead so suddenly no one sees it coming, its presence secreted within the thick grass until the last moment. Zephyr barely has time to yell a warning, the squeal of his brakes screaming through the savannah, before we're upon it.

Chen reacts instantly, throwing us hard right to avoid it even as the other roamer crashes hard against the trunk. Our own roamer jumps as the left front wheel charges up over a tangle of roots, dropping sharply as the brittle wood collapses under the weight. We slew around, the left front tire stuck even as the rest of the roamer keeps going. I catch sight of the sound amplifier flying through the rails just before I pitch backward, dropping my launcher as I cling to the roamer frame for dear life. Wind whips my face and vegetation flies through the air at us as the spiked wheel of the roamer spins in place, unable to pull free of the roots and savannah.

"The amplifier!"

I look up just in time to see Zel leap from the roamer. The tree trunk caves in beneath her feet, the rotting wood too weak to take her weight, and she flies forward. Unable to stop her momentum, she tucks herself into a ball and rolls, springing back to her feet barely a second after hitting the ground. Instantly she takes off, red ponytail flying as she sprints for the device.

"Zel!" Archer yells.

"They're still a full minute out, ATL! I can get it!"

He pauses. "All right, Zel, go! Chen, stay at the wheel. Sorenson and I are going to dig this thing out!"

Even before he finishes giving the command, I'm vaulting out of the roamer and going for the mired wheel. Roots crack and split as I tear at the debris caging us in. While the smaller, more brittle pieces snapped like twigs when we hit, the larger roots still have a lot of fight left in them. My back and biceps strain as I yank at a particularly thick one, the wood strong and unyielding as it resists my efforts. Then Archer's there, adding his considerable strength to mine, and the root cleaves away from the tree with a loud *snap!*

"Try it now, Chen!"

Woody detritus flies up at us as Chen hits the accel. The roamer rocks in place as she guns it forward and back, but otherwise doesn't move. A glance over my shoulder tells me Asriel's group isn't doing much better. Smoke rises from their roamer's hood, and despite repeated attempts by Zephyr, their vehicle isn't moving.

"Heads up, team!" Zel's voice sings through the com as she makes it back, the amplifier tucked safely under her arm. *"We've got incoming!"*

I whip my head around at her summons, and the stench hits me full in the face. *Ghouls.* Five hundred meters out and closing fast. They must have sensed that we stopped and realized we were vulnerable. *Slag!* In a head-to-head matchup, the ghouls can outrun pretty much any human on foot and are basically tireless. If we can't get this roamer moving again, it's all over for us.

I redouble my efforts, ripping through roots and grass, trying to find the hang-up, Zel and Archer at my side. Over the com, I can hear Asriel calling for a pick-up, but Herrera is still two minutes out.

"Archer, status!" Asriel snaps out.

"The roamer's still mired, TL!"

Asriel swears, *"And ours is dead. Keep at it, we're coming over to help!"*

We're not going to make it, I suddenly realize. The shiver is only thirty seconds out now. Even with the others' help, we won't get moving in time. My eyes flick to the field, strangely empty to my eyes, though my nose says otherwise. Beside me, Zel suddenly drops the root she was tugging on and jumps back.

"I think I can buy us some time, TL."

"Zel, what—"

Before anyone can react, she grabs the amplifier and takes off. Blue lights spring to life a few seconds later, whirring up the sides of the cylinder as she activates the amplifier. The enemy's response is instantaneous, the shiver immediately winging around to follow Zel. They whip past us a good thirty meters to our right, hot on the trail of the soundless shriek of the amplifier and the lone woman who carries it.

"I've got it!"

I turn around just in time to see Zephyr yank a nasty-looking piece of debris out of the wheel well. He jumps back, Chen revs the motor, and the roamer pops free.

"Everybody in!"

Nobody needs a second invitation. Within seconds we're piling into the back, nearly falling over each other in our haste to get in, and then we're off, zooming through the savannah after Zel.

We catch up fast, pacing alongside Zel some twenty meters to her left, ready to veer off if the ghouls show any signs of coming for us. I clutch my launcher tight, unable to do anything but stare in awe as Zel runs the race of her life. Her long legs weave through the grass in powerful strides, arms pumping like stutter-cannons as she sprints five meters in front of the shiver. My heart pounds as I watch her go. Though I knew it was conceivably possible for a human—a *very fast* human—to outrun a ghoul, I never thought I'd actually *see* it.

"We need to get Zel out of there, and quick," Asriel is saying. "Zel, drop the amplifier! When the shiver stops to go for it, we'll swing around and grab you."

The amplifier drops from her hands as soon as the words are out of his mouth, bouncing through the grass before getting eaten up within the tall fronds. I up the magnification on my lenses, searching for the cylinder until I spot its bright blue lights rolling through the grass once again. I will it to keep going, far from Zel. *Come on, come on . . .*

The blue lights suddenly wink out, the amplifier disappearing into the grass, and the ghouls zoom straight over the device as though it's not even there, still hot on Zel's trail. I swear as I realize what must have happened.

"Slag! The fall must have triggered the off switch!"

At my exclamation, Zel risks a sniff over her shoulder, eyes widening as she catches their scent. She pushes on with renewed vigor, strong rhythm never faltering as she tears across the ground. She's so fast I half expect her to leave fire trails in her wake. But as fast as Zel is, I realize with horror, the ghouls are *faster*.

They're gaining on her.

My heart's in my throat, palms sweating as I smell the shiver slowly start catching up to her. Almost imperceptibly at first, so that I'm not even sure if what I'm scenting is accurate.

Until I am.

Five meters, four, three. Slowly but surely, they're creeping up on her. While Zel may be their equal in speed, the Specs have one huge advantage. Humans tire; ghouls *don't*. From the others' reactions, I'm not the only one who smells it.

"We've got to get her out of there, TL," Archer says, turning off his com so Zel can't hear. "Zel's fast, but she's not inhuman. She can't hold them off forever."

"Agreed," Asriel says. "Ideas, people?"

"What about using the amplifier to draw them away?" RC suggests. "That's what attracted them in the first place."

"Not a bad idea," Archer says, "only one problem: Where *is* the amplifier?"

As one, we all glance back at the sea of grass, thigh-high strands whipping about within the wind's breath. I scan my head back and forth, trying to remember where I saw it fall, but everything looks the same. Even with my lenses on highest magnification, I can't pick out anything. Judging by the squinting eyes and shaking heads around me, neither can anyone else.

I jerk my gaze back to Zel, nostrils fanning as I smell for the enemy. She's down to a two-meter lead and still losing ground, exhaustion clearly starting to take its toll on her. Wherever that amplifier might be, it's obvious she's not going to last long enough for us to track it down.

"Launchers?" I venture. "Just drive up and blast 'em off?"

"There's gotta be fifty ghouls on her tail," Ty says. "There's no way we can blast away that many, not in such an open space with a steady wind. Even if we launched grenades, the wind would just blow the gas right away."

"So what if we just swing around ahead of her for a quick pickup?" Archer says.

At the wheel, Chen shakes her head. "They're too close. In the time it would take to stop and pick her up, they'd be on us."

"Well, we have to do something!" Ty says.

Before anyone else can speak, Herrera's deep voice booms over the com. *"Someone call for a pickup?"*

The ship drops down through the clouds above us, its gleaming carapace shining like a snow-white charger riding to the rescue. It lands directly in front of Zel, a mere fifty meters ahead, bay door already opening. To my surprise, she instantly veers away from the ship.

"No," Zel huffs through the com, breaths coming fast and hard. *"They're only a couple of meters behind me now. If I go for the Sky-Runner, they'll overrun the entire ship before you can take off again."*

Silence falls over us, broken only by Ty's muttered expletive. Zel's right. If we pause long enough to pick her up, via ship or roamer, they'll grab us all. If we don't, well, sooner or later someone's going to win this race. And it won't be Zel.

"Wait, I've got an idea," Asriel says. "Chen, take us in."

"We can't leave Zel!" Ty exclaims, though Chen doesn't even hesitate, gunning straight for the bay and only braking moments before we fly inside.

As soon as we're in, Asriel immediately begins barking orders to everyone as he explains the plan. I vault out of the roamer along with the others, foot tapping anxiously as Herrera closes the bay doors and fires the thrusters. Though it's only thirty seconds or so before

we're in the air again, every moment feels like an eternity. I jog to the passenger section with the others, arriving just as Archer hits the control to open the side passenger door. It slides open, giving us a good view of Zel still furiously sprinting across the plain, then Herrera banks and we're sailing down toward the grass below.

The ladder unfurls from the shuttle like a banner as we swoop in low. Herrera takes us down, skimming along the plain until the end of the ladder touches the top of the grass, swinging and swaying across the fronds as he strives to hold us in place. Asriel activates the com.

"Zel—"

"I see it!"

And that's when she really takes off.

She might as well have boosters on her shoes, that's how fast she ignites, impossibly long strides pushing even longer, harder, faster as she sprints for the ladder. Her long ponytail streams out behind her, glowing with red and gold fire, her pale skin ablaze under the setting light of Demeter. Spider webs cling to her forearms, fluttering out in gossamer drifts. She looks like an angel.

She's almost here, the shiver only a couple of meters off her tail now. We hover in place, the shuttle swaying in the wind despite Herrera's best efforts, and with it the ladder. It snakes to and fro in the savannah wind, whipping and blowing through the tips of the long grass. My heart's in my throat, fingers white-knuckling over the seat as I realize how easy it would be for Zel to go for the ladder and miss. One fumble, one fall, and she'll be history, buried under an avalanche of ghouls. Only a meter out now, I catch my breath as she spots the ladder, winds up her arms, and leaps . . .

Her hands snag the rungs, legs wrapping through the ropes as she screams, "Go, go, go!"

Herrera guns it, Zel shoots up, and the ghouls sail under her. We skyrocket up from the plain, and in an instant we're gone, hurtling up and away through the bright afternoon sky.

Cheers break out, everyone whooping and hollering as the ghouls fall off, no match for the speed of the shuttle. Archer and RC crank up the ladder, and before long Zel is crawling into the ship to a multitude of backslaps and fist bumps.

She collapses onto the floor with a grin. "Thanks for the lift."

A chorus of laughter breaks out. Even I can't help grinning, adrenaline and relief rushing through my veins in a mixture of giddy triumph, and for a second I'm tempted to join in the camaraderie. Only for a second, though. Then I remember every teammate, every friend, every family member I've ever lost, and the impulse dies, snuffed out like a dying sun finally gone black.

Ignoring Archer's outstretched hand, I settle back against the shuttle wall, nostrils fanned and eyes fastened on that shadowy grass until long after that sour-and-sweet stench has faded away into the wavering savannah below.

———

Herrera takes us out of the atmosphere, and we're off the moon within the hour. Everyone appears to be uninjured, unfazed even, by our wild ride, though I doubt I'm the only one breathing a sigh of relief when we punch through the exosphere and into space. The only casualty of the day is Ty's necklace.

"Ow," she says, unsealing the top of her jacket and picking what appear to be glassy bits out of her upper chest. A silver chain hangs around her neck, the broken end of what used to be some sort of crystal pendant bumping softly against her skin. Blood wells up in tiny pinpricks around the translucent shards.

"It must have broken during the crash," she says, using her shirt-front to wipe away the blood. "Thanks, Zeph."

"Thank the tree," he retorts sarcastically, and everyone laughs.

The trip back to base goes quickly. Asriel uses the time for a short debriefing, then upon our return sends the three involved in the roamer crash to the infirmary for a quick medscan. The rest of us are free to grab some chow and a shower.

It doesn't hit me until I'm standing under the water in the hygiene units. The thrill of the mission fades and the adrenaline drains off, and suddenly every thought and emotion I've locked away comes rushing back in. My hands start shaking, and my heart catches in my chest. Breath stutters in my lungs, and it's only through the sheerest effort that I drag in one breath after another, each inhalation rattling through my windpipe with the greatest reluctance. I ball my fingers into fists and lean against the wall, but it doesn't do any good. It never does. All I can do is wait for it to pass.

Long after the water shuts off I remain, standing in the shower, my body shivering with fear, my fists shaking in anger, and my heart trembling with a grief that just never goes away.

10

SQUISH!

The clear gel spurts out of the cuff of my glove as I sink my fingers deep into what has to be at least half a canister of shaving gel. Laughter peals out around me, filling the armory with deep male chuckles and higher-pitched feminine giggles.

Yeah. *My* team. What a bunch of comedians.

I clench my jaw as I gingerly pull my left hand out of my mission gauntlet. Gobs of gel dribble off my hand in gooey plops, eliciting yet another round of guffaws.

"Hey, Sorenson!" yells Herrera. "Forget to wash your hands after hitting the hygiene units?"

Followed by Ty: "Don't you know you're supposed to shave those hairy knuckles *before* coming to work?"

The heckling is nothing less than I'd expect, the ritual new-guy hazing hardly new to me, but irritation smolders inside me anyway. The old me, the one who existed before Lia died, would've found the whole thing hilarious. He'd already be flipping those nulls the one-finger salute even as he began plotting his revenge.

The new me is *not* amused.

I take a step toward the two hecklers, anger burning in my chest

and fists involuntarily clenching. At that moment, the door opens and
Archer walks in. The temporary distraction cuts through the rage,
and common sense intercedes. Taking a breath, I clamp down my
temper, then scoop up my other glove and exit the room. The soiled
gloves get tossed into a laundry bin before I make my way to the
nearest hygiene unit for a thorough hand-washing. Too late. Those
hairy knuckles Ty apparently objected to are now completely smooth.
So now I've got one girly hand and one normal one. Perfect.

Grumbling, I return to the armory, ignoring the chuckles as I grab
a new pair of gauntlets from the equipment locker. Though it would
be totally deficient to play the same prank twice in a row, I still check
the new pair before slipping them on. I flex my fingers a few times to
check the fit, adjust the fastenings, and reach for my helmet. Raise it
halfway to my head, then stop. Look inside.

"See!" Zel whispers. "I told you he'd check his helmet."

"You were right," Ty agrees.

A clink of chits, no doubt followed by a quick transfer of credits
from one account to the other.

I make another trip back to the equipment locker.

Grabbing another helmet, I shake my head. It's been a week since
I arrived at R&D, and besides a few irritating pranks, I've settled in
without too much fuss. When I'm not training with Delta Team, I
spend any extra hours in the gym or on the shooting range, all the
while trying to dodge the questions of my new teammates: where I'm
from, why I joined up, who's waiting for me back home. The usual
stuff. When I can't avoid the queries, I just grunt or shrug off their
questions. My past is none of their damn business, any more than
theirs is mine. Not that I can entirely avoid learning some of my
teammates' pasts with all the barracks gossip going around.

Asriel, I've learned, comes from a tiny colony on the edge of the
Lower Expanse, one of the few places left where English is not the
primary language, which explains his odd accent and careful enuncia-
tion. Archer is a devoted family man; he sets his chit two hours early
every morning so he can link his five-year-old daughter right before she
goes to bed. RC keeps the image of a beautiful brunette digitized inside
his locker, while Zephyr's has a number: 397. It's the number of days
left in his term of service. The number of days before he can go home.

Once upon a time, that could have been me, counting the days after getting drafted away from everyone I love. Now my home is just a pile of memories and debris floating in space.

We finish suiting up before trooping en masse to the transport bay. Now that we've proven the sound amplifier actually works—though not, perhaps, in the way anyone expected—we're being sent out to set up a whole array of them down on Javeyn so the researchers can do additional testing. We stop long enough to get a last-minute briefing from Dr. Rahman, the project head, before departing, only to find out that we're not expected to actually activate them this time. Confused looks greet this revelation.

"How are you going to continue testing if you don't want us to activate them?" Archer asks.

Dr. Rahman furrows his brow. "We'll use the remote activation sequence, of course."

Stunned silence. It's Ty, eyes practically bugging out, who finally says what everyone's thinking. "There's a *remote control* for these things?"

"Of a sort," Rahman confirms. "A single amplifier has limited application, but an entire network could be potentially groundbreaking. By activating a specific series of amplifiers, one after another, you could not only clear a strategic area, you could lead the ghouls somewhere specific. Like a trail of bread crumbs leading them wherever we want them to go. To that end, we created the amplifiers with the capacity to be networked together. Once you've networked a set of amplifiers, you can activate them all by simply activating one. The amplifiers also have a built-in timing system, so you can preset them to activate at a specific time. Didn't I explain this in the briefing the other day?"

The word *no* has never been conveyed quite so eloquently as it is in the ensuing silence.

We don't go back to our previous testing site but instead set up the network on one of Javeyn's northern continents, per Rahman's instructions. Compared to our last mission, this one goes off with barely a hitch. Though we encounter a few ghouls during the setup and are forced to either drive them off with launchers or retreat altogether, it's nothing compared to the mob we took on during our first mission. We fly to the last site and split into pairs to place the final group of amplifiers.

"Set up or guard?" Zel asks, offering me a choice of launcher or amplifier.

I grab the amplifier, forcing the spiked end into the ground while Zel stands guard over me with her launcher. Once it's secure, we get in our roamer, drive on to the next location, and do it all again. We're on our fourth one when Zel speaks.

"So, Sorenson."

My shoulders tense, and I just know she's about to ask me about my past or my family or something else equally intrusive. I take a deep breath.

"Know any good jokes?"

I laugh in startled relief. For the next hour, we trade bad jokes and funny stories of our time in the service. Zel's got a couple of good ones about Ty—no surprise there, with the two of them best friends as well as roommates. We both agree that the last Javeyn mission is definitely one for the books.

"I still can't believe you managed to stay ahead of the mob," I say, shaking my head in wonder as I pound in another amplifier.

Zel looks away. "It was no big deal."

"No big deal? I never thought I'd see anyone who could outrun a ghoul, and certainly not a mob. It was quite a ra—"

Race. Memory clicks into place, as if my mind were only waiting for that one tiny clue to drop, and suddenly I know who she is. Why she looked so familiar that first day I met her in the briefing room with the others.

"You were that runner from the 18th Cross-Galactic Games. The one who—" I stop, suddenly afraid to say it out loud.

"Cheated?" Zel finishes for me. Her clear blue eyes meet mine, flat and steady, and a slight flush touches my cheeks at the hint of challenge in her gaze.

I nod, the details coming back to me now that I've recognized her. Andreja Zelinski, a runner from the colony world Amaranth. She set a record pace in the five thousand meters only to be disqualified shortly before the medal ceremony when testing confirmed she was illegally gen-amped. Muscles, lungs, bones, joints; all prenatally engineered for one purpose. To win. While it had been widely suspected that genetic amplification was being used to cheat at elite sports, this was the first time they'd been able to successfully test for it. The news had been on all the feeds, Zel's digital becoming a household image in an instant.

What followed wasn't pretty. They stripped her of all honors and awards, and banned her from professional athletics for life. For the next couple of years, the media followed her ruthlessly, trying to get her side of the story, but she never gave a single interview. Never talked, though she probably could've made a fortune selling the story if she'd wanted to. Then a year ago the stories stopped, as if she'd just fallen off the grid, ceased to exist.

No, not ceased to exist. *Recruited.*

What tales had the R&D recruiters spun to weave her into this web? I suddenly wonder. What stories of duty and honor, of glory and redemption, had they whispered in her ear to make her run into fields of ghouls with reckless abandon?

"Why did you do it?" I suddenly ask. "After everything that happened, why did you come to R&D?"

She sighs, a small noise that feels fraught with more meaning than mere words could ever convey. At last, she says, "Because I wanted what I did to matter."

My heart clenches at the reply, the reply of someone who lost everything that meant anything in a single instant, and no matter what she does, can never get it back again. The same way I can never get anything—or anyone—back again no matter how much I might want it.

Her liveliness, her laugh; the thrill of my heart every time we raced through the station without a care in the universe.

The distant howl of a mountain lion cuts through the silence, rescuing us from the twin pains of our past. With a gruff nod, I vault back into the driver's seat, waiting while Zel slides into the passenger side. Wordlessly, we drive on to the next site.

———

An hour later, we dock at OP EQ-1, one of the orbital platforms orbiting Prism, for a quick psychic scan before returning to the station.

I step out of the docking bay after the PsyCorp specialist finishes with me, and my mouth drops open. The place is in chaos.

The plain metal walls are ablaze with holographic displays, every spare centimeter taken up by scrolling data streams and vivid control panels. Scientists in white consult with technicians in silver, typing commands into their tip-pads that then wirelessly sync with the ever-changing feeds along the walls. Others stand in groups of two and three, talking in excited voices and occasionally gesticulating at this display or that. Movement flashes in the corner of my eye, and I turn just in time to see a suited body flash past one of the viewports.

What could they possibly be doing that would require people on the outer hull?

Before I can voice my thoughts aloud, we're approached by the OP commander on shift, a PsyCaptain judging by the patterned half-star and four silver cross-bars on her uniform.

"Team Leader," she greets Asriel, the nod of her head denoting respect though not deference. "My apologies, but we can't grant clearance for you and your team to return to the station just yet. One of our research teams is about to conduct a weapons test. For everyone's safety, all air traffic is being held until the test is completed."

"Of course," Asriel agrees. "I knew of the test, but I was under the impression it wasn't scheduled until sixteen hundred."

"It originally was, but the weather technicians have predicted strong solar flare activity later today, so they decided to move the test up. We have rations in the break room over there," the PsyCaptain says with a sideways nod. "Your team is welcome to kick back and grab something to eat while they wait—it shouldn't be more than an hour—or there's an observation deck at the far end of the platform where they can watch the test, if they'd like."

Just so long as we stay out of the way, I mentally translate.

Asriel thanks the OP commander, then turns to us. "All right, team, you heard the PsyCaptain—break room or observation deck. You know the drill. I'll link you when we've got the go-ahead to leave. Dismissed."

I follow the others down a cross-corridor and into a smallish room with a few tables and a scattering of chairs. A counter runs along one wall holding racks of meal-paks, a couple rehydrators, and a drink dispenser, while the opposite wall is digitized to show the view outside the platform. Everyone immediately makes themselves at home, dropping gloves and helmets on tables and dumping their favorite ration paks into the rehydrators. As I watch their easy routine, it's obvious they've done this before.

I sidle up to the counter next to Archer and grab a pak. "So what's the deal with all this testing, anyway?"

"Oh, that? They're just testing another potential WMGD." At my confused look, Archer clarifies, "Ghoul-killer."

"Up on an orbital platform?"

"Of course."

I frown, not understanding. "How do you test a ghoul prototype on an OP without any ghouls?"

From across the room, Ty laughs. "No, you've got it all wrong, Sorenson! The OP isn't the testing site. It's the *weapon*."

The weapon! But if this whole platform is a weapon, then— "The testing ground?"

"Is the planet," Archer confirms.

My eyes widen as I realize only now just how accurate my earlier assessment of the planet as Angelou's laboratory was. Lab rats, indeed! My surprise must show on my face, for Zephyr puts in sarcastically, "What, you thought the master plan was to give us all little ghoul guns and send us out to kill each one off individually?"

"No, I—"

"Hey, I'd love to have a ghoul gun," Herrera interjects. "Something that would actually kill 'em instead of just pushing 'em away. You give me a ghoul gun, and I'll go out and kill every single one of those bastards."

"As if you could," Ty retorts.

"Hey, you got no idea what I can do," Herrera shoots back with a suggestive waggle of his eyebrows.

"What, make women puke?" Zel hoots, accepting a hand-slap from Ty before dropping into the seat next to her.

"As a matter of fact . . ."

The argument continues on, and I frown, mystified as to how my simple question about testing morphed into a debate about Herrera's prowess with the opposite sex. As if reading my thoughts, Archer grins at me and motions me to a table in the far corner where RC and Zephyr are sitting. Pulling up a couple of chairs, we join them while RC fills me in on the WMGD.

Weapon of Mass Ghoul Destruction. That's the Holy Grail for the scientists at R&D, I soon find out. A large-scale weapon that can kill ghouls without harming people or destroying property. With entire stations and even planets taken by the ghouls, the only way to get them back is to clean them out en masse, preferably without ever having to set foot in those places at all. That's where the orbital platforms come in. With every planet, colony, and space station in the Expanse outfitted with these OPs, they are the perfect way to deliver a single, coordinated strike across the entire Expanse. No heavy manufacturing required; all it would take are some basic modifications to the shield generators and a software upload. Quick, efficient; if we timed our efforts right, we could hit the ghouls before they even knew what was happening. Of course, that's assuming we actually manage to create an effective weapon in the first place.

"Which is a very big 'if'," Zephyr snorts. He shakes his head, and the metallic gold streaks in his hair shimmer beneath the pale lights.

"I don't know. They've been doing a lot of orbital tests lately. Maybe they're on to something this time," Archer counters. "RC, you're the tech expert. What do you think?"

RC considers the question. "The frequency of testing could be an indicator of any number of factors, so without full access to the test data, it's hard to say. Now, supposing we had access to the test results from the last several weeks—or better yet, the last several months— we could analyze the data for any systematic trends that may indicate potential progress. Unfortunately, no one at this table has high enough clearance to obtain the data in question, so all we can really do at this juncture is pointlessly speculate. Personally, I'd rather eat. I'm starving." He shovels his last forkful of Chick'n'Rice into his mouth, and then goes for seconds.

What the . . . ?

Zephyr rolls his eyes. "A simple 'I don't know' would have sufficed," he calls after RC, and Archer just laughs.

I glance around the room, from Ty and Zel joking with Herrera at the next table, to RC at the counter calmly refilling the rehydrator, and back to Zeph and Archer, both casually sprawled out at the table with me. Everyone seems so laidback and relaxed; I can't help envying their serenity. It's barely been twenty minutes and already my feet are squirming impatiently in my boots at the forced inactivity.

Except for Chen, I realize, with another look around. The Delta pilot is nowhere to be seen. She must have gone to the observation deck to watch the test. Smart. I'm thinking about doing the same when a computerized voice speaks out over the com.

"Attention, all research personnel. WMGD Test Rho 13 will commence in T-minus ten minutes. Please report to your designated stations and prepare for testing."

Before the announcement has finished repeating, Asriel appears in the door. "I need a volunteer ASAP. Sorenson!" he snaps when I pop to my feet like a jack-in-the-box. "You're up! Let's go."

I follow Asriel across the platform and straight into the command center. The circular room is filled to capacity, researchers manning all three consoles with another half dozen looking on. Split panels on the wraparound viewscreen show the outside of the OP from every possible angle as well as additional views from the planet and atmosphere below. A tiny woman in a perfectly pressed lab coat seems to be running the show, barking out orders in a crisp alto voice. The name embroidered on her coat says Preston.

"Mason, where are we on the ground feeds?"

"All feeds are online and transmitting, Doctor."

"Good! Be ready to activate the detection lights once the pulse beam shuts off. What about the power levels, Salazar?"

"Power reserves are at one hundred percent. Generators are set to charge at forty-three percent."

"Negative! Drop that down to thirty-eight percent."

"But Dr. Morales said—"

"I'm sure I don't need to tell you that Dr. Angelou takes the safety protocols established for these testing procedures very seriously. Any breach of protocol, and he'll have all our heads. Thirty-eight percent, please. We want to kill ghouls, not give half the human population down there seizures."

"Yes, ma'am!"

"Vorobyev, what's our targeting status?"

"Testing area has been acquired, but we can't set the target lock until Shield Generator Gamma is in place."

"Oh, for vac's sake! Jacobi, where are we on repairs?"

"Almost there, Doctor. I just need an extra pair of hands to hold this piece while I weld."

As it turns out, *I* am the extra set of hands. Before I know it, I'm standing at a control panel on the far end of the room, holding a small blade of metal within a slit positioned lengthwise along a huge metal cylinder while a woman in her thirties wields a welding torch precariously close to my fingers. She's wearing half a pressure suit, and I realize she was the flash of movement I saw floating past the OP viewport earlier.

She winks at me right before she flips her mask down. "Don't worry! I only set someone's hand on fire that *one* time."

Yeah, *that's* a big relief.

"Attention, all research personnel. WMGD Test Rho 13 will commence in T-minus five minutes. Please report to your designated stations and prepare for testing."

I jump slightly at the announcement. Heat singes the back of my knuckles, but I manage to keep my hands steady. I peer at the metal piece I'm holding, identical to another few dozen blades positioned all around the cylinder. *It's like a tooth on a gear,* I suddenly realize, *the blade pushing against the neighboring blade every time the cylinder turns.*

Jacobi welds carefully along the cylinder, soldering the blade firmly into the slit. At last, she switches the torch off, inspecting her work for a minute before gesturing at me to let go. I do so, watching as she gives the cylinder an experimental turn before nodding in satisfaction.

Now that I don't have a hot torch right next to my fingers, I feel free to ask, "What happened?"

"The old blade just sheared in half the moment we tried to reposition the shield generator," she says with a nod to the old blade where it lies on a nearby console as she fits the cover back into place over the control panel. "It's strange. This whole generator shaft is brand new—just arrived on an equipment shipment a week ago. We never even used it before today. I think it must be a flaw in the original casting."

"*Attention, all research personnel. WMGD Test Rho 13 will commence in T-minus one minute. Please report to your designated stations and prepare for testing.*"

"Jacobi! Where's my shield generator?"

"Almost there," she replies, immediately going to the controls. A slight vibration rumbles through the floor as a giant dish on the bottom of the OP starts moving on the viewscreen ahead of me.

"Just a little farther," Vorobyev coaches as the dish slowly inches right. "There! Target lock acquired."

"*Attention, all research personnel. WMGD Test Rho 13 is now commencing. Please prepare for power surge.*"

I brace myself against the metal wall as a low humming starts spreading through the platform. Barely perceptible at first, then gaining strength as it sizzles along the walls, the ceiling, the decking beneath my feet. It thrums through my hands like lightning, raw power coursing into my flesh everywhere skin touches metal until I can't tell if it's the walls that are shaking, my hands, or both. Orders are flying through the command center around my head, excitement pulsing through the room like a living thing, wild and unchecked.

"Generator status!"

"Twenty-eight percent and rising! Twenty-nine, thirty . . ."

The platform suddenly lurches, a hard jolt vibrating through the floor from the lower starboard direction.

"What happened?!" Preston asks.

"The power regulator for Gamma Generator just shorted out! I'm shunting power to the shield gen manually."

"Steady with the power flow," Preston commands. "If the generators power up unevenly, it could tear this platform apart!"

The floor lurches once more and then subsides, any further discrepancies swallowed up within the avalanche of power building just below us. The vibrations intensify, the quiet waves piercing straight through my flesh, and then suddenly they all meld together into one pure pitch, like a tuning fork struck at *just* the right angle . . .

"All generators are at thirty-eight percent! Repeat: all generators at thirty-eight percent!"

In an instant, every voice falls silent, not a single noise but for the humming power surging through the platform. The entire room holds its breath, every eye looking to the woman in charge, waiting on the point of a star for the dawn to fall. Preston takes a breath, chest rising in a ragged breath of anticipation, then—

"*Fire.*"

11

SILVER LIGHTNING JOLTS from the generators arrayed on the viewscreen before me, pulsing down through space toward the planet below. It skips down through the various display panels as it crosses into the atmosphere, streaking through the thin upper layers and the cloudy mid-layers to burst through the clear skies below.

I shift my gaze to the target panel just in time to see a flash of light bloom within the city streets, roiling like a silver Aurora Borealis briefly deigning to come to earth. It shines for one long moment, lighting up the screen like a prayer, and then it's gone, literally disappearing within the blink of my eyes.

I let out the breath I hadn't realized I was holding, only now noticing that the humming has stopped, the platform transforming once more into a lifeless hunk of tritanium and steel. Sweat covers my skin, and my whole body feels limp, like I just finished a hard hand-to-hand workout. I lean quietly against the wall and watch the scientists, only one question on my mind.

Did it work?

"Enlarge the force fence network. Mason, activate the lights."

My eyes dart to the fence network, now prominently displayed on the viewscreen. So far none of the lights have gone red, but that doesn't mean a whole lot. The fences only light when a ghoul travels between two fence posts. Once they're inside the posts, the fence shows nothing.

I tap my foot impatiently, wondering how long we'll have to wait and watch, when white lights burst from every street lamp. They shine brighter than anything I've ever seen, so blinding my lenses automatically kick into sunshield mode, but even with the dimmed lenses, I still see them. Dark, rainbow-hued shapes roiling about within the light, their colors shimmering like oil slicks against the white background.

Ghouls.

A second later, the first red light trips on the force fence network.

Disappointment sings through the command center at the undeniable evidence before us. WMGD Test Rho 13 has failed.

"We'll have to monitor the fences for the next week, try to get a count," Preston is saying, voice all business, as though this were only a routine test and not another stunning failure of humanity's greatest hope for survival. "Until we can get some numbers, we have to allow for the possibility that we destroyed some of the enemy, though clearly not all."

The white lights are out now, the enemy invisible once again, but the roiling cloud is burned into my brain. Maybe the scientists have to cover every angle, but they know as well as I do:

We didn't kill any.

Strangely enough, I'm not nearly as disappointed as I would've expected. Standing here in this control room, surrounded by the excitement of the mission and the passion of the scientists, with the awesome effects of the WMGD coursing through my veins, I can see now the sheer scope of Angelou's vision. For the first time since he recruited me, I'm starting to understand what Angelou meant about being one of the few who doesn't simply fight in the war, but will dictate *if* we win the war.

My hand buzzes. *"All members of Delta Team,"* comes Asriel's voice from my chit. *"We'll be receiving final clearance to depart for the station shortly. Please report to docking ring 2A within the next five minutes."*

With a link to the affirmative, I shut off my chit and jog for the exit. My legs are a bit unsteady from all the vibrations, and I accidently bump into a console on the way out. One piece of the broken blade I helped replace slides toward the edge, and I quickly reach out to catch it. I'm about to put it back when my eyes zoom in on the break. Perfectly straight, perfectly smooth, running at a perfect right angle from top to bottom.

I run my finger lightly over the edge. There isn't a spot of corrosion on the blade, but the lightest dusting of some sort of silvery residue comes off on my fingertip. I stare at the ashy dust in consternation.

"What are you doing?" Preston asks, walking toward me with a face like a storm cloud.

All eyes on me, I quickly put the blade back. "Just leaving, ma'am."

Suiting action to words, I make for the launch bay, where I meet up with the rest of Delta Team. Asriel breezes in a heartbeat later, and before long we're on a transport back to the station. As we descend into the pastel mists, I find myself staring down at my hands once again, at the gray residue still coating my fingertip.

"Hey, Sorenson."

I quickly tuck my hand behind my back at Archer's call.

"What did Asriel want with you earlier, anyway?"

I pause. "Oh, they just needed an extra set of hands for some last-minute repair work."

It's on the tip of my tongue to tell him about the blade, but something stops me. It's none of my business, after all, and no doubt the scientists will go over every little detail of the test, down to that broken blade. If there's anything to find, they'll find it. But for some reason, I can't stop rubbing that silver residue between my thumb and index finger, not powdery soft like dirt accrued over time, but something coarse and grainy.

Metallic dust. Like the sort of residue you might find if one side had been scored by a laser cutter.

———

We spend the remaining hours of the day in training, finally breaking for a quick supper. I follow the rest of the team into the outer ring of the Central Habitat, where we take a cross-corridor between a couple of shops to emerge into the Atrium.

By far the single largest space in R&D, the Atrium is one vast communal area, lightly subdivided into lounges and mess areas by strategically placed couches, trees, tables, and low walls brimming with plant life. Sunlight streams down through the transparent ceiling, illuminating the floor and refracting off three circular tiers of restaurants, offices, and other station amenities lining the outer wall. Unlike the other habitats, which are strictly off-limits to all but those who work or live there, everyone is welcome here. It's the one place in the station where the lines between divisions blur, and we're not scientists or testers or admin, but just people.

We cob a spot in one of the mess areas where several members from other testing teams are currently eating. Halfway through the meal, a live address from the Chairman of the Celestial Expanse begins. Someone from Beta puts it on, queuing up the channel on the back wall with a wave of his chit hand. As the opening commentary rolls, everyone starts making guesses about the forthcoming speech.

"Additional travel restrictions?"

"More jump jamming?"

"Probably just another one of those inspiring *If-we-all-stand-together* speeches," Ty says with a roll of her eyes.

She's probably right, but I turn my chair toward the back wall anyway. The setting is a familiar one—a large, circular dais edged by nine silver chairs arrayed in a semicircle around the central lectern. Floor-to-ceiling viewports give an incredible view of the panorama outside, inky space and silvery stars a perfect frame for the glowing white planet and four small moons hovering just beyond the glass. It's the *Praetoria*, a heavily guarded space station orbiting the Class 10 planet Genevieve. If the far-reaching and irregularly shaped Celestial Expanse could be said to have a center, this would be it.

My eyes zero in on the gleaming chairs, one for each member of the Board of Directors, the Expanse's ruling oligarchy. Tremaine, Nogales, Petrovna. Addison, Jong, Quo. Villanuevas and Margolis.

And the Chairman makes nine.

The faces change with time, but the Directors always come from the nine founding families, the shipping magnates who dared to create an empire from Telluria's castoffs. The far-flung colonies too distant to be worth anyone's while; the untamed planets too recently terraformed to do more than support the roughest of life. Space stations enslaved to this corporation or that, and orbital mining rigs assumed to be transient at best. While others wrote them off, sight unseen, the nine families looked at them and saw untapped potential. It was they who laid down the blunt to create jump paths others considered a waste of credits. They who invested in poor colonies struggling to survive and built way stations to bridge the empty spaces between distant worlds. Each of these nine families took a piece of the Celestial Expanse, a lawless tract of neglected space, and turned them into true empires. Shipping empires, formed through commerce rather than politics, but empires nonetheless. With the improvement of terraforming technology over time, these empires only expanded, as planetoids previously considered untamable became new worlds brimming with life.

As the nine families rose in power, first economically and then politically, Telluria responded. Once little more than a group of planets and colonies sharing close geographical ties, the Tellurians eventually formed into a tight alliance under the leadership of the planet Earth. Together they rose to become the first galactic superpower, using their consolidated military and political powers to dominate on an economic level as well. Unable to compete against the Alliance's superior resources, the nine families had a choice to make. Join together, or be swallowed up within the might of the Alliance. Everything after that, as they say, is history. Nine empires became one, and what was once little more than a name on a map became the Celestial Expanse in truth. So I remember from class, anyway. I was never much for school; no, that was always Teal.

Teal.

My fists clench and my gut burns, grim anger settling over me the way it does whenever I think of my little sister, and yet despite that I can't stop this traitorous voice deep inside that whispers: *I wonder how she is.*

I shove half a roll in my mouth and tell it to shut up.

Minutes stretch on, and the *Praetoria* remains empty, with only the commentators' voiceover for company. I'm starting to wonder if this address is ever going to happen when the lights come up and a figure steps into view. He wears a black suit, high-collared and trimmed in Celestial gold. The tailored tunic shows off his broad shoulders while the polished boots only add to his considerable height. His features wouldn't be described as handsome, but they're strong. Everything about him, in fact, exudes strength. Looking at him, a picture of health, it's hard to believe the stories about how he almost died at birth, a preemie with stunted limbs and life-threatening birth defects. The patterned half-star of PsyCorp glints dully from his left lapel.

The Chairman of the Board steps up to the lectern, though the chairs remain empty, and a hush falls over the mess.

"My fellow Celestians, it is a time of war. Over the past eighteen months, we have seen terrible things and experienced great losses. For some of us the war seems far away, barely a blip on our radar, while for others the war is already at our back door. These are frightening times for us all. Many ask, 'How can we fight an enemy we can't see? How do we destroy them when they can't be touched or heard?' "

Ty holds up a hand. "Wait for it."

"I know you're afraid, but if we all stand together—"

A smattering of laughter breaks out. Ty slams her hand down on the tabletop triumphantly. "Did I call it, or did I call it?"

The Chairman continues on, but the spell is broken, team members talking in low voices over his speech despite shushing from the others.

"Where's the rest of the fraggin' board?" mutters Arturo Evangeline—or 'Vange, as he's known by his Gamma teammates. His scarred face creases in confusion. "Shouldn't they be here?"

"There's a war on," replies his ATL, a hard-nosed woman with razor-sharp eyes called Songbird. "It would be completely deficient for the Board Members to make themselves a target by putting themselves in the same place at once."

"Even the Chairman's not actually on *Praetoria*," RC adds. "It's merely a digitized background."

"How can you tell?" Zel asks.

"Chiron," he answers, pointing at the moon in question. "Its position is completely incorrect for this time of year. Technically, you shouldn't be able to see it at all from this angle."

"Figures," Zephyr snorts. "He's probably boarded up in some hidey-hole somewhere, too afraid to come out, all the while telling *us* to be brave?"

The comment garners a flurry of replies, both agreeing and disagreeing, along with another round of shushing from the more politically inclined. I lean an elbow on the table, one ear on the speech and the other on the conversation, interested enough to listen but not enough to comment. Politics have never really been my thing. I prefer action to talk. A clear target and a plan of action. Not this endless droning on that never results in anything happening.

"Seal it, everyone!"

I snap my full attention back to the wall just as the Chairman says:

"—and now, my fellow Celestians, it is with a heavy heart that I inform you that at 3:36 p.m. Galactic Post-Standard Time, President of Earth Suni Ariadne passed away from squatter-induced organ failure. She was a strong leader, a tireless humanitarian, and my friend. She will be missed."

Silence falls, shock effectively gagging even the most vocal of us. I gape at the feed, still trying to process the news. The Spectres infiltrated Telluria over four years ago, and unlike us, the Tellurians didn't have the benefit of forewarning. No force fences or Sniffers or aero-launchers. The enemy was free to spread through their empire, from planet to colony to station, without anything or anyone to stop them. Only the war between the Alliance and the Expanse kept them from spreading into our territory as well. By the time the Tellurians learned of the invasion, it was already too late for them. Most of the Alliance had been infected by that point. That the President of Earth was infected and eventually killed by the squatter inside her shouldn't be all that surprising. And yet . . . it is.

Xian, a specialist from Beta, shakes his head. "I don't . . . What does this mean?"

No one says anything for a moment until 'Vange finally states, his face brutish and his voice cold, "It doesn't mean anything except that one more person died today. We should just thank the slaggin' stars it wasn't one of us."

"One more person?"

"It was the President of *Earth*!"

More objections fly out, but it's RC, his voice cracking like a whip across the room, who puts into words what everyone else is afraid to say.

"It means Telluria is dead, and *we* put the final nail in their coffin."

Archer puts a hand on his shoulder. "Easy, RC."

"It's not like there was anything we could have done," Zel adds softly.

"Nothing we could have done? That's bullslag!" RC shakes off Archer's hand with a violent shrug and rises. "Do you remember all those refugees who tried to get out when the news first broke over a year ago? All those people who made for the border, frantic to get themselves and their families to safety? And did we put them through force hoops and check them for squatters and take them in? No! We jammed their jump paths and turned them away. We *shot them down*! They came to us for help, and we slammed the door in their faces."

"That's not fair," Songbird objects levelly. "We didn't even have the tech in place to protect ourselves at that point, let alone handle hundreds of thousands of terrified Tellurians."

"Most of whom were already infected by then anyway," Xian adds. "We couldn't have saved them all—"

"But we could have saved *some* of them."

"Well, you know what I think?" 'Vange suddenly stands, brown eyes brimming with hatred. His jaw sets in the familiar clench of a guy spoiling for a fight, and I'm starting to think all the barracks talk about his crude upbringing in the slums of Alara is true. "They're the ones who were so keen to put their fraggin' boots on New Earth that they brought those alien scum-slaggers back! If it weren't for them, we wouldn't even be fighting this war. I think those motherfraggin' Tellurians got *exactly* what they deserved."

Forks are dropped and chairs thrown back, half the people on their feet at the inflammatory words. RC and 'Vange are practically indistinguishable from each other, a blur of black uniforms and flying fists and grappling bodies. I start to rise, unsure what to do—if I should even *do* anything—but the ATLs are already moving in to break up the fray, yelling for the others to back off while going directly for the main combatants. Seconds later, RC is flying backwards as Archer grabs his jacket and yanks him bodily away from his opponent. 'Vange lunges forward, fist flying in a nasty roundhouse, but Songbird is there, sliding in past RC with the grace of a dancer. She effortlessly blocks the punch, snaking her arm around 'Vange's and yanking it up behind his back. An instant later, he's on the floor, face in the decking and Songbird's knee on his neck.

"Ice it down, 'Vange," she says mildly, looking completely at ease even as 'Vange uses his free hand to furiously tap out. "Save it for the real enemy."

He gasps out an affirmative, and a second later she lets him go, rising fluidly from the ground in a single movement. Not a hair of her slicked-back braid is out of place. She extends a hand to her specialist, and 'Vange takes it, grumbling, "Rip my slaggin' arm right out of its slaggin' socket, why don't you?"

"Don't tempt her, 'Vange!" someone hoots, and a chorus of chuckles ring out. With that, the charged atmosphere eases, the tension of the day lessened by the healing power of a good joke.

I laugh along with the rest, watching as Songbird directs the others to pick up the fallen chairs and otherwise set things right. I don't know much about the Gamma ATL. Like Asriel, Songbird's a career soldier, having spent ten years as a Ranger before coming to R&D, but this is the first time I've seen her hand-to-hand skills in play. She's one of the smart ones, I realize, the sort who wins by using her brains when others are using their tempers. I make a mental note never to get into a fight with her around.

Not that Archer is any less ruthless, I note with a glance at RC, whose neck is currently sewn up in Archer's thick arm. His methods may be simpler, going for brute strength where Songbird uses technique, but the results are the same. RC struggles against the hold.

"Take a walk," Archer commands, jerking a head toward the door.

RC angrily tries to jerk away, but Archer only grips him tighter and gives him a hard shake, his eyes colder than I've ever seen them. He leans in, gravelly voice low. "Take a walk *now*."

RC glares at him, but he finally nods, stepping off when Archer deigns to release him. With a disgusted shake of his head, he strides out, only stopping when he reaches the doorway. "Kid yourselves all you want," he says, voice dripping with disdain, "but the Tellurians are dead because *we* left them to die."

Then he exits the room, leaving the rest of us to wonder if maybe, just possibly, he's right.

12

"**THE CITY LOOKS SO** *NORMAL*. It's hard to believe it's already gone."

I jump down from the back of the shuttle and join the others at the railing. Perched atop the north roof of the Rose-Cross Skyscraper, one of the largest interstellar com stations on Prism, we must be at least four hundred meters above the ground. Above us is nothing but sky—klicks and klicks of pastel clouds as far as we can see.

Below us is the enemy.

Standing at the building's edge, I look down at the bustling metropolis and shiver. Ty's right. It looks completely normal, as though it's just a regular city full of regular people, and not a teeming labyrinth of squatters over a million strong. And I suppose that, in a way, it is. Prism's only been infected for a year. Enough time for the Spectres to infect the entire population, but not enough time for people to start dying. With the planet banned from both interstellar travel and communications, there's little for the Specs to do besides settle down inside their hosts and breed. Nor is there anything for the humans to do but live out the rest of their lives, for what little time they have left. It's called the Time of Equilibrium, after the early suicides and crime sprees have died down, but before the mass deaths begin.

I snort. Time of Equilibrium. I guess they thought that sounded better than the Time of Encroaching Doom.

I shudder as I try to imagine what it must be like to live with a squatter in your head. To go about your life making the usual rounds of work and school, family and friends, knowing you only have a precious few years left to live. Not only that, but knowing everyone around you is just as doomed. Do they sit across from each other at the dining room table and wonder who will be the first to go? Do they study themselves in the mirror each morning, looking for the telltale signs of emaciation caused by their Spectres slowly eating away at them from the inside out? Just thinking about it makes me nauseated. I only hope I never have to find out for myself.

"All right, team," Asriel's voice barks out in the silence. "Gamma has everything down to the ninety-fifth floor secure. Let's go!"

Jogging after the others, I ignore the lurch in my stomach as we enter the building and take the stairs two at a time. Theoretically, this should be an easy mission. With interstellar communication banned when the planet was quarantined, this building has been closed and sealed off for a year now, which means no squatters. No ghouls either, as they prefer to hang around their hosted friends if given an option. Still, it's hard to forget I'm stuck in an enclosed space only a few hundred meters above a city with a mil's worth of squatters and God-only-knows how many ghouls! My mind goes back to what Ty said at the beginning of the mission.

"That's the beauty of the whole thing," she said. "We slip in quietly from above, do our thing, and then get out without them ever knowing we were here."

"But won't they be able to sense us up here with their ghoul-dar or whatever it is they use to sense potential hosts?"

She only shrugged. "Maybe."

Yeah. Real reassuring. I fan my nostrils and take a huge sniff. Is that distant scent of sour-and-sweet from down in the city getting stronger? Maybe. Or maybe I'm just being paranoid.

Down on the top story, we fan out toward our assigned positions. The whole floor is one giant control room devoted to operating the com station. Once a central hub for interstellar communications, it's now secretly being used to collect and transmit data from all over

Prism up to R&D. Force fence data, testing equipment—everything goes up through here. For the most part, it runs on its own without human intervention, but every once in a while they need someone to repair parts or install upgrades. That's why we're here.

My position is at a control panel on the far end of the room. I use my multi-tool to crack open the cover, goggling as a maze of wires, fluorescent tubules, and crystalline capacitors meets my eyes. The sight is a familiar one; a couple of the engineers on base took us through the whole process during training the other day. It seemed easy enough then. I try to remember their instructions as I thumb on my tip-pad and search for the right schematics.

Cut the power, replace the main power shunt, reboot the drive.

Locating the schematic, I compare the diagram to the opened console, easily identifying the part that needs replacing. Following the instructions, I quickly replace the main power shunt, reboot the drive, and then close up the panel. Running a quick diagnostic on the console above, I nod in satisfaction as it confirms I completed the task correctly.

I rendezvous with the others back up top, and we lift off after barely an hour planetside. In and out—those were Asriel's instructions. Untaken hosts tend to attract ghouls, which is one of the reasons they've chosen to leave the station unmanned. The last thing we want is for our presence to draw unwanted attention.

My return trip is spent in the cockpit getting a piloting lesson with Herrera and Chen. Apparently, everyone on the teams is required to learn basic piloting skills. When I ask why, Chen and Herrera exchange a look.

"So that if your entire team is lost on a mission, you can still fly yourself out."

Oh.

Strapping into the copilot's chair, I follow Chen's instructions, using voice commands to direct the ship. The commands are fairly simple, and I soon realize that when Asriel said "learn basic skills," he really meant "learn to use the autopilot." Still, I feel a small sense of accomplishment as we lift smoothly into the air and begin ascending through the atmosphere—in stealth mode, to avoid detection by the natives.

By the time we hit the first cloud line, I'm actually a little bored with the lesson. As the mists flow across the viewscreen, I alternate my attention between the glowing dials, numbers, and data scrolling over the wall and holos of Herrera's four nieces and nephews.

"That's Gabriela, there in the middle in the silver leotard. This week she wants to be a ZG acrobat like Zeph. Last week it was an actress, the week before it was a dancer. Anything as long as she gets to be the center of attention. Mateo is the brainy one—always top of his class—and Esteban is mad about animals. I swear, he has an entire menagerie in his room. The shy one in the corner over there is Catia," he says, beaming at a black-haired little girl hovering above his hand. "She rarely talks, but when she sings, she sounds like an angel. Best little singer on Kappus," he boasts with typical Herrera swagger.

"When did you last see them?"

Herrera's face falls. "Not for months, since before R&D. I send them presents whenever I can—spoil them absolutely rotten, my sister-in-law claims—but . . ." He shrugs. "It's not the same."

No, it isn't. I recall all those times I missed my parents after they went off to war. How much I hated them being away, and how I could never understand why they chose what they did. Now I'm the one off to war. Strange how things change.

Herrera continues bragging about the kids, and I glance over at Chen, only now realizing that aside from some basic instruction, she hasn't said a thing. She sits quietly in her chair, face perfectly composed and eyes on the controls as she monitors the shuttle's progress. I try to recall one thing she's ever said that wasn't mission-related—a personal story, a tidbit about her family, even just an opinion—and can't think of one. Curious. While in the field she's as vocal as the rest of us, off the field she carries a graceful solemnity I rarely encounter in other servicemen. I glance at the flag on her upper arm but don't recognize it. No surprise. There are so many colonies and stations in the Expanse that it's impossible to know the flags for all of them.

I have to stop myself from reaching up and touching my own patch. The flag is for Zaia, a small planet one jump path away from New Sol. Zaia was one of the colonies where they evacuated the New Sol inhabitants after Lia went Nova and the station blew. It's where

I was staying with my grandmother and sister when I formally enlisted; hence the flag, though I only lived there a few months. Now I wear its emblem on my upper arm for all to see, the ever-present lie that in saying where I've been only hides where I'm really from. What I really am.

And who I really knew.

Her faithfulness, her face; the blond wisps always escaping her ponytail no matter how often she pulled them back.

My chest tightens, the memory pulling me back toward a familiar well of despair, but before I can start sinking, a low-pitched tone interrupts.

"We've hit the planetary net," Chen says, answering my quizzical look with a nod toward the ceiling. "You'll have to call the Primary AP with a request to open a hole in the net."

I make the call, all the while watching the brilliant blue lattice-work shimmering above us. It's so close I can see that the holes between the individual traceries are surprisingly large, more than big enough to fit a shuttle if they weren't constantly shifting open and closed in rapid patterns across the sky. A solid energy blanket around the planet would not only require impossible energy reserves, but would destroy the planet's ecosystem outright.

As we wait for return clearance from R&D, I ask, "What would happen if we hit the net?"

"The energy matrix in the net creates a polarized field akin to the one found in a typical shuttle's shields. It creates a repulsion effect similar to the way two like magnetic poles will repel each other," Chen explains. "Essentially, we'd bounce off the net with a pretty good jolt, but otherwise we would be okay."

"What if the shields weren't up?"

Again, Chen and Herrera exchange a look. "You'd get sliced to ribbons before you could even think about calling for help."

I grimace at the gruesome image. "So if they didn't open the net for us, would there be any way to get through?"

"Nope," says Herrera at the exact same time Chen says, "Maybe."

Silence. Herrera and I both look at Chen, eyebrows raised in question. She squirms a bit under our joint gaze and finally says, "In theory, if you knew the net's rotational pattern and turned off your shields, you might be able to navigate through the net's holes manually without getting hit. But you'd have to have killer reflexes and be one hell of a pilot to do it, and if you screwed up even *once* . . ."

I nod, getting the picture. R&D radios back just then, and soon after a hole opens up in the net above. I switch my attention to piloting, flying us neatly up into the net with Chen's coaching. Only now as we fly through the shield do I realize: It's not a single latticework moving unbelievably fast, but several latticeworks set one atop the next. From a distance they give the impression of a shimmering wall, the traceries too quick to be passable, but from the inside I see the wide-open holes Chen referred to. I suddenly understand what she meant about navigating through manually, if you're skilled enough.

Not to mention desperate enough.

We ascend out of the net, and I watch as the hole fades away behind us, swallowed up once again by countless bands of seething light. As I set course for the station, I spy some dark clouds hanging back in the distance. I'm not the only one who spots them.

"Storm's coming." Chen rests her chin on her hand and gazes out at the clouds, her expression unreadable.

I frown, suddenly wondering what happens to a sky station during a storm. "What does that mean for us?"

Herrera grins. "It means it's going to be a hot time in the old town tonight."

———

Just as Chen predicted, the storm clouds lurking back along the horizon roll in late in the night. I awake to the sound of thunder, jerking upright in my bunk as the *boom-crack!* splits the darkness. With a hoarse cry, I stumble half out of bed, body and instinct clearly working at cross-purposes as I hit the floor with an awkward thump. A second clap rings out, reverberating through the air around me like plucked strings vibrating violently across my nerves.

Alarmed, I glance over at the others, scanning their bunks by the glow of the emergency lights set into the floor, but aside from a couple of rollovers and a few unconscious grumbles, nobody seems disturbed by the noise. All except for RC, whose bunk is empty. Probably in the hygiene units.

Feeling vaguely stupid, I climb back into bed and close my eyes. For some reason my thoughts drift back to Aurora, to a game Teal and I played as kids. When the next thunderclap booms out, my lips silently count. *One thousand—*

Boom!

One thous—

Boom!

One thousan—

Boom!

Five minutes of rolling thunder later, I resign myself to the fact that sleeping on a sky station in the middle of a fraggin' thunderstorm isn't going to happen. Instead, I get up, throw on a pair of pants, and pad out into the hall.

The barracks habitat is laid out simply enough, with the oblong platform divided down the center by a long corridor with hygiene units and sleeping quarters on either side—women on the right and men on the left. Team Leaders get their own—admittedly tiny— rooms, and ATLs are two to a room. Fraternizing with anyone else on the teams is strictly forbidden, with the threat of permanent de- motion to scut a fairly effective deterrent for anyone who might think otherwise. We were chosen because we're risk-taking adrenaline junkies; the thought of spending the rest of the war taking out trash and bussing tables is enough to make even the most careless of us think twice. Especially when there's company enough to be had among the research personnel, if one cares to look.

Her loyalty, her lips; the tingle of electricity that shot down my spine every time we kissed.

I don't care to look.

The end of the hall opens up into a communal lounge with real viewports wrapping around the circular room on three sides. I swipe the access pad with my chit and walk into the darkened room.

The crystalline windows are lit up from every direction, jagged streaks of lightning flashing in rapid concert across the sky so fast night has practically become day. Deafening cracks of thunder continue to roll and boom, underscored now by the wind, whipping in hard, airy chimes against the crystal walls. Rain adds a percussive rhythm, the silvery drops thrown across the ports like knives, sharp and deadly.

I shiver beneath the onslaught, feeling the storm even within the protection of these walls. The thunder is vibrating right up through the floor into my feet, and my arms are prickling, static electricity crackling along my skin and making all the little hairs stand on end. We're in the heart of the storm—a vengeful, raging, merciless storm—and never have I felt more unprotected and alone. No weapons, no place to run; only a scattering of walls and a lone energy shield.

Against my will, I drift closer to the viewport, compelled by the sheer force raging only meters away. Several more cracks of lightning streak across the sky, and shield polarity notwithstanding, it seems impossible that we haven't been struck yet. The energy shield glows with unearthly light, as though calling to its kindred as it flashes by rather than repelling it, and it suddenly occurs to me how little protection the shield really is. Maybe it can repulse energy and solids, but it's essentially nonexistent to liquids and gas. The storm rages through as though it's not even there, winds whistling in from the east while rains sheet down from above.

A trio of booms crash painfully loud just above my head, accompanied by a series of flashes too quick to count, and in their illumination I see Habitat 6 just across the way. It gleams pearl-like within the maelstrom, its curving walls draped in white lightning and silvery moonlight. The walkway connecting it to the Central Habitat sways noticeably, and even though I know it's made that way, to bend with the winds instead of break, I'm still very glad I'm not in one of those spindly passages. Even just looking at it swing and sway from a distance makes me nauseated.

I shift my eyes away from the walkway. I'm about to head back to my bunk when a yellow light pierces the night sky. I magnify the view, gasping as I realize it's coming from one of the shield generators. It's rocking in place, shifting crazily back and forth in a violent tug-of-war between its positional compensators and the storm's winds. For a second it steadies, and I think the compensators have won the battle. Then it shoots across the sky, tearing out of the shield grid as if thrown by the hand of God himself. The shield winks off, like a string of Christmas lights blowing a bulb . . .

Then it's back on, the other generators already compensating for the lost hardware. Now outside of the protective shield, the stray generator spins wildly about in the storm, its metal carapace gleaming deadly bright in the white sky. The *lightning*-white sky—

Crack!

Lightning strikes the generator, and it explodes in a shower of sparks. Pieces fly in every direction, tossed by the storm and their own deadly momentum. The shield shimmers, blossoming out in a film of gold as a dozen bits of shrapnel hammer against it, but it holds, the tritanium daggers bouncing harmlessly off before sliding down the shield and out of sight.

I sink slowly down on the window seat, eyes wide and heart racing. The station is a fortress, just as Angelou said. If nothing else, the events of the past few minutes prove it. Redundancy upon redundancy. Knowing Angelou, we could probably lose half the generators without any serious mishap. And yet, the exploding generator, the shield winking down for that split second . . .

Spectres. We're hanging over a planet full of Spectres.

After Lia died, it was like I was incapable of fear. I'd always been brave, even a bit reckless at times, but I'd still had limits. Not so once Lia was gone. Nothing was off-limits anymore because I had nothing to lose. It's what made me a good guardian. It's the reason Angelou recruited me. No obstacle was insurmountable, no action too risky, because I wasn't scared of anything.

Then I met Angelou and came to R&D, and suddenly all that changed. Maybe it was the grandeur of the base or the power of the mission. Maybe it was as simple as Angelou saying that what I did mattered. Because as I sit at the window, looking out over a storm-tossed sky with the echo of ghouls in my nose and lightning in my eyes, I realize:

I'm scared now.

———

Back in the bunkroom, everything is just as I left it, except that RC is back from the hygiene units and sleeping like the dead again. I shiver as I sink down on my bunk, only now noticing I'm drenched with sweat. Swiping my chit hand across the access panel on my storage locker, I fumble inside for a change of clothes. Even with the dim emergency lights set into the floor, it's almost impossible to see anything inside, and I spend a frustrating few minutes searching for something appropriate.

Soft cloth whispers under my fingers, and I turn it over in my hands several times only to realize it's my old Celestial Guard uniform. Disgusted, I'm about to toss it back in when something falls from the folds with a loud clank. I pick it up, frowning at the unfamiliar contours beneath my fingers. It feels like some sort of tool, with a thin metal barrel the size of my finger and a switch on one side. *What is this?* As a guardian, it was my job to know all of my equipment by feel as well as sight, and I don't recognize this piece at all.

The lights of the hygiene unit automatically snap on at my entrance. The room is empty, no surprise with it being the middle of the night. I pull out the item from my uniform, and my eyes widen.

It's a laser cutter.

Five-centimeter haft, crystal power cell, dual-blade make. A common enough tool, but not one I've been issued by either the Guard or the Testing Division.

My blood runs cold as I stare at the cutter. I try to think of an explanation for why a tool I've never seen before in my life would be in my locker. Maybe it's just an innocent mistake or part of some deficient new hazing ritual I have yet to undergo. Except my locker is encoded for access by my chit alone, and while I have no doubt the securities could be bypassed by someone with enough skill, that would preclude a simple mistake. Even hazing seems unlikely, with my team's tastes in torture leaning less toward sophisticated and more toward *gooey*.

Hefting the cutter in my hand, I turn it around and examine it. The tool is surprisingly light, though the laser glows with a solid red core when I activate it, neither a blip nor a waver in the beam. A good, high-quality blade then. De-acking the laser, I thumb the catch on the side of the haft, pop open the tool, and carefully lift out the blade assembly. Inside is a standard replacement blade—no surprise there—but something additional is jammed into the space beside it. With a faint frown, I reach inside with my index finger, eyes widening as I pull out a thin object the width of my thumb.

It's a data chip.

I let out a low whistle. *What is this?* Warranty details or instructions for installing the replacement blade, perhaps? Activating my chit, I uplink to the data chip in my hand. My fingers tap anxiously on the sink as I wait to see what's encoded on it. However, the only thing that comes up is a single number.

98J-346279-A248

I frown, thumbing through the data chip in search of something, anything that might tell me more, but there's nothing to thumb through. Just this single, unidentified number. Whatever *that's* supposed to mean. I stare at the number for a minute more, then finally disconnect the chip and de-ac my chit. What the number means isn't important right now. No, the real question here is: How in the universe did this laser cutter end up in *my* locker?

Against my will, my mind flashes back to the broken blade I helped fix during the WMGD test. I remember the coarse residue I found on the back and the disconcerting observation I made as I rubbed it between my fingers.

Metallic dust. Like the sort of residue you might find if one side had been scored by a laser cutter.

I finger the cutter, not wanting to face this new possibility, but unable to avoid it.

We have a saboteur in R&D. And I'm holding the tool they used to do it.

Onboard Sky Station Epsilon-065
Secret Research Base for Division 7

THE BUILDING LAY ACROSS *the ground in ruins. Charred and broken, it tumbled in an uneven pile of jagged blocks and smoldering wood, like a makeshift tomb from some long-lost era.*

Hands clasped behind his back, the Doctor stood at the viewport in his office and watched as the full extent of the destruction unfolded before his eyes. Though a thousand light-years away, he might as well have been there in person, the feed from the officer on site's combat lenses spooling across his own so that he could see everything the other saw, go everywhere the other went.

Together they walked, through mounds of shattered stone and twisted metal, across severed I-beams and crunching glass that glittered under the noonday sun. Odds and ends were strewn around the rubble—a broken chair leg, a scrap of fabric. A hank of hair spilling coppery and bright across the dark stone.

At the far end of the lot, a portion of wall still stood, a broken gravestone for the multitude of bodies that lay buried underneath. The sign nearby was scorched but still readable:

The Nguyen Home for Wards of State.

They'd hit a school. A world with a population of over a billion, outfitted with military outposts and key technological facilities, and they'd blown up a boarding school for orphaned children.

"And this was the bomber's only target?" the Doctor said at last.

"Yes. From the information we were able to gather, this was his sole purpose for coming on-planet."

"Did he say why?"

The officer shrugged a shoulder. "He's a squatter, an ex-military demolitions expert. He thinks he was protecting planetary security by taking down a major terrorist cell. He has no idea he killed three hundred innocent children."

The Doctor nodded. It was how the enemy worked. They settled into your head and warped your perception of reality. Deceived you into committing unthinkable acts by making you believe the most outlandish delusions. Over the course of this war, he'd interviewed hundreds of squatters. The specifics differed, but the basic story was always the same. Ultimately, it was never about the human without, but the Spectre within.

They walked in silence for a minute, the officer pacing the disaster site while the Doctor paced his office.

"Any survivors?"

"Just one. A fifteen-year-old Tellurian refugee. He was out in the garden when the bomb went off. The blast threw him clear, with only minor injuries."

"Is it possible he had something to do with the explosion?"

The officer shook his head. "The psychics already checked him, and he's clear. The boy just got lucky."

"Or unlucky," the Doctor murmured with a shake of his head. It didn't make sense. Ghouls were organized, coordinated. They would wait for their moment and strike en masse, taking whole stations and even colonies in a single attack. Not squatters. Most of them seemed content to simply settle down within their hosts and breed. Though individual squatters could get aggressive when cornered, most of them weren't particularly violent.

Though why would they be? Killing off potential hosts would only hurt their goals, not help. Spying, sabotage, misdirection—those were the squatters' true stock-in-trade. The few that did commit acts of violence did so for a reason, hitting military or manufacturing targets.

Not schools full of homeless children.

"Is there any possible reason why they would have seen that school as a threat?"

"No," the officer answered without hesitation, immediately understanding what the Doctor was really asking. "That school was exactly what it appeared to be. Not a front, not a cover. No key figures hiding there under another guise. It was simply a school."

Uneasiness settled over the Doctor as he contemplated the senseless act of carnage before him. This was the fourth in a series of inexplicable, seemingly one-off attacks over the past three months. Was it a threat? A message? Another test? Some key piece of strategy he couldn't yet discern with his human perception? He didn't know. All he knew was that Nguyen was fast becoming part of a chain of events he couldn't explain. Seo Pak City, the Sniffer's testimony, the bombing of a completely irrelevant target. He'd thought he understood this war inside and out. Knew the enemy's abilities and desires, tactics and strategies. Not anymore. The game was changing, and if they didn't figure out the new rules, and soon, it could be the end of them all.

The Doctor steepled his hands together, thinking. Three hundred dead, and none of them could be saved, but the one . . .

"Has the Admiral seen this?"

"Not yet. You're the first to respond to my link."

"So, where's the boy now? The survivor, what was his name?"

"The boy known as Storm—a nickname, I believe—was treated for his injuries and is now at the local station pending further instruction." The officer consulted his tip-pad. "I'm sure I have his real name here somewhere . . ."

The Doctor waved him away. "Never mind that. I want him shipped off-planet by the end of the day. Find another school, somewhere small and unimportant, off the radar. Delete his name from the files, and tell no one of his survival."

"Of course. I'll link the Admiral and—"

"Tell no one of his survival."

"Sir?" The officer's voice wavered, unable to refuse but equally unable to obey. "The Admiral is my commanding officer. Not directly, but—"

"*In your opinion, do you believe this boy deserves to spend the rest of his life in Interrogation?*"

"No."

"*Then delete him from the files, send him off-planet, and tell no one of his survival.*"

Silence. Then—"*It shall be done.*"

13

SNOWFLAKES FLUTTER AROUND ME in a rust-tinged swirl, the dusty shapes settling like an icy cape across my shoulders. I hold out my right hand and stare in wonder as one tiny, lattice-like flake alights on my palm. It's perfect. Exactly like I always imagined, only better. By early afternoon this flake, along with a million tiny others, will have left an inch or two carpeted across the land, only to melt away within a few hours, leaving the ground bare and ready for the next morning's fall.

I glance around at the others and quickly withdraw my hand. No need to make myself look like a null who's never seen falling snow before—even if it *is* true.

We've put down on Caraquin, the third of Prism's three moons. As a planetoid still in the last stages of terraforming, it's the most rustic of Prism's satellites, with small settlements, dirt roads, solar fields, and rough houses created from a mix of native materials and heavy alloys left over from the earlier days of terraforming. Unlike Javeyn, Caraquin is a Derelict—everyone evacked and relocated to either new homes or squatter colonies, leaving only ghouls to coast along its now-silent plains.

From the open bay of the shuttle, Zephyr pilots a small, open-air skiff out onto the plain, an anti-grav vehicle rather than a roamer now that we don't have to worry about Javeyn's grasses jamming up the exhaust ports. I stand by with Zel and Ty as he runs it through a few safety checks, all of us still waiting for Archer to emerge with the final member of our party: Dr. Inoue, the scientist we'll be escorting on the mission. Per the briefing last night, it's a B&B, a relatively easy mission that requires only a partial complement instead of a full team.

"What's a B&B?" I'd asked, unfamiliar with the terminology.

"Babysit and bodyguard," Ty had promptly snapped out.

While the teams do the majority of the testing, the researchers occasionally go out into the field if the tech is too complex for us or requires constant monitoring and tweaking during the trial. When that happens, we go along as a protection detail. As Archer put it in the briefing, "You have one job for this mission, and one job alone: to keep this researcher safe. If you have to throw yourself between him and a squatter to save him from a pistol blast, you do it. If you have to stay behind so he can escape, you stay. And if you have to take a ghoul for him so he can come back uninfected, you take it."

Even now, I still feel a shiver as I remember his words. It's one thing to die for someone; it's a completely different thing to take a ghoul for them. Of course, there's always the coma capsule, I remind myself, rubbing the little bump on my wrist.

Yeah. Not comforting.

On the positive side, we got assigned some new equipment. In addition to my usual stunner and aero-launcher, I've also been issued a string of light grenades. A recent innovation by R&D that's still in the testing phase. Supposedly, it can create a cloud of light that will illuminate ghouls, though not kill them unfortunately. According to Archer, a single grenade will only last a few minutes and leaves a bitch of a headache, so they're only for emergency situations. The other innovation is on my launcher itself, which has a sight along the barrel using the same light technology as the grenade.

I raise an eyebrow, trying to decide if being able to see what I'm shooting at will be useful or just creepy, and finally shake my head. I'll know soon enough, I suppose.

From beside me, Zel shifts her weight impatiently and wipes a bead of sweat from her forehead. "How long does it take to ready one researcher?"

"Eh, you know these scientist types," Ty answers. "Brilliant in the lab, but put 'em in the field and they can't tell the difference between a combat knife and a laser cutter."

A jolt goes through me at Ty's careless words. *The laser cutter.* When I turned the tool in to my CO the morning after the storm, along with my suspicions that it may have been used to sabotage the shield generator blade, Asriel didn't say much. Just raised an eyebrow and said he'd look into it. Since then I've been waiting on tenterhooks to hear back from him, but if Asriel has found anything out in the last week, he has yet to tell me.

Before I can speculate any more on the situation, the shuttle door opens and out comes Archer with our researcher, a slender man in his mid-forties. Casting my eye over his borrowed gear, I can't help thinking Ty might have had a point. Dr. Inoue looks a bit like a child playing dress-up, his utility belt buckled incorrectly and the testing uniform hanging awkwardly off his thin frame. Despite that, he gives us a game, if uncertain, smile. In his nose, I spy the glint of two metal tubules pushed up his nostrils: the sniffer.

It's what we're out here to test. If it's successful, it could allow anyone who hasn't had the nose modification to smell out ghouls. Due to cost and time constraints, members of the Celestian Military have only been given the nose modification on a need-to-have basis. Of course, with ghouls, "no need" can change to "need to" in an instant. If this device works, they could easily mass-produce and distribute the sniffer across the entire armed forces, and even to local law enforcement and authority figures. It could be a powerful tool in our war against the enemy. It's also the reason why Dr. Inoue is coming out into the field himself. Every member of the testing teams is already outfitted with the nose modification, as well as the majority of researchers and support staff on base.

Zipping up my jacket, I grab a guardrail and vault into the skiff as Archer outlines the plan. Or should I say Team Leader Archer, who was bumped up to TL a few days ago following Asriel's sudden promotion to Division Commander. Nobody told us what happened to the previous commander, though we all have theories, none of them good. Ty has taken Archer's old place as ATL, beating out Herrera for the role, who's been giving her pointed looks ever since.

"Zephyr, you're driving," Archer says, "and I'll take shotgun to cover the front and give direction. Dr. Inoue will be in the middle, flanked on port by Ty and starboard by Sorenson. Zel, you've got the rear, and Herrera will be our ride in the sky." Archer nods at the two women. "Zel and Ty, you'll be our ghoul counters."

"Yes, sir!"

"Affirmative, TL."

"Now remember, our job is to get Dr. Inoue close enough to test the sniffer without attracting any undue attention. We get in, we get out. No fuss, no muss. Got it, team?"

I lock an air cartridge into place and add my acknowledgement to the team's. Three guards seem like overkill for what appears to be a fairly simple task, but who am I to argue? Taking my position on Inoue's right, I wedge myself against the side rails, launcher relaxed but ready. And if my heart experiences the slightest uptick in activity as the skiff kicks into motion, I'm sure it's due to the asteroid's thinner atmosphere and nothing else.

We glide silently over the ground, heading toward a settlement in the distance. The force fence network there still runs, at least partially, powered by self-maintaining solar collectors that churn on, oblivious to lowly human concerns like invasion and evacuation. We'll use it now, tapping into the system wirelessly through our helmets to get a read on where the enemy is, or at least the moving ones. Our noses will have to keep track of the stationary ones. God forbid any of us ever gets a cold.

Before long, we're at the outskirts of the city, skimming through a field of solar collectors. Though the collectors have dust-resistant surfaces and are programmed to regularly rotate in order to dump off any surface debris blown by the wind, the long neglect has still taken its toll. Small particles cling to their surfaces, too stubborn to be shifted by mechanical means, veiling the collectors and reducing their efficiency. It's why parts of the force fence have gone out. Not enough power to run them all.

"I'm not smelling anything," Dr. Inoue speaks up, the sniffer making his voice noticeably nasal and high. "Are they near? Do you smell them?"

"We're not close enough yet, Dr. Inoue," Archer says soothingly. "Don't worry, we'll let you know as soon as they're near."

Though I agree with Archer's assessment, I lift my head slightly and flare my nostrils just in case. I don't scent anything, but a bright glint catches the corner of my eye. Upping the magnification on my combat lenses, I peer off toward the southwest for a minute, but I see nothing. Just more batches of solar collectors.

Solar collectors. A whole section glinting noticeably brighter than the ones around it. Is it a trick of the sun or something far more worrisome?

"See that, Zel?" I subvocalize into my mic, lightly pointing my launcher in that direction.

She turns her head, silent as her eyes search the field, and replies, "*Sure do. TL, we've got a problem.*"

"*What is it?*" Archer asks quietly from the front, keeping his voice low to prevent Inoue from hearing.

"*Looks like this Derelict may not be as derelict as we thought,*" she answers, unzipping her jacket a bit and fanning herself with her shirtfront.

"*Squatters?*" Archer's voice is terse.

"*None that I saw, but Sorenson caught a whole batch of collectors at four o'clock that are shining noticeably brighter than the others. Like they've been regularly maintained, and not by machines but human hands.*"

Archer swears softly. "*Good catch, Zel, Sorenson. Ty, Zeph? You guys see anything on your side?*"

Zephyr's a negative—unsurprising since he's focused on driving—though Ty says, "*No, but I agree with Zel's assessment. I grew up on a planet similar to this, and there's no way the collectors would be that clean after so long without some human intervention. Not with the kind of tech they'd have on a rock like this.*"

Archer goes quiet as he considers the situation, and I wonder if he's going to call off the whole mission. After a moment, he advises, "*Okay, team. It's only one batch in a whole field, so it's most likely a very small group of squatters that got missed. Adjust your helmet feeds to scan for life signs and keep your eyes peeled. The mission's still a go, but be ready to abort at a moment's notice. I'll link Herrera and let him know the situation.*"

A pale yellow tints my visor as I adjust my settings, but the only heat signs I get are far too small to be human. Jackrabbits or voles, or whatever small wildlife they've got here. I reach down to touch the stun pistol on my hip. They're standard issue, even when the mission doesn't call for them. A detail I'm profoundly thankful for at the moment.

Inoue may not have been able to hear the convo, with us subvocalizing into our coms and our faces turned away, but he does notice when we all start adjusting our equipment at once.

"What's going on?" He starts to rise, but Zel puts a hand on his shoulder and gently pushes him back down.

"We've detected signs of possible squatters," Archer explains. "Probably a very small group that got missed in the final mop-up. Most likely they won't even show. For now we're going to proceed with the mission, but at the first sign of trouble, we'll abort."

"Squatters?" Inoue's gone saucer-eyed, and it occurs to me that he's probably never been near a squatter—or a ghoul—in his life. Instead, he sits in a lab located in the securest place in the universe, working on tinker toys day in and day out for a threat he himself has never faced. Even I can see the irony in that. Until he adds, "Not immunes?"

"What?"

"Immunes," Inoue repeats. "They could be immunes."

Zel and I exchange an equally dumbfounded look, but it's Ty who blurts out what everyone's thinking. "Immunes? As in, immune to ghouls? Are you slaggin' us?"

Inoue looks shocked. "No! That is, I don't know anything myself, but I've heard they've found uninfected people in the mop-ups. People that by all rights should have been infected but weren't. Immunes." He glances around at our astonished expressions. "I shouldn't have said anything. It's just rumor anyway, and this sort of research isn't even something allocated to our base. R&D is purely tech. All the bio goes to the Heli—"

He stops, clamping his lips together in a clear sign he's said too much. Stunned silence follows, even Ty speechless in the face of this revelation. Immunity would be a game-changer, especially if it could be turned into a vaccine. But as Inoue said, it's only rumor.

Of course, I used to think the coma capsules were only rumor.

"All right, Team." Archer's voice snaps us back to the present. "Ghoul territory dead ahead. Look alive."

Archer's admonition comes just as we roll through the last of the solar field. The outermost buildings of the settlement loom up before us, and my nostrils involuntarily flare beneath a weak ripple of sour-and-sweet.

"Specs at five hundred meters," Ty snaps out, all business now. "Too distant to pick up numbers."

"Same here," Zel echoes.

"Inoue?"

The researcher shakes his head. "I don't smell anything."

"It would be really faint. Just the slightest hint of a sour-and-sweet odor," Archer elaborates. When the doctor shakes his head again, Archer nods. "All right, it may just be that the sniffer doesn't have the same range as our surgical implants. We'll try getting a little closer. Zephyr, take us through the fence. Doctor, you let us know the moment you get something."

A slight frisson of energy zaps through my skin as we hit the barrier, jolting my already jumpy heart, and then we're through. Past the force fence and into the capital city of Caraquin.

It's a ghost town.

Abandoned buildings stare emptily at us from either side of the broad avenue, their neglected frames a tapestry of dust, debris, and disuse. Lawns wave with snow-strewn weeds, too hardy to be quashed without manmade pesticides, while their cultivated flowery counterparts drape lifelessly over the ground. Open windows and fallen garbage cans and random items littered over lawns and sidewalks speak of a hasty evacuation. A white cat sits curled on a porch step, licking her paw and watching us. Yes, it's a ghost town, all right.

Or rather, a ghoul town.

"Four hundred meters, still can't call numbers," Ty barks, and Zel agrees. Inoue just shakes his head again.

At Archer's nod, we continue on. Zephyr's cut our speed to quarter pulse, more a slow drift than a skim, but the reduced speed only makes me more tense, not less. I force my lungs to stay calm, to continue breathing slow and easy, though I can't seem to stop my foot from jittering inside my boot. Three hundred meters, then two. It seems like Inoue's sniffer is a bust, when—

"I've got something!"

We stop, hovering in place in the middle of the street. Inoue takes another giant sniff, excitement breaking out over his face. "It's distant, but there. Just like you said—a sour-and-sweet smell. It works! It really works!"

Archer raises an eyebrow at Ty and Zel. By prearranged signal, they both flash four fingers. Four ghouls.

"Can you tell us how many are out there?" Archer asks.

Inoue frowns. "How can you tell?"

"The smell gets stronger the more there are. Also, when you get close enough, each has a distinctive odor that allows you to tell them apart."

When Inoue denies an ability to smell it, Zephyr takes us another fifty meters forward. The sun shines brightly through the cold, crisp air, warming my face and making the falling snow glitter whitely. Birds chirp cheerily from their posts high up, and the wind rustles gently through the street. It's a beautiful day, but still my biceps tighten, every muscle in my body on high alert as we stop once again. I push Inoue and Archer to the back of my consciousness and check the force fence grid on my shield. So far nothing. Either there aren't many ghouls in this part of town, they can't sense us, or they simply don't care.

A flash of orange moves at the edge of my visor, and I whip around toward the heat sign, already going for my stun pistol. Two other launchers swivel my way.

"What is it, Sorenson?"

My eyes search around the nearest house, but I see nothing. After a moment, I shrug. "Not sure. Thought I saw a heat sign."

"Enough for today," Archer declares. "We've verified the sniffer works; Dr. Inoue should have more than enough data to refine and tweak it for the next test. Zeph—"

Decimator blasts explode from the windows nearest us. Crackling bolts slice a hairsbreadth past me, flying from buildings on either side of us, and that's when I realize: the heat flash I saw? It wasn't around the house, but *in it*!

I fire back, shifting my position to block Inoue from the lethal energy pulses even as Zel thrusts the scientist down and covers him with her own body. Archer is yelling for retreat, Ty and I trying to keep the heat off with our own fire while Zephyr throws the skiff into gear, and that's when I smell it.

Two dozen ghouls flying from the houses around us.

14

CHAOS ERUPTS, no one prepared for a shiver of ghouls appearing out of thin air. More Specs materialize, another dozen rising up from the ground around us in a billow of sour-and-sweet.

"What the *hell*?!"

"Where in the vac did *they* come from?!"

"Launchers, team, now!"

Archer's already gotten his first blast off even as I go for the launcher under my arm. My weapon swings into position, and I gasp as a beam of white light shoots from the sight atop the barrel, illuminating a swathe of dark shapes writhing in ever-changing waves of black and red and gold. Something clutches in my chest at the sight, at the invisible enemy now suddenly visible to my naked eyes for the first time on the field of battle.

I freeze, every muscle in my body struck dumb at the sight of these roiling ghouls. Someone throws a grenade, and instead of a few, I'm suddenly seeing dozens of them, backlit by a burst of light so bright only the dimming of my combat lenses stands between me and blindness. Inoue is screaming, "They're everywhere! They're everywhere!" and for a split second I just stand there, unable to act. *Oh God, oh God! What do I do?*

Another blast sizzles by me, so close it shakes me from my trance. I fumble between my weapons, momentarily unable to figure out if it's my launcher or my pistol I should be wielding. Though ghouls swarm around us, squatters are continuing to shoot from the cover of the houses, their blasts dangerously close to the mark despite the blinding light. It's the terrifying sight of a ghoul launching straight at my face that shakes me from my indecision. Dropping my pistol, I go for my launcher.

The shot goes off just in time, tossing the ghoul back from its deadly course less than a meter from my face. It veers off, but I know the cloud won't hold it for long.

"On my mark, everyone shoot toward the rear!" Archer orders. "Zeph, as soon as they shoot, gun it! One—"

A blast of heat creases my thigh, burning through my armor, but I manage to point my launcher to the rear.

"—two, three. Mark!"

Three clouds of gas burst toward the rear, and suddenly the skiff is flying backward. The sharp scent of ghouls burns up my nostrils as we sail past, and then they're behind us. The little craft automatically swivels around on its axis, putting Zeph in the front once again without him even having to turn. We zoom down the road, zigzagging to the left and right to avoid the energy blasts, ghouls hot on our tail. Archer yells frantically into his com for airlift.

"*Herrera, we need pick-up* now . . . *ghouls* and *squatters . . . End of town, two minutes!*"

I shoot off another blast from my launcher, but already the ghouls are falling off, unable to outrun a skiff. A few more shots ring out, and I fumble for my own pistol, dropped in the earlier scuffle, but there's no need. The shots don't even get close, and soon we're out of range. The street falls silent, a ghost town once again, and just like that the crisis is over.

Not that anyone relaxes. Ty and Archer still hold position, pistols drawn and launchers at the ready, while Zephyr doggedly drives. Zel managed to shift around in the chaos so she could cover our researcher but still shoot. Sweat covers her face, and her arms quiver from the difficulty of holding the heavy launcher in such an awkward position for so long, but she never wavers. Inoue is just a shivering ball on the floor, barely visible behind Zel's back. Thank God the ghouls didn't come up through the floor, or it would have been all over for him. I keep my launcher aimed toward the ground, balancing it on one of the skiff's guardrails the way Ty is so I can hold my pistol in the other hand.

No one says anything until we rendezvous with Herrera at the end of town, and even then, our conversation is limited to terse phrases and one-word answers as we load up and bug out. Injuries are minor—a few decimator grazes, me included—but though painful, they're nothing our armor couldn't absorb. Inoue is so shaken, though, that he refuses to come out of the skiff at all until Zel manages to talk him out, wrapping an arm around his shoulders and helping him from the vehicle and into a seat. She and Archer sit beside him, telling him he's okay again and again. Zephyr goes up into the cockpit, presumably to fill Herrera in, leaving only Ty and me at loose ends until our return to the station.

Ty silently retrieves the sniffer from the floor of the skiff—dropped or removed in the chaos, I don't know—and hands it off to Inoue. Her eyes meet mine in a moment of perfect harmony, and I know, I just *know* she's thinking the same thing I am.

Five people with nose modifications and force fence grids, and somehow the ghouls still got the jump on us?

Even though the attack is over, the Spectres left far behind on Caraquin, the memory of it is just as alarming, the terrifying situation only made more so by the fact that we can't explain it. It's as though no matter what we do, whatever innovations we come up with, the Specs are still always one step ahead. With the odds stacked against us like that, what chance does the human race have?

"It's okay, you're safe now. We're all right here, and we're not going to let anything happen to you. Everything's going to be okay, I promise."

Zel's voice wafts quietly through the shuttle, her words bearing a gentle kindness I didn't even know she possessed, and as I listen to her alto voice reassure Inoue over and over again, I wish with all my heart I could believe the lie as easily as she tells it.

———

We all pass the psychic check on the OP, much to everyone's relief. Inoue cries when they clear him. No one knows quite what to do with our hysterical researcher, and we're all beyond grateful that a med team is waiting on hand to take charge of him when we finally put boots down on the station.

"He won't be coming out with us again," Ty comments, but her tone is sober, not snarky, like she regrets the loss of innocence we couldn't quite prevent rather than disdaining it.

"What the hell happened out there?" Zephyr asks softly. "How could they have possibly gotten the drop on us like that, without anyone smelling anything?"

"I don't know," Ty replies, glancing at Zel and me in mute appeal. Both of us only shake our heads.

Per Archer's orders, I take a quick pass through the infirmary along with Zephyr and Ty to get treatment for our decimator wounds. I've got a nasty crease on one thigh and a slight graze on my elbow—painful, but not serious. Ty and Zephyr have similar. Afterwards, we hit the barracks for a quick shower and change. Dumping my sweaty uniform into the laundry, I'm following Zephyr into the hygiene units when my chit buzzes. I activate it, grinning when the link—text-only—scrolls over my hand.

Happy 18th birthday, Michael. Take care. I love you. Mom.

I snort ruefully at the message, the terse words a direct contrast to Dad's wordy hmail which arrived earlier this morning. In it, Dad congratulated me on attaining the "hallowed ranks of manhood"—because a year spent fighting an alien invasion apparently didn't qualify me for membership—and both parents deposited a couple hundred milicreds into my account. Gran already linked me yesterday. I've heard nothing from my sister on Iolanthe.

Not that I wanted to.

De-acking the text, I stop in the hygiene units for a quick shower before heading to the mess. A second message arrives just as I'm stepping out: a summons from Asriel. My heart quickens as I realize what it must be about. *The laser cutter.* I don't stop to dwell on it, but dress and get down to the DC's office as quickly as I can. Asriel gets right to the point.

"I've spoken with Dr. Preston, the head of the WMGD team,

regarding the broken shield generator blade from Test Rho 13. She informed me that her people did a thorough investigation of the part in question after the test ended, and they found no signs whatsoever of sabotage. It's believed the part sheared in half due to an error in the manufacturing process."

A factory defect . . . just like Dr. Jacobi said.

A flush rises to my cheeks as I realize how outlandish my story about saboteurs and setups must sound in light of their findings, especially when Asriel adds in a mild tone, "Dr. Preston also suggested that in the future you leave the analysis of any equipment failure to the engineers. After all, that *is* what we're paying them for."

His mouth quirks slightly, and I have a feeling that whatever Dr. Preston said, it was a good deal less polite that what Asriel relayed. And why shouldn't it be? Here I am, a lowly testing grunt, trying to tell these supersmart engineers their job! I must seem completely laughable to them.

Feeling like an utter null, I nod. "Yes, sir."

"As far as the cutter appearing in your locker goes, I went through the electronic records for your storage compartment and found no signs of unauthorized access. Additionally, I had the locker itself checked out, and there was nothing to indicate a forced entry."

No signs of forced entry at all? How can that be?

"Is it possible you accidentally picked the cutter up somewhere without realizing?" Asriel continues. "Remember, we had that training session for our repair work at the Prism relay station not too long ago. As I recall, the engineers running the session had quite an array of tools available. Perhaps you stuck the cutter in your pocket during the session and forgot about it?"

"I . . . I don't know, sir."

"Or could it have been mixed in with your laundry?" he adds. "Someone left the cutter in a pocket, where it fell out during the wash and eventually ended up in your things. It wouldn't be the first time something went astray in the laundry."

My brow furrows as I consider his words. Both theories make perfect sense, especially now that I know the blade wasn't sabotaged. After all, without the sabotage, there's no reason to plant an ordinary tool in my locker. It's the perfect explanation . . . except for the fact

that the cutter fell out of my Celestial Guard uniform, which I've neither worn nor washed since coming to R&D. Of course, it was pretty
dark when I found the cutter. Maybe I mistook where it came from?

Though uncertainty still lurks, I answer Asriel's expectant look
with a nod. "I suppose it's possible, sir."

"Then it sounds like the mystery is solved. I'll just put the cutter
in the lost and found in case anyone is looking for it."

He dismisses me then, going back to whatever paperwork he was
doing on his tip-pad before I arrived, but there's one last question still
unanswered.

"What about the chip, sir? The one I found inside the cutter with
the number on it?"

"Oh, that? As far as I can tell, it's a manufacturer chip. The number is probably the designation of the factory it was produced in or
the quality control inspector who examined that batch. I wouldn't
worry about it." He arches one eyebrow. "Was there anything else,
Sorenson?"

I flush again, suddenly realizing how idiotic I must look to Asriel.
As the new Division Commander, he must have enough on his plate
without having to deal with some rookie full of wild conspiracy theories. I'm about to say no when I catch sight of the digital on his desk,
the one of the original Alpha Team that Asriel showed me my first
day on base. I give an awkward nod to the picture.

"I'm sorry about the DC, sir. I know she was your old teammate."

Asriel's eyes flick to the image and then away again, his stern expression never changing as he acknowledges the words. "Thank you,
specialist." He nods to the door. "Dismissed."

I quickly make for the door, already wondering if I overstepped
my bounds by saying anything. After all, for all the speculation about
Asriel's promotion, I don't actually know that the previous DC died.
I should've just kept my big mouth shut—just like I clearly should
have done about the laser cutter. I wanted to do what was right, and
ultimately all I did was waste everyone's time and make myself look
like a complete null. Still, at least the mystery of the cutter is solved.
I frown. Sort of.

I head down the hall toward the Central Habitat, determined to
put the whole situation behind me. But despite my resolve, uneasiness

hangs heavy in my chest, and not for the first time do I wish with all my heart that this mysterious laser cutter had ended up in any other locker on the station but mine.

———

After the meeting, I catch up with the rest of the team in the mess, where those of us from the Caraquin mission meet up with the Deltas who stayed behind.

"How's the chow today?" I ask as I drop into a seat across from Zel.

"Oh, you know. Tastes like Spectre," Ty remarks mildly, and everyone laughs at the usual joke that shouldn't be funny anymore, but somehow still is.

The nose modification that allows us to smell ghouls has the side effect of either canceling out or diminishing our normal sense of smell. For the most part, all any of us can smell are ghouls, or the absence of ghouls. With smell being such a large part of taste, many of us can't taste much either. I'm lucky; I can still smell other scents a bit, which means I can also taste most flavors, though they're generally flat and weak. Others can't taste anything at all, while most people, like Ty, can only taste strong sour and sweet flavors. Hence, tastes like Spectre.

Or maybe it's just wishful thinking, this idea that for once *we* could eat the enemy instead of the enemy eating *us*.

"So, I heard Inoue came back a basket case," RC comments as we chow down. "What did you guys do to him, anyway?"

"Oh, you know. The usual," Ty says pertly, a shower and a meal apparently enough to restore her former spirits.

Zephyr launches into the story, and before long Ty is putting in her own additions, along with the occasional comment from Archer. I listen silently as they talk the rest of Delta through the solar field, all the way up through our lunar getaway. Unsurprisingly, the rest of the team is vacced to hear about the ghoul ambush.

"No one smelled anything at all?" Chen asks in clear disbelief. "I mean, besides the ones in the distance?"

"That makes no logical sense," RC objects with a shake of his head. "Maybe you wouldn't catch the ones that were hidden underground—

I've heard of ghouls laying ambushes that way—but you should've at least smelled the ones in the houses. Especially with the windows open."

Archer shrugs. "I've already talked to the DC about it. Asriel's never heard of anything like it either. He's going to take it straight up to Dr. Angelou."

"I'm just glad they finally came out with a new batch of light grenades," Zephyr comments. "These leave a headache, but at least you can see straight afterwards. After the last batch we threw, I was seeing spots for three days straight."

"Well, *I'm* just glad Zeph didn't drive us into a tree this time," Ty remarks dryly.

Everyone bursts into laughter, with the exception of said driver, who promptly flips Ty the bird, and then everyone is talking at once, exclaiming over Zeph's insane driving and our frantic getaway. Even I can't help getting buoyed up, a small rush of adrenaline spiking my system as I think of our triumphant escape in the face of crazy odds. It may have been a close shave, but we all got out alive and uninfected. Though I've only run a handful of missions here, I'm starting to understand that that's all anyone on the teams can really ask for.

Ty throws a comment to me about the cleared solar panels, and I agree, turning a grateful smile on Zel for backing me up. That's when I realize she's the only one not talking. In fact, she's not reacting at all but just sitting there, staring down at the fork in her hand as if she's not sure how she got here.

"Zel?"

She looks up, startled, and I stifle a gasp. Her light skin is even paler than usual, her pupils strangely dilated. Sweat beads her face, and it suddenly occurs to me that she's been sweating every time I've seen her today: on Caraquin, a rock cold enough to produce snow; in the shuttle after the mission; and here in the temperature-controlled mess which, if anything, is on the chilly side.

"Zel—?" I start to repeat.

She suddenly stands up, head cocking as if catching a sound in the distance, though I hear nothing. She blinks a few times, clearly disoriented. "I'm s-sorry, I—"

Then her eyes roll up in her head, and she starts seizing uncontrollably.

15 ZEL DROPS TO THE FLOOR with a thud. Her body writhes in erratic jerks, hands flopping with abandon against the metal tiles while foam bubbles over her lips in a rich froth. Her head rolls around helplessly on her neck and her pupils have completely disappeared, only the whites of her eyes visible, like twin moons shining wetly within their sockets.

"Zel!" Ty is the first one there, sliding to the floor by Zel's side, heedless of the hard tiles beneath her knees. "Zel! Oh my God! Archer!"

Horrorstricken, all I can do is hover in place, half-standing, half-sitting, as Archer vaults over the table. He kicks Zel's chair well out of the way and drops to his knees a safe distance from her. "Stay back, give her room," he cautions as the other Deltas gather around. He puts his palm to his face, activating his chit with a few swift finger movements. "Medical emergency in the Atrium mess. I repeat, medical emergency in the Atrium mess."

A voice comes on, asking for more details, and Archer explains the situation in quick, terse words.

"Archer!"

My eyes shift back to Zel. Blood is coming out of her mouth now, streaking the white foam red with fire. At first I think she just bit her tongue until I see more blood—so much blood!—rimming around her eyes, her nose, her ears, welling up and trickling down her pale skin in strips of crimson. Painful rasps scrape from her mouth, loud and labored. Archer takes one look at Zel's swollen throat and swears.

"Someone get me a med-kit now!"

Chen goes running for one as Archer unzips Zel's collar and yanks it away from her throat. He drums on his thighs furiously, swearing under his breath as he waits for the kit. Then her seizure abruptly stops.

Along with her breathing.

"Chen, I need that kit *now*!"

The med-kit is in his hands within seconds. Archer fumbles with the box, hands trembling as he goes for a scalpel and tube. Zel's face is an ominous shade of blue, the kind of blue I've only ever seen on dead people, and I frantically search for a sign, any sign, that she's still alive. Archer seems to think so, for he's already swabbing her throat with alcohol. Blood wells up as he slits her throat with the scalpel, preparing to trach her.

Her body suddenly jerks, knocking the tube from his hand. Zel convulses hard, shivering in one long, violent paroxysm . . .

. . . and then it's over, the only sound within the silence her limbs falling limp and lifeless to the floor.

Voices call out around me, jumbling together in a cacophony that no longer holds any meaning, while images flash before my eyes like pictures in a frame: Archer, his hands limp and helpless by his sides; Ty, grabbing his uniform and screaming something; Zephyr on his knees and Chen open-mouthed and RC, his eyes wide with shock.

And Zel. Her skin blue and waxen, the bloody whites of her eyes shining moist and swollen under the sterile station lights.

I try to tell myself that it doesn't matter. That I barely knew her and her absence doesn't make any difference to me.

But of course it does.

————

"It was a tick."

Silence reigns. I exchange glances with my team, all of us propped up in various spots just outside the infirmary, and all of our gazes saying the same thing: *What* the *hell?*

Dr. Solstice elaborates. "During the autopsy on Specialist Zelinski's body, we discovered a siren tick—a small parasite that will attach itself to a living creature and feed off its blood. It's similar to the deer tick originating on Earth, which has been known to transmit Lyme disease, but is far more deadly. Our sources say this particular type of tick evolved during terraforming on one of our moons. Javeyn, to be precise."

Javeyn. The name tolls out over us like a death knell.

"We were on Javeyn a two-square back for a mission," Archer says slowly.

The doctor nods. "That would explain it, then. Apparently, Specialist Zelinski picked up this tick during the mission, and it's been on her ever since, pumping minute amounts of poison into her blood. The poison finally reached critical levels and her system overloaded, causing her fever, seizure, and the swelling in the trachea which caused her asphyxiation."

More silence. Then—"A *bug*? She was killed by a slaggin' *bug*?"

Ty's eyes are bulging out like the creature she just swore at, and it looks like she's perilously close to vaccing out. Archer puts a staying hand on her shoulder.

"I'm very sorry for your loss," Dr. Solstice continues. "From what I could glean, the siren tick population is fairly small and is a main food source for the grass-back spider. Deaths from the tick are rare, and as long as the tick is caught in time, the poison is very treatable. Unfortunately, this one was not."

Spiders. My mind flashes back to Javeyn with its spider webs shimmering across the grass in the early morning light. Zel ran right through the thick of them, racing for her life while glistening webs trailed from her arms in every direction. I wonder if that siren tick was there, carried along in a web only to crawl up her arm and make a home for itself on her body, a ticking time bomb biding its time until it could strike the fatal blow.

Laughter rings out. I swivel my head around to the source of the noise. Ty is laughing, an ugly, harsh sound borne through lips curled in utter disgust. Everyone stares at her in shock. She gives us all a grotesque grin. "What, you don't think it's funny? Here we are fighting brain-sucking ghouls and mindless squatters, narrowly escaping being infected or shot on a daily basis, only to be brought down by a *bug*? How stupid. How *fragging stupid*!"

She laughs again. Archer leans over to speak to her, but Ty abruptly yanks away. "This is bullslag," she tells him, "and everyone here knows it."

Then she turns and strides away.

No one says anything. Ty is right; Zel's death was senseless and stupid. Though we've all seen death before—touched it and held it and rinsed it from our hands—this time it's different. Not because of who or even where, but *how*. Because we can understand being gunned down by squatters or trampled in a riot or infected by a ghoul, but this? Ty is right—this makes no sense. But right doesn't change anything: not this war, not this place, and not Zel's body, lying on some slab in the morgue, never to rise again.

"Training is cancelled for the rest of the day," Archer says at last. "I'll be scheduling medical exams for everyone on the team ASAP, but in the meantime, please check yourselves over for anything suspicious and report to medical if you experience even the mildest symptoms.

"I'll arrange for Zel's burial and link you all with the place and time. Dismissed."

For a few seconds, no one moves, as though by tacit agreement we're all observing a moment of silence for our fallen teammate. Then the moment breaks, and everyone gets up and leaves. Veterans of death all, no one sheds a single tear. At least, not in public.

The next day at 0900, Zel is given a burial within the net. Chen flies us down in a small shuttle to a point just above the planetary net and releases her coffin. I see it for just a moment, framed within the shimmering blue latticework below—

And then it's gone, atomized on contact by a single band of energy, just one of a thousand more rushing by across the pastel sky.

A basket of gengineered flowers shows up in the communal lounge two days later, an unsigned note gracing the petals.

I'm sorry about your teammate. She saved my life. I won't forget.

It sits there for half a day until Ty comes back from training and sees it. She reads the note, then picks up the basket without a word and spaces it out the nearest airlock. For a few glorious seconds, the petals fly through the air like brilliant butterflies, shining and bright. Then gravity takes hold, and away they fall through the sifting mists.

———

We lose Herrera a week later, infected while testing out a new mix of launcher gases. The scientists on base told us the new formula would act as an even stronger repellent against ghouls. Too bad no one told that to the Specs. They flew right through the cloud as though it wasn't even there. By the time we could shoot them off with our normal cartridges, it was a hair too late for Herrera. As they dosed him with Spectranol and took him away, all I could think about were the holos of four little kids who would never see their favorite uncle again.

We're not the only ones who suffer casualties. Not long after our botched launcher mission, Gamma Team's shuttle gets mobbed en masse by ghouls when they attempt to go planetside for a mission. They manage to get away in time, all except for the Team Leader, who steps out an airlock two minutes after being infected. Instant promotion for Songbird, not that she can appreciate it given the circumstances. Beta manages to squeak by without any losses, but Alpha Team loses a couple of members, one shot through the head by a squatter and another infected and sent off to a high-security internment facility. As the weeks continue to pass, a pall falls over R&D, or at least the Testing Division. It's as though Zel's death was some sort of signal, a catalyst setting off a chain of casualties that no one can seem to stop.

We carry on as best as we can, and despite the early losses, things aren't all bad. Though we lose Herrera, we get a transfer from Beta Team—Kagawa, a former firefighter who was recruited after distinguishing herself during a ghoul invasion—to up our numbers until the next group of recruits arrives. We also go on several other test runs that are more or less successful. Less in the case of the pulse net and ghoul goggles—the former shorted out five seconds after we dropped it on our incorporeal prey, while the latter didn't accomplish anything more than making us look like total nulls. More in the case of the Psi-darts, tranquilizer guns filled with a highly concentrated dose of Psi-Lac. A direct hit in the chest area sends a burst of the drug directly into a squatter's bloodstream, suppressing the psionic power of the Spectre and confusing the host for up to several minutes. We could all vouch for the fact that the squatters we tested them on seemed fairly disoriented, though whether that was because of the drug or simply the natural result of being randomly attacked by soldiers with trank darts is still in question.

Additionally, after a few more runs—sans Inoue—and some major tweaking, the sniffer is declared a go, with schematics being sent to all the major manufacturing facilities in the Expanse for immediate production and distribution. The light grenades, light sights, and a basic flashlight version generically referred to as a "ghoul light" also go into mass production, along with a few other gadgets tested by some of the other teams.

All of this, of course, is in addition to serving at the beck and call of the WMGD team, who have stepped up their efforts to questionable avail. They've continued to run tests, sometimes as many as two a week, and we're often called upon to upgrade data collection equipment or even act as rudimentary data collectors ourselves, perching high up in the target area during the tests and using our noses to determine if anything has changed, at least in an olfactory capacity. No one can decide whether the increased testing is a good thing or a bad thing—a sign they're close to a breakthrough or an indication the war is only getting worse. Closeted away within the pastel mists, away from the invasions, riots, and evacuations, sometimes it's easy to lose touch with the universe outside.

The chance to reacquaint ourselves with the real world comes unexpectedly several weeks into my hitch at R&D. We're racking our gear in the armory after a mission when I get linked into Archer's office along with Chen, Ty, and RC.

One hour later, we're lifting off from the station, on course for the next jump path out of here.

———

Ships hover around the planet in droves, their metal hulls gleaming brightly beneath a yellow sun that's already begun to set around the far side of the world. Evacuation carriers, defense corvettes, refugee transports. All it takes is a single glance to know that this is a world under siege. Not by the ships, but by the invisible army sweeping across the land below.

I feel a strange pang in my chest. I've seen this sight a hundred times, lived it on a daily basis at one point, but after only a few months at R&D, already my former life feels distant and estranged. Every piece is identifiable, every movement I know by heart, and yet as familiar as it all is, I feel no real connection to the world I see outside. Of course, maybe that's because I was never very connected to it to begin with.

After fourteen straight hours in flight—six to the path, one in jump, and seven to this place before us—we've finally arrived at our target destination, a planet called Nomia. We've been sent to collect a shipment of highly specialized equipment created especially for the WMGD team at R&D. Normally the equipment would have been shipped off-planet to a military depot near Prism for pickup, but with the unexpected invasion, all shuttles have been commandeered for the evacuation effort. Either we grab that equipment now or lose it to the enemy forever.

Chen lightly dances our shuttle farther into the chaotic web while in the copilot's seat beside her, Archer transmits our clearance codes every thirty seconds so that some itchy trigger finger doesn't blow us out of orbit. Not that anyone really cares about the ships going down at this point, not with the number of squatters groundside already in the millions and growing with every minute.

"The *Resilient*." Ty's quiet voice points me to an evac carrier orbiting just above the secondary OP. "That's my old carrier."

Meaning that if she hadn't joined R&D, she'd be down there right now, just one of a multitude of guardians working to get as many people as possible out before the final net drops. The same way I would be—if not here, then somewhere else—if I hadn't taken Angelou up on his cagey offer. Strange how some choices only seem to lead us back to the beginning, as though we never really had a choice at all.

"How long has it been?" I ask. "Since you were there?"

"Six months, twenty-eight days."

I raise an eyebrow at the exact count. "Tight unit?"

"You better believe it. Anyone in that unit would've taken a ghoul for me and vice versa. We knew the meaning of loyalty." Her eyes flick toward the pilot's seat, and in a sharp voice she suddenly adds, "They would never betray their own."

At the forward console, Chen's back stiffens for just the slightest instant, though I can't tell whether it's a reaction to Ty's tone or something outside the viewport. There's a discordant undercurrent running between the two women that I've never felt before, and it occurs to me that I've never once seen them together outside of team activities. Even at group meals they usually sit at opposite ends of the table.

They don't like each other, I suddenly realize. They cover it well—if not for this one slip-up, I would never have guessed they felt anything worse than indifference for each other—but it's there, lying just beneath the surface. I wonder what happened to cause the rift. Probably guy troubles. Isn't that what women always fight about?

Perhaps Archer feels it too, because after a quick glance around the cabin, he puts in, "Hey, when you do what we do, you have to count every day."

"Amen," RC murmurs.

Amen, indeed.

We continue to make our way through the labyrinth of ships, careful to keep out of the way of the myriad shuttles flying evacuees up to the waiting transports above before returning to the surface for another load. Through the far corner of the viewscreen, I can just make out a couple of nasty looking storm-class warships lurking just aloft of the chaos. Though they don't exactly wear a sign, I know what they're doing there. They're waiting for the moment when the command is finally given to quarantine the planet. Then, come hell or high water, they'll drop the planetary net.

No matter who may still happen to be down there.

I'm not the only one who seems to be thinking along those lines. Chen takes us down into the Qyoto manufacturing district with a speed bordering on recklessness, and Archer is flinging open the doors only seconds after we hit the loading dock. Sirens greet us the moment we step out, and it's clear from the empty streets below that this part of the city has already been evacuated. Luckily, Angelou got us the entry codes before we departed, and within seconds we're inside.

With the last military update showing ghouls only three hours from the city, we snap to like a well-oiled machine, locating the shipment toward the front of the warehouse and loading it onto carts for transfer to our waiting shuttle. We work quickly, everyone fully aware of the potential consequences should we waste even a second, but still the time ticks by far faster than anyone would like. Minutes turn to an hour as we move almost as one, our pulses pounding in time to the same frenetic rhythm. *Load, transport, unload, return. Load, transport, unload, return.*

With only forty-five minutes to go, we're down to our last load. Chen's on the ship getting the cargo secured, and RC and Ty have just headed that way with their carts. I'm closing up the storage area when I hear a noise.

I stop, ears pricking as it comes again. A soft bang, neither automated nor machine-made, but something more random. Like the wind blowing over a stylus holder or a small animal knocking over a cup.

I finish locking up, then com Archer. "TL, I'm picking up a noise nearby. It's probably nothing, but I'd like permission to check it out just in case."

"Granted, Sorenson. Let me know if you need backup."

"Affirmative, TL. Sorenson out."

Pulling out my stun pistol, I stalk down a corridor toward the source of the sound. The noise comes again, and my eyes go to the door at the other end of the hall. I put my ear to the door and immediately hear more sounds—the sort of varied, irregular noises only a human could make. Definitely a person, then. A looter, perhaps, or an employee who managed to evade the evac teams.

My lip curls in disgust. As a guardian, I ran into people like this on evac runs all the time. People too scared or stubborn to leave, or else criminals taking advantage of the chaos to steal and vandalize. We were working our asses off to save these people, putting our own lives on the line, and they made our job ten times harder. I don't know which sort the person behind this door is, but it doesn't matter. Whoever they are, they don't belong here. The ghouls will be rolling in en masse in less than an hour, and anyone left at that point will be ghoul bait.

I should just leave them here. Whoever it is, they've made their bed; might as well let them sleep in it. However, I already know I'm not going to do that. I was a guardian, after all, and old habits die hard. We could easily take them out on our shuttle and drop them with one of the refugee transports in orbit. Decision made, I swipe open the door and walk in.

I'm in an employee break room, the small space kitted out with a few tables and chairs, a narrow counter, and several glass-fronted food and drink dispensers. A lone woman stands in front of a dispenser, back to me as she peruses the selections. A backpack sits at her side, stuffed to overflowing with various odds and ends including a couple bottles of water and an emergency blanket. As I watch, she suddenly pulls back and gives the dispenser first one, and then another massive kick. Something drops inside the machine, and she quickly grabs a candy bar from the access panel. She only pauses long enough to pull off the wrapper before shoving roughly half of it into her mouth at once.

A strange mix of disdain and amusement bubbles up in me as the irony of the situation takes hold. Here we are in the middle of a full-fledged ghoul invasion, with barely forty minutes remaining until they hit the city, and the only thing this woman cares about is stealing candy from a food dispenser. Unable to stop myself, I let out an incredulous laugh.

The figure jumps at the sound, knocking the backpack over as she whirls around in alarm. Her mouth drops open, and the gob of half-chewed candy comes tumbling out. It hits the floor with a gummy *splat. "Michael?"*

Now it's my mouth dropping open. It's been well over a year, but it hardly matters. I could never forget the face of the girl who betrayed us that long-ago day on New Sol Station. We had a plan. A plan that included Lia *living* . . . until this glitch ditched us at the last moment, forcing us to change everything with only minutes to go. If not for her, everything might have happened differently.

Lia might still be alive.

"No, that's impossible." Shar is shaking her head, the response coming so quickly on the heels of my thought that I know she must have taken it straight out of my head.

A bolt of white-hot rage shoots through me. *How* dare *she . . . !* Shar's face blurs, eclipsed by a violent haze raking across my vision. The ground seems to shake beneath my feet, and from some far-off place, I hear Shar's voice squeak my name again. Then her throat is under my hands, and everything shatters.

16 GLASS FLIES, the display window exploding under Shar's shoulders as I slam her back against the vending machine.

"Stay out of my head!"

Shar falls back into the broken machine, candy raining from the racks as she thrashes within my grasp. She kicks at my shins and slaps at my arms, but her blows are like an insect's bite—inconsequential. Somewhere in the back of my mind, a voice is telling me to release her, that she's no threat to me, but my rage is so strong. Shar's pulse flutters under my fingers, and for a long moment, I hover over the edge of an abyss, one I might not ever be able to return from should I take the plunge.

Sanity wins, the world coming back into focus in one startling instant. I force my fingers to loosen, to relax my grip while I fight to regain control—

Stars explode in my brain, memories and thoughts cleaved apart and sent flying by a searing pain knifing red-hot through my mind. Disoriented, I fall to my knees, unable to think, to remember, to process . . . *anything*. Mind asunder, I huddle on the floor, body shaking and hands thrown protectively over my head as I drift within the dark void of my psyche.

White flowers with blue centers.

The creak of a porch swing, children laughing.

A raging storm and a scared girl's voice. "Can I stay with you tonight?"

"Michael? Michael! Please wake up!"

Hands shake my shoulders, fingertips pressing hard into my biceps. A woman's face hovers over mine, skin ashen and eyes wide.

A closing train door.

The rumble of a shockwave streaking out through the floor.

Then it's only debris. Silver shards everywhere.

"Oh God, not again. *Please* not again. Michael? *Michael?*"

Clarity comes back in a blinding rush, the sound of my name snapping back the splinters of my memory like iron filings drawn to a magnet. My heart is pounding, and my head feels like a concussion grenade went off inside it, but everything seems to be intact. I blink at Shar through watery eyes. "What the hell happened?"

Shar nervously bites her lip, not answering. I reach out a hand to her, and she springs back; hands up, pleading. "Michael . . . please. I don't want to hurt you."

Despite her words, she looks genuinely afraid, though I'm not entirely sure it's me she fears. With a wary nod, I get to my feet, trying to do it in the least threatening way I can. Not difficult, considering I'm still reeling from the psychic concussion I received. I'd known she had psychic abilities, but I never guessed she was capable of *that*. Either she never revealed the full extent of her powers or they've gotten stronger since New Sol. A lot stronger.

It's been a year and half since I last saw her, not since that final, fateful day on the space station. No one knew about the Spectres then. No one . . . except Lia. As one of the last members of the Tellurian Resistance, it was her job to reveal the enemy to us Celestians. To give us a fighting chance against an enemy no one could see or hear or even touch. Only her memories went haywire, and by the time she recalled her mission, it was almost too late. Ghouls had spread through New Sol, poised to strike, so we decided to strike first.

Using the ventilation system, we forced the enemy into the Central Hub by pumping ghoul-repellant gases into the Habitat Rings. Once they were sequestered in the hub, away from the station's population, we separated the rings from the hub by setting off a core breach alarm. The plan was for all of us—Lia, Shar, Teal, and me—to grab a SlipStream train to the rings, where Shar would use her psychic gifts to reveal Lia's memories of the enemy to the station commander. The stationers would be safe in the rings, the enemy would be revealed, and Lia would remain alive.

Everything was going perfectly until I met up with Lia and Teal at the SlipStream station only to find out that Shar wasn't coming. She'd turned coward at the last minute, sneaking onto an outgoing ship and forcing us to change the plan at the last minute. Forcing Lia to stay behind in the Central Hub . . .

. . . where she went Nova.

The light from her explosion revealed the enemy for all to see, but it came at the cost of her life. Now not a day goes by when I don't wonder: If not for Shar's last-minute desertion, would Lia still be alive? But Shar *did* desert us, and Lia *did* die, and all I can do now is curse Shar for getting away scot-free from the mess she left behind.

Well, maybe not completely scot-free, I reluctantly revise. A single glance is enough to tell me the months have not been kind to her. She's wearing a stained and tattered shipsuit two sizes too big for her, belted at the waist and sleeves rolled up to her wrists. Her boots are scuffed and dirty, and a peculiar, unwashed odor is emanating from her greasy hair. Dark shadows ring her eyes, and even her cheeks have taken on a sallow, sunken look. A thin, white latticework of scars creeps almost invisibly across her forehead.

"You look awful," I blurt with a nod toward her scarred head. "What happened? You pick a fight with someone your own size for once?"

She flinches at my sarcastic words, strangely cowed considering she was able to drop me with one blow. Her fingers lift, involuntarily reaching for her forehead, but at the last second her hand drops. "Something like that," she finally mutters.

I shake my head in disbelief, still stunned to find *Shar*, of all people, here in Qyoto. Last I knew, the ship she'd snuck onto was bound for the lower colonies. Clearly she's been on the move since then. "What are you doing here, anyway? Besides looting vending machines?"

She shrugs, not answering, and the flippant brush-off only reignites my anger. Contempt rises in me, spreading through my chest like liquid nitrogen, a cold fire that burns and yet freezes everything in its path. Contempt for her cowardice, for her disloyalty, her selfishness. Does she even know what happened? Does she even *care*?

"Lia's dead, you know," I suddenly say; casually—conversationally, even—as though I'm talking about the weather or a bit of news, and not the passing of the girl I loved. "Went Nova just an hour after you turned tail and left."

"I know."

Of course she knows. Who in the known Expanse *doesn't* know what happened to Lia?

"I was sad that she died," Shar adds in an unexpected addendum. I wait for her to say more, but she doesn't, her six words apparently enough to render her mute once again.

"That's *it?*"

"What else do you want me to say?"

"Oh, I don't know, maybe that you're *sorry*!" I burst out. "That you regret ditching us at the last minute and forcing us to change the plan? Some sort of acknowledgement of what you've done?"

Shar only stares at me silently.

I lean down until our faces are only centimeters apart and whisper, my voice like a frosty wind on an Aurora morning, "That if not for you, Lia might still be *alive*."

Now she moves, chest popping in an audible breath, like a holo character suddenly startled back to life. Tears well up in her eyes, her lips pressing together in an obvious attempt to hold them back, but all she does is softly shake her head. "No, it was always fated to be that way."

I jerk back, appalled as much by the words themselves as the ring of truth they carry. There's a faraway look in Shar's eyes, like she's seeing into a world no one else can see, and once again I can't help wondering if she's reading my mind with her psychic gifts.

"If you're trying to brain-drain me again—"

"Trust me," she interrupts, mouth flatlining and eyes going cold, "I have far better things to use my powers on than *you*."

The sudden fierceness catches me off guard, makes me look at her a second time—*really* look at her. The gaunt frame and ill-fitting clothes, the scarred head and defeated air. Misery wraps her from head to toe, and whatever she's done, whatever she's guilty of, it's clear her flight from New Sol has only brought her more pain, not less. A fitting punishment for her desertion, and one worse than anything I could ever tender. Yet despite her misery, there's still fight in her. A dogged refusal to give in to whatever ugliness fate's dished up for her. Whatever her past, even I can admire that, at least a little.

"*Sorenson,*" Archer's voice emerges through my com. "*Status report.*"

Shar's eyes widen, panic lighting her face as she shakes her head violently at me. Without taking my eyes off her, I activate my com. "It was nothing. Just an animal like I thought."

"*Acknowledged. We're almost ready to shove off, so I need you back here ASAP. I've been listening in on the fleet's com reports, and I don't think they're going to hold off on that net much longer.*"

"On my way. Sorenson out." I de-ac my com and turn back to Shar. "There's a shiver of ghouls coming. If you don't want to end up as ghoul bait, I suggest you get yourself to one of the evac shuttles now. The nearest evac station is ten blocks east and another five blocks south," I tell her after checking the location on my chit. "I'd run if I were you."

She looks away, exposing the vulnerable arch of her neck, and with it the red marks from my fingers still imprinted on her skin. Shame passes through me as I eye those marks, no part of me able to justify my behavior now that the searing rage that accompanied it is gone. Once again I'm struck by how tattered she looks, how vulnerable. I think about how long it would take Shar to make it to the station on foot and realize: Lia wouldn't have left her in the lurch.

Her compassion, her kindness; though she'd had no reason to, in the end she'd shown Shar forgiveness.

Something inside me loosens at the memory, some unflinching resolve relenting under Lia's example. I sigh and rub my aching head. "Listen, forget the evac station. We can take you—"

"Save your pity! I can take care of myself!"

I stare at her in surprise for a moment, then let out a rueful laugh, recalling how easily she hitched a ride off New Sol. I should've known—when it comes to her own survival, Shar always has a plan. She certainly doesn't need any help from me.

"Yeah, I guess you can take care of yourself," I concede after a moment. "Goodbye, Shar."

Without another word, I turn around and walk away. As I reach the door, Shar suddenly calls out, voice brimming with certainty, "I'll see you again, Michael."

For a split second I pause, heart quickening at the ridiculous assertion, then shake my head. "I doubt that."

If she has an answer, I'm already gone before she speaks.

———

I make it back to the shuttle in a minute flat, jogging up to the dock just as they're stowing the last load. After helping Ty and RC secure the cartons into place, I make my way to the cockpit, where Chen is already doing preflight checks. Holo gauges fill the viewscreen in front of her, feeding data to her from various ship systems, while in the copilot's seat beside her, Archer listens intently to the com traffic from the fleet up above in orbit.

"Resilient, *this is Captain Crae of the* Meridian. *What's your status?*"

"Meridian, *this is the* Resilient. *Our guardians on the ground are finishing up their last sweep for stragglers as we speak. The final shuttles should be loaded up and back onboard within thirty minutes tops.*"

"*Acknowledged,* Resilient. *Keep us posted.* Meridian *out.*"

Archer catches sight of me and jerks a head toward one of the seats. "Good, you're back. Strap in, Sorenson. We'll be taking off any minute now."

With a nod, I do as he says, grabbing a seat in the back and pulling on the harness. RC and Ty join us a heartbeat later and immediately follow suit while Archer continues to scan through the com frequencies.

"*. . . are the preparations for the net coming?*"

"*Admiral, we've finished seeding all the generators into the atmosphere and are initializing the grid now. We should be ready to activate within fifteen minutes.*"

"*Good. Scans are showing large masses of ghouls converging on a few dozen key targets. They'll be in range of the first cities within a matter of minutes. Continue initializing and stand by for further orders.*"

"Hear that?" Archer asks, shutting off the com. "That's our signal to leave. Chen, take us out."

"Yes, sir."

Chen makes a few motions with her hands, and a host of lights spring to life across the viewport. Another motion, and the holo gauges fly out from the center of the forward port, rearranging themselves along the top and bottom to give Chen a clear view out. A nearly inaudible purr hums through the cabin, followed by the familiar roar of the thrusters.

"Engines hot and thrusters primed. Lifting off in three, two, one . . ."

A loud boom cracks through the cabin. The starboard thruster goes out, and the shuttle lurches, the right side suddenly dropping to slide across the landing bay with an earsplitting *scree!* I grab for my seat, bracing myself as the port side follows, hitting the tarmac with a hard jolt.

Archer draws himself upright. "Report!"

Chen's fingers scroll through the air, bringing up data scans and systems gauges as she searches for the source of the blow. Suddenly her hand flies out, bringing the shifting holos to a halt. A ship schematic hangs in the air before her, one section glowing red in the pale cabin lights.

"There." She enlarges the schematic with a few flicks of her hand. "Something caused the ignition regulator in the starboard thruster to overload."

"Can it be fixed?" Archer asks.

"Not before the net drops. We might be able to bypass it."

"RC!" Archer barks out.

"On it," he replies, shucking his restraints and running for the thruster.

"Chen, you work with RC. See if you can talk him through the bypass from here. Ty, go back and assist RC if he needs it. I'm going to see if I can get a link through to one of those cruisers up there."

Everyone leaps into action, Ty disappearing through the door while Archer fires up the ship's com system. Chen is already flipping through numerous schematics as she speaks with RC in a low voice through her helmet com.

"Okay, you're going to need to start by opening up the forward maintenance panel on the starboard thruster. Look for the catch located at the base of the panel near the manufacturer's mark . . ."

"This is the shuttle *SkyRunner* of the CE Military Support Corps calling any ship in orbit. Please respond immediately."

I sit up in my chair, hand hovering over my restraints, itching to help but having no appreciable way to contribute. Instead I tune my helmet com to the traffic high above, flipping through the frequencies as I listen to the voices in the sky with one ear and my teammates with the other.

"*. . . your status,* Resilient?"

"*This is the* Resilient. *We've completed the evacuation efforts, and the last shuttle has just docked. All our people are aboard, and we'll be jumping out of system in the next few minutes.*"

"Once again, this is the shuttle *SkyRunner* of the CE Military Support Corps in Qyoto on a classified mission. Can anyone read me? Please respond."

". . . been disconnected, you'll have to reroute the conduction coils through the secondary regulator on the internal frame . . ."

Minutes tick by, and still we sit unmoving on the ground. Judging from Chen's quiet instructions, RC has disconnected the blown regulator and is in the process of routing everything through a secondary system. Meanwhile, Archer has managed to raise someone on the com—a communications officer from the sounds of it—and is fighting to get patched through to someone in command.

"As I said before, we were here on an RD-3 Classified Mission when our thruster broke down and we became grounded. Repairs are underway, but we need more time. It's imperative I speak to your superior *now.*"

"*I'll see what I can do, Team Leader. Please hold the line.*"

I jitter my foot impatiently and switch back to the feeds overhead. Voice links are crackling back and forth in rapid succession, and it's clear we don't have much longer before they drop that net.

"*. . . clearing the area now, per your orders.*"

"*Phantasm to the* Meridian. *The net is charged, initialized, and ready for deployment. I repeat, the planetary net is ready for deployment.*"

"*Acknowledged,* Phantasm. *Stand by for further orders.*"

"*Meridian, sensors show the outer fences around a dozen major population centers including Hibiscus, Langford, and Qyoto have all tripped. I repeat, the outer fences have tripped in over a dozen cities. We have ghouls inside. Your orders?*"

Silence hangs over the com, dark and forbidding, then the words I've been dreading to hear finally drop.

"*Activate the net.*"

I glance over at Archer in alarm. He's finally managed to get through to the admiral of the fleet, but the answer he receives is a death knell.

"*Negative, Team Leader,*" the admiral's voice crackles through the shuttle's com. "*The net is already in the process of being deployed and cannot be recalled. If you don't want to be grounded, I suggest you get yourself into the air within the next five minutes.* Meridian *out.*"

"Damn it!" Archer throws down the transceiver and switches to his helmet com. "RC, where are we with that thruster?"

"*Almost there,*" comes RC's voice, slightly muffled through the group channel. "*We completed the bypass, and we're just double-checking it before closing up.*"

"They're dropping the net. Close up now!"

The minute it takes for RC and Ty to finish with the thruster and get back onboard is the longest minute of my life. Even before they finish strapping in, Chen is revving the engines, preparing to take off. She mutters something that could be either a curse or a prayer, then eases back on the throttle.

The thruster ignites, and I'm thrown back into my chair as we rocket up, ship pitching backward as the nose rises in the air. The shuttle bucks once, and for a second I think we're going to fall again . . . then it steadies, and we're soaring up through the skyline, the city at our backs and the open sky before our eyes. Before long, we leave Qyoto behind, pushing up into the atmosphere at full throttle.

My eyes rake the sky before me, searching frantically for any signs of the net—and then I see it!

Blue energy ripples against the sky, filling my peripheral vision with light as it shoots from one shield generator to the next. It snakes across the sky from every direction, its deadly energy crackling through the atmosphere and lighting generator after generator. As each tiny unit lights, it throws out rays to half a dozen more, lacing out in a pattern so swift and complex I can't even begin to track its movements.

"Chen—"

"I see it!"

The shuttle kicks as Chen pours everything she's got into acceleration. I hold onto my harness, fists clenching and pulse pounding as we race against the net's deadly weave. We're flying faster than I've ever flown, but the net's flying too, eating up the sky with a raging hunger that can't be denied. The empty space is closing, holes knitting with frightening frequency. Chen adjusts our course, aiming for the biggest open section.

It's going to be close.

I press my lips together, foot fidgeting in my boot as we get nearer and nearer. The net is closing up, the network almost whole now, and I'm not sure we're going to make it. The suspense is agony, cutting through me like a knife as I watch our destiny bear down on us. *Come on, come on!*

We shoot through the bottom layer a hairsbreadth before it closes, charging up inside the latticed tiers of the net itself. Blue light sizzles around us on every side, flashing like lightning through the viewport, cracking like thunder in our ears. For a split second, I'm *sure* we're going to get caught, fried deep within the net's core, never to be heard from again—

—and then we're out, bursting through the top layer like a comet streaking through the night, on course for oblivion. We soar out of the atmosphere seconds later, sucked into the vacuum of space as the planet falls away below us, and then there's nothing left standing between us and the stars but distance itself.

Relief pours through me as we make good our escape, every other emotion subsumed by the basic human drive to survive. Yet even as we disappear into the black of space, I can't stop thinking about all the millions of people left behind, consigned to an imprisonment beneath the net even as we fly freely away into the universe above.

———

After a quick stop to refuel, we leave the system and head for home. From within the shuttle's small hygiene unit, I brace myself against the sink as we make the transition to jump, waiting until my body adjusts to that familiar sense of inward compression before turning the water back on. Now that the mission's complete, I'm taking advantage of the lull to wash some anxiety-induced sweat off my face. My skin feels grimy after the dusty halls of the warehouse, and there's a hollow ringing deep in my head. A lingering gift from Shar, no doubt.

My lips twist into a grimace at the thought. I'd wanted to kill her the moment I saw her, infected by a rage so potent I couldn't see straight. It was as though all anger over Lia's death transferred to Shar in the blink of an eye, taking me over, controlling me, turning me into something else completely. Something monstrous.

I relented in the end, loosened my hands when I could have tightened them. Even before Shar struck me down, I'd regained control and chosen not to kill her. Still, the thought of what I *could* have done frightens me more than I care to admit. If only I'd had some warning, some inkling Shar would be there. The shock alone was at least partially responsible for my loss of control. For that matter, what the hell was Shar doing on Nomia—and in Qyoto, of all places!—anyway?

After her defection on New Sol, I didn't expect to see her ever again. Why would I? The Expanse is vast beyond compare, and Shar made it clear her only goal was to run as far away as she could. I'm no math genius, but even I know the odds of meeting her again were too high to even calculate. Well, too high for *me* to calculate. No doubt Teal could calculate the odds down to the last fraction or ratio or whatever! But I don't need the odds to know that we should never have met.

At least, not by accident.

Not that meeting on purpose makes any more sense. How could

Shar have possibly arranged to run into me when I didn't even know I'd be there myself until yesterday? Not to mention the fact that she looked as shocked to see me as I was to see her. No, our meeting was no more Shar's design than it was mine. Call it whatever—an accident, a coincidence, a twist of fate—but it occurred for no purpose and meant even less. At least that's what I tell myself.

With a shake of my head, I reach for a towel. I've been in here for ages; the others are probably wondering where I am. Quickly, I pat my face dry and wipe my hands, then exit the hygiene unit.

A noise originating from the opposite end of the hall pauses my journey back to the cockpit. I take a quick detour, hunting for the source of the sound, and find RC in the engine room, his sharp eyes combing through a twisted cylinder of glass and metal. He jumps up at the sound of my footsteps, momentarily startled, then relaxes.

"Oh, hey, Sorenson."

"That was a great job you did back there. When the engine crashed, I thought we were dead. I can't believe you managed to get us back into the air in time."

"I did an internship with Creight Shipyards a few years back," RC explains. "They're one of TruCon's biggest shipping facilities. I learned a lot there."

"So if you're such a good engineer, why are you in the barracks with the rest of us testing grunts?" I ask curiously. "Shouldn't you be with all the other R&D engineers?"

"I appreciate the note of confidence, but compared to those geniuses, I look like a complete null." At my incredulous expression, RC nods. "It's true. The recruiters brought me in because of my joint background in both engineering and athletics. I played several sports in college, even played on a few championship teams. They were hoping with a little training, I could be a bridge between the testers and the research personnel—strong enough to keep up with the testers and smart enough to understand the tech. *Really* understand the tech, enough to make modifications in the field when needed."

"That must have been a big change, going from a university to R&D."

His expression suddenly shutters. "It was better than being thrown into a refugee camp after the Spectres invaded."

Ah. No good response to RC's acid comment, I nod to the cylinder at his feet. "That the regulator?"

"Yes. I was analyzing the damage to see if any of the internal parts might be salvageable, but—" He finishes the sentence with a luckless shrug.

"Too bad. Maybe the mechanics at R&D will have better luck with it." A ribbon of scarlet on his hand catches my eye. "That looks like a nasty cut. Here, let me take the regulator. I'll stow it for you while you clean up."

RC hesitates. "Sure, why not? Thanks, Sorenson."

I take the damaged regulator from RC, grasping it gingerly to avoid stabbing myself with any of the broken pieces. The regulator is little more than a charred piece of metal, glass, and ash now, and even I can tell it's unsalvageable in any way, shape, or form. Still, it's the mechanics' job to make the call one way or the other. With a nod to RC, I bear it down the corridor and into the cargo bay in back. Opening up a storage bin, I'm about to dump the regulator in when something inside it catches my eye. Picking away the outer pieces of rubble, I lean down for a closer look.

Cold washes over me as the silvery glint resolves itself into a very familiar-looking object. Heart sinking, I slowly reach into the regulator and pull it out, my suspicions confirmed the moment the device hits the light.

Hidden amidst the broken glass, a twin to the one I found just days before, is a data chip.

Onboard the Personal Space Station *Solaria*
Home of the Chairman of the Celestial Expanse

THEY'D LINKED IN AS SOON as they'd gotten the word.

R&D had gone down.

Not the real Division 7, of course, but the "official" R&D. The real one was still safely buried away within its pastel mists under the unassuming title of "Military Support." Not that he was supposed to know its actual whereabouts, per se. No one besides the Doctor was. But he'd figured it out, as undoubtedly the Admiral also had. If there was one thing he'd learned as Chairman, it was that it was never a question of if someone knew a secret, but how many *knew.*

By tacit agreement, neither he nor the Admiral spoke, both looking to their colleague for the first words on the situation.

"Do we know how they did it?" the Doctor finally asked.

"We're still trying to determine that," the Admiral replied. "From what we've been able to gather, the ghouls somehow managed to breach the defense platforms without setting off the fences. Instead of spreading into the station, the newly created squatters recalibrated the shields, turned off the safety protocols, and sent a massive power overload through the shield network, in effect—"

Frying them with their own shields.

She waved a hand at the charred, electrified corpse on the screen in lieu of stating it, a rather uncharacteristic show of squeamishness for her. Or perhaps it wasn't squeamishness so much as an uncharacteristic deference toward their colleague.

The Doctor casually laced his hands behind his back, face composed, as though the destruction of his division's façade meant little, if anything at all. "It served its purpose," he finally said, voice empty of emotion. "It was meant to be a decoy if ever the enemy came looking, and because of their sacrifice, the real R&D is still alive and untouched."

He said it all quite matter-of-factly, but somehow the Chairman doubted the Doctor was as unfeeling as he seemed. If anything, the Doctor was the soft one of their little triad—always had been, with his talk of ethics and morals and lines that must not be crossed. Unlike the Admiral, who didn't seem to think lines existed at all.

The Admiral shook her head. "Between this and the latest casualty reports, I think it's time we revisited the possibility of enacting Protocol 325."

The Chairman arched an eyebrow. "Banning any and all interplanetary travel for the foreseeable future? That's a little extreme at this point, don't you think? We're supposed to be quarantining the squatters, not our own people."

"Protocol 325? Absolutely not," the Doctor immediately objected. "There are stations and colonies out there that depend on imports to survive—food, water, air. If we enact this protocol, we'd essentially be condemning them to death."

"Yes, we'd suffer casualties, but we'd stop the spread. Look at the numbers. Nine percent infected, up from four percent only a matter of months ago. From almost ten years to the projected annihilation of the human race, we've dropped to 7.3. A year from now, we could be kicking ourselves for not implementing it when we still had a chance."

"No, I disagree. While the numbers have spiked, we still have the situation under control. My division is working around the clock to find a solution. We just need a little more time. Besides, if the Infiltration Hypothesis is correct, it wouldn't make a difference anyway."

The Infiltration Hypothesis. A theory by an obscure scientist in the Lower Expanse positing that, unbeknownst to everyone, the Spectres had already infiltrated every single planet, colony, and station in the Expanse before the war even began.

A chilling theory, to say the least, but thankfully one for which they had yet to see actual evidence. Still, the scientist who had dared to voice the theory had been quietly disappeared, all trace of her theory carefully eliminated. No need to start a panic over nothing.

The Chairman sat back in his chair, a slight smile touching his lips as the argument continued before him. As usual, the Doctor and the Admiral were at loggerheads, and it was up to him to break the tie. Ironic, considering that at one point in time, shortly after the Admiral's abrupt ascent to power, he'd been convinced the two would join together to make an unstoppable team. Who wouldn't assume that, considering? However, the rumors of their falling out hadn't been mere rumor, but reality, and if anything they were more likely to work against each other than together, making him the perpetual tiebreaker.

Convenient.

A silent alarm vibrated through his chit. With a twist of his hand, he shut it off, absently stroking his injector as he considered the situation. While technically the decision was up to the Board of Directors, realistically the other Directors would follow his lead. That said, all of them had financial interests that would be rudely disrupted if they instituted the protocol, and the public outcry such a policy would engender would not be pretty. Widespread panic, rioting—he didn't even want to think about the potential consequences.

"We should wait," he finally said, breaking the argument with his powerful voice. "Continue monitoring the situation closely and reconsider if need be."

Predictably, the Doctor looked pleased and the Admiral stone-faced as usual, but both nodded. Later, after the Doctor had linked off and he was alone with the Admiral, the Chairman voiced the question that had been on his mind ever since hearing the news.

"Do you think they know? The Spectres, I mean. Do you think they know that the R&D they hit wasn't the real one?"

The Admiral folded her hands behind her back, not a trace of doubt in her voice as she spoke. "They know."

17

"DO YOU RECOGNIZE THIS?"

Asriel sets the small metal scrap on the desk before me with a soft *clink*. I raise my eyebrow in question, and at the DC's nod, pick up the piece and examine it. Approximately four centimeters by one, the paper-thin plate is so scorched that its golden color is almost completely obscured. I trace my thumb around the edges, sensing something familiar about the piece, though I can't put my finger on exactly what. After a moment's consideration, I shake my head.

"Look closer," Asriel advises.

Anxiety trickles through my gut at his stern voice. I flick my eyes between him and Archer, who stands just over his shoulder, but neither one's expression gives me a clue as to what's going on. Nothing that might tell me why I've been so summarily called into the DC's office, with neither warning nor explanation, the morning after our return from Nomia.

I do as Asriel bids, lifting the plate to my face and peering closer. Now I see what he means. Though charring covers most of the plate, I manage to make out four letters glinting through the black soot on the right side.

NSON

My hand involuntarily goes to the left side of my chest as I realize what it is. It's a nameplate from the breast of a uniform. Not just any uniform, but an R&D uniform. An R&D uniform for someone whose name ends with the exact same four letters as mine.

I gape at the little nameplate. "I don't understand. Where did this come from?"

"Our maintenance crew found this last night," Asriel says with a glance at Archer, "in the thruster core of the *SkyRunner*."

The *SkyRunner*! That's the shuttle we took to Nomia, the same one that almost grounded us in a city full of ghouls due to a thruster malfunction. A malfunction caused by an ignition regulator containing a data chip exactly like the one I found in the laser cutter.

My mouth flaps helplessly, my brain at a complete loss for words. When I'd found the chip in the ignition regulator, I'd almost had a heart attack. Especially after I'd uplinked with it to find, just like with the cutter, a single unidentified number.

19L-287098-B3948

Make, model, size—except for the number encoded inside, the two chips I'd found were exactly the same. Clearly the data chips were related, but as for the particulars—the *who*, *how*, and *why*—I hadn't a clue. My first instinct was to bring the chip directly to my CO . . . until I remembered how that worked out the first time. The laser cutter incident was downright humiliating, my outlandish story about saboteurs and setups not only making me look like a child with an overactive imagination, but casting me as the proverbial Boy Who Cried Wolf. And since the generator blade wasn't even sabotaged, I had no reason to think that the ignition regulator had been either. Asriel was probably right; the data chip was just a manufacturer tag of some sort. While the cutter and regulator came from different makers, both manufacturers were subsidiaries of TruCon, so it was certainly possible both companies followed the same equipment procedures. Still, there was something about that data chip that made me uneasy, and when I finally stowed the ignition regulator, the chip was safely tucked away in my pocket. Undecided on the right course of action, I finally decided to sleep on it, hoping everything would be clearer the next day.

Of course, that was before I knew I would get hauled into Asriel's office the next morning to find that my nameplate had somehow ended up in the thruster assembly.

"Well, Sorenson?" Asriel raises an expectant eyebrow, clearly waiting for me to speak. "Do you have any light to shed on this situation?"

It's on the tip of my tongue to tell him about the data chip I found. But if I do that, I realize with a sinking heart, it will look like I'm guilty of messing with the regulator, then trying to blame it on my imaginary saboteur. Besides, what do I actually have? A data chip with a single number whose meaning is unknown at best and nonexistent at worst? It's not proof of anything—not another person's guilt or even my innocence. Not to mention the fact that, technically speaking, I *stole* the chip out of a piece of classified R&D tech.

Yeah, if that doesn't convince them I'm guilty, I don't know what would.

Confused and torn about what to do, I finally go with the truth. At least, part of the truth. "I'm sorry, sir, but I have no idea how that nameplate got into the thruster assembly."

"Did you ever approach or touch the thruster assembly in the *SkyRunner*?"

"No, sir."

"Did you ever handle the ship's ignition regulator in any way?"

"Yes, sir. Just once. On the trip home, I helped RC secure it in the hold so it could be properly recycled upon our return."

The questions continue, all of which I answer truthfully, if not always completely. At last, Asriel asks to see my mission uniform from Nomia. I silently lead them down to my locker in the armory and show them my uniforms, each of which still has its nameplate neatly sewn onto the breast. Once again, I catch Archer and Asriel exchanging looks, though I have no more idea what they mean than I did their earlier one.

Back at Asriel's office, I wait in the anteroom while the DC and my TL confer quietly in the room beyond. My feet tap furiously in my boots, and I wish more than anything that I had gen-amped hearing so I might have some idea what they're saying. Guilt gnaws at me as I think about how I held back about the data chip. By admitting I stole the chip, I might very well end up on scut for the rest of my measly life, regardless of what they decide about the nameplate. Still, if there's any possibility the data chip could be significant, isn't it my duty to report it, whatever they may do to me?

By the time they call me back in, I've made up my mind to tell them about the strange chip I pulled out of the regulator. My mouth opens to speak, but Asriel beats me to the punch.

"I have just one more question for you, Tech Specialist Sorenson." Asriel pulls out a helmet and sets it on the desk before him. *My* helmet, I realize after a moment. "Why did you lie to your Team Leader while on an official mission?"

"Sir?" I ask, glancing back and forth between the two men with a confused frown. Asriel looks stern while Archer simply looks disappointed.

Asriel makes a few motions with his chit hand, and a holo feed springs up from my helmet to hover in the air before us. It's the feed from the Nomia mission, and standing smack dab in the middle of the holo is *Shar.*

———

"*Sorenson,*" Archer's voice emerges from the holo. "*Status report.*"

"*It was nothing. Just an animal like I thought.*"

Shock ripples through me from head to toe as I hear myself damned aloud by my own voice. I should have realized they would check my helmet feed from the mission to see if I'd gone anywhere near the ignition regulator. Lucky for me, I wasn't wearing my helmet at the time I helped RC stow the regulator and nabbed the data chip. Not the case for my meeting with Shar, though.

My cheeks flush as I remember our encounter, though it's not the physical altercation so much as the heated words we exchanged that makes me burn with humiliation. Figures! Separated by months of time and countless light-years, and still Shar manages to come back into my life and frag everything up all over again!

"I'm still waiting for an answer," Asriel says. "Why did you lie to your Team Leader during a mission?"

Because I didn't want to have to explain Shar to anyone.

I couldn't, because explaining Shar would mean explaining Lia, and I can't talk about Lia, not to anyone. Not to the Division Commander, not even to my Team Leader. Even now, with both of them staring expectantly at me, I can't seem to make myself speak. All I can do is stand here silently and watch as my career—my entire life— falls apart before my eyes. Strangely enough, it's Archer who comes to my rescue.

"It must have been quite a shock to be attacked by a PsyCorp Renegade on a routine pickup mission," he prompts, "especially considering that area of the city was supposed to be evacuated."

"Yes, I—" My brain stops as his words sink in. "Wait, a PsyCorp Renegade?"

Archer nods. "Yes. We matched the image from the feed with the PsyCorp database, and it turns out she's on the PsyCorp Watch List as a Class 5 Renegade. Although from the sound of your conversation, it appears you know her?"

"I encountered her once over a year ago," I admit, "but I didn't know she was a criminal or that I was supposed to detain her."

Asriel shrugs. "Technically, you weren't. A Class 5 designation is given to psychics who are considered too dangerous to be apprehended by regular military or law enforcement. That means anyone encountering her should inform PsyCorp of her whereabouts immediately but not attempt to capture or detain her in any way."

A PsyCorp Renegade. I frown, still trying to wrap my mind around that particular revelation. I hadn't known Shar well, but I'd certainly never suspected *that*. No wonder she ran out on us. We're just lucky she didn't put us all in psychic comas first. Although as I recall, Lia did mention something to me about a near-death experience with Shar. It never occurred to me she meant it literally.

"Why don't you tell us what happened, starting from the moment she attacked you," Archer suggests, his expression strangely encouraging. "When you told her to get out of your head and tried to counter her psionic attack with a physical one."

When I told her . . . ? I frown, unsure what he's talking about, when suddenly it hits me. They think it was *Shar* who attacked *me*! That I yelled at her to get out of my head because she was hurting me, and that my subsequent shoving her through a vending machine was merely self-defense against an attack I had no real defense for. A logical assumption, considering she's a dangerous PsyCorp criminal.

It all makes sense now. If they believed I'd actually assaulted a civilian, lying to my Team Leader would be the least of my worries right now. Instead, my only real crime seems to be that I lied to my TL and hid the fact that I was attacked. A much lesser crime, and one I might actually manage to scrape through with my skin intact, if I play my cards right.

"I—I've never felt anything like that before," I finally stammer, which is the absolute truth. I've been angry plenty of times, but the sheer rage I felt when meeting Shar was something else entirely.

I go through the rest of the incident as best I can, playing up my shock and confusion at encountering Shar and intimating that my subsequent lie was a result of my brain getting scrambled by her psychic wallop. Judging by their occasional nods, the story is pretty much what they expected. Though I phrase my responses in such a way as to avoid any actual lies, I feel terrible about the deception. I'm not a liar. But the truth would be the end of my career and, strange as it may seem, the more I think about the encounter, the more I have this nagging feeling that it wasn't my fault. As though I was somehow forced into the situation by powers beyond my control, though for what reason I can't even begin to guess.

My story apparently passes muster, because there's no talk of bringing me up on charges for assaulting a civilian. What's more, Asriel absolves me of any wrongdoing concerning the ignition regulator. While the plate did look suspicious, with only four letters it couldn't truly be connected to me, especially when my helmet feed and uniforms said otherwise. As for the lying, Asriel delegated my punishment to Archer, who assigned me a two-square of garbage detail in H9 along with a med session with one of the PsyCorp Specialists to ensure Shar caused no permanent damage.

I take the punishment gratefully, fully aware it could have been much, much worse. As Archer strides down the hall to his office, I can't help calling out.

"Team Leader!"

Archer stops, one eyebrow raised in question.

"I'm sorry, and . . . thanks."

He acknowledges my comment with a curt nod. "I won't lie, So-renson. I expected better from you."

I look down, heart sinking at his rebuke, though I know it's nothing I don't deserve.

"That said, you're a good soldier. You just made a mistake is all. Keep your nose clean from here on out, and you'll do fine."

With that piece of parting advice, he disappears into his office. As I stand in the empty corridor, still reeling from everything that happened, my mind goes back to the data chip, still secreted inside my jacket pocket despite my earlier resolve. With the revelations about Shar, I completely forgot about it. Not that I could have revealed it, not after they caught me in a bold-faced lie. With my credibility shot and my career on the line, they certainly wouldn't have believed me about the chip, even if I had told them. Not to mention that with the blade revealed to be nothing more than a defect, I have no real reason to believe the chip is related to the damage in the ignition regulator.

Pursing my lips, I cast my mind back over the strange events of the laser cutter and now the ignition regulator. Asriel's supposition about the cutter being a laundry mix-up or an accidental grab on my part made sense . . . all the way up until that nameplate showed up in the thruster assembly. Individually, the two instances could be construed as random happenstance, but together? This is no coincidence. Lack of evidence notwithstanding, someone *did* plant that cutter in my locker, I'm sure of it. As for the data chips—I don't know if they have any significance to this whole mess, but I do know one thing.

Someone in R&D tampered with that ignition regulator, and unless I miss my guess, they tried to set *me* up to take the fall.

18

"OVER HERE, TL! I'm open!"

Shouts ring out through the gym, players from both sides calling to their teammates as they vie for the scoring ball. In my spot by the doorway, I drop my recycler bag and lean forward, eyes intent on the game before me. So far Delta's up by eight points, but Gamma seems intent on coming up from behind. Songbird passes the s-ball to 'Vange, and he nails it for an easy floor basket.

Make that a seven-point lead.

I'm in the south training gym in H7, also known as the Testing Division's unofficial g-ball court. Regulation baskets bookend the enclosed space, a nod to the game's old Earth ancestor, while above the floor hang a variety of clear platforms ranging in elevation from two to twenty meters and held in place by their own anti-grav units. More baskets dot the upper and mid levels, and large grav pads are situated along the walls at strategic positions. Though I haven't played an official game since high school, my experienced eye still easily follows the play.

"Pass, Annah! Pass!"

"Watch out! The grav ball isn't in play yet!"

The impromptu game started up almost an hour ago, occasioned by the rare opportunity afforded by both Delta and Gamma Teams having the afternoon off. Ty, Archer, and RC are the grounders for our team, all pounding along the main floor after the scoring ball, while our flyers, Kagawa and Chen, perch on a couple of islands mid-level. Zephyr crouches just above the action on the lowest platform, g-ball in hand, scouting the play. Gamma Team's members are arrayed similarly, with three below and three up in varying positions.

My eyes flip to the action on the floor. Gamma Team's got the s-ball and is taking it down the court, but Delta is stuck to them like glue, looking for the steal. With RC practically on top of him, the Gamma shooter has no hope of making a shot. He fakes to the left, then pulls up to shoot a high pass over RC's right shoulder just as Zephyr wallops a grav pad with the g-ball.

A loud buzzer sounds as the gravity cuts in half. Instead of arcing neatly into 'Vange's hands, the ball sails over him, its trajectory skewed by the sudden change. Zephyr is already going for it, dropping from the platform just in time to intercept it. He runs two steps and leaps, using the lighter gravity to soar up into the air. He somersaults neatly onto one of the lower platforms, landing as lightly as a cat, before pushing off for the next platform. Now the game has taken to the heights, with Gamma's flyers in hot pursuit of Zephyr. All I—or anyone—can do is stare in awe as he flies from platform to platform, his lithe form flipping and soaring through the air with liquid ease. When he finally passes the ball off to Chen, it's clear he's only doing it to be a team player, and not because anyone has a prayer of catching him.

"Careful, Chen!" I call out as I catch sight of one of Gamma's flyers going for the other ball. "They've got the g-ball!"

A high-pitched alarm goes off as the flyer slams another grav pad. Chen passes off to Kagawa mid-leap before using the ten-second delay to land safely on the next platform. Standard gravity returns just as Kagawa slam-dunks the ball in a basket on one of the highest levels. I glance at the scoreboard just in time to see the fifty-three under Delta's side change to fifty-eight. I smirk as I eye Gamma's score. Forty-six. No surprise with a player like Zeph on our team.

As the players reset for the next point, I sidle up to the recycler nearby and pretend to be emptying it. Technically, I'm supposed to be in H9 on scut duty right now, but one of the maintenance crew sent me up to manually retrieve some garbage from a malfunctioning recycler unit. When I passed by the gym and saw the others playing, I couldn't resist stopping in to check out the game. As a result, I'm lurking here in the doorway like a null while everyone else plays and wishing like crazy I'd never gotten put on scut in the first place.

Back in the game, Gamma has the s-ball again and is taking it down the court. Annah passes to Songbird, who hands it off to 'Vange. He moves in toward the basket and goes up for the shot, only to be blocked by RC at the last second. The two smack into each other in mid-air, and both hit the floor.

"Hey, watch it, glitch!"

"Who are you calling a glitch? You're the one who fouled me!"

A pulse whistle blows, no doubt in response to 'Vange and RC. The two are off the floor and up in each other's faces now, loud voices and flagrant motions making it clear an out-and-out brawl isn't far off. Luckily, the two TLs are on the situation in a flash, pulling them apart and calling a general time-out so everyone can cool off before things get too heated. Everyone scatters, most going for the hygiene units while a few others go for water or just collapse on the court where they are for a brief rest.

Ty catches sight of me in the doorway and grins, dropping down onto a nearby bench with a towel around her neck and a water bottle in hand. "What's orbiting, Sorenson? Sick of garbage duty yet?"

"Wouldn't you be?"

"Hey, at least you don't have to put up with Tweedledumb and Tweedledumber over there," she says dryly with a nod to RC and 'Vange who, though separated, look like they're about to take another go at each other anyway.

I smirk at the imagery, and Ty adds, "Although to be fair, I can't really blame RC. His wife was Tellurian. She was on Earth when the news of the invasion hit and the borders closed. Never made it out. If I were RC, I'd want to take off 'Vange's block, too."

"RC has a Tellurian wife?" I murmur. "No wonder he vacced out during the Chairman's speech."

"You didn't know that?" Ty asks, surprised.

I shrug one shoulder, not wanting to admit that I didn't know because I'd never asked. I'd never asked who the raven-haired woman in the digitals in RC's locker were, the same way I'd never asked 'Vange if the rumors about him doing time in a labor camp are true or Archer to explain the meaning behind the prayer amulet he carries in his right vest pocket. Because by asking questions about their pasts, I would be inviting questions about mine, and those I couldn't bear to answer.

I cast my eyes over the court, scanning my fellow testers, and wonder what else I should know about them but don't. Is there a story behind 'Vange's hot temper or Zephyr's sarcasm? Is Songbird the Gamma TL's first name, last name, or simply a nickname? My gaze falls on Chen, who's doing a few stretches to keep warm during the break, and I remember my earlier observation about her and Ty during the Nomia mission.

Seeing a chance to rectify at least one information gap, I ask, "What's the deal with you and Chen?"

"What about me and Chen?"

"What do you have against her, anyway?"

Ty blinks, the question clearly taking her by surprise. "What makes you think I have something against Chen?"

Again I shrug, at a loss to explain the feeling I got on the *SkyRunner*, and finally settle for giving her a knowing look. It seems to work, for after a moment, she shrugs back.

"You got me, Sorenson. The truth is, I'm just really jealous of Chen's beauty. Even without ever wearing a smidge of makeup, she always looks better than me."

She laughs, and I give her a light shove, recognizing the sarcasm for what it is. "No, seriously. Why don't you like Chen?"

Ty gives me a sidelong look. "Let's just say we have . . . philosophical differences."

I raise an eyebrow. *Philosophical* differences? If that's not code for "man troubles," I don't know what is. I grin, amused by the idea of two such different women fighting over the same guy. Not that any guy wouldn't be seriously lucky to have either of them—Chen with her solemn beauty or Ty with her fun-loving humor.

Something lurches in my chest. *What am I thinking?* These women are my colleagues, my comrades-in-arms. Even if there weren't strict rules against fraternizing with other members of the Testing Division, I know better than to get involved with people who regularly put their lives in my hands and who regularly hold my life in theirs. Although if I'm honest with myself, it's not the idea that I could be interested in any of my teammates that bothers me, but the idea that I could be interested in anyone who's *not* Lia.

Her individuality, her élan; everything about her, from her spirit to her smile, was unlike anything I've ever known.

I shake my head. Lia was one of a kind. There is no replacing her.

The time-out ends, and everyone returns to the court to finish the game. As Ty huddles up with RC, Archer, and Chen to discuss some strategy, it suddenly occurs to me that I'm looking at the four other people who were with me on Nomia when the ignition regulator blew. Out of everyone on the teams, those four would have had the best opportunity to tamper with the regulator *and* slip in the nameplate that would set me up. It would have been easy, really, in the chaos of the loading.

My mind churns with unspoken suspicions, and I scowl, not liking the direction my thoughts are going. They're my teammates, and I trust them with my life. I have to, and yet I can't deny that something's going on, and right now they're the likeliest suspects. Or at least they would be, except for the fact that if their work had been successful, they would have been stuck too, grounded just as a shiver of ghouls was about to descend upon the city. So wouldn't that make them the least likely to have sabotaged the regulator? Besides, I get along well with all of them; I can't think of a single reason why any of them would want to set me up. Or perhaps it wasn't a matter of want so much as a matter of convenience?

I honestly don't know. Sometimes it seems like my thoughts are an ever-growing tangle of questions with no answers ever forthcoming.

A soft buzzing in my chit hand saves me from further deliberation. It's the maintenance head from H9 wondering why the hell it's taking me so long to collect one little bag of garbage. With a sigh, I link back a quick response and shoulder my bag once again. Three days down, eleven to go. One thing's for sure—it's going to be a long two-square.

———

The rest of the month passes with far less excitement. In between missions and training, every spare moment of my time is spent in H9 on garbage detail, during which time I get far more up close and personal with the workings of the main recycler than I hope to ever do again. Aside from the hard work and exhaustion, which aren't so bad, it's the sheer boredom that gets to me. With so much time to think, my thoughts often go to the one person responsible for putting me here: Shar.

Did she make it off Nomia in time? Or did she overestimate her own abilities and end up as ghoul bait like the rest of those poor unfortunates down there? There's no way for me to know, and yet something in my gut says she did manage to get away. If nothing else, Shar has proven herself to be fairly resourceful, able to get in and out of tight spots with ease. Why should Nomia be any different? All I hope is that wherever she ended up, fate has seen fit to dish up as big a pile of garbage for her as it has for me.

Meanwhile, a new influx of recruits for the Testing Division arrives on base. Replacements for all the testers lost on missions, though no one mentions Herrera or Zel. Kagawa chooses to stay on with Delta rather than transferring back to Beta where she originally started, and we receive one of the rookies as well: Raisman, a former Aquatic Forces commando from ocean-covered Kaloth. Her skin carries the telltale blue tinge brought on by certain underwater conditioning therapies which, coupled with her platinum hair and cerulean eyes, gives her a striking look. I'm curious what need we'd have of an underwater specialist, but Raisman turns out to be proficient on land as well as excellent in ZG. When asked why she joined R&D, she says, and I quote: "Because you don't get to blow up much stuff underwater."

Yeah, somehow I have a feeling she'll fit right in.

My two-square on scut finally ends, and I gratefully return to normal duty. Archer says little as he puts through the paperwork letting me off, except to warn me, "Step out of line even once, and I'll put you straight back on scut."

Fair enough.

After he finishes with the paperwork, we meet up with the rest of the team in one of the small training rooms in H7. It's Friday afternoon, which means one thing: new equipment. Replacement gear for items lost or damaged, drug refills, and whatever new technology the researchers have come up with for us to test over the coming week. Archer checks off items from the shipment manifest while his ATL hands them out.

"Let's see, new leg guards for RC," Ty says. "Wear them with pride. New helmet for Zephyr. Next time a squatter throws a large projectile at you, Zeph, try to block it with your face instead of your visor. We need to save money on equipment."

"Ha, ha," Zeph shoots back sarcastically, and everyone snickers.

She hands out a few more pieces, then moves on to the refill drugs. We each wear a pouch on our belts which contains an injector plus a dose each of Psi-Lac and Spectranol. The Spectranol is in case a teammate is infected. The medicine will prevent their squatter from breeding a ghoul while they're being transported to a squatter colony for permanent internment. The Psi-Lac is for ourselves. If you're newly infected or about to get infected, it will prevent the squatter from exerting its psionic influence over you for a short period of time. Just long enough to complete a last mission or neutralize yourself so you don't harm anyone else.

No one needs any refills today, but the powers that be surprise us with something entirely new: Spec 1280. Or as Ty calls it: The Spectre Detector. Simply put, it can allow a non-psychic to determine if someone is a squatter.

While a squatter is still basically incorporeal and can only be sensed psychically, its psionic bond causes small changes in the host's brain chemistry, which can be detected through a blood test. By mixing a bit of the suspect's blood with the drug in the vial and seeing what color it turns, one can determine if someone's a squatter. If it turns clear again, they're safe. Purple, you've got a squatter.

I turn the little vial over in my hands. The letters *TCP* are printed on the bottom in stylized script. The manufacturing company? I have no idea, only that all Spectre pharmaceuticals are produced somewhere else entirely and shipped in as needed. They're also in short supply, especially the Spec 1280, so we're only to use them if absolutely necessary.

I've just stowed the new vial in my belt pouch along with the others when a voice rings out over the habitat's com.

"Attention, all personnel. The light test will begin in T-minus five minutes. For safety purposes, we ask that you please don your protective eyewear at this time in preparation for the coming trial. Thank you."

A flurry of blinking greets the announcement as everyone activates the maximum sunshield level on their combat lenses. The researchers took the light technology used in our launcher sights and grenades and have created a network of lights throughout R&D, similar to the network of lights in the WMGD testing areas on Prism. Since the lights require tremendous amounts of energy and are too hard on the human eye and brain to use regularly, they'll be programmed to activate only if a force fence trips. Assuming the system works, anyway. Today is the first ever test run.

Archer and Ty check off a few more items on the list while we wait, until finally the station com activates once again.

"Attention, all personnel. The light test is now commencing. Please don your protective eyewear and prepare for the trial."

The announcement has barely finished before the test begins, light flaring from the ceiling to illuminate the room in a frenzy of white. The crystalline walls glow brighter than I've ever seen as they refract the light back at us in a brilliant torrent. Even with my darkened lenses, I have to squint against the brightness. I can't help thinking someone must have seriously missed on the power level—what's the point of ghoul lights if you can't keep your eyes open long enough to see them?—when something overhead bursts in a shower of sparks. Every light in the room, ghoul or otherwise, flickers like hell.

Then they all go out.

19 DARKNESS DROPS OVER US like a shroud. My lenses compensate almost immediately, the armory coming back into view as my night vision activates, but still my muscles tense, ready for action. Around me, the others are doing the same, bodies moving into attack postures and hands reaching for nonexistent weapons. Several people start talking at once, their voices the expected mix of confusion and concern.

"What the . . . ?"

"Hey! Where'd the lights g—"

"Shh! Listen!"

Everyone falls silent at Kagawa's terse command. I strain my ears in the darkness, listening for whatever the former Beta specialist thinks she heard. A rustle of fabric, the shifting of a boot. The heavy breathing of eight people suddenly plunged into darkness for unknown reasons. All the sorts of noises I would expect to hear.

"What is it? I don't hear anything," Zephyr finally admits, voice hushed.

"Not the foreground, but the background," Kagawa whispers, and that's when I realize what she's getting at.

Something in the ambient noise is off. The steady hum of heat and ventilation and anti-grav engines, the unassuming sounds of life, are faltering. Stuttering in breathy little fits and starts—*ptu-tu-tu-tu-tu*—until they disappear altogether, the noises of life gone and in their place an eerie quiet, the sort of silence that within a contained habitat speaks of only one thing: Death.

Life support has gone off.

Nearby gasps tell me I'm not the only one who's noticed, but before anyone can speak, the hum returns. Lights come back seconds later—not the detection lights, but normal illumination. My night visions kicks off, the armory coming back into normal view, and then everything is just as it was before. I can almost feel the collective sigh breathing through the group.

After a quick chat via his chit, Archer has an update. "All right team, I just checked with the DC, and it looks like it was merely a minor equipment failure. A power relay blew in H3 and knocked out an entire power grid. Backup systems are on, and the issue is being fixed as we speak. So forget any illusions you nulls might have had about getting out of training for the rest of the day," he adds in an attempt at levity.

After a few forced chuckles, we return to our equipment allotment and training continues as usual. I try to keep my mind on the business at hand, but something about the whole situation gnaws at me, like a worm chewing through an apple one bite at a time.

I ask RC about it a few hours later while we're running fitness drills. He gives me a sharp look, eyes flashing with an expression I can't quite comprehend, and answers, "Power relays burn out and get replaced a lot more often than you'd think. We just don't usually notice it because a single burnout doesn't generally cause such a large disruption in the grid. My guess is that they way overestimated the power level needed for the lights and blew out several relays at once. Embarrassing as hell for the person who screwed up, but nothing to worry about."

Maybe. Or maybe someone *wanted* it to burn out.

I mentally shake my head. It was just an equipment failure; it's none of my concern. Of course, the shield generator was *just* an equipment failure. The ignition regulator was *just* another one. Is there a power relay sitting around somewhere containing a plate with my name on it? I think about those ten cold, hard seconds when life support went down and no one knew when—or even *if*—it would come back on. An awful thought occurs to me.

What if it hadn't been the lights—and the life support—that went off, but the propulsion units that hold the station up?

A vision of all those ghouls down there, ghosting across Prism just waiting for hosts, flickers through my head, and I can't help shuddering at the thought.

My fists clench at the image. If there really is a saboteur on board, they're not just messing with the equipment; they're putting the life of every single person on this station at risk, including mine. And if they set me up to take the fall for one crime, there's no reason to think they won't do it again. For everyone's sake, especially my own, I have to find that burned-out relay. I have to know if there's a nameplate with my name on it lurking somewhere within. Or, vacuum forbid, another one of those strange data chips.

Tamping down my anger, I keep my voice level as I casually ask, "So, what happens to the burned relay?"

RC shrugs. "All equipment refuse eventually ends up in the main recycler in H9, where they salvage what materials they can and dump the rest."

Habitat 9. Damn! I only have access to 5 and 7. There's no way I'd even be able to get to the recycler, let alone find and examine the damaged relay. My mouth twists in a wry smile. If only I were still on garbage detail.

Step out of line even once, and I'll put you straight back on scut.

Then again, maybe it's as simple as breaking a few rules . . .

———

I stand in a pile of junk up to my knees, hands covered in grease as I sift through the garbage once more. Mounds of equipment litter the floor in a kaleidoscope of shattered crystal, twisted metal, and burned plastic—the remnants of old tech that couldn't be saved and only have the gaping jaws of the recycler yet to brave.

From the northeast corner of the room, I look out over the sea of refuse. It stretches for meters across the compactor floor in a stagger-

ing display of useless prototypes and old parts, a hymn to failed genius and sheer, dogged persistence. Though whether it's persistence
on the scientists' part or persistence on mine, I'm not quite sure. Between the time I've clocked before, during, and after my scut duties,
I've been in here for hours, searching for the power relay. Not the
easiest task when there are about a zillion old relays hidden in the
trash and no concrete way to identify the one I'm looking for. I've
already checked half a dozen of the power rods, but whether the relay
I'm looking for simply doesn't have anything to find or I haven't
found the right one yet, I have no idea. On the upside, I have learned
one useful thing: not a single power relay I've searched contains a
data chip. In other words, the chips are *not* an integral part of the
equipment, at least, not the power relays.

Tossing down a coil of old cable, I move on to the next pile and
start methodically sorting through the slag. After three days of alternating between scut duties and my own harebrained quest, it's hard
to remember why I ever thought this was a good idea. A two-square
of scut is not my idea of fun, and for all I know, I already found the
relay in question and didn't realize it. But even though I know I
should give up this fool's errand, something in my gut tells me I'm on
the right track.

A familiar nodule pokes out from the very bottom of the heap,
and I give it a hard tug. Junk crashes down in every direction as the
rod pulls free. I awkwardly heft it to a free spot on the floor. Over a
meter long, and half that in diameter, the relay's a pain in the ass to
lug around, but I eventually get it there. Pulling out my multi-tool, I
carefully open up the blackened cylinder and start picking through
its innards, pulling aside wires and other crap as I search for anything
suspicious. After ten minutes of searching, I'm about to give up and
toss it aside when a glint from under the lip at one end catches my
eye. Prying back a blackened metal spring, I reach in and pull out a
data chip.

My heart sinks even as my gut clenches in triumph. Despite a bit of
charring on one side, it's the exact same type as the two I found before.
What's more, when I link to the chip, it reveals a single number.

89R-786524-P103

Another chip, another number. Clearly the three chips *do* mean something, though I don't yet know what. Part of me is smug at being right; the other part is scared. Because the more evidence I find, the harder it is to deny that something is going on. Someone is tampering with key equipment at R&D, wiring it to either blow or fail, and leaving these strange chips behind, and somehow I've gotten caught up in the middle of it. Now I just have to figure out what I'm going to do about it.

Stowing the chip in my pocket, I snap several digitals of the power relay from multiple angles, making sure to get images from end to end. This relay will be crushed to bits within a couple of days, and I want evidence of the damage in case I need it for later.

Evidence? I snort, dropping my hand as my good sense finally catches up to my actions. Evidence of *what*? That I'm sneaking into places I'm not supposed to be, going through classified R&D tech, stealing pieces out of the equipment? Even if I did turn this chip in, along with the one from the ignition regulator, the only criminal it would convict is *me*. Forget scut duty—what I've done would probably earn me a court-martial and jail time!

I try to imagine what Asriel would say if I came to him with yet another wild story about saboteurs and data chips. He would think I was completely unstable, some paranoid space case full of conspiracy theories—an idea only supported by the fact that I'm an established liar who was caught fibbing to my TL. Even supposing he believed me long enough to have the engineers check out my story, what if they simply declared the power relay another factory defect, like the generator blade? One crazy story Asriel could probably shrug off as that of an overeager rookie with an active imagination, but two? It would be a death knell for my career, here or anywhere.

Not for the first time, I cast my mind over the members of R&D, wondering who could possibly be behind all this. I think of RC's tech expertise and Chen's enigmatic air. Archer's cold voice, as cold as the vacuum itself, when he told RC to take a walk. Even Asriel comes to mind. Supposedly he checked my locker from head to toe and couldn't find a single sign of tampering. Were there really no signs of the person who planted the laser cutter, or was he hiding those signs from me for some reason? The fact of the matter is that until I know who the saboteur is, there's no telling who I can trust. Someone has targeted me on two separate occasions. If I were to accidentally tip my hand to the wrong person, who knows what might happen? No, my only solution is to investigate this myself. The minute I find concrete evidence of something, I'll turn it in.

Satisfied with this compromise, I pack up and get out of the recycler ASAP. No need to stick around any longer than I have to now that I've found what I was looking for. Besides, I have a job to do.

I have to track down a saboteur.

My investigation begins the same night. While everyone else sleeps, I sit up in the hygiene units, making a list. Since the chips don't tell me who the saboteur is, it's up to me to determine who the saboteur *isn't*. Simply put, I'll use the process of elimination to narrow down the suspects until I'm left with only one. The common denominator, the person who had access to every piece of sabotaged equipment. Then all I'll have to do is find hard evidence of their guilt, turn it in—with*out* incriminating myself—and I'm home free.

Yeah. That's all.

I almost give up right this moment. The task seems monumentally impossible. Then I think of the way we were almost grounded on Nomia, the lights going out in R&D, and I know I can't give up so easily.

Turning back to my tip-pad, I get to work. Three thousand people in R&D seems like an impossible number until I remember the laser cutter. The cutter was planted in my personal locker; that means the saboteur has to be someone with access to H5. Since all of the cleaning and maintenance is done by 'bots, it has to be someone from the Testing Division. Except for Angelou, I don't think anyone else has access to the barracks habitats except the residents themselves. With that in mind, I pull up the division roster and carefully list the names of each and every member.

Forty-five names. Now let's see if I can narrow it down any further.

The first act of sabotage happened within a week after my arrival, which means that anyone recruited since couldn't possibly be guilty. I go through the list and cross off twelve names. That leaves me with thirty-three.

I go through the list again, this time stopping on two specialists from Alpha. Garvey was shot and killed by a squatter a week ago, so I no longer have to worry about him. Nori was infected on the same run and has since been sent to a penal colony. Deciding to work on the assumption that the saboteur is still alive and present, I cross both names off the list. Scanning through the names again, I stop as my eyes light on the top four members of Delta Team.

Ty. RC. Archer. Chen.

All the people who were on the Nomia mission with me when the ignition regulator blew. My stylus hovers over their names uncertainly. Should I cross them off? Or should I be crossing off all names *but* theirs? After a long minute of deliberation, I finally settle for starring them and leave it at that.

I take another couple of passes through the list, but no one else's name jumps out at me. So now I'm down to thirty-one. Still a lot of names, but better than forty-five, and certainly better than the three thousand names that comprise R&D. Now I just have to keep finding ways to narrow down the list until I find my culprit.

Before it's too late.

————

The next day I stop by the lost and found on my way back from breakfast. When I leave, the laser cutter is once again in my possession, tucked safely away in the inner pocket of my jacket. As I stride through the halls, I can't help feeling like all eyes are on me, as though the people around me *know* what I carry in my pocket and just what it means. A deficient idea, but one I can't seem to shake. How is it that someone else is perpetrating crimes against R&D, and yet *I'm* the one feeling guilty?

At my first available opportunity, I examine the three data chips together. Do they denote a person, a place, a point in time? Something else altogether? The possibilities are too widespread for me to make an educated guess. I try researching both the chips and the numbers on the net, but I come up with nothing. Struck with a sudden bit of inspiration, I try following that up with a link to the manufacturers of the equipment. Unfortunately, their customer service personnel are even more clueless than I am. As a final resort, I try searching the numbers in several databases on R&D, all the ones I can think of and have access to anyway, but even after twenty minutes of searching, I turn up nothing. If the numbers correspond to anything on R&D—a weapons test, a location on base, a ship or shuttle—I can't find it.

Discouraged by my lack of leads, I finally de-ac my tip-pad. Though I didn't expect this to be easy, I didn't exactly expect it to be so hard, either.

With a sigh, I lean my forehead against the wall and wonder if I'm doing the right thing or if I'm already halfway down the road to hell without even knowing it.

20

MY SKIN CRACKLES as the last of the energy discharge falls away around us, dropping through the city below in brilliant silver rays before dissipating into the bright afternoon light. Per instructions, I tip my nose to the wind, flaring my nostrils as I try to determine if anything's changed in that distant sour-and-sweet odor. Nothing, as far as I can tell. I take another thirty seconds, then link my answer—*No change*—back to the station above.

From my helmet com, 'Vange's voice crackles out over the group channel. *"What exactly is the point of this again?"*

"We're searching for indications that the WMGD energy has harmed the ghouls in some way." RC's tone is like that of a teacher instructing a slow child. *"Just as an animal will give off distinct pheromones if wounded or cornered, the researchers on base believe the ghouls may behave in a similar fashion when exposed to the correct stimulus. If we can scent the changes given off after various tests, the scientists may be able to narrow down which types of energy are more effective and concentrate their focus there."*

"This is completely deficient—"

"You're completely defi—"

"The point is that the scientists on base told us to do it, so we do

it, Specialists," comes Songbird's no-nonsense response. *"Does any-one have a problem with that?"*

Silence, followed quickly by a chorus of, *"No, Team Leader!"*

"Good. Then open your noses and seal your mouths."

With a rueful shake of my head, I settle back against the base of the spire to wait for the next test. We've been on a joint op with Gamma Team, spread out over the high reaches of the city on sky-scrapers and transmission towers, for over four hours while the scientists on base test out one WMGD setting after another. Despite the fact that we have eight two-person teams scattered around the city, we have yet to be bothered by Specs. The ghouls don't seem to be able to sense anything up past four hundred meters, so as long as we stay up high, we remain unmolested. Which makes for a safe mission, but also a boring one. With nothing much to do during tests and even less between them, everyone's more than a little antsy, and downright testy in some cases. Nor does it help that RC and 'Vange can't stand each other. The two are polar opposites, RC educated and thoughtful while 'Vange is graceless and tough.

I drum my fingers impatiently on the roof, catch myself, and settle for pulling on the neck of my new suit for the millionth time instead. Not that it feels uncomfortable, exactly. Just odd.

They handed them out a week ago, these supposedly "ghoul-proof" suits. The one-piece hooded outfit is almost exactly like a standard pressure suit—albeit the sleekest, most expensive pressure suit I've ever seen—with one key difference: a two-centimeter core of air pumped through the outer skin of the suit. The air is a mixture of gases repellant to ghouls, not much different from the air found in our launcher cartridges. Theoretically, any ghoul aiming for us will sense the gases and automatically turn away. Realistically, the suits are awkward, strange, and never actually work. As Ty explained to me, the good researchers of Habitat 2 have been trotting out some version or other of this suit for eleven months now. Everyone is forced to wear them on missions until someone inevitably gets infected, at which point we go back to our old uniforms and wait for the designers' next batch.

Yeah. It's a hell of a cycle.

Checking my timekeeper, I inwardly groan as I see that only ten minutes have passed since the last test. Already my feet are getting antsy and my hands are back to drumming on the roof. I glance over at my partner, Tech Specialist Annah, a former Ground Forces commando from Gamma Team. From her compact form to her close-cropped hair and narrow features, everything about her suggests economy, efficiency. Right now, she has her blond head back against the spire, hazel eyes closed, looking for all intents and purposes like she's sleeping, though she rouses promptly and reports in with every test. Is she merely resting her eyelids or does she have some sort of internal alarm clock capable of waking her on command? I have no idea. Talkative she is not. In this entire mission, we've exchanged maybe a dozen words. About the only thing I know about her is that she got engaged a few weeks ago. Which is fine by me. The less you know someone, the less it bothers you when they inevitably die.

Her earnestness, her eyes; those last few hours we spent together, believing we had all the time in the world when really we had none.

It always comes down to time, doesn't it, standing still when all we want is for it to move on, and flying away the instant we beg it to stay.

The ad hoc philosophy not exactly helping, I decide to check my hmail for the millionth time, eyes lighting up when I see I've got a new message. I key it up with a flick of my hand, smiling slightly when I see it's from Gran. For all that we don't always see eye-to-eye on certain things, I still miss her. While my parents have been off to war for so long I've become accustomed to their absence, Gran still comes to mind in those small moments when I find myself longing for home.

I send the hmail wirelessly to my helmet with a few quick hand motions, and soon her face is smiling across my visor and her voice is speaking in my ear. As she patters on about her new apartment and her job and every little thing on New Sol that's changed, I can't help wishing I had her resilience. Her ability to put the past behind her, or at least hide it away from constant view, and focus on the future.

At the end of her message, she included several short holoclips of the new hub at New Sol Space Station: the shopping area on Level Five, the cafeteria on Nine, several views from the lift station as she rode up and down, including glimpses of the PsyCorp offices and the two main docking levels. I'm amazed by how similar the hub looks to the old one, as though they simply followed the old blueprints down to the last lift step and concourse light.

The last holoclip is titled *Turquoise Flower in Bloom*. I frown at the label, uncertain what that could be referring to. Maybe Gran got a new window box for her apartment? I click open the image.

It's Teal.

I suck in a rapid breath as my little sister's face beams at me from my visor. It's clearly a school holo, a list of her academic achievements marching along the bottom of the clip—all top honors, *of course*—while above she smiles and waves from a beautiful, vine-encrusted, wrought-iron bench set in front of an elegant stone building. Bright greenery twines around the brick in a profusion of life, its curling leaves decked out with colorful blossoms as large as my hand, while exotic birds sing in the background.

My lip curls as I take in the clip. *Perfect*. All this time I've been wishing my sister to hell, and here she is in fraggin' paradise!

The short clip ends, then automatically restarts, my sister set to perpetually wave and smile at me through eternity. Now that the initial brilliance of the setting is starting to wear off, my eyes focus on Teal herself. Only fifteen, but already she looks as grown up as any of the women on Delta. Not to mention tall, like Mom, with that same long-legged slenderness and swanlike neck. She must've had a hell of a growth spurt since I left. But despite the bodily changes, it seems to me it's her face that's changed the most. Her cheekbones look just a bit higher, her cheeks slightly narrower, like she's dropped any last vestige of childhood and finally grown into the full beauty of her face.

I glance at the date in the bottom right corner, and my stomach lurches as I see it was taken only a week ago. My sister is part of a past I've spent months trying to leave behind; to have her pulled suddenly, violently into the present, placed in a time not so distant from my own, creates a sort of paradox in my mind, a disturbance in the space-time continuum I can't seem to compute.

I shut down the holo and yank off my helmet. Damn Gran for sending this! She might as well have punched me in the gut; it certainly would have been more merciful. I glance at the holo label again. *Tur-*

quoise Flower in Bloom. Turquoise = Teal? Yeah, I should've seen that one coming a klick away. Gran's cunning is only outmatched by her sense of humor. And to think people think she's *sweet.*

I rub my eyes, as though I can somehow blot out the image, but it's already too late. Memories from the past come flooding in, and I'm helpless to stop them. Scenes from our childhood on Aurora, moments from those years base-hopping with our parents, our short time on New Sol together, and of course, The Argument. That final bitter argument we had the night before I left, enlisted and shipped out for parts unknown, never to speak again.

"For God's sake, Michael! Haven't you punished me enough? When are you finally going to let this ridiculous grudge against me go?"

"Never! I'll never let it go. You can make excuses until the universe ends, but the fact is, you betrayed *me."*

"I betrayed y—"

"You knew she was going to get off that train; you knew *what she was going to do! How could you've ever let her go?"*

"I let her go because I knew *what she was going to do."*

My chest tightens, and of its own accord, my head shakes in furious denial. Even now, the explanation makes no more sense than it did to me then, the statement nothing more than some ridiculous line to excuse something that can never be excused. I try to shut down the memory, unable to hear any more, but it continues to play on in my mind anyway.

"Bullslag! You could have stopped her, but you didn't. *Instead you hugged her goodbye and then sent her off to die."*

"It wasn't like that. It was Lia *who made the final choice, Lia who chose to go N—"*

"Don't! Don't you dare try to blame this on Lia!"

"Why not? It's true! Admit it, Michael! It's not me you're really mad at, it's her!"

"You're completely lunar! Why would I possibly be mad at Lia?"

"Because she chose everyone else *in the universe over you!"*

Yes, she chose everyone else in the universe over me; only Teal would be cruel enough to point that out. But then, it was all so easy for her, wasn't it? Easy to condemn Lia, easy to let her go. Easy to let her die.

"You think it was easy? You think it was easy to let her get off? Because it wasn't! It's the hardest thing I've ever had to do in my life! But I did it, and it was only because of me that you didn't have to!"

"Oh, is that how it was? You had to let her get off, you had to let her die? Well, guess what? I wouldn't have let her get off, and that's why I'll never let it go—because it's your fault. It's your fault Lia's dead, and I can't ever forgive you for that."

Even now, months past their speech, those words still have the power to hurt. I close my eyes, wanting them to stop, but I'm not to be spared Teal's final words, the last words she ever spoke to me, moments before she walked out the door.

"You know, you're not the only one who cared about Lia."

The words run through my head again, quiet and defeated, and my chest clenches up in spite of myself. In all the words and all the arguments and all the explanations, yelled and linked and thrown at me over the course of all those months, somehow this was the most damning of all.

You know, you're not the only one who cared about Lia.

Because despite everything, I know it's true. It's truer than anything she's ever said to me in my entire life.

It's true . . . but it's not enough.

Because in the end, no amount of affection or regret, of explanations or apologies, of stony silences that echo on across the light-years, can ever bring Lia back. And without her, nothing else will ever be enough.

———

We've been up on the skyscrapers six hours going on seven when Songbird's voice suddenly emerges from my com. *"Heads up, team. The next WMGD test is gearing up as I speak. Be prepared for the next test to go live in ten. Songbird out."*

I link my affirmative, grateful for the diversion. Teal's face still lingers in my mind, an anathema I can't banish no matter how much I pace this godforsaken roof, and I was starting to think even a ghoul attack would be preferable to this misery.

Snapping on my helmet, I point my face to the sky, blinking my eyes quickly to magnify the view in my combat lenses. It's an abnormally clear day for Prism. High winds are dissipating the mists as quickly as they form, providing a clear view of the planetary net shimmering like a blue-tinged bubble overhead. Without the heavy mists, the net is surprisingly transparent, more so than I originally realized. While I can't see R&D, which is protected by its own shield, I can see the two closest OPs hanging overhead in orbit like two giant moons. They're part of a planetary network of sixteen platforms—the standard number for most planetary OP networks—which was originally created to service Prism's interstellar travel and communication needs. Until the war came, and they became a way station to filter out any potential ghouls and squatters. Not that it was ultimately successful.

I squint my eyes, looking for a telltale shimmer of silver. When my lenses are on their highest magnification, I can actually see the platform glowing with gathering energy. It's a beautiful sight, for all that it was created to be a deadly weapon meant to destroy our enemies.

There! I see it. Just a faint glimmer way up in the heavens. I watch as the energy gathers, the silvery light glowing brighter and brighter, a shining flame beaming in the gathering dusk. It spreads outward across the underside of the platform, held together by the combined power of nine shield generators working in perfect concert. I remember what it was like to be on the OP, to feel such awesome power coursing through the platform. The energy continues to build, its light blotting out the neighboring stars, it's so bright. I hold my breath, every muscle in my body tensed as I wait for the moment when the energy releases . . .

Then the entire OP goes up in a ball of fire.

Onboard the *CES Retribution*
Flagship of the First Admiral of the Celestial Fleet

"*. . . **THREE PLANETS**, one colony, and an entire chain of mining rigs. In this past month alone, the infection rate has trebled—*"

"*More than trebled,*" the Doctor interjected, scanning a batch of numbers on his tip-pad, "*if these stats are correct. We haven't seen an IR like this since the first six months of the war.*"

"*Exactly.*" The Admiral threw the Doctor's image from palm to wall with a flick of her fingers, simultaneously pulling up a new image over her hand. "*And I think I know why. Take a look at the enemy's latest target.*"

"*Lark's Calling Shipyard.*" The Doctor stared at the image in dismay. "*You think they're building an army.*"

"*It would fit the uptick in infection as well as the target. There's no point in creating an army if you can't transport it.*"

The Doctor shook his head, lips pursing in that way they did when he began to immerse himself deep into a new strategic puzzle. "*An army? It doesn't fit. The enemy has revealed themselves to be many things, but not outright violent. Not on the sort of scale you seem to be proposing.*"

The Admiral lifted a shoulder. "*Perhaps they don't intend to kill, but capture.*"

"*Round up hosts like cattle?*"

"Or maybe they aren't creating an army but a series of surgical strike teams, recruited for one specific large-scale offensive. We've certainly witnessed squatters making strategic strikes in the past."

The Doctor nodded slowly, turning his head to affix his steely gaze on hers. "Or maybe the uptick and shipyard are indicators of nothing except that the front line is fast losing its effectiveness."

The Admiral leveled a cold gaze on the Doctor, his air of condescension an all too familiar refrain. "Is that what you think?" she answered, an edge of acid creeping into her voice. "Rest assured that we on the front lines have been doing everything in our power to halt the spread of the invasion."

His eyes narrowed at that, and she knew he hadn't missed her subtle insinuation that while her people fought and died on the front lines every day, he was huddled away in his mists doing nothing. Ever so slightly, his jaw tensed, a herald to the disapproving thinning of his lips she knew too well. She waited for the inevitable retort, but at the last instant his eyes softened, the usual hardness seeping away to reveal something soft, almost kind even.

His lips quirked in the barest of movements. "I know."

She barely managed to hold back her surprise, torn between drinking in the near-approbation and rejecting it entirely. As if she needed his approval! Anger wound through her gut that he could still hold such power over her even after all these years, after everything that had happened.

"Of course you do," she replied, letting the carefully crafted sarcasm drip from her lips like honey. "After all, there's never been anything you don't know."

Instantly his gaze hardened, and any iota of tenderness, whether it was ever truly real or merely pretense, vanished in a heartbeat. "Do not think for a moment that—"

His words cut away as if severed, eyes widening as they shifted focus to look through her rather than at her. He slowly rose, gaze transfixed on some vision outside of the feed. Though his expression never changed, all the color drained from his face at once.

The Admiral frowned. "Doctor?"

"Forgive me," he said abruptly. A second later, his holo winked out.

After so long, she'd thought nothing he did could surprise her, and yet he'd managed it twice in a matter of minutes.

Forgive me.

She'd waited fifteen years to hear those words, and even though she knew he didn't mean them—not in that *way, but only in thoughtless apology for his sudden disconnection—hearing them still delivered a jolt she couldn't ignore. Her jaw clenched as she remembered their last confrontation, nearly fifteen years ago, when she'd taken the assignment he'd refused.*

"How could you have even considered agreeing to this madness? What's happening here is wrong! It violates every basic research ethic imaginable! How can you possibly justify being a party to this?"

Followed by her answer: "Don't you see what we're trying to accomplish here? You're a scientist! Even more than me, you should appreciate what we're trying to achieve, and if it requires some sacrifice, so be it. It's worth it."

He'd only shaken his head. "Some prices are never worth paying. I can only hope one day you see that."

Things had changed forever between them that day, all connection severed inasmuch as realistically possible, and from then on he'd been simply the Doctor and she the Admiral. He'd left the service, moving to the private sector, while she'd remained, waiting for her chance to move up. Who would have guessed that fate would eventually force them face to face again, not once, but time after time?

At least they had the buffer of a holoscreen between them, if nothing else. Thank God for small mercies.

The Admiral leaned back in her chair and regarded the empty wall panel before her. His abrupt departure—as well as his hasty words—had been uncharacteristic, to say the least. She wondered what could have possibly occasioned such behavior. Nothing good, certainly, but he would handle it, whatever it was. He always did.

Still, a frisson of anxiety trickled down her spine, and despite her confidence she continued to wait, all day, for a return call that never came.

21

SOBS SHUDDER THROUGH the Atrium in a quiet whisper, shrouding the habitat in a web of sorrow from corner to corner. Numb with shock, I sit with the rest of my team in one of the mess areas, looking out over a sea of frightened faces. Research, Testing, Admin, Support—in the wake of tragedy, all have come, gravitating to this common place in search of answers. In search of the explanation that will somehow, impossibly, render the deaths of twenty-six researchers, two PsyCorp agents, and seven military officers okay. It's a search I know all too well. A vain search, but one that must be undertaken anyway, no matter how hopeless the cause.

No matter how hopeless the survivor.

Her gravity, her grace; with the weight of the world resting on her shoulders, she never bowed.

I briefly close my eyes, the grief in this room so palpable it's hard to keep my own ever-present sorrow at bay. Though most of us on the teams didn't actually know any of the people on the OP that blew, it's clear many of the people in this room did. Shoulders shake, and heads are in hands; gazes stare around, vacant and scared. Waiting for someone to take care of them, for someone to tell them what to do. When direction finally comes, speaking out from on high like

God himself, the whole world stops, heads raised and ears cocked to listen.

"As you all know, a terrible accident occurred during one of our weapons tests earlier today, which ultimately resulted in the deaths of thirty-five people on this base. Some were military, some were civilian, some were PsyCorp, but all of them were here for the same reason. They were brilliant at what they did, yes, but all were here because they wanted to make a difference. They wanted to fight. They wanted to help us win this war, and though some of them didn't see themselves as such, they were all soldiers fighting the most important war of our lives. They may be gone in body, but they remain with us in spirit and ideal. For their wills shall be echoed in the hearts of those here, and their ideas will continue to shine out upon us like the stars in the night sky."

I rest my chin on my hands, strangely moved by the unexpected poetry in Angelou's words. Mysterious, demanding, cold, untouchable. There are so many ways I would've described the Director of R&D if asked, and poetic wasn't one of them. Yet as I sit here, his words whispering in my ears and his thoughts echoing in my heart, I find myself thinking that beneath his cagey exterior and frost-ridden eyes, he loves R&D and everyone in it more than all the universe.

I replay Angelou's speech in my mind. *As you all know, a terrible accident occurred during one of our weapons tests earlier today.*

An *accident*, he said. Or was it? If I were to search that field of debris up in orbit down to its last twisted piece, would I find a data chip in its wake? Part of me needs to know, while the other part is terrified to ask. For if there *is* a data chip bearing a single number floating amidst the remnants of OP NE-2, every single one of those thirty-five deaths is on my head.

The thought makes me go cold inside. To think that I might have prevented this terribleness somehow, if only I'd been smarter, savvier, able to put the pieces together in a way that's eluded me all this time. Guilt worms its way into my gut, a miserable, unfamiliar feeling I don't quite know what to do with. For so long, *I've* been the wronged party. The one who was betrayed, lied to and left behind by the people I cared about most. To be the one on the other side of that line is a new sensation, one I'm not sure I want to experience in any shape or form.

"Does anyone know when the memorial service will be?" RC asks in a quiet voice.

A murmur of "no"s and scattered headshakes answer his question. The silence broken, the specialists begin speaking in low voices, their faces a mixture of confusion and sorrow. Mostly Gammas and Deltas, though I see some Betas and Alphas a little farther off. As I watch them talk amongst themselves, a sudden thought hits me from out of the black.

One of them may be the person who blew up OP NE-2.

My eyes harden, gaze sharpening as I study each one in turn. Nearest me stand Ty, RC, and Zephyr, discussing the situation in worried voices. RC's shoulders are hunched and Ty has her arms crossed over her chest, and everyone's face is a textbook study in pained denial. Past them are Archer and Songbird, their heads bent together in probable conversation, though with their backs to me, I can't tell for sure. Over to my left, 'Vange paces and Kagawa fidgets, her hands constantly clasping and unclasping as she shifts her weight from one foot to the other. Chen stands off by herself, posture ramrod straight and face a perfectly poised mask, though her eyes stare somewhere far away. Annah is slumped over a table. Asleep, I assume, until I see her shoulders heave and realize she's crying.

I turn away, both surprised and discomfited by this outward show of grief, especially coming from such a stoic and stalwart specialist. My eyes land on an assortment of Alphas, Betas, and Gammas sitting or milling around, but their actions tell me no more than those of anyone else I observed. If the saboteur is indeed here, they're hiding their guilt well enough.

Archer turns back to the group, chit still glowing, and I realize he must have been linking someone.

"What's happening?" RC asks.

"Do they know any details about the accident?" I add, eyes intent as I watch Archer for any sign of a reaction.

Archer only shakes his head. "They're still looking into it."

"So what do we do now?" Ty asks, the uncertainty in her voice mirrored in everyone else's eyes.

"What do you think we do?" a hard voice interjects. "Mistakes happen and people die, but the war doesn't stop just so we can blow our noses and wipe our eyes."

All eyes flick to Chen, shock registering on more than one face at the harsh words coming from the usually soft-spoken pilot. There's an unfamiliar sharpness to her demeanor that I've never seen before, an edge of steel I'm not quite sure what to make of.

"She's right," Archer says at last. "We do what we always do. Train, test, fight. Do everything we can to win this war."

It's the only thing we can do, and yet standing in the crowded cafeteria with the grief of this small nation rising up in waves around us, the answer feels completely inadequate. As though continuing to fight could in any way stem the tide of despair echoing around us.

From the other side of the table, 'Vange abruptly stops, pacing coming to a halt as his jaw sets. I tense, uncertain whether the volatile specialist is going to have another outburst or simply storm out this time. To my surprise, he does neither. Instead, he walks over to a sobbing engineer in a silver coat at a nearby table, reaches into his vest, and pulls out . . . a handkerchief?

Everyone silently watches as he shakes open the cloth, places it in her hands, and presses an encouraging hand on her shoulder. He moves on to an elderly man in blue at the drink dispensers next. The biologist is trying to fill a cup with tea, but his hands are shaking so badly that the liquid keeps sloshing over the sides and burning his fingers. 'Vange takes the wet cup away, fills a new one, and escorts the man back to his table. He's across the aisle a heartbeat later, wrapping his uniform jacket around the trembling shoulders of a laundry tech who can't seem to stop shaking.

Unsure what to make of this very un-'Vange-like display, we continue to watch his efforts in silence until finally his TL snaps, "Tech Specialist Evangeline, over here now!" When he complies, Songbird asks, "What are you doing, Specialist?"

"They're our scientists, right?" 'Vange says gruffly, an unexpected hesitancy tingeing his usually brash demeanor. "Isn't it our job to protect them in whatever way we can?"

My eyebrows lift at the unexpected insight, especially coming from someone like 'Vange, but it's the gentle ownership in that phrase—*our scientists*—that really gives me pause. As though our job, to protect them from the rigors of the outside world by taking them on ourselves, somehow grants us a greater responsibility for them than I ever imagined.

"This is deficient," murmurs someone on Beta Team. "It's not like they care when any of us bite the vacuum."

She turns on her heel and walks out, half a dozen specialists following with murmurs of "She's right," and "Forget this!" Not that I blame them. We put our lives on the line, if not every day then most days, in order to protect the very people in this room, and when we die, they don't even know we're gone. It's only today that I finally understand: They put theirs on the line, too. Maybe not in the same way, but Angelou's right. They're soldiers as much as we are, and we're all fighting this war together.

Archer and Songbird exchange a quick look and nod, the two TLs apparently coming to the same conclusion.

"Well, Specialists, what are you all standing around here for?" Songbird suddenly snaps. "You heard 'Vange; we have to protect our scientists."

"If you don't feel up to it," Archer adds, "go back to H5 and take the rest of the day. Dismissed!"

The orders snap us out of the fog, and within seconds everyone is scattering, a few heading for the door while most fan out into the hall, handing out handkerchiefs and fetching hot drinks, anything they might do to lessen the blow. I hover in place, knowing I should join in but held back by a hesitation I can't quite explain. Ty lingers beside me, face an expressionless mask, and I wonder if she's thinking of Zel.

"She's wrong," Ty suddenly says.

"What?"

"Karapova was wrong. They do care when it's us."

My mind flips back to the basket of flowers that arrived after Zel died, to that short note tucked within the petals. The handwriting was crabbed and the wording awkward, but the sentiment . . . The sentiment was *real*.

I don't know what value a single note can hold or why it should matter either way. All I know is that whatever was holding me back suddenly eases, and when Ty determinedly strides forward into the chaos, I follow her.

———

Moonlight shines down through the crystalline ceiling, illuminating the three data chips laid out on the window seat before me. Each one bearing a single number; each one a clue to a much larger puzzle.

The laser cutter.

The ignition regulator.

The power relay.

And now, just possibly, OP NE-2. Or whatever remains of it, floating shattered and lifeless up in the black of space.

I pick up the nearest data chip, turning it over and over in my fingers. Three chips, three numbers, no discernible connection. Though I've looked at these chips many times and found nothing, something keeps nagging at the back of my mind—a sense that I've missed something. Something obvious, something important. So much so that instead of sleeping like every sensible person on this station is doing, I'm up, sitting alone in the H5 lounge staring at these blasted things once again.

I link to each of the chips once more, but if there's anything on them besides the single number, I don't see it. Could it be that the significance isn't in the numbers themselves, but something else altogether about the chips? But every chip is exactly the same, as far as I can tell. Finding myself at a loss once more, I decide to pull up my digitals of the power relay. Maybe something about the damage to the relay will strike a chord with me, give me a new idea I haven't yet thought of.

The digitals spring up over my palm, vivid and glowing in the darkened room. I flip through them one at a time, sometimes enlarging the images, other times rotating them this way and that with a swipe of my finger. The damage is as I remembered—charred metal and fried wires and shattered crystal. Nothing different from every other damaged relay I examined in my hunt for the chip. I'm about to de-ac the digis when something in the last one catches my eye. I magnify the digital, zeroing in on the right end of the cylinder. Hidden almost completely by the charring is a single number. The relay's serial number, I assume. Squinting my eyes, I try to make it out.

19L-287098-B3948

Recognition hits me over the head like a tritanium weight. I *know* that number. It's the number I found on the data chip I pulled out of the ignition regulator. Which means I had the serial number of the sabotaged power relay *before* it blew. I just didn't know it.

My eyes fall on the other two data chips, still sitting on the window seat. Quickly, I de-ac the digitals and pull up R&D's Inventory Database. Inputting the number I found on the chip in the power relay, I do a quick search, eyebrows raising when the database comes up with a single hit. Dread coiling in my gut, I scan the result.

Serial No. 89R-786524-P103
Part Desc: Main Flow Inverter
Installation: Shield Dish Array Beta
Location: OP NE-2, Prism

OP NE-2. The location says it all. I would bet every milicred I have that the main flow inverter is exactly where that ill-fated WMGD test went so terribly wrong.

Hands shaking, I search the remaining chip number, the one I found secreted within the laser cutter planted in my locker so long ago.

Serial No. 98J-346279-A248
Part Desc: Forward Blade Assembly
Installation: Shield Generator Gamma
Location: Orbital Platform EQ-1, Prism

I gasp as I realize what that is—the broken blade I found during my first WMGD test. I hadn't even thought to add it into my equation, probably because I never actually pulled a data chip out of it. So much for a factory defect! This chip proves without a doubt that the saboteur was at that blade, regardless of what the researchers found when they examined it. No doubt if I went back to the Primary OP and dug around in that blade assembly, I'd find another data chip hidden somewhere inside. A data chip with the serial number for the shuttle's ignition regulator, perhaps?

Now that I know the pattern, the pieces fall together easily in my mind. The laser cutter planted in my locker contained a chip leading to the broken blade. The blade assembly probably has a chip leading to the ignition regulator. The regulator has a chip leading to the power relay, and the power relay has a chip leading to the shield dish that destroyed OP NE-2. Which means if I can find the data chip from the shield dish on OP NE-2, I may just know the saboteur's next target.

I roll my eyes spaceward, and my heart sinks. Too bad OP NE-2 is currently shattered across the vacuum in about a billion pieces.

22 THE WAN LIGHT REFRACTS through the halls in panes of gray, lighting the station with a bleak fortitude that feels reluctant and forced. I stand at a bench in the outer corridor around the Central Habitat and look out at the sky. The mists are particularly thick today, and even with the double suns, little light is getting through. Without the sunlight warming the halls and illuminating the walls, the station feels dim, faded. Cold, even, as though Demeter and Persephone have both recognized our cause is lost and have taken themselves away to light other, likelier endeavors.

With a shake of my head, I move on, occasionally pausing to nod at the others passing by. It's early afternoon, and the corridors are loosely filled with an assortment of scientists and support staff, civilians and military. As I walk by, I can't help noticing the similarities between them all. Their identities may differ, but their faces all look the same, grim and set and washed away within the pale gray light. Defeat hangs off their shoulders and doubt clouds their expressions, as though they, like the suns, have already realized some wars can't be won.

The loss of OP NE-2 was a blow that, while not fatal, struck us to our very core. The powers that be classified the explosion as a simple accident—a malfunction in the shield generators that resulted in an unexpected backflow of power to the main energy matrix. A memorial service was held for the thirty-five people who died, which I attended along with the rest of R&D, but if it was meant to bring closure, I'm not sure any of us found it. Though outwardly we've moved on, in the weeks that have followed, I can't help sensing that we've lost something else besides equipment and personnel, something abstract and intangible yet just as important.

We've lost our heart.

The work continues, but since then it's been one failure after another, and while we haven't experienced any other catastrophes of that order, still its aftereffects linger about the station like a storm that lurks overhead and never breaks.

From the outer ring of the Central Habitat, I catch a tender to the Tertiary Atmospheric Platform surrounding R&D. Junk greets my eyes the minute I step out onto the platform, crates of metal shrapnel and barrels of burned-up crystal sharing the corridors with massive sheets of blackened tritanium and twisted duro-steel rods still cold from the vacuum. Though weeks have passed since that awful explosion, the salvage efforts continue, ships going out daily to pick up yet more remains in a cycle that seems never-ending.

I stride through the labyrinth of debris, eyes peeled for the officer in charge. The Tertiary AP has become the primary site for the salvage operation, receiving the countless loads rescued by the scavenger shuttles as they're brought in. The piles are then sorted through, with salvageable parts being plucked out for future use and the rest getting sent to the recycler.

"Afternoon, Specialist," comes a voice from my right. It's one of the engineers, a volunteer like me who's honoring his fallen comrades by giving up his free time to help with the salvage efforts.

I give him a polite nod. "Afternoon, Doctor. Find anything useful today?"

"Not so far, but the suns are still up, so there's hope yet."

Hope. A faint smile passes over my lips. As beaten down, as defeated, as grief-stricken as we all are, there's still hope to be found in the most unexpected places. I laugh quietly. "Yeah, I guess there is."

Halfway down the platform, I finally run down the officer on duty, PsyCaptain Kato. She immediately sets me to work on a pile of new salvage at the other end of the platform. I arrive at the designated spot to find Chen already there, picking through some bins of half charred tech. She acknowledges my presence with a quiet greeting. I drop down at a heap near her and start sorting through the junk. Our job is simple: to evaluate each piece for salvage potential and either set it aside for an engineer to examine later or toss it in the recycler pile. That's the official job, anyway. Unofficially, I have a completely different mission.

I'm looking for the data chip that will tell me the saboteur's next target.

Not that I'm hopeful. I've been volunteering to help with the salvage efforts for three weeks now, with no luck. Even I'm smart enough to know that if there's something to find, my chances of actually finding it are astronomically remote, to say the least.

"Hey, Sorenson. Have you done this pile yet?"

Chen stands at a heap to my left, head cocked in question. I wave her on to the refuse. "It's all yours."

Going back to my own salvage, I watch her covertly from the corner of my eye as she starts in on the pile. As usual, she's impeccably dressed in the black-and-gold service dress of the teams. Though the platform is stuffy and most everyone has their sleeves rolled up or jackets unzipped, she remains impeccably turned out, with her collar fastened to her chin and sleeves secured around her wrists. Her inky hair is slicked back in a neat bun.

It's how she always looks, I observe. Neat to the point of being downright formal, as though pushing up a sleeve or unhooking her collar might reveal something quintessential about herself she doesn't want anyone else to see. Once again, it strikes me how little I know of her despite running on the same team for months now.

"You came from the navy, right?" I ask, curiosity getting the better of my strict no-questions rule for once. "As a fighter pilot?"

She blinks, my random question clearly taking her by surprise, and nods. "Yes. I did a few tours with the Golden Aces before I came here."

I let out a low whistle, impressed by the credential. Even I've heard of the Golden Aces. Among fighter units they're considered the best of the best, the elite squad every pilot aspires to reach. I cock my head at her curiously, wondering why she'd leave such an elite unit to come to R&D, where any flying she gets to do is routine at best.

"Seems like a huge leap," I comment with a shake of my head. "How do you go from an elite fighter pilot unit to a place like this?"

"How do you go from being an ordinary guardian doing evacs and riot control to a place like this?" Chen counters, and I tip my head, conceding the point.

"I suppose you'd have to ask Dr. Angelou that."

"Same here."

The corner of her lip curls up in a slight smile. I grin back, enjoying the unexpected repartee, and several heartbeats pass before her last words actually sink in. "Wait a second. You were recruited by Angelou, too?"

Her smile fades, hands going still as if suddenly realizing she gave away something she shouldn't have. She finally shrugs. "I came to Dr. Angelou's attention after a particular op I flew. One thing led to another, and I ended up here. Arrived only a couple months before you did."

She was personally recruited by Daedalus Angelou? Something shifts uncomfortably in my chest at the revelation, though I'm not sure why it matters either way. She was probably just in the right place at the right time, same as me. *Or the* wrong *place at the* wrong *time*, I think wryly, remembering Ty's words upon my arrival at R&D.

Yet despite my explications, I can't help thinking that it does matter, as though Angelou has connected us in some invisible way by seeing in her the same thing he saw in me. Whatever that thing might be. Somehow I doubt Chen could explain Angelou's motives any more than I could.

We continue sorting through the junk, enveloped by a companionable silence as we sift through broken relays and charred crystal. Chen pulls out a wedding ring, its band still shiny and new, from the bottom of a retrieval crate, and the two of us exchange a pained look.

"We should try to find out who this belonged to," she says softly, a look of pure sorrow piercing her normally impassive demeanor.

I have to clear my throat a couple of times before I can speak. "Perhaps the officer in charge could ask around among the researchers."

"I'll bring it to the captain when my shift is over," she agrees.

I go back to work, trying not to think about that shiny ring and its now-deceased owner, while across from me Chen no doubt tries to do the same. I reach for the last piece of junk in the crate, a blackened concave dish that is miraculously still in one piece. Shifting it into the light, I methodically start examining it to see if it's potentially salvageable, and that's when I find it. Buried in the wreckage of this burnt shield dish—a single metallic data chip.

My mouth drops open. Against all odds, I've found the proverbial pebble in the asteroid belt. Is it fate? Luck? Or perhaps there really *is* a higher power out there.

With a quick glance to either side, I palm the chip in one quick movement and then surreptitiously tuck it into my pants pocket. I can practically feel the chip burning a hole straight through the fabric into my skin, and more than anything, I want to run from the room and check it out this moment. Instead, I force myself to continue with the work, scanning and sorting salvage until I think I'm going to crawl out of my skin with impatience.

When my shift ends, I immediately go hunting for a private place to examine the data chip. The barracks, the H5 Lounge, the training rooms—everywhere I go I find someone or other. At last, I end up locking myself into an out-of-the-way hygiene unit in the Central Habitat, where I link to the chip to find, as expected, a single number. But not just any number. If my theory is right, this number will tell me the saboteur's next target.

Uploading the chip number into the inventory database, I tap my foot impatiently as I wait for it to search. When the results finally come, I can't believe my eyes.

Error: No Match Found

What in a black hole . . . ? I must have accidentally uploaded the number wrong or something. I key in the number manually this time, triple-checking my work before I start the search, but the result is still the same. Nothing in the inventory database matches this chip number. Frowning, I widen my search, running the number through every other database I can think to access. Still nothing. As far as I can tell, there's absolutely no record of this number anywhere in R&D.

I toss the chip aside and pace the small unit, too agitated to sit still. After all this time, I've finally cracked the chips' code only to find the code has changed. Frustration fills me at being thwarted right when I thought I had things figured out, but I force my irritation aside and try to think about the situation logically. As far as I've seen, all the chip numbers have been for parts that have been or will be sabotaged, right? So either the next sabotaged part is located somewhere outside of R&D, or it's in R&D but was never entered into the database at all.

Or the saboteur has changed their MO and the number means something completely different.

Slag! What am I doing? I'm a soldier, not a detective. I have no idea what any of this means. All I know is that once again I'm back at square one with a saboteur on the loose, strange clues that never add up, and absolutely no idea who to trust.

———

Over the next few days, I continue to check the inventory database, not to mention every other database I can think of, but the chip number remains a mystery. The situation is frustrating to say the least, but while the number seems to be a dead end, I have managed to pare down my suspect list a bit.

Remembering what Dr. Jacobi told me while we were welding the broken blade on EQ-1, I went back and checked the installation records for the blade. Just like she said, the blade apparatus arrived at R&D only a week before it broke, which means none of the four Division Recruiters could be involved, as all of them were off-base on recruiting missions during that time. Similarly, I was able to cross off two more specialists, both from Alpha, as they were laid up in the infirmary after a mission accident during that same time period. This brings the list down from thirty-one to twenty-five. Still a lot of suspects, but it's a hell of a lot better than the progress I'm making with the chips.

At the end of the week, a drone ship—a relic from the late war with Telluria—drops into orbit as a replacement for the destroyed OP. We see it come in as we head out to Javeyn on a mission, a dull shape settling like a vulture within the scattered remnants of NE-2. Compared to the platform, the ship is a crude thing, designed only for minor recon ops, but once modified and linked into the OP network, it does the job. At least insofar as any of the platforms do the job, which is to say they still can't get a working ghoul-killer.

As an alternative, the engineers design a smaller, portable version of the WMGD with a more concentrated beam to see if it will yield better results than the large-scale weapons, but though we gamely take it out, driving it around in the back of a roamer and shooting it at unsuspecting ghouls, our efforts don't account for anything in the end.

As Ty so adroitly asks Archer after our tenth round of tests, "Sir, do you ever get the feeling the Specs are just playing with us? They fly around a bit, give chase once in a while when they feel like it, but mostly just sit back and laugh their asses off at our futile attempts to hurt them?"

Archer sighs. "All the time."

I glance at Archer in surprise. There's a weariness underscoring his words, a fatalism I'm unaccustomed to hearing from our TL. I wait for him to crack a smile, a wink, something to show it was just a joke and he didn't really mean it, but it never comes. Instead I see a deep exhaustion in his eyes, as though the weight of the job has become just the tiniest bit too heavy for him.

Judging by the worried frown on Ty's face, she sees it too. She musters a cheeky grin. "Just you wait, sir. We may be down now, but in the end, we'll be the ones having the last laugh."

Now comes the grin, albeit a bit late. "I'm sure you're right, ATL."

Archer gives the order to pack it in shortly after, his demeanor back to its normal confident self. Still, I can't help wondering: If even Archer is starting to bow under the constant pressure and endless setbacks, what chance do the rest of us have?

We put boots back on the station soon after, going through the psy check with little ceremony before catching a tender back to the main station. Thirty seconds after we arrive at the Central Habitat, my chit buzzes.

Report to my office.

No time or date. The sender is Dr. Daedalus Angelou.

I glance around uneasily. Was the message unable to reach me off-station, or did Angelou just happen to know the exact moment I returned? While the former seems more probable, I have this creepy feeling it's the latter.

A few quiet words to Archer, and I'm off to Angelou's office. The director of R&D's workspace takes up all of Habitat 1, a tiny orb located directly above the Central Habitat. I swipe my chit hand across the access pad on the top tier of H1, and after a brief scan, the doors open. Apparently Angelou already programmed in clearance for me. Stepping in, I let the lift platform take me up. One more access plate at the top, also preprogrammed to admit me, and I'm in.

My eyes widen as I get my first glimpse of Angelou's private sanctuary. A large, circular desk, split down the middle to form two opposing arcs, dominates the dome-shaped room. A tip-pad, stylus, and other personal effects are laid out on top, while a collage of holos pool between the glass panes of the desk itself. More holos line the walls, nearly every inch of the curved surface covered with data dumps, star maps, and image feeds. I peer closer at the feeds, my eyebrows raising as I realize what they show: real-time footage of every major section of R&D.

I stifle a snort. So Angelou has the whole place staked out. Why am I not surprised?

Even as I think it, every holo goes out at once, leaving only static in their place. The sound of a throat clearing comes from my left. I flick my gaze in the direction of the noise, hand going to my nonexistent stunner out of sheer reflex.

Angelou stands in the far corner, hands folded loosely before him. His eyes drop to my hand, lips curling up slightly in amusement. With a flick of his wrist, the static on the walls is replaced by one giant viewport. An actual viewport, I realize, not simply opaque walls digitized to show the outside feeds. I can tell by the white streaks shot through the clear surface in various spots. Demeter has just begun to set, the falling rays deepening the normally pastel drifts into bold hues of red, gold, turquoise, and violet. The sight is lovely, but somehow I doubt Angelou invited me up here just to watch the sunset with him.

Dropping into parade rest, I acknowledge his command. "Sir, reporting as ordered."

I keep my tone level, though my mind is fraught with questions. Unlike the last time I was called before the top brass, this time I don't even have a guess as to the reason for my summons. It's nothing to do with my work, I'm sure. That's Asriel's domain, and despite my time on scut, he hasn't shown any signs of true dissatisfaction with my performance. I suppose Angelou could feel some responsibility for me since he's the one who originally brought me onboard, but he doesn't strike me as the type to care much whether one lowly testing grunt is settling in.

I try to gauge the head of R&D, but as usual his expression gives nothing away. Nothing helpful, anyway. I tilt my head expectantly, waiting for Angelou to get to the point. He doesn't disappoint.

"Did you know that a portion of your official file is sealed, Sorenson?" Angelou unclasps his hands and moves to the desk, leaning his hip against the edge in a way that should be casual yet strikes me as anything but. "And not just sealed but hidden. Only someone with high enough clearance would even be able to see it's there, and of those, even fewer would be able to read it."

He pauses momentarily. "I happen to be one of those few."

Dread congeals in my gut, hard and heavy. There's only one reason my file would be sealed. One thing MI would consider need-to-know only on the highest levels. Angelou pauses, almost as if expecting me to fill in the answer, and says:

"You were there the day New Sol blew."

23

WE FACE EACH OTHER once again, the white-haired doctor and I. But while last time it was across a table in a conference room on a naval evacuation carrier with an admiral in attendance—*my* territory—this time it's in Angelou's office within the highest habitat of Sky Station Epsilon-065, and there's no one, absolutely *no one*, who can come to my aid.

Angelou lifts an eyebrow as though waiting for a response, though he didn't actually ask a question. *You were there the day New Sol blew.*

I grit my teeth and answer it anyway. "So were a lot of people."

"Not who knew the bomber."

I laugh, a bitter snort I can't quite keep in. "I didn't even know she was a bomb until after she was dead, so I couldn't have known her all that well, could I?"

"Then tell me what you did know."

That she loved me, she lied to me, and then she killed herself along with a station hub full of squatters.

"They debriefed me back on New Sol when it was all over. Everything's in the original report. If you've got my file, you've seen it all."

"I'd like to hear it from you," he says, taking a seat at the desk and casually folding his hands atop the glassy surface.

My muscles clench; shoulders, neck, back, and biceps all involuntarily tightening in one quicksilver motion. "I don't see what difference it makes."

"You might be surprised," Angelou says in an easy lilt only belied by the intensity in his frost-blue eyes. "The whole of the Expanse hinges upon us creating a weapon that can take down the enemy. Any small detail could mean the difference between success and failure."

"I don't know any details, small or otherwise."

"Perhaps you do, and you just don't realize it."

"I swear to you I don't know anything about the Nova technology." I shake my head once, hard, to hammer in the words. "Lia never told me about it, not once, in the entire time I knew her. I don't even think she knew much about it herself. Everything she had was on that data chip we turned over to the authorities on New Sol. If you just go back to that—"

"We've been over the chip again and again. It's a dead end."

"So am I! I'm sorry your trials have failed all these times, but I'm not the answer!" A thought suddenly occurs to me, so chilling it freezes me from the inside out. "I-is that why you recruited me? Because of my connection to New Sol? Did you think I was just some source you could pump for information?"

"Not exactly. I was on the ScyLab to recruit research personnel and was intrigued by your daring rescue during the evacuation. Imagine my surprise when I checked out your file, only to find your history with the New Sol bomber—classified, of course, so that only those with the highest clearance could read it. It occurred to me that your past association might be useful at some point, and . . . Well, let's just say I saw an opportunity and took advantage of it."

"An *opportunity*?"

Anger boils deep down in the pit of my stomach, but before I can say anything more, Angelou pushes violently to his feet. His face is set, his eyes like two chips of blue diamond glittering coldly under the white station lights.

He whirls around to the nearest viewport, flicking on the feed with a hard jerk of his wrist. A planet springs to life across the port, a glowing orb painting the starry night in streaks of reds and blues and browns. Ships hang in orbit over the entire northern hemisphere—

defense corvettes, refugee transports, evacuation carriers—their metal carapaces gleaming brightly beneath a yellow sun that's already starting to set around the other side of the world, and I know without a doubt that this is a world under siege.

"Oberon. Our enemy's latest victim, being evacuated as we speak. No doubt its sister planet, Titania, will go next."

He flicks to another scene, this one of a planet so blue it's almost blinding.

"Oceania."

Another flick, and three interconnected space stations pop up.

"The Triple Colonies."

Flick! Up comes an enormous planet swathed in pearly white clouds.

"Everest Prime."

Flick!

"Evadne 5."

Flick!

"Orbital Mining Rig Gamma 12."

Flick!

"Colony 08571, so new they haven't even ratified a name for it yet."

The *flicks* and the accompanying names are coming so fast now I can't keep up with them, a new planet or station replacing the last almost the moment it comes up. They blur together under my gaze, bleeding into a meaningless whirl of shapes and colors until at last the feed stops on a single image. Angelou doesn't have to name it for me to know what it is.

New Sol Space Station.

Not as it is now, but as it was after Lia went Nova: Two habitat rings floating alone in space with the debris of the hub still scattered around them in every direction.

I jerk back as if struck, shock quickly turning to rage as I'm forced to take in that terrible view before me. *How dare he—!*

"So many places destroyed, and for what?" Angelou asks. "We are on the verge of a breakthrough that could save humanity if only we can take that final step and reach it! Yet for some reason, that step continues to elude us again and again. There has to be something! Something she *said*."

"She never said anything about the Nova technology!"

"Something she did—"

"She never *did* anything!"

"Some small clue she left behind then. A note—"

"She didn't leave a note!"

"A link."

"*She didn't leave a link!*"

The words rip straight from my heart, torn by an anger that can no longer be denied, and suddenly I'm yelling and yelling and unable to stop.

"*Don't you get it?! There were no notes or links or explanations or apologies! Not even a fraggin' goodbye! Lia lied to me! From the very beginning, she pretended she was just another refugee from the camps, an old friend who turned up out of the blue after so many years! We talked, and we played games, and we hung out, and we kissed—*" My voice chokes up. "*—and all that time she was lying to me! About who she was, what she was! Even when she finally told me about the Spectres, she didn't tell me she was a bomb! And then we came up with that plan and separated the station and everything was supposed to be fine! She was supposed to come to the rings with the rest of us and* live, *and instead she got off that SlipStream! She got off—*" A sob tears from my throat. "*—and she died! She went back into the hub, went Nova, and* died, *scattered across the void amidst the debris of half a space station! So if you want to know her secrets, you'll have to walk out into the vacuum yourself and find them, because they all died with her, and nothing in the universe can ever bring her back!*"

Tears are streaming down my face, and I can barely talk anymore through the torrent of sobs ripping through my chest. Lia's face flashes into my mind, and then the memories are flying through my head one after another. The little dimple in her cheek, left side only, when she smiled. The wisps of blond hair always escaping her ponytail. The sound of her voice, and the way she scrunched up her nose when she laughed. The day I stood outside that cargo bay on New Sol Space Station, curious to see the returned POWs, only to see Lia's name flash on the screen. How my heart had practically leapt out of my chest when she walked out of that bay, looking all lost and alone, and I realized I was still as crazy about her as I was that day all those years ago on Aurora when she'd first knocked on my door and said, "Hi, I'm Lia! I live next door." How tongue-tied I was during our first meal, back together again after seven years, sure I'd say the wrong thing and make a total null out of myself, only to go home and babble nonstop about her until Teal was ready to whack me over the head with her tip-pad and Gran sat me down and told me to take it slow. That after all she'd been through, the thing Lia probably needed most was just a good friend. Our first race through the corridors; our first dinner at my house; our first kiss.

Our last kiss, on the roof of my apartment building just hours before she died.

That moment she got off that SlipStream train and walked back into a hub full of ghouls . . . and never came back. And that awful moment after it was all over, when I'd looked out into space and seen the wreckage of the Central Hub, only to have Teal tell me the terrible news.

"Oh my God! Was Lia there? Please tell me she wasn't there!"

"Michael."

"She got off, right? Managed to catch another SlipStream some-where else. The one over by green quadrant always closes last—"

"Michael."

"She couldn't have been caught in the blast, just couldn't—"

"Michael!" Her voice caught slightly, a throaty catch I'd never heard before. "She wasn't caught in the blast. She was *the blast."*

I'd refused to believe it. Refused and refused until finally . . . I did. But by then it was too late. Lia was nothing more than memories and ash.

I'm on the floor now, head in my hands while my shoulders shake and shake like they'll never stop. But eventually they do stop, or at least slow, leaving me hollowed out and empty, as though everything inside of me has been scooped away, leaving only a vacant husk. The room is so still, at first I think Angelou must have left sometime during my breakdown, but then—

"It's like a betrayal, isn't it?" Angelou's voice is paper-thin within the quiet room, whispering across my consciousness like a wind that barely dares breathe. "When the ones we love turn out to be some-thing completely different than what we thought. And only when we see what they're truly capable of do we realize we never really knew them at all."

A hand briefly touches my shoulder. "It's all right to be angry at the dead."

I'm not angry at Lia. At least, that's what I want to say, but Angelou's words snake through my mind, fingering something I've been unable to admit for a year and a half. I'm *angry* at Lia. As much as I miss her, as much as I mourn for her, as much as I love her, I'm *angry* at her! She betrayed me, lied and left me alone with all the truths she never told me. Maybe she had her reasons, and maybe they were even good reasons, but my mind can't comprehend them and my heart doesn't want them. And yet as angry as I am, I would forgive her in a heartbeat if I could, except there is no *her* left to forgive. No explanations to hear, no apologies to accept. Lia is dead, and there is no confronting the dead. No satisfaction to be found in the vacuum of a grave. Just a soul-abiding anger that goes on and on and can never find resolution.

The hand withdraws. "It's all right to be angry at the dead," Angelou repeats, "for a little while, but eventually anger turns to resentment, and resentment to hatred. So you have to decide: Do you want to remember her with hatred? Or with love?"

The question hovers in the air, deceptive in its simplicity, but though my mind says the answer is easy, my heart knows it's not. All I can do is shake my head—not a no, not a yes, just one more I-don't-know in a string of too many questions I can't seem to find any answers for.

Thankfully, Angelou doesn't seem to expect a response, only remarking mildly, "Think about it."

I silently nod. Reason is fast returning, self-awareness hot on its heels, and I'm suddenly horribly conscious of how ridiculous I must seem to Angelou, swollen-eyed and crouched on the floor like a null.

Rising to my feet, I surreptitiously swipe at my face a few times, grateful that the black cloth of my uniform hides any wetness from view. My heels snap together as I come to attention, and I keep my eyes fixed over Angelou's left shoulder, unable to look him in the face after everything that happened. My voice, when it comes, is more or less steady. "I-is there anything else, sir?"

From the corner of my eye, I see the doctor slowly shake his head no, which seems to be as much of a dismissal as I'll get. Dropping my stance, I'm about to turn tail and flee as quickly as possible when he speaks.

"Sorenson."

I pause, eyes on my feet as I wait for him to continue.

"I can't bring her back—only God has that prerogative—but this I can promise you. I will do everything in my power to make sure her death wasn't in vain."

His voice carries a cold implacability, the tone oddly familiar, and it's only after several seconds that I recognize it. It's the same voice that ordered sixteen survivors to their deaths, consigning their broken ship to hell while around us the debris field rippled and rolled with the remains of an empire.

I didn't fully comprehend that tone when I first heard it on the Colt Crawler all those months ago, thinking him a madman, a lunatic, but I understand it now. It's the sort of voice that takes vows to the grave and carves promises in blood. It's the sort of voice that will either do . . .

Or die.

Though he isn't technically a member of the military, hasn't been for decades, still I raise my hand in salute. And when I finally lift my eyes to his, it occurs to me I could live a hundred years and never know him better than I do in this moment.

24

A STRAY BOOT catches the slim metal relay scanner and sends it flying off the catwalk. It pitches through the air, tumbling end over end as gravity drags it down until it's out of sight.

"Oops." Ty stares down at the city far below, soon to be one relay scanner richer. "Hey, Sorenson. Go on down and grab that for me, huh?"

"Hey, it's your scanner."

"But I've got rank *and* seniority."

I consider that. She's got a point. "In that case, I resign."

"Damn."

It's been months since I first set foot on Prism, and now I'm back again. Only this time I'm not installing a replacement shunt from the safety of an enclosed room but clinging to a narrow maintenance walkway halfway up a massive antenna affixed to the roof of a skyscraper.

Reaching into my vest, I rummage around until I find my own relay scanner. Ty accepts it with a nod and finishes scanning the sensor feed we just installed. Everything checks out, and in a minute she's linking Archer to let him know we're done with this round of modifications.

We've been making adjustments to the sensor hardware since before the start of Prism's abnormally long sunrise. The old equipment wasn't giving specialized enough data, so the researchers on base designed some hardware modifications that would collect better readings. We've been installing and adjusting equipment for over three hours, per the continually changing instructions linked to us from R&D. In between modifications, they've been performing WMGD tests to determine which modifications work the best. Besides Ty and me, there are twenty other two-person teams spread out on spires across the city. Talk about one hell of a mission.

I wrap one hand around the straps of my harness and the other around the flimsy guardrail. The view is dizzying. Except for a few other building spires rising up in the distance, we're completely alone up here—above stone and steel, flesh and blood, in a place few birds dare fly. It's breathtaking.

Maybe a little too breathtaking.

I force my lungs to inhale, casually sidling back from the edge and tilting my chin as though I'm simply trying to catch the sights from a slightly different angle. Ty notices anyway, the side of her mouth quirking ruefully. "You have a thing about heights, Sorenson?"

Fairly certain there's nothing I can say that won't be used against me somehow, I only shrug and grunt, "Never been on the antenna of a skyscraper before. What about you? They have buildings like this on your home world?"

"These metal death traps? Hell, no! The quakes would tear them down around our ears in a week. Our buildings are mostly low-lying structures of heavy cloth and flexible plastics—tethered to the ground for added support, but with enough give to allow them to roll with the ground shifts. Nothing like this place," she says, shaking her head in awe. She shoves my scanner into her utility belt before adding, "Not that I haven't been in plenty of cities like this before, as a guardian."

"Same here."

The smile fades from her voice. "Usually to evacuate them."

Yes.

The word is unnecessary, my agreement echoing clearly enough in my silence. Just as Ty's response to that unspoken agreement echoes clearly back in hers:

At least we don't have to evacuate this one.

No. Because it's already too late for this city.

As one, we look down at the gleaming city below. Prism at sunrise is truly a sight to behold. Only the earliest risers up, the streets quiet and the air crisp. The rising suns intensify the sky's pastels into deep hues, painting the silver skyscrapers in swathes of fuchsia and indigo, turquoise and gold. Captured within the stillness of the morning, there's a serenity so deep and abiding even I can't help but be touched by it, the fidgety feet and impatient hands nowhere to be found though we've been sitting at least an hour. Only the distant odor of ghouls meters and meters below mars the perfection of the day.

"Zel always loved this view," Ty comments suddenly. "She told me once that she was born in the mountains, that no matter where she went, the heights always called to her."

I glance over at Ty in surprise. By tacit agreement, no one really talks about fallen team members once they've been consigned to the net. However, like most of the testers who came from the Celestial Guard, Ty still slashes when a teammate is lost. It's a warm day, and she's got her sleeves rolled up to the elbow, revealing the myriad slashes down her forearms. My eyes fall on the thickest one—a centimeter-wide band of red wrapping her right arm just below the elbow—and I know it's for Zel.

Ty catches me looking and, with a glance at my own bare arms, asks, "You came from the Guard, right?" At my nod, she adds, "Why didn't you ever slash? Or wasn't that something the guardians in your unit did?"

I blink, startled by the question, though I got it often enough in the Guard. The answer automatically fills my mind.

Because if I had, I would be one giant red band from head to toe. Lia would've taken every centimeter of me and left no room for anyone else.

Not that I ever told anyone that. Anyone in the Guard who made the mistake of asking me either got a *Frag off!* or a punch in the face. The question never failed to arouse the constant anger lurking just a hairsbreadth beneath my skin.

I meet Ty's questioning gaze. Strangely enough, I don't feel compelled to curse or hit her. It's as though the anger that's been rustling beneath my skin for so long has vanished. No, not vanished, but faded, its toxins leached away leaving it a pale remnant of its former self. Maybe I used it all up on Angelou that awful day I melted down in his office, or maybe I'm just too confused to be angry right now. All I know is that the lump in my throat that usually comes whenever someone asks me about *her* is gone today.

"It's because of Lia," I finally answer, eyes fixed to the Prism sunrise as it glimmers and glows across the horizon.

"Who's Lia?"

I let out a soft sigh at the question. Ever since my breakdown a few weeks ago, I haven't known what to think or feel about her. *Who's Lia?* There are so many ways I could answer that question, I wouldn't even know where to begin. My childhood best friend; my first love. A Tellurian prisoner and a Celestian patriot. A girl eighteen months dead, and a ghost still very much alive. A traitor I trusted, and the human bomb who killed herself so that the rest of us might live. Too many names, too many labels. I can't even sort her out in my own mind, let alone explain her to anyone else.

Finally I just shrug and say, "Lia was my friend, and now she's gone."

Ty nods once, expression grave, then turns back to the sunrise. Relief fills me at her easy acceptance. Six months ago, she wouldn't have let it go so easily. She would've badgered me with questions, made wild guesses and teasing remarks. But Zel's death changed her, spread a layer of gravitas across her flip demeanor. She's still Ty, overly mouthy and quick with a line, but somehow it's a strength now, as though she found some way to absorb Zel's death into herself, to reshape its unfairness and transmute its ugliness, and come out the stronger for it on the other side. I wish I knew how she did it.

Her humanity, her heart; the way she worked so hard to reclaim everything she'd lost, only so that she might give it all away again.

I wish I knew how both of them did it.

A soft *hiss* from my com has me grabbing my discarded helmet. It's Archer, linking us through the group channel to let us know another WMGD test is about to begin. I put on my helmet while Ty does the same. Though technically the WMGD energy is supposed to be harmless to humans, we're still under orders to wear full uniform, including helmet, during all tests. Nor have I forgotten Preston's sharp comment all those weeks ago about giving half the humans on the planet seizures.

Seizures. I think of Zel, and something pops in my chest, hollow and hard.

I check the timekeeper on my gauntlet. Twenty seconds until the next test begins. Following Ty's lead, I scoot away from the edge until my back hits the spire. I slide down the wall into a crouch, arms resting on my knees. Though we've already sat through a dozen tests today, still I hold my breath as I wait for the light to come. After what happened with NE-2, every test is enough to put a flutter in my belly, no matter how much I tell myself everything will be okay.

It starts slowly, only the most distant spark of silver tingeing the pastel sky, then comes faster, like a spreading stain, as the deep arc of energy drops ever nearer. Energy crackles along my skin, static electricity shocking me in a dozen little pinches as it falls around us in a shimmering mercury shadow. Bathed in a pool of deep, deep silver, I watch as it plunges away into the depths of the city, rippling out in a great wave before dissipating as quickly as it came.

Test complete, I rub my arms to get rid of the tingling sensation running along my skin. Ty shakes her own arms out a couple of times, presumably for the same reason, then turns to the control array.

"Do you have the next set of freqs, Soren—" She stops suddenly, eyes widening as she takes a big sniff. Then in a faint voice, she asks, "Do you smell something, Sorenson?"

Frowning, I shake my head. "No, I—"

My mouth drops open as I suddenly take her meaning. Flaring my nostrils, I take a huge sniff, sucking air deep into my lungs—but I don't smell anything. Not a single thing at all. The distant but ever-present odor of ghouls is *gone*.

My heart drops out of my chest. "You don't think . . . ?"

"I don't know."

For a minute, we just stand there staring at each other, this small shred of hope more terrifying than any enemy we've ever faced. It's the chime of Ty's com that breaks the spell. Turning, she takes a few steps away and answers the call. I watch her profile as she listens to the voice on the other end, but with the rising sun gilding her face, it's hard to make out her expression let alone read her lips as she subvocalizes into her com. At last she signs off with a louder, "Understood, sir. Ty out."

My foot is dancing in my boot now, my earlier serenity gone as I wait with bated breath for her to brief me on the call. She meets my gaze and suddenly grins, eyebrow raised and eyes glinting with life, the old Ty temporarily resurrected. "Feel like taking a walk?"

———

Since the com station building is completely sealed up except for the roof, we take the shuttle down to a landing bay in the southern half of the city. I wonder about the security of leaving our ride off-planet in a strange place, but as Ty points out, the shuttle looks like any other Prism ship used for intraplanetary transport. Nothing to raise eyebrows over, especially with so many others already filling the pad.

Following Ty's orders, I take off my armor and remove my insignia. Dump my helmet and rip off my uniform patches. Strip away my identity piece by piece until anything that can identify me as R&D is gone and I'm left with nothing more than a pair of boots and a fitted black jacket and pants.

I touch the plain fabric on my chest, not even plain so much as bare now that all identifying marks have been taken away. It's a perfectly respectable outfit, the sort of casual suit any working-class civil servant might wear, but somehow I feel almost naked in it. As though my own identity were lost the day Lia died and only by putting on the uniform did I find some definition once again. And now that the uniform is gone, there's no one left underneath.

Or perhaps I just don't know the person underneath anymore.

The last two things to go are my weapons. I cradle them in my hands, the slim stunner in the right and the heavy launcher in the left.

"The launcher's too big to hide, and both could identify us as R&D," Ty says from the shuttle door.

I know she's right, but still I hesitate. If we're wrong, if the scientists floating a hundred klicks up in the air are wrong, it'll be the end for us. We'll simply be sitting ducks waiting for a couple of hungry ghouls looking for hosts.

Or maybe it's just that these weapons have become as much of my identity as the R&D insignia and the false flag patch now absent from my arm.

"You don't have to come. I won't order it."

Ty's expression is steady, her bearing radiating a quiet strength, like the faint rays of a sun that seems too pale to provide any heat—until you stop long enough to realize its light has already warmed your face. With a shake of my head, I carefully stow my weapons under the seat. "You don't have to."

Then together we walk out of the shuttle and into the fresh air.

Onboard Sky Station Epsilon-065
Secret Research Base for Division 7

THE DOCTOR SAT BOLT UPRIGHT *in his seat, pulled awake by the thundering of his heart and the hammering in his head. Momentarily off balance, he clutched the arms of his chair, gripping the supports tightly between his fingers as he waited for the initial alarm to fade.*

He'd fallen asleep at his desk again. An occurrence that was starting to happen with frightening regularity these days. He'd always put in long days and short nights, but after the destruction of NE-2, he barely slept at all anymore. Exhaustion hung over him like a shroud, pressing him down and down toward an early grave, and even when he did sleep, it was only to be awoken again by nightmares. Or should he say the nightmare—*it was always the same one.*

Spectres. Thousands and thousands of Spectres surging around him in a pool of black.

The Doctor shuddered. Others may call them aliens, but they seemed to him nothing so much as demons, like those in the vision of Leo XIII, a Tellurian holy man of old. As the stories went, he'd fallen into a deep faint while in conference with his men, only to have the most terrible of visions: evil spirits charging up from the depths of hell, falling upon the Eternal City that they might damn every last living soul.

Evil spirits.

A vision of blackened rainbows writhed through the Doctor's head, and he let out a noise somewhere between a laugh and a sob. Evil spirits, indeed. After all these centuries, the spirits of that holy man's vision had finally come, descending upon the human race in an endless shiver that would not cease until they had taken every last man, woman, and child in the universe. Only in Leo's vision, the mighty Archangel, Saint Michael himself, had swooped down to do battle with these spirits, never resting until he had cast Satan and all his demons back into hell.

Without thought, the Doctor's lips silently moved in prayer to that mighty defender, the words taken straight from those written by His Holiness himself.

Saint Michael The Archangel,
Defend us in battle.
Be our protection against the wickedness and snares of the
 Devil.
May God rebuke him, we humbly pray,
And do you, O Prince of the Heavenly Host,
By the Divine Power of God,
Cast into Hell Satan and all the evil spirits
Who prowl about the world seeking the ruin of souls.
Amen.

Even the familiar words did little to soothe him. It had been over four years since the Spectres had come, seeping into the human race without anyone the wiser. Time was running out, and yet neither faith nor science had yielded an answer to this plague of spirits sent to destroy them all. Though the Doctor normally considered himself a patient man, a thread of desperation had slowly begun winding its way through his subconscious, creeping into his slumber and subverting his dreams, suffusing his consciousness with a restless urgency almost strangling in its insistency.

It had made him reckless, pushed him to do things he wouldn't otherwise have done, like interrogating a heartbroken kid in a quest for answers that no longer existed, if they'd ever existed in the first place. It was a futile ploy, but with the WMGD technology still inoperable, he couldn't leave any stone unturned. Not when they were so close to success. All it would take was one thing. One small detail that could well turn out to be the key to everything. Yet no matter how many times he went through the data, ran the numbers and scanned the test results, still the answers hovered just out of reach, hanging in some shadowy place between victory and madness.

The Doctor snorted. He wouldn't be surprised if he did go mad one of these days. He certainly had enough cause.

A low buzzing in his chit temporarily stayed the thought, and with a flick of his hand, he threw the incoming link onto the wall beside him. Dr. Preston appeared on the screen, face flushed and normally staid eyes flashing. The Doctor frowned at the interruption, raising one eyebrow as he asked, "Yes?"

Preston's lips fluttered, opening and closing slightly as though she couldn't quite find the words . . . then faith and science combined in a single instant, bursting like a supernova across the blackening void, as she uttered the two words he'd been waiting over sixteen months to hear.

"It works."

PHASE THREE

25

"OUR NEW MISSION begins *today*."

Angelou's voice rings out across the packed hall, echoing off the crystalline walls to fill the Atrium from end to end. I stand at the back with my fellow Deltas, listening as the enthusiastic clamor abruptly ceases, replaced by the anticipatory silence of an audience three thousand strong, all waiting for the doctor to speak. After one year, five months, and twenty-seven days, the time for running and hiding is over.

The fight for the human race is about to begin.

Angelou flicks his chit hand, and the entire front wall of the Atrium seems to dissolve into the black arena of space. Stars ripple into place, the bright points of light creating a framework for the huge orbital platform hanging in the foreground: OP N. The command platform for Prism's entire orbital network.

"You are looking at the first ever offensive weapon created to destroy our enemy: an orbital platform modified to emit a specialized energy pulse that can effectively disperse and disintegrate the enemy while in their incorporeal state. When linked together and operated in tandem with the other OPs in a planetary network, this weapon is capable of blanketing an entire planet in one unbroken swathe of energy. In effect, it can clear an entire planet full of ghouls in a single strike."

Gasps and murmurs break out over the hall as the implications of the doctor's words sink in. Angelou flicks his hand, and every wall in the Atrium disappears, replaced by starscapes brimming with planets and colonies, space stations and suns, jump paths and mining rigs. Even though it's just a map any child would recognize, something swells deep inside of me at the vision, my heart instinctively knowing this place for what it is. Not simply the Celestial Expanse, but—

Home.

A sigh murmurs through the auditorium, and I realize I'm not the only one feeling this way. Though we all come from different planets and stations, different backgrounds and customs, different experiences and memories, still we're connected by this quintessential truth: We are Celestians. Together we stand and together we fall. As I look out over the crowd, at the faces of the people I've lived with and worked with and sweated with all these months, I suddenly feel connected to them in a way I've never felt before, and I know this is a tie that will bind us together for an eternity and never be severed.

Angelou waits for the noise to die down, then continues. "However, the Expanse is a not a single planet, and we will not win this war through minor measures. Which is why, in exactly one hundred seventy-nine days and eighteen hours, we will fire this weapon from every orbital platform in the Celestial Expanse at once. Every ghoul, known and unknown, will be destroyed."

Shocked silence ensues, the previous gasps and mutterings felled by the sheer magnitude of Angelou's announcement. *Every* platform in the Expanse? The numbers are nothing short of staggering. I look around at the others, seeing my own disbelief mirrored in the expressions of those nearest me. In the hush that follows, the entire universe seems to hang on a thread, salvation dangling like a mirage before our grasp if only we dare to believe in it.

"And this weapon of mass destruction, which we will use to launch our first ever offensive against the enemy, is called—

"The Archangel."

Archangel. The word whispers through the hall, borne on the lips of military and civilian alike. Idea morphs into reality, the very existence of a name giving the concept substance and form, and in that moment every doubt vanishes in the blink of a pulsar, replaced by something we'd all thought long lost.

Hope.

———

Everything changes with the birth of the Archangel. In the days and weeks that follow, all of R&D falls under the thrall of our new warrior angel. Projects are put on hold, resources diverted, personnel reallocated—all in service to the Archangel, of course. With an offensive of such magnitude to plan and prepare for, not a single person can be spared.

The plan is surprisingly simple. Since nearly every planet and colony is already outfitted with its own OP network, it's not a matter of creating new technology but modifying the existing tech. To that end, schematics with the shield generator modifications will be sent to each location for the locals to implement, along with a software update that will allow us to link each OP into a master system controlled from R&D. Rather than risk the enemy learning of our plan, the schematics and software will be passed off as a minor shield generator improvement—useful, but not particularly significant to the war effort. For locations where OPs are lacking or destroyed, modified drone ships will be sent in to take the places of the missing platforms.

I nod as I listen to Asriel's explanation along with the rest of the Testing Division, for the first time seeing how Angelou's scheme might actually work.

"Where are these drone ships coming from?" asks RC. "Will we be responsible for modifying them?"

"The ships will be pulled from existing military reserves and modified at a few of our most secure shipyards by local personnel. Due to the amount of modifications required, we'll only be able to modify a small number within the established time frame, so the drone ships will only be used where absolutely necessary. A handful of our own engineers will go to oversee the modifications, but otherwise R&D will not be handling this part directly. I believe the Chairman himself is actually overseeing this portion of the plan."

"And the squatters?" asks Xian, Beta's ATL. "The Archangel can wipe out the existing ghoul population, but won't all those squatters out there just breed more ghouls?"

"As soon as the Archangel is deployed, military personnel will immediately drop into newly cleared areas and begin an Expanse-wide evacuation. Squatters will be dosed with Spectranol and relocated to designated quarantine colonies until a cure can be found. In locations where the squatter population is simply too large for full-scale evacuation, those places will remain under full quarantine. The First IG Admiral will be coordinating and directing the relocation efforts."

"What about the orbital platforms that have already been infiltrated by ghouls?" Songbird asks. "We can't exactly ask the enemy to upload our secret weapon for us."

Amusement tinges Asriel's eyes. "I'm so glad you asked, TL. As a matter of fact, that's where *we* come in. It will be our responsibility to infiltrate all enemy-held platforms and complete the modifications ourselves. With*out* tipping our hand to the enemy."

In the silence that follows, I can practically hear the simultaneous dropping of thirty-eight jaws. Predictably, it's Ty who says what we're all thinking. "Ho-ly *slag*."

I close my mouth with a shake of my head. Yeah. That pretty much says it all.

"With all due respect, sir," Archer interjects, clearly having done the mental geography, "I don't see how we could possibly reach all of the OPs in the Expanse within the designated time frame, let alone infiltrate and modify them."

"Yes, and Dr. Angelou has already accounted for that. We will only be modifying the OPs in our quadrant of space. The rest will be carried out by special ops teams chosen personally by the First Admiral for the task. Even so, we'll still have a lot of work to do. So if there aren't any more questions, let's get to it."

Over the next several weeks, everyone in R&D works around the clock preparing for our big offensive. The researchers and engineers continue to test and retest the Archangel, changing up the target areas, enlarging the beam spread, networking and firing various OP combinations, anything and everything that might help them refine and improve upon the prototype. Any perceived flaw no matter how tiny—a questionable line of code in the software, an older bit of hardware—is ruthlessly seized upon for repair, replacement, or redesign. With so many lives riding on the Archangel, even the remotest possibility for failure is unacceptable.

Meanwhile, those of us in the Testing Division are busy gearing up for our own part in the offensive to come. When we're not assisting the researchers, every minute is spent learning the tech modifications, studying OP schematics, developing infiltration methods, and ruthlessly drilling our missions again and again. Recruitment officers bring in wave after wave of new recruits, our numbers first doubling, then tripling with the onslaught of new bodies. As the recruits come in, additional teams are formed and promotions are handed out like candy.

I wait with the other members of the Testing Division in one of the small training rooms as Asriel barks out promotions with the efficiency of a drill sergeant.

"Ty—Team Leader, Zeta Team."

"Zara—Team Leader, Eta Team."

"Evangeline—Assistant Team Leader, Gamma Team."

"Sorenson—Assistant Team Leader, Delta Team."

I blink, not sure I heard right. Me? An Assistant Team Leader? Inwardly, I exult. Not only have I been promoted, but I get to stay with Delta as Archer's ATL.

The rest of Asriel's list goes fairly quickly. By the time he's done, all of the ATLs have been promoted to Team Leaders, and a good number of specialists have been promoted to assistants or even TLs. As the base's best pilot, Chen's been jumped to Pilot Commander—which seems to be roughly equivalent with Team Leader—and put in charge of coordinating the other pilots, as well as plotting and training the aerial maneuvers needed for the mission. A number of other specialists aren't promoted, but reassigned to new teams in order to intermix the newcomers with the veterans. For all that the new recruits are military elite, compared to us they're two-square rookies in need of seasoning.

Later that evening, Delta Team gathers in the Atrium for one last meal before we all move on to our new assignments. The celebration is short but sweet as we reminisce about our best missions and congratulate each other on our promotions. As I raise my glass with the others, the moment cuts like a knife, joy poisoned by the unalienable knowledge that this is *it*. The last day we'll all be together as a team. Not that this is anything new. In the Celestial Guard, people were transferred and reassigned all the time. It never bothered me in the least. But then, I guess there was never anyone in the Guard I cared that much about.

I pause, my heart drenched with the bittersweetness of it all even as my glass hovers halfway up in the air. On my left, Ty frowns at my grim hesitation.

"Cheer up, Sorenson!" she orders in typical Ty fashion. "Half of us got promoted today, and nobody even had to die."

"Amen to that," Archer remarks dryly, a nod to the fact that normally Ty's promotion would've only come upon *his* death, and everybody laughs.

After a second I join in, suddenly feeling sheepish at moping on a night when there's only cause for celebration. Then raising my glass the rest of the way, I toast my fellow Deltas—the ones that have come before and the ones that will come later, but most of all the ones standing here with me today, voices raised in cheer as we celebrate what's to come.

———

"These times are terrible, team! At the rate you're going, the ghouls will get you before you're halfway through. Let's reset and go again."

At Archer's signal, I activate my chit and wirelessly reset the training consoles lined up against the wall. We've been running software drills all morning, teaching the new Deltas how to upload the Archangel software into the OPs, and then timing them as they do it again and again.

With a wave of my hand, I restart the clock. "Go!"

As everyone furiously leaps into action, Archer and I compare the previous training results, withdrawing to the far corner and speaking in low voices about which specialists might be ideal for the actual computer work and which ones would be better off as guards. I covertly watch Archer from the corner of my eye as he jots notes on his tip-pad about each team member, mentally taking my own notes on his methods as TL.

It's only been a week since I was promoted to ATL, but already the role feels like second nature to me. Teaching weaponry and technical skills, running drills, coaching specialists, and assisting Archer. Not only does the work come naturally, but it turns out I'm actually *good* at it. At least, in the training room. Whether this continues to hold true in the field remains to be seen.

"And stop!" Archer calls. "All right, let's see how you all did this time."

We evaluate the current batch of results, provide some coaching tips, and take them through the drill a few more times before breaking for the evening meal. Afterwards, Archer heads to a meeting for TLs while I take the team down to H8.

Habitat 8 is essentially a large cargo bay, used primarily for storing low-security items like extra uniforms, spare parts, and old testing equipment. Cargo lockers line the walls, and the main area is split into two sections: one containing racks of gear, while the other is left open for larger crates and barrels. We walk in to find the place abuzz with activity: shipments streaming in from the landing bays, teams going through cartons of gear, engineers checking items against their specs, and equipment *everywhere*.

With only a matter of weeks before we launch, preparations for the Archangel Offensive are in full swing, which means that the amount of incoming shipments has more than trebled. Additional food supplies, gear for the new recruits, specialized equipment, and hardware needed for the mission itself flow in, among other things. While normally the inventory personnel would handle all incoming shipments, they're not staffed to handle the overload. As a result, some of the testing personnel have been granted temporary access to H8 in order to help with the influx.

I introduce myself to the officer in charge, who checks my clearance and links me a shipping manifest. It will be our job to help check and stow the incoming shipments, verifying the correct items were sent in the correct quantity, visually inspecting the equipment for any signs of damage, and then stowing it in its designated area. The officer in charge gives us a quick demo, pulling a ration pak from a box, scanning it with his chit to verify the serial number, giving it a quick once-over, and then moving on to the next piece.

I arrange my team into a loose assembly line—some fetching the cargo, others scanning and checking it, and the last few stowing—while I watch the manifest for any discrepancies between their scans and the list. It doesn't take anyone long to get the hang of it, and soon we're churning away like a well-oiled machine.

As I watch my team, I can't help feeling a sense of pride. Though the work is mindless and boring, it's essential to the upcoming offensive, an offensive that could change the face of the war permanently. An offensive that *I'm* a part of it. What's more, it's the first command assignment I've led completely on my own. Maybe it's not the same as leading a mission, but somehow I know that if Gran or my parents could see me, they would be proud.

It's late evening when we finally start our last shipment. I program my chit to alert me if it detects any anomalies in the manifest, then grab a stabilizer, thinking to move the work along faster by assisting with the scans. As I go to scan it, a number jumps off the stabilizer at me.

37W-397823-B276

My heart sinks as I stare at the serial number lightly emblazoned on the side of the stabilizer. I *know* that number. At least, every digit up until the last two. Excusing myself from the others, I slip between a couple of equipment racks and discretely pull up the last chip number, the one I found on the shield generator dish from the blown OP. The one I've looked at so many times since that I know it by heart.

37W-397823-B231

The numbers are too close to be a coincidence, which means that the designated piece is *here*. Probably brought in with one of the previous shipments we've been receiving over the past week, assuming the parts were shipped to us in sequential order. However, what I really need to know is whether the part is still in its original carton, bundled up somewhere for loading, or already on a ship.

Rejoining my team, I help them finish the current shipment, purposely keeping our progress slow in the hopes that my team will be the last one here. As we work, I discretely check part numbers. 37W-397823-B277, 37W-397823-B278, 37W-397823-B279. Definitely sequential order. Based on the numbers, I try to calculate how long ago we might have received the part in question. One week, two? If only Teal were here. No doubt she'd be able to calculate it down to the hour without even breaking a sweat. For that matter, she would have this entire mystery solved by now, the perpetrator identified and the problem resolved.

A pang echoes through me at the thought, the usual tightness in my chest that my sister's name evokes for once mixed with something softer.

I miss her.

Maybe I've always missed her, and was just never able to admit it to myself before. I only lived with Gran a few years, and Mom and Dad have missed whole chunks of my life, off doing their duty to the Fleet, but Teal . . . While everyone else came and went, it was always Teal and me.

Until Lia died.

She died and I enlisted, walking off into the galaxy never to look back. Unable to forgive Teal for her part in Lia's demise, even if I'd wanted to. And now that I've walked away, I don't know if I can ever return.

"ATL, we've finished the last carton. Your orders?"

Casting an eye over the habitat, I'm pleased to see that we're the last ones left. I check over the area, verifying the manifest and nodding in satisfaction as I confirm everything is properly inventoried and stowed. "Good work, team. You're dismissed until the training session at 0600 tomorrow morning. Go grab something to eat. You've earned it."

Pulling up the manifest again, I watch them from the corner of my eye as I pretend to be checking a last couple things. Only when the last one has shuffled out do I spring into action. Quickly, I bring up the inventory database, searching for the serial number. I find it on a manifest for a shipment that arrived almost a week ago. According to the records, it was cataloged and stowed but not yet transferred shipboard. So theoretically it should still be in Carton #146D, which is—I glance up at the bay—in that absolutely astronomical pile of cartons over at the west end of the habitat. Of course. With a sigh, I jog over to the pile and get to work.

Though I know the carton number and the pile is arranged in relatively numerical order, it still takes me a good half-hour to clear enough boxes away to get to the one I want. Praying that I remain undisturbed for just a little longer, I pull out my multi-tool and unseal the carton. The stabilizer is more difficult, no obvious catches or fastenings to indicate how I might deconstruct it, and I have to search out a schematic on my chit before I can haltingly pull it apart. When the carapace finally splits open, I let out a breath I hadn't realized I was holding.

There, nestled within the boards and wires, is a small metal chip.

The saboteur is back.

26 "AS I SAID THE FIRST TIME, there's absolutely nothing wrong with this stabilizer."

From the other side of the desk in H8's small office area, I frown at the equipment officer in consternation. "Sir, maybe not on the outside, but did you check the inside? I swear I heard something rattle in there when I dropped it."

"I assure you I did a thorough check. The stabilizer is in perfect condition," she repeats, an edge of impatience in her voice.

"So there was nothing . . . *odd* about the stabilizer when you examined it?"

"Odd? In what way?"

Unable to think of any response to that question that won't eventually end with me in a court-martial, I settle for a *you-got-me* shrug.

She arches an eyebrow as if to imply the only odd thing she sees around here is *me* and replies, "Trust me, it's a simple device. If there were anything broken or 'odd' about it, I would have detected it." When I continue to stand there dumbly, her face softens slightly. "We're all under a lot of stress, ATL. I'm sure whatever sound you heard was just an echo from elsewhere in the bay. Please return to your duties. I'll just put this away for you, shall I?"

"No!" The objection jolts out of me before I can hold it back.

"That is, what I mean to say is, no need, sir. I've already wasted enough of your time. No sense wasting any more when I already know exactly where it goes."

Straight out an airlock!

I extend a hand, and after a sharp look, she passes the stabilizer back. With a nod, I pivot on my heel and walk briskly away—*before* she can change her mind and decide I'm not merely stressed, but bat-slag crazy. Which I'm not entirely convinced I'm not. After weeks of worrying over chip numbers and wading through junk, I've finally discovered the saboteur's next target . . . only to discover they never actually sabotaged it. Of all the twists and turns in this whole affair, this one is easily the most bizarre.

At my first opportunity, I slip the stabilizer into a carton of supplies bound for H7 and take it straight out the door. Back in my small ATL quarters, I pull it out again and try to figure out what to do. Clearly my plan to take it to Asriel, along with the chips, is out. After all, what does a perfectly sound stabilizer prove? Nothing. I'm just glad I decided to get another opinion before taking it to the DC. I would've looked like a total glitch bringing him a "sabotaged" stabilizer that was anything but. It would have been the laser cutter all over again. Which leads me to the real question: Why hasn't it been tampered with?

The saboteur must have handled the stabilizer, or I wouldn't have found the chip inside. However, what kind of saboteur doesn't actually sabotage the equipment? The only explanation I can think of is that whoever it is must have been interrupted before they could finish the job. In that case, maybe I could use the device to set some sort of trap for them? Only, no. With so much traffic going in and out of H8, it would be impossible to monitor a single stabilizer. Besides, who's to say they'll try again with the same part? I consider the issue further and finally shake my head. Maybe I can't determine what the saboteur's up to or even who they are, but perhaps I can determine who they *aren't*.

A quick search through the inventory database shows the stabilizer was part of a shipment delivered directly to H8 seven days ago, which means anyone who didn't have access to the habitat during that time couldn't be the saboteur. Using my newly acquired ATL clearance, I immediately start pulling training and work schedules for everyone in the Testing Division. Despite the upcoming mission, Angelou's natural paranoia is still in full effect, so access to H8 is being granted on a day-to-day basis only. Simply put, if a specialist didn't have a work assignment in H8 for the day, they didn't have access to the habitat.

With so many new specialists, it takes me nearly an hour to go through the schedules, but my hard work pays off. From my list of twenty-five, almost a third have been crossed off by the time I've finished. I review the remaining names, heart sinking as I see who's left. Ty, Archer, and RC. Songbird, Annah, and Evangeline. Chen, Xian, and even Asriel, among others. Almost everyone I've worked closely with since coming to R&D. In fact, the only former Delta I'm able to cross off is Zephyr. No big surprise there. As the best zero-g expert in R&D, he's been running teams through ZG drills on OP EQ-5 almost nonstop since preparations began. It would be ludicrous to put him on supply duty when he's so much more valuable in the vacuum.

So now I'm down to seventeen names. Seventeen suspects is hardly a blinking X on a treasure map, but it's sure a hell of a lot better than thirty-one. With nothing more to be done for now, I'm about to close the list when my eyes go back to those four starred names: Ty. Archer. RC. Chen. The four people with me on Nomia where we were almost stranded. It doesn't escape my notice that even after all the suspects I've managed to eliminate, all four are still on my list. Is that mere coincidence, or is there a reason for that? I have no idea.

With a sigh, I de-ac my chit. My investigations into the stabilizer are getting me nowhere. Even the metallic chip I found inside it, with its lone serial number, yields nothing when I run it through the database. If that number corresponds to yet another piece in this wild goose chase, it's not on the station. At least, not yet.

A buzz from my chit followed by a link from Archer puts an end to any further postulation on the subject, at least for now. With training in ten, I hide the stabilizer in the hygiene unit vent until I can decide what to do with it. Then, with a quick text to Archer, I'm on my way. It's only as I'm stepping into the main training room in H7 that the strangest part of the whole thing suddenly hits me. The stabilizer arrived less than a week ago, and yet I found the chip with the stabilizer's serial number on it over a month earlier.

So how in the universe did the saboteur have a serial number for a part that wasn't even on the station yet?

The extender panel flies through the vacuum toward me, flipping end over end like a giant throwing star aimed directly at my head. No time to run, I de-mag my boots and push off from the platform. The panel whistles past a hairsbreadth from my ear to smash into the generator dish with a noiseless crunch. Broken bits spew from the dish as the panel bounces off the platform and back out into space, flipping and rolling through the void with reckless abandon. Everyone scatters, jetting up or down as they attempt to dodge missiles large and small. By the time anyone thinks to try and catch it, the panel is gone.

"All right, enough! Simulation's over." Archer waves his chit hand, and immediately the lights come back on, followed moments later by air and gravity.

I automatically reorient myself toward the floor as the returning gravity takes me down, landing catlike on my feet among my teammates. Most of the others land as easily, though Jos doesn't quite manage to orient himself in time, flopping onto his stomach with a loud *whumph* that elicits a chorus of chuckles.

Archer, on the other hand, does not look amused. "Would anyone like to tell me what went wrong with that mission?"

"We lost the extender panel," Kagawa volunteers after a minute.

"We broke the generator dish," Jethro adds.

"We almost killed our ATL?" Raisman suggests.

There we go! I roll my eyes, mildly exasperated that my near-death only made third on the list.

We've spent the morning running simulations in preparation for the upcoming mission, but though we know the basic hardware modifications cold, doing them in ZG is turning out to be a different story. Though the lack of gravity is a godsend when dealing with the heavier pieces, the benefit is more than made up for by bulky suits, runaway equipment, and maneuvering errors. Along with my close shave with the panel, we've had two other near-accidents, and everyone is hot, sweaty, and thoroughly exhausted.

Archer doesn't seem to notice, though, intent on getting the modifications 100% perfect. He reads us the riot act for a good twenty minutes, going over every single thing we did wrong. At last, I seize a moment to pull him aside.

"TL?" I say quietly with a nod to the time. "It's been six hours. They need a break."

Archer blinks, clearly surprised at how late it is. He looks stressed, as though the weight of the Expanse is on his shoulders, and I wonder if it's just the pressure of the mission or something more personal weighing him down. Before I can inquire further, he nods.

"You're right, Sorenson." He rubs his forehead with the heel of his hand. "Give them a lunch."

"Yes, sir."

I dismiss the team, catching more than a few grateful looks in the process, and then deactivate the training room. Briefly, I debate the merits of a shower versus a meal and go for the meal, jumping a slidewalk to the Central Habitat, where I head for the nearest mess. I'm taking a seat at a table in the corner when I hear:

"Sarai? Sarai Chen!"

In the next aisle over, Chen stops, arrested by the sound of her name. She searches the crowd, eyes widening as she catches sight of Hawkins, one of our new pilots, bounding toward her. I barely have time to murmur, *What the . . . ?* before Hawkins throws his arms around her in a giant bear hug.

I goggle at the pair, uncertain which surprises me more: Hawkins' temerity in daring to hug the staid Chen or the fact that she actually seems to be hugging him back. When they finally separate, my astonishment only grows.

Chen is *smiling.*

In my entire time at R&D, I don't think I've ever seen her smile. Not like this, with her eyes shining and teeth showing, words flying back and forth between her and Hawkins with an enthusiasm almost the polar opposite of her normally stoic demeanor. The transformation is nothing short of mind-boggling.

"My God, Hawkins! How did you . . . ? I mean, when did you get here?"

Hawkins shrugs. "They came to the Aces looking for pilots for a dangerous mission, so I thought, what the hell? Shipped out the next day and arrived on base a two-square ago."

"I can't believe you're here!"

"*You* can't believe *I'm* here? I almost died when I looked over and saw you standing there. God, how long has it been now? Thirteen, fourteen months?"

"Just about." Chen nods, amazement and joy radiating from her face.

I'm so blown away by the remarkable change in her that it takes a second for their words to sink in. Thirteen or fourteen months? But Chen only arrived a couple of months before me, maybe seven or eight months ago. In our conversation, she'd made it sound like she'd transferred directly from the Aces to R&D. So where the hell was she for the six months in-between?

"The old team is going to spit stars when I tell them who I found here," Hawkins continues. "Damn! Star Pilot First Class Sarai Chen, back from the dead."

"Dead?" Chen's smile drops from her eyes, the lights inside fading though her mouth never changes, and in that instant the real Chen is back. Or at least, the Chen I know. If Hawkins notices the change, he doesn't indicate it.

"You know what I mean. No hmails, no links. It was like you dropped into a black hole."

"Oh, that. Sorry, I just—"

"No, I get it," Hawkins interrupts with a sidelong look around the habitat. "You'd moved on, you were part of something bigger. I didn't get it then, but now that I'm here, now that I'm part of this place, I understand. You chose to do something greater, Sarai. No one can fault you for that."

His words are nothing but complimentary, and yet if anything, Chen's eyes only go graver. It's a strange contrast, the serious eyes juxtaposed against the effervescent smile, as though two completely different versions of Chen, past and present, have been suddenly, abruptly thrown together, with neither version able to quite fit together with the other. Once again, I find myself wondering where she was in those six months between the Aces and R&D. What happened to wipe the radiant smile from her face?

Her conversation with Hawkins wraps up a minute later, the two sharing another quick embrace before splitting off in opposite directions. I watch Chen disappear across the Atrium and shake my head. Perhaps I'm reading something into nothing. As Gran always used to say: *War changes us all.* I, more than anyone, know how true that is.

Forking down my last few bites of Snap'n'Pesto, I bus my tray and head back to H7. The rest of the day brings more training, as well as an evening meeting with the other TLs and ATLs to brainstorm possible infiltration strategies for the upcoming mission. With many of the OPs infested with ghouls, squatters, or both, getting in to upload the software and then safely out again is the primary concern on everyone's mind.

"It's not the squatters that worry me so much as the ghouls," Xian, Beta's TL, says. "Trapped in an enclosed space on foot, with no vehicles and nowhere to run. We might as well just paint the words 'ghoul bait' on our foreheads and be done with it."

"It's too bad they never got those sound amplifiers figured out," Ty comments. "Repelling ghouls with a few amplifiers would be a lot easier and more effective than using launchers."

I frown, recalling the field of amplifiers we laid on Javeyn and never heard about again. "What ever happened with those anyway?"

Ty shrugs. "I asked Dr. Rahman about them a week ago, thinking they might be useful on the mission. He said they'd run multiple tests using the field we set up but that the results were—in his words— 'puzzling.'"

I raise one eyebrow. *Puzzling?* Whatever that means. Sometimes I think the good researchers of R&D are purposely obscure just to make themselves sound smarter. For now, I suppose we'll have to make do with launchers and gas grenades.

A memory from my last day on New Sol Space Station pops into my head, and I stop, a smile slowly curling around my lips as I recall just how we forced the ghouls into the Central Hub, away from the people. Leaning in close, I clear my throat to grab everyone's attention. "I have an idea."

With all eyes on me, I explain my plan. Nervously at first—*what if they think it's completely deficient?*—but encouraged by the nodding heads and thoughtful looks, I grow more confident with every word I say. When at last I finish and Asriel says, "We could do something with that," I feel as exhilarated as if I had just finished a fifty-meter dash with a shiver of ghouls on my tail.

We continue conferencing for the next hour before finally breaking for the night. Exhausted after an endless day, I return to my quarters, ready for nothing so much as a good night's sleep. It's only when I grab my towel and walk into the hygiene unit that I realize my day isn't done yet. Directly before me is the air vent, and still hidden away inside—

The stabilizer.

———

The soft vibration of my chit stirs through my palm, waking me from sleep. I flick my index finger to quiet it, blinking several times as my eyes adjust to the dim emergency lighting. I glance across the floor to my roommate. 'Vange lies atop the opposite bunk like a felled tree, arms flung out and chest heaving slowly in and out. Definitely asleep.

Rising from bed, I pull on a pair of trousers and slip into the adjoining hygiene unit. The stabilizer is exactly where I left it, hidden within the vent. I tuck it into my pants pocket, yanking my shirt down to cover the protruding cylinder. It blouses out in an obvious bulge, and I casually position my arm to block the shape as I make my way out of the room and into the corridor. My caution is unnecessary, though. The corridor is completely empty.

The nearest airlock lies in an alcove just off the main lounge. In theory, it's a secured door that can only be opened with the authorization of the DC or other higher-up. In practice, it's been the site of many a rookie hazing or drunk dare, and most anyone who's been in the Testing Division for a few months knows how to open it without setting off any alarms. Including me.

The inner doors hiss open with a crisp puff, the cool air raising goosebumps along my bare arms and exposed neck. Through the clear crystal of the outer doors, the moonlit sky beckons, the curling mists awash in a silvery glaze, flickering and twisting up through the dark. I rest my forehead against the cool crystal and look out. In the dark of the night, with the whole station sleeping and the lilting silence echoing through the halls, I feel like my heart might split apart with loneliness.

Her presence, her poise; I never knew I was incomplete until she made me whole.

I close my eyes, Lia's face hovering just out of reach in the facets of my mind. Then lifting my head, I push away from the crystal, breaking free from the siren song of night beyond the door and all she might offer. Grabbing the stabilizer, I toss it to the floor and step back into the station. Warm air surrounds me as the inner doors shut behind me, locking away the chill of the night. The stabilizer lolls on the floor just inside, cold and alone. For a moment, I just stare at that mysterious device and all it might represent.

Then with a twist of my wrist, I open the outer doors, depressurize the airlock, and send the stabilizer hurtling into space.

No doubt the energy shield around R&D will vaporize the stabilizer on contact, and if not, the ever-shifting bands of the planetary net lurking just below will do the job. And yet for some reason, when I finally go back to bed and close my eyes, I have the strangest dream:

That of the stabilizer soaring down through the darkened mists to land deep within the ghoul-ridden city waiting far below.

27

SHADOWS FLICKER DOWN through the sky-light above, casting the room in a web of shifting light. From my place at the far end of the observation lounge, I lift my gaze to the ceiling, stomach clenched as I look up through the swirling mists. Sunlight drapes across my face, dappling my cheeks in a ripple of warmth. It flickers once again, in a quick pull between light and dark, then goes out entirely, blocked by something unseen just beyond the veil. I stare up into the sky, searching, searching for the thing blotting out the sun on the other side of the curtain . . .

Through the mists she comes, sleek and strong, her black carapace glinting like the darkest obsidian against the pale pastel furls: a raptor-class carrier. Heavy armor plating wraps her hull, armaments bristling across it like rows of vicious teeth beneath the transparent flicker of the shields, and despite her small size, it's clear she's a predator. A very *fast* predator, judging from the shape of her thrusters and the size of her exhaust core. From my vantage point, I can see at least three shuttles fitted into her sides, like missiles, slim and deadly.

More shapes appear in the mists, identical to the first, dropping down on all sides of us in perfect sync, like a wolf pack moving in for the kill. Gasps ring out around me, stunned murmurs whispering through the deck, but I don't make a sound. I don't do anything but stand at parade rest, hands clasped behind my back as I watch the fleet settle into a perfect circular formation around us. The faintest smile cracks my lips.

Our ride is here.

A frisson of excitement passes through me at the thought. In exactly two weeks, every member of the Testing Division will board one of those ships, scattering through the Expanse on a mission to install the mighty Archangel on every ghoul- and squatter-ridden OP in Celestia. But we won't be working alone. While we're facing off against the enemy, schematics for the required shield modifications and software uploads will be sent to all human-held platforms so that local personnel can begin the upgrades, while drone ships are sent in to cover any missing or blown OPs. Entire naval fleets will be on the move, evacuation transports and carriers laden with Celestial Guardians and other infantry moving into position so they can begin the squatter evacs as soon as the Archangel does its work. It could be the offensive that wins us the war . . . or loses it. The knowledge of all that's riding on this one strike is terrifying when I stop to think about it.

"Now that is one sick ship," 'Vange says, a cocky grin on his face as he surveys the nearest raptor. "Maybe we're all gonna get blown to hell, but at least we're going in style."

"Hey, speak for yourself! I fully intend to live," Ty puts in.

"They've got a lot of weaponry considering they're essentially transport ships," Chen remarks.

"Good!" comes 'Vange's response. "Means those mother-fraggin' Specs will think twice before tangling with us."

Chen raises an eyebrow at that, a speculative look in her eyes, but otherwise doesn't respond. I find myself intensely curious as to what she's thinking right now, but before I have a chance to ask, a quiet voice speaks.

"They look like death. Appropriate, considering we're going off in them to commit genocide."

All eyes go to the speaker. Songbird stands at the far viewport, hands braced on the sill as she looks out through the mists at those black raptors crouching just out of reach. When no one speaks, she glances over her shoulder at us. Her normally sharp features seem downright forbidding; her expression could cut glass.

"That is the word for it, I believe," she says mildly, "when you set out to wipe another species off the face of the universe."

Stunned silence. Then—

"Because they're about to wipe *us* out!" Ty bursts out.

Several shouts of agreement back her up, choruses of "Yeah!" and "No kidding!" A specialist from Iota starts to move toward Songbird, a dangerous look on his face, only to be checked by a sharp look from his TL.

"This is lunar talk," someone mutters, followed by another's, "I can't even believe we're discussing this."

"What choice do we really have?" RC intercedes, his easy tone the very voice of reason. "We have no method for imprisoning them, and all communication efforts have failed. Maybe if we had a way to cure squatters once they're infected it would be different, but we don't. If we sit back and do nothing, we could all be infected in a year from now."

"Perhaps," Songbird agrees, "but just because they would wipe us out, does it make us any less a monster, that we would do the same?"

Denials greet her assertion, but they're fewer and less emphatic than the ones from a minute ago. Gazes drop and heads bow, and it's clear Songbird's words haven't fallen completely on deaf ears.

After a moment, Ji, the ATL of Kappa, points out, "There's still tons of Specs left on New Earth."

"Sure, until we finish with the ones *here*," a specialist from Alpha mutters.

"You don't really think—?"

"Why wouldn't they?" Xian says. "Once we wipe out all the ghouls in the Expanse, what's to stop anyone from going straight to New Earth and finishing the job? All it would take is a handful of drone ships. Purely in the name of self-defense, of course."

"So what if they slaggin' do?" 'Vange jumps in. "They're just *animals*. Brain-suckin' alien scum! Species go extinct all the time and no one cares. Why should we now?"

"You can't really believe that," Ty objects. "We may not like them, but these things are as intelligent as we are. They work in concert, they coordinate and plan attacks using solid strategy—"

"Plenty of animals hunt in coordinated packs," 'Vange interrupts. "That doesn't make the fraggers intelligent, only cunning predators."

"He may have a point," RC says reluctantly, his face pained at the prospect of actually having to agree with 'Vange. "If you analyze the Spectres' overall strategy, it doesn't really hold up."

"How do you mean?" Ty asks.

"We all know that in order to reproduce, the Spectres require physical hosts to breed, right? So a species with higher intelligence— an intelligence at least on par with our own—would maintain and breed a preserve of uninfected hosts so that they might continue to reproduce indefinitely. However, if you analyze their patterns of attack, the Spectres don't seem to be doing that at all. Rather than trap or hold hosts for future use, they simply infect all humans within a given target area. While this allows them to harvest more hosts now, those same hosts will be deceased within a few years. If they continue with these tactics, all they'll end up with in the long run is an empire of dead humans, an enormous number of ghouls, and no hosts for any of them. Take Telluria as an example. In a few years, the entire Alliance will be nothing more than a ghost town."

RC stops, face falling at the words, and I'm suddenly reminded of what Ty once told me about his Tellurian wife, lost to the Specs on the other side of the Alliance. Clearly he still feels her loss deeply. Does he blame the Expanse for what happened to her? Enough to sabotage the Celestian war effort? My mind flashes to my list, to the star next to his name. With his engineering background, he could easily rig basic equipment to malfunction or blow, and possibly even override the security on my locker to plant the laser cutter without being caught. I watch him from the corner of my eye, torn between guilt and unease at my suspicions.

"Just because their strategy seems nonsensical to us doesn't mean they're not intelligent," someone from Gamma objects, pulling me from my train of thought.

"True. Look at all the deficient things *we* do," another adds, eliciting a chorus of wry chuckles.

The discussion continues, but the longer it goes on, the more I find my attention drifting from the words themselves to the people who are speaking them. Or rather, to the people who *aren't* speaking. The taciturn Chen's silence doesn't really surprise me, but what about Archer? Annah? Both have stayed out of this debate about our genocidal mission. Do they have reason to hide their true feelings about this war, or does some other reason keep them silent?

My mind unwittingly goes to the stabilizer I found not so long ago. While flushing it should have quelled my nerves, they've only increased since then, knotting my gut into a tangle of anxiety that only tightens more with each passing day. Once again I find myself wishing that laser cutter had never shown up in my locker. Finding that cutter was like stepping in quicksand, treading over a seemingly harmless patch of mud only to find myself sunk up to my waist before I even knew what was happening. Everything I've done since then has only made it worse, burying me deeper in the muck with no way out. If I tell anyone what I've found out, I'll be court-martialed and jailed for sure, if only for all the rules I've broken in the course of my investigation. Maybe it would be worth it if I could finger the saboteur . . . but I can't. Not that I haven't tried.

I've continued to check the inventory database every day to see if the serial number from the stabilizer's chip has shown up, but to no avail. Additionally, I've used my higher clearance as ATL to research all five items, checking installation and service logs to see if there was a common denominator—a single person who installed or serviced all of the parts at some point. However, nothing in the records indicated a common party. Storage records didn't help either. The five parts were stored in three different habitats manned by three different sets of equipment personnel, so any suspicions I might have developed toward the equipment officers evaporate before they can form.

In fact, given the catalog of affected locations, I'm not certain how anyone in R&D could be getting access to all the items that have been sabotaged. OP EQ-1, H5, Landing Bay 6, H3, OP NE-2, H8. The sheer array of locations is nothing short of mind-boggling. While OP EQ-1 is open to all incoming and outgoing traffic, OP NE-2 could only be accessed by the OP's staff and a select team of WMGD personnel. H3, where the blown power relay originated, is for power and maintenance workers, while regular access to the landing bays is restricted to flight personnel. Only members of the Testing Division are cleared for H5, and H8 is the Inventory Personnel's domain. While someone might manage to gain access to one or two normally off-limit areas for mission or prep purposes, I don't know how anyone could conceivably gain access to all areas. So how could a single saboteur move from place to place so easily?

I'd almost think it was Angelou—who else could get such unfettered access across the station?—but for the gleam in his eyes when he looks upon R&D, the tenor of his voice when he speaks of his sky home. For beneath his cagey exterior and cold brilliance, his love for R&D is the truest thing about him, and I can't help thinking that like the proverbial captain on his sinking ship, the death of R&D would mean the death of Angelou himself.

"You okay, Sorenson?"

Archer's hail breaks me from my trance. I look up to find that at some point during my ruminations, the debate ended and everyone began scattering. Only Archer, myself, and a few others remain.

"I'm okay. Just thinking."

Archer raises an eyebrow. "Oh?"

My hand strays to my jacket pocket, mind going to those five chips secreted inside. Confession rests on the tip of my tongue, the sudden urge to tell him what's really on my mind almost overpowering despite the consequences that would come as a result, but I can't quite make myself do it. Though I trust him with my life, there's still some small part of me that doubts, though I'm not sure whether it's him I doubt or just my own judgment. Instead I ask, "Do you believe what Songbird said back there? About us being instruments of genocide?"

Several heartbeats pass. "It doesn't matter what I believe," he finally answers. "It doesn't matter what any of us believe. We have a job to do, simple as that."

"So you would do it even if it turns out to be wrong?" I ask.

"I'm a soldier. It's my job to follow orders, not question them."

"Then you *do* agree with Songbird."

Archer's eyes harden. "I didn't say that."

I peer at him through narrowed eyes, trying to make him out. To determine once and for all if he truly is the man I believe him to be or someone else altogether. His normally genial demeanor is gone, eclipsed by a set jaw and knitted brow, and try as I might, I find it impossible to see through the stony exterior to the man below.

"Are you having doubts about the upcoming mission, Sorenson?"

"Sir? I . . ."

"Because if you go out into the field with doubts, you won't only get yourself killed, you'll get everyone under you killed. Songbird may disagree with our mission, but when she's out there, she's committed one hundred percent. And if her people die, it won't be because she let them down. Understand?"

I slowly nod. "Yes, I think I do."

"Good."

He claps me briefly on the shoulder and walks away, but though those five chips are still burning a hole through my jacket pocket, I don't call him back. For despite all the names I've managed to eliminate, Archer's is still sitting squarely at the top of my list, and as much as I may want to, I can't cross him out.

———

The next couple of weeks pass quickly, everyone in R&D working like mad to complete the final preparations for our upcoming launch. Supplies and equipment are allocated and loaded onto each ship, last-minute tweaks to the Archangel are tested and finalized, and mission strategies are endlessly drilled. With so much to accomplish before we launch, interdepartmental lines are blurrier than ever as everyone pitches in to get the necessary jobs done, regardless of where they're from. Even Angelou, once a distant figure I only occasionally spotted in passing, is now often seen in this habitat or that, directing operations or coordinating with one of the department heads.

I see him in the Atrium one morning, and the idea of talking to him about the chips flits briefly through my mind . . . but no. In the hierarchy of R&D, Angelou is God and I'm an ant. Anything I had to say to him would have to go to my CO and up the chain of command. Not to mention that I'm still humiliated by the way I broke down in his office. I'm not sure I could go back and face him one-on-one for any reason.

Angelou's is not the only familiar face I encounter. Afternoon comes, and I find myself loading a cargo hold with a flight mechanic on my right and a familiar researcher on my left.

"Dr. Inoue," I blurt in surprise, recognizing the slight man from the Caraquin mission where we tested the sniffer.

He drops the carton he's holding, eyes widening as he takes me in. "Tech Specialist Sorenson?"

"It's Assistant Team Leader now, but yes."

Awkward silence descends over us, neither quite sure what to say. I help him retrieve the carton he dropped, stowing it back in the hold with ease. Together we finish unpacking the grav sled he brought in.

"Preparations are nearing completion," Inoue says. "I suppose you and your team will be shipping out soon."

"Only a few weeks now," I agree.

"Have you been assigned to a carrier?"

"Not yet. According to my TL, we should be finding out any day now."

"Good, good."

Silence descends again, Inoue's supply of small talk apparently exhausted and mine nonexistent. We finish securing the cargo, and I reactivate the sled in preparation for another load.

"I was sorry to hear about your teammate," Inoue offers suddenly. "When the shooting started, she was the one who pushed me down, used her own body to block the shooters. She was a very brave woman."

"She was."

Inoue looks down, fingers fidgeting nervously as he studies the floor. "I behaved badly that day. You and your team must have thought I was a terrible coward. I'm sorry."

I have a sudden vision of a basket of flowers, and with it a note, its words awkward but sincere.

I'm sorry about your teammate. She saved my life. I won't forget.

How much courage must it have taken to offer that clumsy token? After spending the past year running away from my emotions, the courage to speak from the heart is something even I can appreciate, if not always do. I offer the engineer a wry smile. "Courage comes in many forms. It's just that not every type holds up well under gunfire."

He laughs at that, and together we go for another load.

Despite the weeks of hard work, everyone remains in high spirits, excited to take the war to our enemy instead of merely waiting for their next inevitable strike. And strike they do, taking down a series of small orbital mining rigs two systems over. The population of the OMRs is small, and the losses relatively minor compared to some of the targets the Specs have previously hit; however, the sheer proximity of the rigs to R&D gives everyone pause. Are the OMRs simply a gateway, a stepping stone as the Specs make their way inevitably toward R&D, or is their location mere happenstance? Whatever the answer, an edge of fear creeps into the station, tingeing the edges of our anticipation with a frisson of encroaching danger impossible to ignore.

Meanwhile, final teams for the launch are confirmed. Delta is assigned to the carrier *Infinity* under the command of Major Estes, along with Songbird's Gamma, Xian's Eta, and Iota Team, where RC was transferred. Though I've never met Estes before, I've seen her around the base a few times during my stay here. A tall, humorless woman in her fifties, she nonetheless has an impeccable reputation among the military staff, and the TLs agree she's a good choice for CO. After running mission scenarios with her at the helm for a week, I'm inclined to agree.

As the days drop from the calendar with dizzying swiftness, I look toward Launch Day with a combination of excitement and fear, only one question on my mind. Will this be the offensive that wins us the war?

Or loses it?

28 CRUNCH! The energy converter breaks apart into a million bits, crushed to death by the recycler's mammoth compactor. I survey the mangled pieces with satisfaction. *That's* never going to convert anything again. If, in fact, it was ever intended to convert anything in the first place.

I sweep the pieces into the recycler and lean back against the wall with a sigh. The energy converter arrived on base eighteen hours ago, part of the very last shipment received before our launch tomorrow. The data chip from the stabilizer I spaced led me right to it. Good thing I continued to check the inventory database for the serial number from the stabilizer chip every day. Like all the previous items I'd found, the energy converter contained a data chip with a single serial number programmed on it: 62M-071837-J572. A number which has since proven to be nonexistent in R&D's database. Even more confounding, the converter, when checked over, turned out to be perfectly sound.

Not that the fact was enough to stop me from putting it through the compactor anyway. After what happened to OP NE-2, I'm not taking any chances.

With a shake of my head, I leave the recycling facility and head back to the Central Habitat. It doesn't make any sense. I could believe the saboteur missed one device—failed to sabotage it properly or got interrupted before they could finish the job—but two? Either this is one inept saboteur—an unlikely theory, given the effectiveness of their earlier work—or there's more going on here than simple sabotage. Maybe these latter two devices weren't meant to blow up or malfunction but do something else entirely. Not that I have any idea what that might be.

Nor have I figured out how the saboteur could know the serial number of an item that hadn't even arrived on the station yet. Could it be that the saboteur is off the station? A supply tech or manufacturing grunt who's tampering with the equipment and adding those strange chips before the items even arrive on base? The idea makes a lot of sense until I remember the laser cutter. *Someone* planted it in my locker, which means that even if they have a partner off-base, there's still a saboteur on R&D.

It all comes back to the data chips. Why leave a data chip with the serial number of the next device in line to be tampered with in each item? It's like they *want* their plans to be foiled. In which case, why bother with the sabotage at all? Either that or the chips are a message, even a map of sorts. A trail leading to something much bigger lurking somewhere down the road. The thought sends chills through me. They already blew up an entire platform; how much bigger can they go? My gaze flicks up to the ceiling, my mind's eye envisioning the Archangel with its network of platforms spreading out across the Expanse, and I shiver.

Engrossed in thought, I grab a slidewalk in the Central Habitat, letting it take me around the outer ring while I continue to ponder the situation. While I still don't have an answer to my biggest questions, the one good thing is that I caught the energy converter within hours of its arrival on R&D. With only a handful of teams in the supply habitat during that time, I was able to cut my list from seventeen all the way down to six. On the list of people I was able to eliminate were Kagawa, my roommate Evangeline, and Chen, who's spent the week stuck on flight duty doing supply runs 24/7. Her schedule was so tight, I doubt she had time to take a leak between flights, let alone sabotage anything. I count off the remaining suspects in my head.

Archer
RC
Ty
Songbird
Xian
Annah

All people I've worked with for months in one capacity or another. What's more, with the exception of Ty and Annah, all of them are on my carrier, the *Infinity*. Something lurches in the pit of my stomach at the thought of one of my fellow testers being a traitor. Javeyn, Caraquin, Prism. In the months since coming to R&D, we've been through so much together, from crazy missions to painful casualties, all in pursuit of one united goal: to win this war. Though I've known from the beginning that the saboteur had to be someone from the Testing Division, I can hardly bear the thought that one of them has sold us out. Nor can I comprehend it. What could someone possibly gain from sabotaging our efforts? Despite my misgivings, I've continued to hunt for the saboteur, closing in on them a little more each day, but with Launch Day almost here, time is quickly running out.

I arrive back at H5 to find that my new mission uniform has arrived. Jacket, pants, gloves, utility belt. A sleek black EVA suit so thin I can barely believe it'll withstand the vacuum. New body armor with matching helmet, custom-made just for me and outfitted with the latest tech. I run my hands over each piece in turn, marveling at the sheer quality inherent in each and every part, from the perfect stitching of my name across the jacket to the flawless plating of the armor. I remember what Ty said that day OP NE-2 blew:

They do care when it's us.

Looking at this uniform, at the obvious craftsmanship that went into it from design to creation, I realize she's right. They do care, and somehow that knowledge only makes the attire before me that much greater.

Well, better make sure it fits, right?

Stripping off my service dress, I kit up one piece at a time. The uniform comes first, followed by the EVA suit, the utility belt, the mag boots, and then the armor. Everything fits perfectly, from the cut of the fabric down to the shape of the plating. My helmet comes last, the solid carapace sliding smoothly over my head in one easy motion. All I need is my launcher and stunner to complete the picture, except that both are currently in the armory with the rest of my tech equipment. Waving that minor detail away, I digitize a portion of the wall into a mirror. I've never seen myself in full battle dress before, and the sight raises an eyebrow.

Is that how I look?

The man in the mirror looks strong, capable—commanding, even, in the gold-trimmed black mission suit. He's the sort of man who could lead a team into ghoul-infested platforms and just possibly bring them out again alive. The sort of man who could go toe-to-toe with a delusion of squatters and come out on top. But even more than that, he's a man who cares about something much greater than himself. A man who would sacrifice his life for a cause for no other reason than because he *believes* in it.

Just like Lia did.

I slowly step back from the mirror, stunned by the revelation. Lia gave her life because she believed in something greater than herself, and though I understood her choice with my head, I never grasped it with my heart. Until now.

Did she once stand where I'm standing now, staring into her soul only to discover a hidden depth, a greatness she never knew she possessed? I suppose I'll never know. Still, just the thought that I'm standing in her shoes and walking in her steps makes me feel closer to her than I've felt since the day she went up over New Sol in a blaze of light.

———

I rise early the next morning, too anxious to sleep. Launch Day is finally here, and though I know our first platform run is a couple of days out yet, nervous anticipation still simmers in my gut at the thought of our impending mission. Dressing, I hit the gym for a workout and then the showers, the familiar motions doing much to steady my nerves.

Back in my room after a quick breakfast in the mess, I check the time once again: 0710. Plenty of time before I have to catch my ride out of here. Too much time. I glance at 'Vange with envy, still snooz-ing away on the bunk across the room, face buried in his pillow. If he's nervous about the offensive to come, it's sure not affecting his sleep at all.

Dropping onto my bunk, I drum my feet against the floor, trying to decide what to do. It occurs to me I should link my folks, and Gran, too. I haven't spoken to them in ages, and who knows when my next oppor-tunity may come. Depending on how the mission goes, it might never come at all. I should take the chance while I have it, though the thought of linking them and telling them I'm about to go off on a mission and may never return seems overwhelmingly morbid, even if it's true.

In the end, I decide to send them all hmails instead of linking in per-son, worrying over the words for a full half-hour until 'Vange rolls over and sits up with a huff. He lobs his pillow at me with a cranky scowl.

"Geez, Sorenson! Just tell them you love 'em and leave it at that."

"Is that what you did?"

'Vange lets out a bitter snort. "Hell, I don't have anyone *to* tell."

Yawning widely, he grabs his towel and disappears into the hy-giene unit we share with the ATLs in the room on the other side. As the door shuts behind him, I consider his advice with an approving nod. *Not a bad idea.*

The messages I finally record are short and sweet, saying I love them and hope to see them again soon. Sending off the three mes-sages, I'm about to de-ac my chit, only to pause as one more face flits into my mind.

Teal.

I haven't spoken to her in almost a year and a half. Not since the night before I enlisted and shipped out, that day we had our last ar-gument. No matter how many links she sent or how hard Gran begged, I just couldn't bring myself to talk to her. I was too angry. Too mired in pain and betrayal to listen to words that seemed no more than an empty salve. But it's been months now, and the rage that once seemed so uncompromising has vanished. Or at least di-minished into something smaller, less hurtful, as though the flow of time has leached the worst of the poison from the wound, leaving only an ordinary pain.

I stare at the open hmail window and sigh. She *is* my sister.

Opening up a new message, I slowly crook my index finger to start recording. I draw in a deep breath, preparing to speak . . . and release it. Take in another breath, sudden and quick, only to let that one, too, slip from my lungs unspent. The minutes stretch out, and still I stand there, staring at my chit as I breathe in, breathe out. But no matter how hard I try, the words don't come. Maybe the pain has lessened, but the wound is still there.

With a shake of my head, I erase the message and deactivate my chit. Then, grabbing my duffle, I take one last look around and leave the room.

Out in the station, it's chaos. Support staff running here and there, frenzied looks on their faces as they complete whatever last-minute tasks have slipped their minds till now; testers heading to the landing bays where they'll catch their rides out; researchers lining the outer viewports as they wait to see our fleet off, their months of labor finally come to fruition.

I catch a tender to the Secondary AP, where the *Infinity* awaits me and the rest of my team. Striding through the corridor, I scan the walls, looking for something that will tell me which landing bay is mine. I'm outside Landing Bay 7 when my chit buzzes to signal an incoming text. It's from Ty. Probably linking with a final farewell. I flick my finger to pull up the message.

EMERGENCY IN LANDING BAY 4! COME ASAP!!

The words spool across my palm in a blaze of red. Images of Zel flash through my head, and I don't think, I don't ask questions, I just drop my bag and take off across the platform. Over a stack of cartons and around a grav-sled, I run helter-skelter through the maze of personnel and cargo, my only thoughts of getting to the loading bay before it's too late. My feet pound hard against the decking, eyes scanning the signs for my destination as I fly by.

Landing Bay 6.

Past an officer with a tip-pad and between a pair of engineers in silver tunics, their startled shouts echoing through the crowded terminal behind me. I glimpse a med-kit on a wall up ahead, and I detour just enough to rip it from its moorings. It slips through my grasp, nearly dropping to the floor in my haste, but I manage to tuck it under my arm and keep going.

Landing Bay 5.

I dash through a knot of support staff and leap over a pile of ration paks, long stride clearing the sacks with ease. Through the crowded concourse, I can just make out the edge of the fourth ring up ahead, and I put on a burst of speed as I skirt around a heavy bulkhead. Another few strides and I'm there, charging through the hatch, med-kit in hand as I scan the room for the emergency.

Quizzical looks meet my entrance, heads turning and brows knitting at my dramatic arrival. The bay is surprisingly full, a good thirty people or so milling about the space, seemingly at loose ends as they stand in clumps and talk. A couple of supply personnel are stowing a last load onto the ship, while an officer on duty oversees the final prep. I don't see anyone who looks to be in distress.

Ty steps from the crowd just then. She catches sight of me, eyes flicking down and back up again, and bursts out laughing.

I frown, sensing something's off but not quite sure what it is. "I'm here. Now what's the emergency?"

"Oh, that," she says. "Zephyr's transport is about to take off, and we haven't gotten a digital of the old team yet."

My mouth drops open. "*That's* the big emergency?"

"Would you have come if I'd said to turn out for a photo op?"

I scowl, which is apparently all the answer she needs.

"Exactly. But hey, full marks for speed and preparation." She claps me on the shoulder with a cheeky wink and a nod toward the kit in my hands. "I'd drop the med-kit for the digital, though."

My cheeks burn, but I drop the kit and follow her over to the far end of the bay anyway. All of the original members of the Testing Division—pre-Archangel—are here, at least the ones who are still alive. Ty and Archer. Zephyr, RC, and Chen. Kagawa and Songbird, 'Vange and Annah, Xian and all the rest from Alpha, Beta, Gamma, and Delta. Even Asriel has turned out as DC and former Delta Leader. I raise an eyebrow, wondering if this team picture will eventually join the other one already digitized on his desk.

"Come on, people! We don't have much time. Group together now, group together!"

Everyone starts bunching together, forming into a ragged mass in front of a line of shuttles. I hover on the fringes, not quite sure where to go, before slipping in near the back. Hands grab my arm, pulling me through the crowd until I find myself surrounded by Deltas. Ty and Archer on either side of me, RC, Raisman, and Kagawa in the row just before us, with Chen and Zephyr down front. The officer on duty holds up her chit hand, palm toward us as she prepares to take the picture.

"Smile, Sorenson." Ty gives me a shove on the shoulder. "It's a digital, not a funeral."

So I do. Surrounded by the people I've trained with and sweated with, eaten with and risked my life with, I grin as the duty officer captures the moment forever in a digital image that will continue to endure long after the people in it have fallen.

An hour later, I'm standing on the lower observation deck of the *Infinity*, watching as the pastel glow of Prism falls away beneath us and wondering if I'll ever see it again.

Onboard Sky Station Epsilon-065
Secret Research Base for Division 7

THE CARRIERS ROSE UP FROM the mists, breaking atmosphere to sail up past the exospheric line and into space. Black on black, they soared almost invisibly against the void's dark expanse, sleek and silent like a fleet of predators on the hunt. For survival, for vengeance. For the taste of redemption slicked hot and heavy across the blood-soaked stars.

Hands clasped behind his back, the Doctor watched them fly away through the night until they were gone from every last feed flickering over the curved walls of his sky-lit office. Though he didn't consider himself a sentimental man by any means, he couldn't help feeling a surge of pride at their passing. Pride, hope . . . and fear. The sort of icy disquietude that only comes when the very highest of hopes are pitted against the very worst of repercussions should one fail. But, as he reminded himself time and time again—

Failure was not an option.

Clearing away the center feeds, the Doctor linked into the interstellar communications buoy in orbit. Both recipients responded directly to his links, faces filling the ports on either side of him. He greeted them with two words:

"They're away."

The Admiral nodded once. "As are my people. And everything else?"

"*The schematics and software for the OP modifications are being transmitted to all staffed OPs as we speak, under the guise of a routine security upgrade. Once the software uploads have been completed, we should be able to link every OP into the master system.*"

"*Good. What about the ships?*" she asked with a glance at the Chairman.

"*The drone ships have been modified and sent out as ordered,*" the Chairman confirmed. "*All should reach their target destinations on schedule. Additionally, all hardware necessary for the modifications has been manufactured and distributed where needed.*"

They consulted on specifics for another half-hour, verifying drug supplies and military deployments, communication lines and contingency plans, but even the Admiral was eventually forced to concede that everything was, so far, going to plan. She idly clasped her hands behind her back and shrugged a shoulder.

"*Then I suppose all we have left to do is wait.*"

Silence descended, its thick web fraught with hidden fears and tacit dissent. The Doctor scanned the Admiral, trying and failing to read what lay behind her studied indifference. At one time, he'd been able to read her like a tip-pad, but in the intervening years she'd made concealment an art, and even he rarely knew what she was thinking anymore. The Chairman, too, was uncharacteristically quiet today. With a minute shake of his head, the Doctor spoke, compelled by the silence and his own unquiet thoughts.

"*It will work.*"

Now the Admiral's reaction came, a twist of the lips that disappeared as quickly as it came. She leaned forward, face looming up on the holo feed.

"*I've heard that before.*"

The urge to slap her cracked through his palm, never mind that she was a thousand light-years away and he'd never raised a hand to anyone in his life. That she should bring that up now, of all times! But he stilled his temper, knowing she was only trying to provoke a rise from him, and simply repeated his original statement.

"*It will work.*"

She shrugged one shoulder. "*We shall see.*" With that, she linked off.

The Chairman followed soon after, linking off with only the tersest of goodbyes, leaving the Doctor alone once again. Sinking down into his chair, he tried to put aside the Admiral's words and couldn't. Even after all this time, the reminder of his worst failure still rankled.

The failure of the Nova Technology.

They'd followed the specifications to the letter, using the Tellurians' schematics and data to create a weapon identical to the one that took out New Sol Space Station and its entire complement of ghouls so brilliantly. But although they'd done everything as instructed, they could not duplicate the results. Planets, colonies, evacked stations teeming with ghouls—they'd used the weapon in every possible location, but though the bombs always worked and the Spectres appeared, when the light finally died, the ghouls never died with it.

The worst was Luna Internment Camp 3. Not a Derelict, like all their other testing sites, but a squatter camp. The carnage was horrific, the death toll unspeakable. Out of a camp of ten thousand, 7,843 dead in the blink of an eye, and for what?

A weapon that did not work.

Not that the rest of the Expanse knew. Everyone had meekly accepted the official story: that the weapon was simply too destructive to be effective. An easy story to push, as it was essentially true—with one minor detail excluded. Only a handful of people in the highest echelons of command knew the real story, and all of them—the Admiral, the Chairman, the engineers working for R&D—simply believed the Tellurians had provided faulty or incomplete schematics for their weapon. It was the only logical answer. But though it was the only explanation that made sense, the Doctor had never been able to accept that. There was a reason it had worked on New Sol and nowhere else. Had the Spectres somehow found a way to defeat the Nova Technology? To withstand its killing effects so that when the explosion came, they stood firm? Or perhaps they'd found some way to sabotage the Nova bombs themselves. As a scientist, he couldn't reject the possibility no matter how much he might want to, nor could he deny the inevitable conclusion that followed:

If they'd found a way to defeat the Nova Tech, the Archangel might be next.

For months they'd been seeing the signs; that of an enemy poised on the brink of a new offensive, one whose nature could never be fathomed nor timing discovered. If the enemy had somehow uncovered the plan, or if they struck against them in some other way before the Archangel could do its holy work . . .

No, he couldn't afford to think this way. He was a scientist, not a strategist, and for all her faults, he trusted the Admiral to do her job and keep the enemy at bay until the time was right. In ninety days, he would personally input the commands that would send the Archangel surging across every planet, colony, and station in the Expanse. And then, bathed in the glory of its light, every ghoul would die.

They would die, because if they didn't, the entire human race would.

29

THE PLATFORM APPEARS upon the viewscreen before me, flat gray against the brilliant ripple of star-studded space above and the glowing white aura of the planet below. Skysa OP SE-3. From a distance, it looks like any other OP I might see out in orbit. It's only as we draw nearer—near enough to see the scorch marks scoring the thick tritanium, the hatches that have been welded shut, the portals that have been rendered inaccessible—that it starts to sink in. This isn't an orbital platform anymore.

This is an enemy stronghold.

I stare grimly ahead, heart thumping as the shuttle dances closer to the target, its course carefully calculated to avoid any sensor sweeps. Melted stumps and burned metal dot the platform at various intervals—vestiges of the platform's weapons system, destroyed by the navy during the original evacuation—while entire docking arms have been sheared off completely. Most have long since floated away, but a few remain, caged by the wreckage still partially attached along the scored metal.

"*Infinity*, this is *StarRunner*. Approach vector is set and confirmed. I repeat, approach vector is confirmed."

"*Acknowledged*," comes Major Estes' voice through the com. "*You're cleared to engage. Happy hunting,* StarRunner."

"Understood. *StarRunner* out."

Our pilot cuts the com, and a moment later the ship noticeably picks up speed. It's our first mission since leaving R&D, and adrenaline runs through the shuttle like rain. Silver stealth lights drench the cabin in a cold sweat, bathing everyone inside in a sickly aura that only enhances the climate of dread. I set my jaw, unwilling to give in to the fear. This mission is too important to frag up through overeager nerves and rookie mistakes.

The OP's port deck looms up on the viewscreen, blistered and black, before sliding away beneath us as we pull up over the platform to skim along its top. The glow of the planet disappears, blocked by the platform's heavy hull, and darkness falls across the lower viewscreen. I shiver at the sudden blackness, face turned to the target just below. Can they sense us down there, through the meters of tritanium and the cold of the vacuum? Do they know we're here, or for once have we managed to turn the tables on our enemy, becoming the silent specter coming invisibly in the night for them?

We coast lengthwise down the platform, gliding past fried docking ports and seared hatches until we reach the halfway point. With a slight shiver, the ship perches delicately on the OP's hull, its magnetic landers touching down against the metal as softly as a butterfly's feet alighting on a flower. My muscles tense, every sense on high alert as I wait for the pilot to complete the landing process and give us the go-ahead to move. It's not long in coming.

"Delta Team," comes the pilot's voice a minute later, "landers have been extended and locked into place. You're clear for debarkation at your convenience."

"Acknowledged, *StarRunner*," Archer responds. He signals us to seal our helmets, switching over to the team channel as he says, *"All right, Delta, we're up. Let's go."*

He issues a few commands with his chit hand, and a circular hatch set into the floor begins to open. I climb down first, along with three specialists, to form a human assembly line along the ladder and into the airlock below. Under Archer's supervision, the others pass down several large canisters to us. As soon as they're in the airlock,

Archer and the remaining specialists climb down, hatch closing behind them.

"*Helmets secure?*" comes Archer's query.

I check my seals, adding my own affirmative to everyone else's. Shortly after, I hear the soft *hiss* of the air being vented from the airlock. The process seems to take forever, but eventually the indicator light on the control panel turns red, and I know we're ready to go. Archer glances at me.

"*You want to do the honors, Sorenson?*"

With a curt nod, I hit the large round button on the control panel. The circular hatch set into the floor opens, and we're looking down into space.

Sheer awe has me surreptitiously grabbing a handgrip to steady myself. This is no digitized vista projected across a perfectly solid wall, no view through a pane of glass or chunk of crystal. Just the deep, yawning black of the void, nothing between us and its endless chasm but the platform below.

"*Raisman,*" Archer calls, "*you're up.*"

"*Yes, sir.*" Lifting a dual-gauge magnetic grappler to her shoulder, Raisman crouches by the hatch, takes careful aim, and fires.

The heavy cord shoots from the grappler in a perfect arc, the magnetic end attaching to the platform three meters below. Raisman gives the line several hard pulls to ensure it's secure, then ties off the other end inside the shuttle. After another couple of tugs, she nods at Archer. "*Safety line secure, sir.*"

Archer nods. "*Acknowledged. All right, team, it's go time. Just like we practiced. Keep your clip secured to the safety line until you're magged onto the platform, and don't forget to keep an eye on the fences.*"

I glance at the force fence grid on my face shield. With our noses rendered ineffective in the vacuum, the fences surrounding the OP will be our only warning if the ghouls decide to come out and play. A nerve-wracking proposition, though we've all pre-dosed with Psi-Lac just in case. They may be able to possess us, but at least they won't be able to control us. Not at first, anyway. The last thing we want is one infected team member to take down the rest before they even know what they're doing.

Archer takes his place by the hatch and gives me a single nod. I spring into action, running to the hatch where I immediately clip onto the safety line. Adrenaline is pumping in my veins, but I don't feel scared anymore, only confident and strong. This is what I've been training for all these months, through simulation after simulation and test after test. The enemy has hit me hard, robbed me of the people and things I love the most. Now it's my turn to fight back.

I don't hesitate, but jump feet-first through the hatch toward the platform, pushing off from the shuttle and allowing the safety line to guide me down. I spot the hull coming up and activate my boots, letting the sharp tug of the magnets pull me the rest of the way to the duro-steel hull. The shock of the landing reverberates through my legs, but I'm on, safe and sound. I unhook from the railing, letting the cord recoil into my belt with a quick snap. Taking a few steps across the hull to clear the way, I signal to the rest.

"Sorenson reporting. I'm safely on and secure."

"Acknowledged. Kagawa, go!"

Within a minute, Kagawa, Jethro, and Raisman have joined me below. The canisters are sent down next, clipped to the security line and pushed into our waiting arms. The rest of the team follows them down, brought up by Archer in the rear who promptly releases the security line the moment he's magged to the platform.

"StarRunner, *this is Delta. All equipment and personnel have completed debarkation. You're good to go any time.*"

"Roger that, Delta." Up above, the airlock hatch closes, sliding firmly shut with a finality that only serves to emphasize just how exposed we are. *"Departure in thirty. StarRunner out."*

The landers retract, and the shuttle lifts off, its stealth-draped carapace a transparent ripple barely visible against the deep black sky before it disappears altogether. A wave of vertigo hits me as I stand there, only a pair of mag boots between me and the endless vacuum. For the first time, I realize just how insignificant I am, one small life form within a vast universe that neither knows nor cares if I live or die. It's the single most exhilarating—and terrifying—thing I've ever felt in my entire life.

Archer's voice snaps me back to reality. *"Sorenson, Kagawa— take your triads and execute the first stage. Triad One, follow me."*

"Yes, sir."

"Affirmative, TL."

At my nod, Raisman and Jethro each grab a canister while I activate the tracker that will allow me to pinpoint our assigned location. Splitting apart from the others, we head north along the platform's outer ridge. I walk in ponderous strides, unaccustomed to the constant tug of the mag boots as they continually seek to pull my feet back to the platform. Not that I'm complaining. I'll take sore calves over a one-way trip into the vacuum any day.

We stop at a cluster of exhaust vents at the far end. It's one of the few places where the ventilation system comes up to the platform's surface, allowing it to vent excess waste gases or heat into the vacuum where they can harmlessly disperse. It's a key part of any orbital habitat's self-sustainability, and they're the only outside portals not sealed up upon evacuation. Now the very ventilation system that makes life possible will become our greatest weapon.

Taking off my pack, I start pulling out charges, all specially made for use in the vacuum. Briefly forgetting where we are, I lob one to Jethro. Instead of arcing neatly into his hands, it sails up and over his shoulder. He twists in a last-minute grab for it, but just misses. As one, we all watch it soar into space and out of sight.

"Retrieving that's going to be a bitch," Raisman observes dryly. *"Talk about a long walk off a short pier."*

Jethro snickers. I just shake my head.

Luckily we have extra charges, though I settle for handing them to the others this time instead of tossing them. We set our charges in an equilateral triangle to the right of the vents, each charge roughly a meter apart. Backing well away, I take cover behind the charred remains of a weapons mount with the others. Once we're all secure, I detonate the charges with a twist of my hand.

The outer plating blows off the hull in a flurry of tiles. Shrapnel flies in every direction, soundlessly winging its way into space, the silence of the explosion at odds with the violent vibrations rippling through the hull beneath my boots. I keep low and tight, making myself as small a target as possible, though the weapons mount should be enough to shield us from any debris. We wait until well after the area has cleared, then go back to survey our work. A gaping hole perhaps two meters in diameter waits for us. The outer hull has blown cleanly off, leaving only a layer of silvery insulation between us and the guts of the platform.

"*Nice,*" Jethro comments.

"*Sure, if you like wanton destruction,*" replies Raisman.

The two look at each other, then burst out laughing at the same time. I grin ruefully. *Yeah, that's a no-brainer.* I give them their moment, then wave my hand for silence.

"All right, enough. We've still got a job to do. Jethro, you got the cutter?"

"*Affirmative, ATL,*" he says, all business as he wrestles the large, two-handed laser cutter from his pack.

I run the tracker over the hole, looking for the right spot. The monitor stops me a meter from the far edge. Pulling a marking tool from my belt, I sketch out the area in bold white lines. Stepping back, I make sure to give Jethro plenty of room as he fires up the huge cutter.

"*Sorenson, status report.*"

I flip to the command channel in answer to Archer's summons and say, "TL, we've blown the outer hull and are about to cut through the insulation. I estimate breakthrough in approximately thirty minutes."

"*Understood. Keep me posted.*"

We take turns with the cutter over the next thirty minutes, swapping it between us as the precision beam work and exacting muscle control required for the job take their toll on us. At least the lack of gravity means we don't have to support the cutter's weight, which is considerable. Despite the hard work, the time flies, and before I know it, we're pushing through the last of the barrier. The insulation peels away, and suddenly we're in. Below are the emergency O_2 tanks that feed directly into the main ventilation system in case of system failure. Now it's just a matter of unhooking the oxygen tanks and connecting our own gaseous brew.

"Jethro, schematics."

He digitizes the system plan over his suit arm, reading out the instructions while Raisman and I each take a canister and begin the complex process of bypassing the security and switching out canisters. Hoses, nozzles, and control keys fly across my vision in a kaleidoscope of colors and lights as I work steadily to get the job done as fast as I can without making any mistakes. Finally finished, I check and double check the work until I'm satisfied everything is correct.

I link Archer. "Team Leader, we've attached the canisters and are ready to dispense on your command."

"Acknowledged, Sorenson," Archer's voice comes back a moment later. *"Kagawa, sitrep."*

"We're just hooking up the final hoses now." She pauses. *"Checking the connections . . . and we're a go."*

"Good. Sorenson, Kagawa—go ahead and dispense the gas."

Excitement bubbles up in me at the command, though I keep my reaction to a hard grin. Reaching down, I twist the nozzles on both canisters until the indicator lights go from red to blue. Though I can't hear it, I can imagine the gas hissing through the nozzle and into the ventilation shafts. Sitting back on my haunches, I wait as the gas goes to work.

While we can't gas squatters—the safety protocols programmed into the platform would trip if we pumped in anything harmful to humans—that same limitation doesn't apply to ghouls. Just like our launchers, these canisters hold a concentrated mix of gases repulsive to our incorporeal enemy. By dispensing the gases into specific parts of the OP, we can essentially clear out those areas for Gamma Team, giving them precious time to get in and upload the software before the ghouls come flying back for them. It's similar to something we did on New Sol Station the day Lia died, gassing the habitat rings in order to push the Spectres away from the people and into the comparatively empty Central Hub.

I smile slightly at the memory. Here we are, a professional military strike team in the midst of the most important offensive of the war, and we're using a strategy originally pioneered by my *fifteen-year-old sister*—who, in point of fact, was only thirteen at the time. Brotherly pride washes over me at having such a brilliant little sister, and I grin with pride . . . until I remember I'm supposed to be pissed at her, not proud.

The canisters finish dispensing their gaseous cargo within a matter of minutes, blue indicator lights flicking off to show they're empty. I link Archer with the news, then direct my team in reversing the process: switching the empty canisters out for the original O_2 containers, repacking the insulation, then securing it all down with flexible sheets of plastoid from our packs, which we bolt over the hole to replace the blown plating. As we work, I can hear Archer linking the others to let them know we've finished this portion of the job.

"Infinity, *Gamma, this is Delta. We've finished dispensing the gas. I repeat, we have finished dispensing the gas.*"

"*Understood, Delta,*" comes Songbird's reply. "*We'll time our breach accordingly. Gamma out.*"

We've just finished bolting down the last piece of plastoid when a flicker of red dances in the corner of my eye. My heart jumps, eyes flicking to the force fence grid on my face shield, but it's just one of the fences inside the OP tripping as our gas begins to do its work. The ghouls aren't coming through the hull of the platform to get us.

At least, not yet.

First part of the mission finished, it's time to turn our attention to the second part of the job: modifying the shield generators. All of which are located on the *opposite* side of the platform, of course. After a brief check-in with Archer, I turn to my triad.

"Let's take a walk."

We set off across the hull, width-wise toward the nearest edge, detouring around crumbling weapons mounts and an interstellar antenna that's so charred as to be practically unrecognizable. Our boots play along the smooth hull with soundless clanks, nothing but the in-and-out of my breaths echoing through my helmet and whispering in my ears. Now that I've gotten used to being in the open vacuum, there's something almost peaceful about being here, enveloped within the heart of the starry night. The silence, the stillness; the strange feeling that I'm part of something so much larger than myself and completely alone at the same time.

We reach the edge of the platform, and I lean my head out over the side. Though I know that there is no real up or down in zero-g, that it's solely my mag boots keeping my feet on the hull, the drop is still dizzying. Just a yawning chasm of black hovering over the distant glow of the planet below.

My stomach kicks as I take my first step over the edge, making sure my boot's magged tight to the side before following with the other. I take a couple of steps down, and just like that my world reorients, the platform's wall now becoming my new floor. Jethro and Raisman join me, flanking me on either side as we make our way down toward the bottom—side?—of the platform. Along the way, we pass a bank of viewports—real viewports, not simply digitized wall screens.

I peer inside, unable to make out much more than a host of shadowy shapes, half lit by the dim emergency lights still powered after all this time by solar fumes shunted from the collectors lining the platform. This particular OP is a Derelict—no squatters, only ghouls—so there's no one inside to impede our progress, at least not physically. However, as I look inside that shadowy den, I can't help wondering if there's a shiver of ghouls on the other side of that viewport, looking back at me with a million ghostly eyes and a hunger that can never be satisfied.

Once on the planetward side of the platform, we meet up with Archer's and Kagawa's triads at the Central Shield Generator. It's here where the Archangel's power will be born, concentrated within the massive dish array before being transmitted to the planet below. Eight additional generators located in a giant ring around the central generator will help bolster and focus the power even further, enabling the generator to sweep the entire target area down below before rotating back up to sweep the OP itself. However, in order for it all to work, we have to make some serious modifications to the hardware along the planetside of the platform, starting with the Central Shield Generator.

"StarRunner, *this is Delta requesting first CSG equipment drop. Please respond.*"

"Acknowledged, Delta," comes the pilot's voice a second later. "*Mobilizing now, with ETA in one minute.* StarRunner *out.*"

Hours pass as we labor on the generators, enlarging the Central Dish Array with huge extender panels, adding additional power relays, and changing the energy converters. Everything required to turn a defensive energy shield generator into an offensive weapon capable of wiping out an entire alien species. After everything is installed, we have to recalibrate and sync it all with the original hardware before we can reactivate the system. Once we finish with the central dish, we split into triads to work the remaining eight generators which, to everyone's relief, are significantly smaller and only require minor modifications.

While we attack the platform's exterior, Songbird's team goes to work inside.

"Infinity, *this is Gamma. Fences show the enemy has relocated in an optimal spread. Requesting permission to breach the target.*"

"*Gamma, this is the* Infinity. *Permission granted. Stars be with you.* Infinity *out.*"

Perched on the rim of a shield generator, scanner in hand, I listen in on Songbird's team as they breach Starboard Hatch 3 and enter the platform. In some ways, their job is the easiest. Get in, upload and initialize the software, then get out again. However, with ghouls potentially lurking around every corner, it's also the most dangerous job. If the ghouls don't all evacuate the gassed areas as planned, or if they return earlier than expected, Gamma could get caught in an ambush impossible to escape.

Not that we're entirely safe out here, but at least we could push away from the platform if the outside fences start to trip, use our jets to get as far away as possible, and call for a pickup. That's assuming the ghouls even realize we're here to begin with. According to the theorists, the ghouls are blind in the vacuum, unable to sense potential hosts through the airless void. I have no idea if that's really true, but there would be a certain equilibrium in that, if so. We can't smell them through the vacuum, but nor can they sense us with their ghouldar. It's a fair exchange. Fairer than most match-ups between us.

"*Sorenson, where is your triad on the modifications?*"

I activate my com. "Our first generator is complete, and our second is nearly done. We're just finishing up the last few modifications now."

"*Good. Choose one person to finish the mods with you, and send the other on to the last generator. Someone from Kagawa's team and I will meet up with them there.*"

"Understood. Sorenson out."

Keeping Raisman at my side, I send Jethro on to help Archer with the remaining shield generator while we finish up on this one. Meanwhile, Songbird's team seems to be moving along quickly. They've reached the Control Room and are three-quarters of the way through the upload. So far the gases seem to be working, keeping the ghouls well out of the way on one end while Gamma works on the other. Nor have any of the fences surrounding the platform tripped, though I've kept a constant eye on them. When we finally jump ship an hour later, piling into our shuttles and heading back to the main carrier, not only is everything installed and uploaded, but everyone is alive and uninfected. In other words, a textbook mission.

Sitting in the back of the shuttle, I exchange backslaps and fist bumps with the rest of the team. Though I'm drenched with sweat and my heart has yet to relax its guarded beat, I feel pumped. More than pumped, but victorious, like we just came up against our first real trial only to crush the opposition with ease.

However, as I watch the platform fall away through the aft viewport, its dark visage gleaming dully in the night, I somehow doubt the subsequent ops will be so easy.

30

WITH THE UNQUALIFIED SUCCESS of our first platform modification, we're plunged into a harrowing, three-month-long mission spanning two and half sectors, nine systems, and fourteen planets. Within the first week, my earlier prediction is borne out when we sustain our first casualty: a specialist on Gamma who gets taken by a ghoul during an Inside Op. Though we all knew casualties were inevitable, the first one is a blow that hits everyone hard. Even after he's dosed and stuck in the brig for the remainder of the mission, it's clear we're all thinking the same thing:

Who will be the next to join him?

That question is answered soon enough. As the days spool out into weeks, the casualties continue to come—a specialist from Eta, two from Iota. The worst loss comes on my own team when we return from a seemingly easy mission only to have PsySergeant Han Di stop our final team member, a rookie named Kalloway, with a hand to his chest and a shake of his head.

"I'm sorry, Specialist."

Just three words, but no one is under any illusions as to what they mean. Only Kalloway, who shakes his head, consternation awash on his face as he tries to deny them.

"No, no, I can't be." He shakes his head again, as if he denies the truth enough times it will cease to be true. "I mean, yeah, I smelled something on the way out, but it was . . . I mean, it wasn't . . . No, it can't be."

Han Di puts a gentle hand on Kalloway's shoulder, face composed though his eyes reveal pain. As a PsyCorp agent, he's no doubt had to tell more than his fair share the bad news, a tough job for someone whose psionic gifts afford him greater empathetic abilities as it is.

"Come on, son," Han Di says, guiding Kalloway toward the opposite exit.

Kalloway starts to follow, then suddenly stops, jerking away from Han Di with a hard yank. "No! No, I won't be bagged and tagged and sent off to some squatter colony! I won't!"

His eyes go wild, and his chit hand twitches spasmodically. I lunge forward, certain he's going to go for his pistol, though whether he means to use it on us or himself, I have no idea. Before I can take two steps, he lets out a high-pitched gasp, face contorting in a web of agony. His whole body seizes up, muscles clenching in a shuddering frenzy . . . then his eyes go blank, as though every grain of intelligence has been wiped from his mind at once, and he keels lifelessly to the ground.

I jump back, hands going for my launcher as my nose automatically scents for the released Spec, but I smell nothing. Just the cold, sterile air of the *Infinity*'s docking bay. It's only then that I finally understand what happened.

He coma-capsuled.

Killed off his cerebral cortex and liquefied his medulla, leaving only enough life left in his body to trap the Spectre in his head. The soldier's way of suiciding without putting any of his teammates in danger. It's both manically simple and elegantly horrendous at the same time. Of course, his body will eventually die if no one takes care of it. His body still requires the basic necessities of life to survive, such as food and oxygen and water. But though we can tend his body, there is no cure for his mind, now permanently vegetative for as long as his body should last. It's a horrible fate.

I lightly finger my own coma capsule, recalling how Angelou shot the thing into my wrist upon our arrival to R&D. Though I'd understood in theory what the capsule did, I didn't really *understand.* Until now.

The coma-capsuling hits everyone hard. Though we're used to infection and death, there's something about the brutal, dehumanizing efficiency of the coma capsule that is especially vicious. Long after Kalloway's body has been removed, I can still see it in my mind. That moment when his body seized and his eyes went blank, and every little thing that made him human was stripped away in a single instant. It haunts my dreams, jerking me awake deep in the night, though usually I sleep without dreaming.

Eyes wide, I lie there in my bunk, waiting for the rapid patter of my heart to slow again. I'm so vacced from my nightmare that it takes me a moment to realize it wasn't the dream that actually woke me. Movement is coming from the other side of the tiny room, rustlings and stirrings that sigh in the dark. I freeze, sure an intruder has broken in, but then my eyes adjust and I realize it's just Archer, my roommate for the duration of the mission. He's shoving his legs into a pair of trousers, pulling on a shirt and grabbing his boots before silently slipping out the door.

In a heartbeat I'm up, fumbling for my clothes where I tossed them over the end of the bunk before crashing. I make it through the door just in time to see Archer disappear around the corner at the end of the hall, and I hurry to catch up, led on by gut instinct. My uneasiness grows the farther we go, passing the hygiene units, the turn-off for the mess, even a small lounge where a couple of ship personnel are watching a holo. *Where the hell could he be going in the middle of the night?* When at last he swipes himself into the armory where we prepare for missions, my uneasiness turns to full-fledged dread.

I pause just outside, back to the wall as I try to decide what to do. Everything in me revolts at the idea that Archer could be the traitor, and yet even I can't deny that sneaking into the armory in the middle of the night does not look good. Is my hunt to find the saboteur about to end here? I suddenly wish my stun pistol were on this side of the door, with me, and not on the other side. With Archer. If only I'd known I'd be trailing my TL to the armory in the dead of night, I could have prepared better. Nothing to be done about it now, I reach for the door.

Rather than use the automatic control, I go for the manual release lever at the side of the door. It pops the seal with a soft click, and ever so slowly, I slide the door open a crack. Putting my eye to the gap, I scan the room. To my surprise, the main armory is completely empty. I frown, trying to decipher just what happened, when I spy the door to the locker room where we gear up for missions. I'm across the room in a dozen quick strides. Even before I put my ear to the door, I can hear voices, though I can't make out the words. My whole body tenses. Who's he talking to? All this time I assumed there was a single saboteur, but perhaps he's got a partner. Only one way to find out. Popping the manual release, I slowly crack open the door.

". . . is you, this is me, and this is Mommy. And see? This is our old house, before we had to come to this place. You can tell 'cause of the flowers over here by the door."

Tuning out the voice for a moment, I take in the scene before me. Archer's sitting in the locker room, one leg up on the bench beside him, his hand resting on his knee as he watches an hmail. I tilt my head slightly as it continues to play, noting the cheap shelters and bare ground behind the little girl, who's holding up a small tip-pad with some sort of drawing scrawled across the screen. She flips to another picture.

"This is the one I did of my two best friends. See, over here is Jandra, and this is Holly. Holly lives in the same houseblock as us, but Jandra I met at school . . ."

A light goes on in my head as I finally see what's going on. The girl in the holo is Archer's daughter, and the place in the background? It's a *refugee camp*. I recognize it easily from my time on Zaia, where I was evacuated with Gran and Teal after New Sol blew. Archer's family is just one of tens, even hundreds of thousands of families whose homes were taken by the enemy and have been left to rot in the refugee camps.

But maybe not for long, I suddenly realize. If the Archangel offensive goes off as planned, we can clear out entire planets and colonies in a single strike. Families like Archer's would be able to go home, to pick up where their old lives left off. I recall the conversation I had with Archer before we left, when I asked him if he agreed with Songbird about our committing genocide and he refused to answer. Looking at him now, his face suffused with love for the little girl before him, I know: He would do anything for her. Even if it meant violating his deepest ethics, he would wipe out every Spec in the universe if it meant that she could go home. Threatening the Archangel project is the very last thing he would do.

". . . love you, Daddy."

"Love you, too," Archer answers softly.

The hmail ends, and Archer cues up another. Feeling like the worst sort of spy, I close the door as quietly as I can and slip out of the room.

Back in my quarters, I pull up my list of suspects and silently cross Archer's name from it. After a bit of digging in the personnel files, I discover that Xian, too, has kin who have been displaced by the war—a sister and her entire family. I doubt he'd do anything to jeopardize his family any more than Archer would, so I go ahead and cross him off as well. Which leaves me with just four names.

RC. Annah. Songbird. Ty.

It doesn't escape my notice that of the four remaining, two were on the Nomia mission. Is it significant or is it just coincidence? I suppose that remains to be seen, assuming I ever manage to figure out the identity of the saboteur.

Closing the list, I de-ac my chit and climb back into bed. I shut my eyes and try to sleep, but as tired as I am, I can't seem to drift off. Those four names continue to dance around in my head, and it occurs to me, not for the first time, that by the time I figure out who the traitor is, it will be too late.

———

The seal around the hatch softens and melts, the metallic compound dribbling away bit by bit to float in silvery strands around our heads. I apply more solvent while the three others assisting me do the same. We continue brushing aside the gooey filaments until the last barrier between us and the hatch has dissolved away into the black of space. I shiver slightly as I watch the final few strands drift away. How long must the navy's welding ships have spent sealing everyone in, never expecting that within a matter of months we would put in equal effort to break back in.

I glance over at Archer where he's splayed against the platform on the other side of the hatch. "Sealant neutralized, Team Leader."

"Acknowledged, ATL. Go ahead and input the code."

"Inputting now, TL." Activating my chit, I manually key in the security code it feeds through my helmet com. Through the hatch, I feel a soft click as the locks disengage. "Code entered."

"Let's open it up."

I glance at the force fence grid inside my face shield. The pattern of lights shows that the gas diversion delivered by Xian's team has worked, pushing the ghouls to the far end of the platform. As far as I can tell, anyway. Without being able to use my nose, it's impossible to know for sure. For all I know, there's an entire shiver waiting for us on the other side of this hatch, ready to grab us the moment we walk in.

Taking a deep breath, I enter the command to open the door. For a moment, nothing happens. Then, ever so slowly, the hatch grinds open.

Lights blink on inside, automatically triggered by the door's motion. I poke my head around the opening, scanning for any signs of life, but the airlock is empty. Empty of squatters, at least. A light grenade thrown through the door confirms no ghouls, either. I shield my eyes from the garish glow as I wait for it to die down. Then, after a nod from Archer, I grab my launcher and vault inside.

The hard floor reverberates beneath my boots as I land, tremors snaking through my legs as the gravity of the station pulls me down into the airlock harder than I expected. Even though the grenade already confirmed the place is empty, I still scan the light sight on my launcher around the compartment just in case, checking for any sign of hostiles while I wait for the others to finish boarding. I won't feel truly safe until I can unseal my helmet and smell for myself.

As soon as the hatch closes, the airlock begins its automatic repressurization protocols, air hissing in through vents on the ceiling. I watch the indicator lights on the control panel as they change from red to orange to yellow, foot tapping impatiently in my boot as they slowly trudge up the spectrum. When the lights turn blue, a low tone chimes.

"Pressurization complete."

Despite the system's verbal assurance, I pause for a moment before switching my helmet over from Vac-Mode to At-Mode. As soon as the seals disengage, I take a huge sniff, breathing the station air deep into my lungs. Around me the others are doing the same, everyone's nose confirming the same thing: *no ghouls.*

At least, not in this airlock. Outside it? Who knows. None of the fences in this area have tripped since Xian's team gassed it, though, so that's something.

"Security feeds," Archer orders.

I use my helmet to wirelessly jack into the surveillance system, minimizing my force fence grid so I can flip through the image feeds on one side of my face shield. Scanning through the images, I stop on the view right outside the door. We're in an auxiliary 'lock on the planetward side of the OP, which leads directly into a maintenance level situated below the main deck. It's here, beneath the feet of all the unsuspecting people who live and work above, that the real guts of the platform, the machinery that runs this habitat, reside.

The areas directly adjacent to the airlock are all clear, as expected. The platform's support systems are automated and mostly self-maintaining, with only minimal human intervention needed to keep them operating. While small crews will come down and visually inspect the equipment from time to time, most diagnostic work is actually done via computer from the main control room. Good for us, as it means we have undisturbed access to the entire length of the platform.

"Maintenance floor is clear," I confirm.

"So are the stairs," Kagawa adds a moment later.

The others continue sounding off, each reporting on their assigned area.

"Sporadic traffic in the administration corridor. If we time it right, we can probably get through without running into anyone."

"Two officers in the control room."

Archer acknowledges the reports and turns to our tech expert. "Jethro, cameras."

Our tech expert nods. "Patching into the system, initializing command protocols . . . Done! I should be able to freeze individual feeds at will as we pass through."

"All right, team, it looks like our infiltration strategy is a go. Keep an eye on your sector and immediately report if you see movement. The ghouls have been gassed to the opposite side of the platform, so we shouldn't have any from this direction, but keep your noses open anyway." Archer glances at me. "Let's go."

From my spot by the control panel, I acknowledge his command with a nod. Then reaching up, I hit the button to open the airlock.

The inner door slides open with a barely audible swish. We step out into a shadowy expanse, subdivided by a labyrinth of humming machinery arranged into long, loose corridors across the vast floor. Cargo lockers line the walls and piping runs along the ceiling, life-giving conduits that transport water, energy, and air to the rest of the platform. Unlike most places, the lights don't come on automatically when we step into the room—perhaps to discourage unauthorized visitors from poking around down here—leaving only the emergency lights set into the floor and walls at regular intervals to guide our way.

As soon as we're in, Perseus and Quinn take up positions near the hatch so they can guard the airlock and neutralize any threats that might compromise the maintenance level. If we lose our exit out, we're all completely fragged. The rest of us fall in after Archer, who takes point to lead the team through the maze of equipment, and I bring up the rear. We move quickly, jogging across the level with swift steps to the emergency stairwell. It's the easiest way to access the main level where the control room is located. My nostrils flare, scenting for the distant stench of ghouls, while my eyes continually search the shadowy nooks and crannies between the machinery for any possible threats the security feeds might have missed. However, we make it without any problems, using the codes Angelou secured for us to access the stairwell.

We pause on the first landing to review the camera feeds and plot our best course to the control room. Though the platform was partially evacuated, there are still plenty of squatters left onboard who could potentially derail the mission. Military squatters who, playing off the natural inclinations of their hosts, tend to shoot first and ask questions never.

After a quick camera check, Archer outlines our route. "We'll take this set of back halls all the way down to the second junction, where we'll detour around through the tech corridors. This should keep us mostly out of sight of the regular station personnel. If we need to, we can duck into rooms *here*," he points, "or *here* as needed."

A flurry of acknowledgements rings out as Archer finishes outlining the plan. Stun pistols in hand, we jog the rest of the way up the stairs, check the feeds once again, and enter the codes into the control panel. The door slides open with a low hiss.

A man in the standard coveralls of the maintenance corps is standing directly in front of us.

"Hey—"

The maintenance man falls, shot in the chest by Archer before he can get another word out.

"Well, that was bad timing," Raisman comments as we tuck him in the stairwell to sleep off his stun bolt.

No kidding. Camera feeds are all well and good, but sometimes the placement of the security cameras leaves something to be desired.

We move off into the station, taking a circuitous route and ducking into side rooms whenever necessary to avoid running into more squatters. Jethro freezes the cameras as we go through each section so security won't pick us up on the feeds. Despite our precautions, we end up having to neutralize two more people on the way—a corporal out on rounds and an IT specialist doing work in one of the tech corridors. Adrenaline pumps through my veins with every encounter, palms sweating at the thought that we might not neutralize someone in time.

Within ten minutes, we make it to the control room. Both officers are down with stun bolts before they even realize we're here, slumping limply in their chairs as they fall soundlessly unconscious. I take one and Raisman grabs the other, pulling them from their chairs and depositing them out of the way at the side of the room. They'll have splitting headaches when they awake, but otherwise they'll be fine. While we take care of the officers, Jethro pulls off his glove and uses his chit to jack into the main console. His fingers fly so quickly over the console, it's easy to see why Archer chose him to do the Delta uploads.

"Adewola, Kirst, take up position in the doorway across the corridor," Archer commands. "Kagawa, take the control room port door; Jos, take the starboard. Sorenson, monitor the camera feeds. I want to know the instant anything moves in this direction. Raisman, you'll stay with Jethro."

Taking up a position near the door, I keep my stunner ready as I continually flip through the camera feeds on my visor, eyes vigilant for any possible threats. Five minutes pass, then ten, then twenty. The wait is killing me, the tension winding me tighter and tighter the longer we linger in enemy territory. My foot jitters in my boot, and I silently will Jethro to hurry up, though I know he has little control over how long the process takes. When he finally speaks, I want to sigh with relief.

"Software is uploaded," Jethro says. "I'm starting the initialization process now."

"ETA?" Archer asks.

"Five minutes, Team Leader."

"Five minutes, team," Archer repeats. "Be ready to move as soon as he's done."

I add my acknowledgement to the others', flipping through the feeds once more, and then one of the camera feeds flickers. The pit of my stomach goes cold.

"Team Leader, a camera just flickered."

"Where?" he snaps.

"One corridor over, about five hundred meters north."

"Cause?"

I shake my head. "Unknown. Could be a random glitch, or could be they figured out we jacked their system."

Archer keys his com. "Team, we may have squatters on the way. Prepare for possible incoming from the northeast corridor. Jethro!"

"One minute!" he calls, not even needing to be asked the question. He taps his fingers rapidly on the console; not typing, I realize, but nervous tapping as he waits for the initialization process to complete.

I'm flipping through the feeds again when another camera flickers. "TL, we just had another camera go! Same corridor, two hundred meters closer."

Archer acknowledges the info with a hard nod, both of us knowing: One camera might be a malfunction. Two is not.

Everyone is getting antsy now, the tension frosting the air like ice.

The control room is situated at the end of a dead end, which means there's only one way out. Perfect for a squatter ambush. My heart thumps, all too aware that the longer we wait, the more time they'll have to bring backup. We have go, and we have to go *now*.

"Got it!" comes Jethro's voice from across the room. He grabs his gauntlet, already backing away from the console, even as the rest of us get ready to move.

"Let's go," Archer orders.

We're halfway down the hall when half a dozen squatters in security uniforms burst around the corner ahead. Everyone dives for cover, ducking into doorways and behind bulkheads as shots scream back and forth across the corridor. One of their people goes down, followed quickly by a second, and then a third. Even with decimators, they're clearly no match for us. Before long, everyone is stunned and on the ground. Knowing only more will come, we swiftly jog past them and down the passage, picking our way around stunned bodies and fallen weapons. As I pass the last one, I sense movement from the floor behind me. A body flashes in the corner of my eye; an arm rising, the barrel of a decimator glinting smooth and deadly under the cold station lights. Even as I turn, I somehow know it's too la—

A hard shove sends me reeling to the floor in a heap. The decimator flashes, energy shooting from the barrel with a golden crackle, and then the bolt that was meant for me takes Archer point blank in the chest.

31

A LOUD *CRACK* rends the air as the blast blows apart his shoulder plate, snapping Archer's armor in three places and searing a path deep into his neck and shoulder. He drops to the floor, suit torn open and chest heaving, breaths grating erratically from the charred flesh of his windpipe. It's Kirst who reacts the fastest, whirling around to hit the squatter with a shot from his stunner. Three more shots follow right on its heels, courtesy of Kagawa, Jethro, and Jos, but it's already too late. Sirens are going off all around us, their klaxon calls ringing high and shrill through the platform. The squatter must have triggered station security just before being shot.

I crawl to Archer's side. His pulse is rapid and his skin clammy, and it's clear he's going into shock. I direct a glance at Kagawa, our most experienced medic after Archer, but she only shakes her head. The message is clear: We get him medical help, and *fast*.

Or he dies.

Slapping a clear cauterizing patch over the wound, I start snapping orders. "Jos, you help me carry Archer! Kirst and Adewola, you take point. Raisman and Kagawa, cover our six. Jethro, use the cameras to find us a path out, if they haven't frozen them all yet. We're getting the hell out of here!"

I grab Archer's right arm, Jos grabs his left, and together we heave him up off the floor. Our TL tries to help as much as he can, feet fumbling to gain purchase on the decking, but it's clear he's fading fast. Looping an arm over each of our shoulders, we support Archer between us, taking as much of his weight as we can. As I straighten up, the sound of running footsteps patter in my ears. I start flipping through the camera feeds on my visor, searching for the source of the steps, but Jethro is already on it.

"Raisman, Kagawa! Three coming up the corridor behind you."

The squatters don't even know what hits them, all of them going down with stunner shots within a second of turning the corner.

"Eastern corridor is still clear," Jethro continues. "If we move fast, we can make it to the first junction before the squatters catch up."

"Let's move it, team!" I order, already suiting action to words.

We race through the corridors as fast as we can, twisting and turning through the various junctures at Jethro's instructions. Kirst and Adewola lead, clearing the way for us all, while Raisman and Kagawa follow up on our tail, watching our backs and frequently throwing grenades full of stun gas to keep the squatters from getting too close. Normally we'd be able to get back to the hatch in two minutes flat, but with Archer practically deadweight, we're forced to move at a snail's pace. We duck into a disused customs office to avoid a delusion of squatters, and that's when we hear it: a low whirring sound sweeping through the platform.

"What is that?" Adewola asks.

"Fans," Raisman says after a beat. "They're trying to clear the ghoul gases."

I take a huge sniff. The distant odor of sour-and-sweet tickles the back of my nostrils, and I realize she's right. As if we didn't have enough to worry about!

No time to linger, we duck out through the back of the office and drop down to the maintenance level below. Weaving between hunks of machinery, we make a beeline for the airlock. Footsteps clang on the stairs between levels, followed by several shots as Raisman and Kagawa work desperately to cover our rear, and I know it won't be long before our pursuers catch up. I force myself to move faster, but it's difficult. Archer's legs are barely moving now, and my back and shoulders are screaming in agony from the prolonged weight thrust upon them. Gritting my teeth, I ignore the pain and keep moving. The airlock comes into view ahead, and I activate the command channel on my com.

"*StarRunner*, this is Delta Team requesting pickup now! I repeat, we need pickup now!"

"*Understood, Delta. ETA in two minutes. StarRunner out.*"

We tumble into the airlock only meters ahead of the enemy, Jos and I half carrying Archer while the rest crowd in behind us. Archer is sagging heavily between us now, his weight hanging off our shoulders and his feet dragging against the floor. Blackish blood oozes through the charring on his neck and shoulder, and I can just smell the stench of burned flesh beneath the distant odor of ghouls. Panic jolts through my heart, and I try to rouse him. "Archer? Sir!"

He lolls between us, completely unresponsive, and I know he doesn't have much time.

Shots ring out against the other side of the inner airlock door, and I whip my head around in the direction of the sound. The airlock hatch is going crazy, repeatedly opening a few centimeters and then closing as Kagawa plays a life-or-death game of tug-of-war with the squatters outside.

Bam! She punches the command to close, and the door slides shut, only to jackrabbit open a second later as the squatter outside counters her move.

Open. Close. Open. Close. Open.

Her fingers fumble on the control pad, and the door keeps going this time. Shots fly through the widening gap, crackling past my cheek so close I can see the bolts reflected off my visor. I lunge awkwardly to the left, trying to get out of range and hold up Archer at the same time.

"Sorry!" Kagawa yells as she slams the hatch shut again.

"We need to get that door shut!" I tell her as it starts opening again. "The outer hatch won't open if the inner door isn't sealed."

"The override isn't working!" Kagawa shoots back. "I could destroy the panel, but with the squatters playing Jam the Door with me, the timing is too risky."

Close. Open. Close. Open.

I see the problem immediately. If that door isn't one hundred percent sealed when she destroys the panel, it'll freeze open, preventing us from opening the outer hatch and effectively trapping us inside the airlock.

Slag! The mission is falling apart. Archer is down, we've got ghouls on the way, and we're trapped in an airlock with squatters beating down the door. Everyone is looking to me—

"ATL?" Kagawa asks uncertainly.

—and I haven't the faintest idea what to do.

I minutely shake my head. I can't speak, I can't breathe. I try to marshal my scattered thoughts, but terror runs through me, freezing me in place and making all thought impossible.

A loud *clank* echoes through the air as the *StarRunner* appears at the portal ahead. The entire 'lock shivers, vibrations rumbling through the walls and floor as the shuttle attempts to make a connection. Already off-balance from Archer's weight, I stumble under the tremors and almost fall, throwing a hand against the wall at the last second to steady myself. Archer's arm immediately starts to slide off my shoulders, and I grab for it again, using my stance to brace myself as best as I can. After what seems like an interminable interval, the pilot comes on the com.

"*Delta Team, this is the* StarRunner. *Docking is complete. I repeat, docking is complete.*"

I take a quick breath, awakened by the pilot's voice speaking into my ears. The fear eases slightly, and I find I can think again.

"Acknowledged, *StarRunner*," I snap out, the answer coming before I consciously make the decision to speak. "We're taking heavy fire and are having trouble sealing the inner door. Stand by!"

I go back to my team, mind clear and wheels turning. "We have to clear out those squatters long enough to get the inner door sealed. How are we on ammo?"

"It's not ammo we lack," Jethro answers, "but cover. As soon as we let that door open, we'll be sitting ducks."

"Do we have any grenades left?"

"Half a dozen light grenades and two stun grenades."

"So if we just gas them with stun grenades—"

Kirst shakes his head. "They've already masked up."

Slag! A couple of grenades would make everything so much easier. Although now that I think about it, maybe we don't actually need to *gas* them . . .

An idea takes shape in my mind. Quickly I explain my plan, and almost immediately everyone starts pressing against the side walls, getting as far away from the opening in the door as possible. All except for Kirst and Adewola, who flatten themselves against the wall on either side of the inner door, and Kagawa, who stays by the control panel.

As soon as everyone is in place, I give the signal. "Kagawa, now!"

The door slides open again, keyed by the squatter on the other side, but this time Kagawa lets it go. Bolts fly through the gap, charring the opposite wall, only to be cut off as Kirst and Adewola fire back, pumping pulse after pulse through the widening crack. Another second, and then Raisman is there, tossing two grenades underhand across the threshold.

Boom! Boom! Light explodes through the gap as both grenades go off in quick succession. Screams cry out from the other side of the door, and even with my visor and combat lenses, the effect is almost blinding. Before the squatters can regroup, Kagawa punches in the command to shut, pistol poised over the panel as she waits for the door to close . . .

It slides shut, a blue light flickering on at the top of the control panel as the inner hatch seals. Kagawa brings her pistol butt down across the pad, hitting it once, twice, three times. Sparks fly from the panel, a nasty crunching noise ringing out through the airlock, but my eyes are fixed on that blue light, the inhale caught in my throat as I wait to see if it'll flicker out—but no. The light remains.

The inner door is *sealed*.

"*StarRunner*, we're coming out!" Even before I finish speaking, I'm hitting the controls to open the outer hatch. It slides open with a grinding screech, still rusty from disuse after all this time, but it opens. Jos and I dart through, dragging Archer with us, while the others pound through the hatch after us. Kagawa is the last one through, punching the hatch shut and calling to the pilot, "We're clear!"

Immediately the docking clamps begin to retract as the shuttle gears up to leave, but I barely notice. All my attention is on Archer, who hangs like a sack between Jos and me. I yell for a medic, heart pounding in terror as I search for the nearest med-kit, but I can't seem to spot one. Someone throws down a blanket, and we make for the makeshift bed, hauling Archer across the deck with frantic steps.

But as we lay him down on the shuttle floor, body limp and face a cold, lifeless mask, I don't need a medic to tell me he's already dead.

———

My promotion to Team Leader is made official the next morning. Major Estes calls me into her office, hands me my new insignia, and shuffles 'Vange over from Gamma to help even out our numbers and give me a seasoned ATL. Her manner is brisk, though not unsympathetic, and I find myself grateful that she isn't making a big deal out of Archer's loss or my promotion. This matter-of-fact gravity I can handle; sentiment I cannot.

Afterward, I go to the armory to start prepping for the day's ops. I pause outside the door, unsure if I'm ready to go in and face my team. Unsure if I'm even ready for them to be *my* team. Guilt sears through me every time I recall that moment on the OP, when Archer pushed me aside and took the decimator blast meant for me, and doubts prey upon my every thought. *Maybe I'm not good enough to be Team Leader. Maybe I'll just end up letting my team down.* For a moment I'm tempted to turn tail and run, but that's not what Archer would have done. Or Xian, or Songbird, or any of the other TLs. They would walk into that room and take care of their team.

So that's what I do. Through the morning prep work and on through two outside ops and one inside. Everyone accepts my promotion without comment, the advancement taken for granted with Archer now dead and gone. Taken for granted by everyone except me, that is. Though the commands come easily, etched into my head after hearing them so many times from Archer's mouth, I can't help feeling like it's still Archer's team, and I'm merely a stand-in.

We finish the day with no casualties, a triumph any day, but especially today. The last thing I want is to get everyone killed my first day on the job. After they rack their gear, I dismiss the team to their own devices for the handful of hours we get before hitting the next system. 'Vange is the last to leave.

"I can't believe I have to call you 'sir' now," he says, clapping me on the shoulder to show there are no hard feelings. However, we both know: Our roles would have been reversed had it been Songbird who'd fallen and not Archer.

After he leaves, I collapse on a bench in front of my gear locker. I made it through my first day as TL with surprising ease, and yet more than ever I'm suffused with guilt. Archer took a decimator beam meant for me, and because of that I'm alive and he's dead. Though I know it was his choice, that in fact I would've done the same for him if our positions had been reversed, I can't help feeling like his death is on my head. Even the success of the day is marred by guilt, as though it was somehow wrong to not only take Archer's job, but perform it well.

"You okay, Sorenson?"

I glance over to find Songbird standing in the doorway and let out a snort. I should've known I wasn't going to get through the day without some sort of uninvited pep talk. As though there are any words in the universe that could make this better! I glare at her, voice edged as I ask, "What, you lose the chit flip or something?"

Walking in, she leans against a gear locker and regards me. "Xian was promoted to Assistant Team Leader when his ATL was permanently demoted to scut for fraternizing with someone on his team. He got one of the extra TL slots when the new recruits came onboard for the Archangel mission. 'Vange became my ATL the same way."

I look down, the pointed words reminding me that, unlike Xian and 'Vange, her rise was also built on the back of someone else's demise. She was an ATL when I first came to R&D, rising to Team Leader only when her own TL was infected on a mission and chose to step out an airlock rather than be exiled to a squatter colony. She didn't lose a chit flip; she came because, unlike the others, she's been where I am.

Humbled by the realization, I swallow past the lump in my throat. "I'm okay."

She nods, needing nothing more than to hear this one small assurance. Or perhaps she never needed to hear it at all, but rather asked because she knew *I* did. The same way somebody else once asked that of me so long ago.

Her sympathy, her solace; that night she waited on me for hours for no other reason than to make sure I was okay.

I blink, surprised at the sudden memory. For so long, Lia has been a ghost I could never shake, a memory that clung to my waking thoughts and never let go. Yet it's been ages now since her memory's come to find me, as though she understands: I don't need her so much anymore.

The revelation doesn't bring fear or anger or even the heartbreak I would've expected, but a quiet acceptance that endures on through them all, continuing long after such paltry emotions have faded and fallen away.

"I'm okay," I repeat again, stronger this time, and now Songbird smiles a little, as though she knows something changed between the first answer and the second, though she doesn't know what. As she turns to go, she pauses at the door, head turning to look back over her shoulder. "Do me a favor, Sorenson."

I raise an eyebrow in question.

"When I go, you do this same thing for 'Vange. You make sure he's okay."

Her sentiment is clear, and her wording isn't lost on me. Not *if* she goes, but *when*. I want to deny those words, but I can't. We're soldiers in a war, and all of our time is borrowed. We take the time we're given and give up the time that's taken. It's just that simple.

Raising my head, I meet her eyes and nod. "You have my word."

But even as I make the promise, I hope to God I never have to keep it.

32 MY EYES SNAP OPEN as I emerge from sound sleep in a single instant. I roll out of my bunk, not needing to check with command to know we've just dropped from jump. After days of the same routine—Arrival, prep, mission, jump. Arrival, prep, mission, jump—the physical decompression that comes with the drop is like a subconscious alarm clock I can't ignore.

Activating my chit, I check the time. 0500. Almost six hours of sleep this time, practically a luxury these days. Flipping to the mission schedule next, I check our ETA. There's only one target in this system, a planet called Zayghara, but it's a round robin, which means that instead of one or two OPs, we have to do all sixteen. Unusual, as the military is generally able to lock down the remaining platforms once the first few OPs in a network become infected. As the uninfected platforms still staff skeleton crews to maintain the planetary net and fix any potential malfunctions, we're free to leave the Archangel modifications on those OPs to them. Zayghara is different. With every OP taken in a single coordinated strike, every platform is a sealed stronghold of ghouls and squatters, watched over only by a distant pair of small cruisers.

Suppressing a yawn, I make a quick stop in the hygiene unit, dress, and hit the galley for a ration pak before heading down to the armory for mission prep. I go through prep almost in a trance, refilling air tanks and power cells, checking gear for any potentially harmful wear and tear, and restocking equipment packs. Every cell in my body is calm, completely unperturbed by the dangerous mission ahead which, in the space of days, has become mere routine. Not that the danger has disappeared, not by a long shot, but rather the sheer repetition of mission after mission has somehow served to inure me to it all—the adrenaline, the fear, the inevitable losses.

Or perhaps it's simply exhaustion that numbs me to everything but what's happening in the immediate moment. Long, hard days, sometimes twenty hours or more, filled with manual labor and continuous peril, broken only by brief rests as we jump to the next system on the list. Lhasa OP SE-3. Nissou OP N. Manara OP EQ-1. Shoshana OP EQ-6. Agra OP SE-1. Ptolemy OP NE-4. The names run together in a kaleidoscope of missions—inside, outside, some easy, some hard, some we barely scraped through by the skin of our teeth. Each is an imperceptible presence, but when added together, they become a weight across my shoulders that only grows heavier with each passing day. Still, as heavy as the burden gets, I always seem to have just enough strength to carry it, as though each added weight only serves to make me stronger rather than causing me to bow and snap.

We finish our prep and deploy at 0610 on the dot to start the first platform. We're overwhelmed with squatters on OP N and barely get out alive, but an emergency hatch in the control room saves us. OP EQ-1 is a spacewalk by comparison, though rampant equipment issues keep us on the hull almost twice as long as usual. Delta's off for OP EQ-2, so after a quick shower, I make my way to the bridge to tune into the mission with the officers.

I take a seat at one of the back consoles, watching the feed from Xian's helmet on the main viewscreen as his team breaks through the seal on the outer hatch and enters. As the airlock cycles, Xian takes a few readings with his tip-pad.

"*Something's wrong,*" he says with a shake of his head. "*Not only is the surveillance system down, but I'm not getting any life signs. Are you sure this OP isn't a Derelict?*"

"Not according to the records," Major Estes replies. "However, it's always possible they're in error. Proceed with the mission, but be prepared to deal with possible ghouls *and* squatters."

"*Understood.*" Though Xian's voice is firm, his unease is palpable, a frisson of fear underlying the confident reply, and I find my own heart rate pick up just the slightest bit in response.

The airlock's control panel flickers red, indicating a pressurization malfunction. Xian examines the panel, plays around with the controls for a bit, and finally shakes his head. "*Airlock is malfunctioning—it won't pressurize for some reason. We're going to have to override it and manually force the door.*"

He keys the override codes into the panel, and after a minute, the red light on the door turns blue to indicate the lock has released. His ATL pops the panel with the manual release lever, and at Xian's nod, pulls it down. Even before the door pops open, I know, I just *know* something terrible is awaiting them on the other side. The door slides open, and I tense, waiting for a delusion of squatters to pop out and charge the airlock.

Bodies litter the floor in every direction, perhaps a dozen all told, all in a similar state of decomposition. Xian jumps back with a curse, the image on the screen swinging wildly back and forth as he snaps his head left then right in quick succession. His breaths steam through the audio feed, a rasping counterpoint to the gasps ringing out on the bridge of the *Infinity*. I bite my knuckles in shock, the murmurs around me matching the appalled thoughts in my head.

What the hell . . . ?

Oh my God!

"*Xian,* Infinity? *What's going on up there?*" Songbird's quizzical voice intrudes over the com—her team's got the Outside Op—and I realize she can only hear the reactions to the horror, not see it herself.

No one answers at first, the shock too great for organized speech. It's Xian who finally responds, voice hoarse as he answers Songbird's call.

"*Songbird, th-this is Xian. They're all dead.*"

Silence, then—"*I'm sorry, I didn't read you. What did you say?*"

"*They're dead, Songbird. Every last one. They've been dead for months.*"

"*Stars save us.*"

With an effort, Xian raises his tip-pad, scanning the area and examining the results. The tip-pad screen wavers, moving to and fro in little jerks, and it takes me a moment to realize it's actually the shaking of Xian's hands, not the pad itself.

"It looks like the ventilation system went down," he says. *"That's why we couldn't get the airlock to pressurize. They all asphyxiated. Suffocated from lack of oxygen or else drowned in their own carbon dioxide."*

Asphyxiated. Everyone is quiet, unable to avoid thinking about what an awful way that is to go. To choke to death, trapped inside with nowhere to go even as they gathered down on the maintenance level desperately trying to get the machinery working again.

Wait a second. An awful idea starts forming in my mind as the repercussions of the situation suddenly dawn on me. *If the ventilation system is down . . .*

"Major!" I snap out without thinking. "If the ventilation system isn't working right, that means the gas compounds they pumped in won't have circulated like they should. The ghouls might still be in the area."

"But the fences—" objects the com officer.

"All it takes is one ghoul to trip a fence," I point out. "If only a few of them left, as a diversion, and the rest stayed, we might still have ghouls in there. With their helmets still sealed—"

"Eta won't even be able to smell the enemy coming," the major finishes, already hitting the com. "Xian, light grenades now!"

Four grenades go off at once as both Xian and his ATL respond to the major's order. At first, I think the grenades must be malfunctioning, only small streaks of white showing here and there. Until I realize: *There are so many ghouls, they completely block out the light.*

"Abort, Xian!" the major orders. "Get out of there! Get out of there now!"

The coms crackle to life, the communications officer calling back the pilots while the major orders Songbird's immediate evac. Xian's team scrambles for the hatch, every single one of them seeing with crystal clarity the danger they're in, but we all know—

It's already too late.

The call comes from PsySergeant Han Di only minutes later. Still on the bridge with the major and the rest of the senior officers, I listen with bated breath.

"Major, I've just scanned all the members of Gamma and Eta Teams . . ."

"And?"

"Everyone on Gamma checks out, but every single member of Eta Team is infected. They've been dosed with Spectranol and are being incarcerated by security as we speak."

"Understood. Stand by for additional orders within the hour. Estes out."

An entire team, including Xian! The sheer magnitude of the loss is enough to thaw even my numbness. I close my eyes, lips moving in a soundless prayer I thought I'd forgotten long ago. It's the buzz of my chit that breaks me out of it. I glance at my hand. It's Songbird. Retreating to the corner of the bridge, I answer it, hand to my face as I subvocalize into my chit.

"Sorenson here."

"You heard?"

"I heard."

She pauses. *"It could have easily been either of us in there."*

"Yeah. Yeah, it could have."

Silence hangs over the com, no words in existence that could portray the depth of feeling, of guilt and sorrow, relief and despair, that haunts us both. At last I ask, "How's Gamma?"

"Pretty shaken, but they'll handle it. They always do. We always do."

"We do," I echo. "We came here for a reason, and no matter what, we keep going, we fight, and we get it done."

"We get it done," she agrees.

Now I only hope we can.

Linking off, I return my attention to the room. Like Gamma, most of the bridge crew is still pretty shell-shocked; the images from Xian's feed will be the stuff of nightmares for weeks, months, and even years to come. The only one who seems remotely collected is the major, who's speaking with Dr. Chiwafor, our engineering expert, in a low voice.

"—there any way to get the ventilation system up and running from outside the platform?" Estes is asking.

Chiwafor shakes his head. "I'm sorry, but judging from the small amount of data Xian was able to gather before they evacuated, we would have to access the system from the inside if we wanted even a prayer of repairing it. If it even *could* be repaired," he adds with a knowing look.

I think of all those people slowly suffocating to death even as they frantically struggled to repair the system, and I see his point. If they couldn't repair it, who's to say we could?

"That's an opportunity we don't have." Estes shakes her head, catches sight of me, and straightens. "Team Leader. Allow me to express my regrets at the outcome of today's mission. Eta's loss will be felt by all."

I nod, in outward acceptance, at least, if not inward. "They did their duty."

"They did," Estes agrees. "Now it's time we did ours."

I frown, uncertain what she means, but the major has already turned away. Striding across the bridge, she begins issuing rapid-fire orders.

"Initiating Protocol Royal Sweep. Martinez, switch us back to standard view, please. Jaffa, take us around to heading one-two-five mark eight. Riegert, begin priming all forward beams."

A slight kick ripples through the deck as the ship accelerates from its holding drift and begins to move. I grab ahold of the nearest console to steady myself, head whipping back and forth as I try to figure out what's going on. On the viewscreen, the earlier mission feeds wink out, replaced with the view from outside, magnified to compensate for the distance. Holo gauges appear around the outside of the screen, showing basic information like heading and speed, defense shields and weapons status. A targeting circle appears on the forward view, centering in on a distant object growing larger by the second.

The orbital platform.

A bad feeling keens in the pit of my stomach as we continue to advance. My eyes fall on one of the gauges on the forward screen, its spiraling translucent wheel turning steadily gold. Though I'm no pilot, even I know what that gauge is for. Weapons. My eyes widen. *Surely we're not . . . I mean, we couldn't . . . ?* But as the ship tilts on its axis, settling into an attack arc I would recognize whether I was on a corvette, a transport, or a ship of the line, my bad feeling is only confirmed.

"Coming around to heading one-two-five mark eight . . . now."

"Acknowledged," replies the major. "Lieutenant Riegert?"

"Weapons primed and ready, sir."

Estes nods, posture steady and eyes front. "Fire."

Triple beams explode from the hull of the *Infinity*, arcing through the dark in a hail of white lightning. They envelop the platform, lighting it up for one brief moment like a miniature sun shining silver through the black of space, brighter and brighter. The nearest side of the platform implodes in a ball of light, collapsing in on itself in a wave of destruction that sweeps down the platform from one end to the other. Walls cave in and ceilings fall, the entire OP crumpling up as though it's being squeezed by a giant fist, until finally it shatters altogether. Pieces fly out in a cloud of debris, spinning in a frenzy of shattered bulkheads and cracked pipes and bits of insulation now rendered defunct within the cold of the vacuum.

"Sweeper bots!" the major commands, and a host of tiny drones flies into the wreckage, their beams vaporizing debris upon contact while the *Infinity* presides over the work at a safe distance.

I watch in dumbstruck amazement, too shocked by this unexpected destruction to do anything more. In the background, I can hear the major giving orders to prep the drone ship—a replacement, I see now, for the OP we just destroyed. I hadn't even known we were carrying one.

My mind flashes back to the day we stood in the Central Habitat Lounge and watched the carriers arrive, to Chen's shrewd observation about the sheer amount of weaponry present on what were ostensibly transport ships. *She knew,* I realize. She put together in minutes what the rest of us didn't even begin to guess: that each carrier isn't simply a transport, but an ever-present fail-safe should we fall short in our mission.

As I watch the cleanup efforts continue, I try to remind myself that the OP was empty of life—at least human life—and that this is perhaps the best burial those poor souls could've hoped for. However, with that reminder comes one question, a cold and unforgiving presence hanging in my mind that can't be ignored.

What if that OP had still had people alive on it?

Only I don't really need to ask the question because I already know the answer.

Onboard the Personal Space Station *Solaria*
Home of the Chairman of the Celestial Expanse

THE INJECTOR HISSED, ITS NEEDLE puncturing and retract-
ing in the blink of an eye as it pumped his latest dose deep into his
veins. A low buzz hummed from the device as the needle underwent
sterilization, and the Chairman waited for it to finish before loading
his final dose and injecting it.

Done for the moment, he put the injector away, nestling it care-
fully into his lower desk drawer between vial upon vial of medica-
tion, all neatly labeled and sorted into racks. Locking the drawer, he
leaned back in his chair, a grim expression on his face.

It was getting worse.

The dosages required to control his condition stronger, the injec-
tions more frequent. The side effects—harder to cover up. Despite
all his efforts, he was running out of time, and he knew it. He'd
known it ever since he'd come back to his station all those months
ago, knowing he would never leave it again.

Not that he was the only Director to lock himself away from the
big bad universe. Most of the others had long since gone into hid-
ing, preferring to conduct their business from the safety of their
ships or stations rather than go out themselves. It was certainly
easy enough, with the miracle of interstellar communications al-
lowing them to handle most everything from a distance, aided by a

few select military personnel or high-level managers to do anything requiring a more personal touch. There were exceptions, of course, but to the rest of the Expanse, he seemed no different from everyone else on the Board.

No different at all.

The Chairman shook his head. No! He was different. He was stronger. He could conquer anything, if only he willed it hard enough. As a child, the doctors had said he wouldn't live, but he had. He had, and he would.

An alert trilled out from his desk, information pooling over the surface in a web of light. He scrolled through the holostream with curt strokes of his index finger, scanning over the message before letting out a swift curse.

Thud!

The desk vibrated under the force of his blow, holo-feed quivering off at the strike of his hand. His chit activated in a bluish glow. Minutes later, the Admiral appeared on his hand before him.

"I see you've received my report," she said in greeting.

"What the hell is this?!"

She shrugged one shoulder. "Was the data not self-explanatory?"

"Don't you dare play games with me!" The desk reverberated again at his sudden smack. "Twenty-one planetary nets, all in different sectors of the Expanse, taken down within twenty-four hours of one another. We're only weeks away from the greatest offensive in living history, and you've allowed twenty-one planets' worth of squatters loose to do who knows the hell what! For all we know, they've just released twenty-one planets' worth of shock troops."

"I'd hardly say we 'let' them escape," the Admiral replied icily. "The military crews overseeing the nets are there for maintenance and operational purposes only. They're not equipped to fight in the event that the nets fail entirely. Perhaps the squatters found some way to take down the nets from the inside. Or perhaps," she added with a pointed look at the Chairman, "the nets failed on their own for some reason."

A muscle twitched in his cheek at the implication. "Those nets, like every other piece of technology TruCon has manufactured for the war effort, underwent rigorous quality control tests before leav-

ing my factories. If there's any fault to find with the nets, it's in the design, not the manufacture."

"No doubt we'll see, once we learn more information."

"I'm not funneling funds to you so you can sit on your ass while a bunch of vac-spooks poke around the wreckage."

She arched a single eyebrow. "No, as I recall you're funneling money to me for a much different purpose."

Helios.

Neither spoke the name, but still it quivered in the air like a word whispered too quietly to hear.

"You're right, I am," he admitted softly after a moment, "but according to your reports, you don't seem to be making any more progress on that than you are with the nets."

"Results take time." She eyed him sharply. "When I took over the military's Bioresearch Division, you said I would have complete autonomy. Full control, all the funding I needed, and most importantly, no questions asked."

"I made that deal when I thought you would get results," the Chairman fired back, "but it's been months now, and I have yet to see any real success. There are billions of squatters out there, infected and waiting for a miracle. Where's the cure you promised me? The vaccine, the treatment, the method for extracting the squatters from their hosts?

"You were the one who argued that normal bioresearch was not enough to find a cure. That in order to make real progress, we needed to take—how was it you put it?—extraordinary measures, unhampered by the usual ethical standards and prying eyes of the politicians. So I gave you the Helios Project, just as you requested, and what have you brought me so far? Nothing."

"You disappoint me, Chairman," the Admiral sniffed. "Vaccines, cures. You think too small. We have an opportunity unprecedented in the history of the human race—a chance to push the bounds of humanity in a way we've only dreamed of!—but only if we have the vision to take our opportunity while we can."

The Chairman barely resisted the urge to snarl. He'd heard this speech before. Just as the Doctor had R&D, she had Helios. They thought they were so different, the Doctor and the Admiral, and yet in some ways they were exactly the same. The only difference between them was in how far they'd go.

"Enough! I will not cater to your insanity. Find the cure, or I'll find someone else to do the job. Or perhaps the Doctor's impending success has dimmed your motivation?"

The Admiral's expression never wavered, but her eyes went glacial, the way they always did when he compared her to the Doctor. "There's nothing wrong with my motivation. You want results? Then stop wasting my time with useless links."

With that, she cut the feed.

The Chairman smiled slightly. If nothing else, that little conversation should light a fire under her to get the job done.

His smile faded. Whether it would be done soon enough remained to be seen.

33 THE CRACKLE OF A DECIMATOR wings past my ear. I take cover behind the entrance to the control room as I exchange fire with a squatter in a gas mask about ten meters away. From the other side of the corridor, Raisman and Adewola do the same, stunners on max as we try to hold back the enemy.

"Jethro, how long on the update?"

"I've completed the upload and am initializing now," comes his swift response. *"Three minutes."*

"Make it a fast three minutes," I tell him as four more squatters appear in the corridor ahead of me. "'Vange, sitrep!"

"Our exit's still clear, but the ghouls keep coming. If we don't get the hell out of here, those fraggers'll overrun us!"

"Understood. Keep your triad throwing those gas grenades! We need three minutes."

"Acknowledged, TL."

I fire a few more bolts with my stunner, taking down a squatter with a neat shot to the chest before ducking back into the control room to avoid a flurry of crackles. Behind me, Jethro is still working on the software, fingers flying over the console as he works to get the initialization completed.

I resist the temptation to ask him again how long it's going to be. Instead, I use the brief respite to reload, ejecting the spent power cell and popping a new one into place. My head is ringing from the firestorm, and my left arm is burning from shots to the shoulder and elbow, but I hardly notice the pain. I only care about one thing, and that's getting the software uploaded and my team out of here.

Leaning around the frame, I fire off several more shots just as three squatters in station security uniforms make a rush for us. One falls, dropped by a pulse from Adewola's stunner, but the other two make it to the cover of the doorframe just beyond us, and I know it won't be long before the others try the same.

"Jethro—"

"Got it, TL! Software initialized and sweeper program released."

I fire another quick pulse and alert my team. "Team, we're out of here! Rais, Jeth, and Ad, grenades on my mark. 'Vange, keep holding that corridor; we'll be there in thirty." I switch over to the command channel. "*StarRunner*, we'll be coming out hot!"

"Understood, Delta."

With a flick of my wrist, I pull a light grenade from my belt. "Grenades—now!"

The grenades are clattering into their midst before the squatters even realize what's happening. Light explodes around them in a burst of white, blinding everyone within a five-meter radius. The shots abruptly drop off, replaced by cries of fear and confusion.

We don't hang around to watch the effects of our handiwork but take off in the opposite direction, Jethro and Adewola taking point while Raisman and I cover the rear. We take a left at the first junction, then drop straight down a lift shaft to the maintenance level below and keep going. The smell of ghouls, a dull scent in the background, is getting stronger with every step we run, an acrid sweetness that runs through my nose like rancid honey.

"Launchers!" I command, my own already off my back and in my hands. My team immediately follows suit, ready to blast anything incorporeal that might come our way.

We turn another corner, and there's 'Vange waiting at the head of the corridor. He falls in with us as we blaze past. The gas is so thick I can barely see two meters in front of me, but that's the least of my worries. Ghouls hang back just beyond the cloud, their ranks swelling every second as more punch in through the walls, the floor, the ceiling, all waiting for the second our shield falters. I shoot off round after round from my launcher, coughing like mad from the cloying gas, while around me the others do the same. Everywhere I turn, the light from my sight illuminates writhing black shapes, like oily shadows, hiding back behind the clouds. Predators waiting to pounce.

Halfway down the corridor we pick up Jos, the second member of 'Vange's triad, and a little farther down we grab Kagawa. Now the only one left is Kirst, frantically dropping grenades and firing his launcher as he tries to keep the airlock clear.

Come on, come on . . .

We blaze down the homestretch and pound into the airlock in a mass of bodies. Kirst hits the panel, and it closes behind us, narrowly missing Raisman's heel.

"Helmet seals!"

The sour-and-sweet odor abruptly disappears as I hit the control to seal up my helmet. Oxygen starts flowing the moment my suit seals, and a blue indicator light appears in the corner of my visor.

I scan my gaze across the others, counting the blue indicator lights as they appear on each helmet. Three, four, six. Seven! No time for decompression, I punch in the override and jam my hand down on the control panel. The airlock slides open—

—and we're all blown out into space.

———

By some miracle, we all pass the psy check back onboard the *Infinity*. Well, we all pass it once our pilot has finished fishing us out of space like a bunch of flopping carp, that is. Our chit signals made us easy enough to find, but the half hour spent floating in space while people went—

"*What do we do now?*"

"*What do you think we do, dumb-bot? We wait.*"

"*I'm hungry.*"

"*I'm bored.*"

"*Hey, how 'bout we start a pool on who gets picked up first?*"

—was more than enough to strain my less-than-patient nerves. Not that I could really blame them. They were babbling out of relief that we'd made it out in time, and babbling with the suppressed fear that maybe we *didn't* make it out in time. If the inane chatter was what it took to keep everyone from vaccing out, I wasn't going to stop them. God knows, they had plenty of reason to.

The loss of Xian's team, while not a complete catastrophe, has left us painfully short-handed. With barely two and half teams left, everyone is constantly on the job, only getting occasional breaks as we rotate specialists in and out of the two working teams. The only real rest anyone gets is during our jumps between systems, which we all use for one thing: sleep. Whether it's four hours or twenty-four hours, no one misses those precious opportunities to sack out for as long as possible before rising to start another long, endless round of mods.

Despite the exhaustion, no one complains. Over the weeks that have passed, every last one of us has taken this mission to our hearts. The Archangel may be our best, possibly our only, shot at saving our friends, our families. The human race. We may be short-handed, but we are determined to get the Archangel modifications implemented before Angelou's timetable runs out no matter what it takes.

Our return to the *Infinity* marks the end of a particularly tough op—a round robin for a small planetoid. Only ten OPs instead of sixteen due to its unusually small size, but grueling nonetheless. After racking our gear in the armory, I dismiss my team to grab whatever chow or rack time they can before our next op. I stay to examine what looks like a hairline crack on my visor, relieved when a little scrubbing reveals it's just a random stain. I'm about to stow it on the rack when the light catches the lower inside edge of my helmet. I stop, lifting the helmet closer to my face and peering inside. Embossed on the shiny plastic is a single number. Not just any number, but a very familiar number.

62M-071837-J572

My heart stops. *No, it can't be.*

I hurl the helmet away, sheer gut reaction driving me to get that thing away from me as soon as possible. It hits the wall with a sickening crack, bouncing hollowly off the metallic surface before dropping to the decking below. I stare at it with a mixture of fear and disgust as it lolls on the floor like an unexploded grenade, caught in some bizarre standoff as I wait for it to blow up or worse.

Nothing happens, though, and after a minute I pull myself together. Enough to force myself to walk across the room and retrieve the helmet. I turn it over in my hands, examining the outside for anything strange while feeling around the inside for anything anomalous. At the edge of the lining, right up near the face shield, I find something: a hard, triangular shape just barely tangible through the padding. Drawing my combat knife, I carefully slit the edge of the lining. A data chip falls out.

Even though I was half expecting it, I swear aloud as the chip drops into my hand. It's undeniable now. This is where the data chip I found in the energy converter on R&D was leading me—to my helmet!

My own custom-made helmet manufactured solely for *me*.

Everything inside of me goes cold as the implications of that sink in. While the laser cutter and ignition regulator seemed tailored to me, none of the other items tried to finger me in any way. In fact, I'd started to think that maybe my initial belief—that I was the saboteur's target—was faulty. The laser cutter in my locker could have been a laundry mix-up, like Asriel suggested, and the nameplate in the ignition regulator could have spelled out any number of names. But a customized helmet with my name engraved on the side? There can be no mistake now. *This is personal.* Someone is deliberately toying with me, manipulating me with this bizarre set of clues leading me from one item to the next. Again, I have this feeling that I'm being inexorably led toward something on the horizon. The question is what?

The chip itself doesn't shed much light on the subject. Like the others, it contains a single number, no doubt a serial number for yet another piece of gear or equipment, although strangely enough, the format is different: 002432862367. Different manufacturer, maybe? The others were all made by subsidiaries of TruCon—hardly surprising, as they have a near monopoly on all military manufacturing contracts—but maybe this piece was manufactured elsewhere. I go ahead and check the manifests for every item we brought onboard, but the number doesn't match any of my other gear or the mission equipment. Nor am I able to match the number with anything in any of the *Infinity*'s other databases. I have a sneaking suspicion it's for something on R&D, although without access to their inventory database out here, I have no way to confirm that.

Checking over my helmet again, I feel around for any other anomalies I might have missed during my initial quest for the chip, but if there are any, I can't find them. Not that I'm surprised. In fact, if I had to bet on it, I would guess that there's absolutely nothing wrong with my helmet, the same way there was nothing wrong with the stabilizer or the energy converter. I've been using this helmet for weeks; if the saboteur meant to hurt me, they would have done it by now. Probably.

It all goes back to the laser cutter. That was the item that originally started me down this twisted path. I think back to that stormy night when I went searching for clean clothes and pulled out the cutter instead. How I took it to Asriel, only to have him tell me that my locker hadn't been tampered with in any way. Something is bugging me about that incident, nagging at the back of my mind. I have the strangest feeling, like I'm missing something important about that laser cutter, only I can't quite put my finger on what.

Four names left on my list: Songbird, RC, Annah, and Ty. One of them could probably give me the answers to my questions. The only problem is that I have no idea which one to ask.

————

Within a day, we've finished the remaining platforms and jumped for the next system. Expected transit time is almost two whole days—practically a holiday for us. We sit around a table in the mess one night, Songbird, RC, 'Vange, and I, eating and talking in low voices. About our homes, the war, what will happen if the offensive is successful and we really do destroy all the Specs. Or at least the incorporeal ones.

"You realize all we have to do is hold out for three years, and the war is over," RC points out. "We quarantine all the squatters, fire the Archangel regularly to take care of any new ghouls, and once all the squatters have died, it's over. There will be nothing left but to figure out what to do with ourselves once we have no more enemy left to fight."

"No more war?" Songbird shakes her head. "I can't even imagine that. I don't have the first clue what I'd do. Re-up, I suppose. Go back to fighting humans instead of aliens, just like the good old days. What about you, 'Vange?"

"Are you kidding me?" he replies. "I'm gonna be a fraggin' war hero! If that won't get me laid in every port 'cross the Expanse, I don't know what the hell will."

Everyone chuckles, as he meant us to, and yet I can't help thinking the answer is a deflection more than anything. I remember what he said to me once, about not having anyone he loves to say goodbye to, and I suddenly wonder if he regrets the road that took him to this place, alone.

"What about you, Sorenson?" RC asks with a nod to me. "What will you do once the war is over?"

I blink, taken off guard by the question. The truth is I've spent so long mired in the pain of the present and my memories of the past, I've never spared much thought for the future. Or perhaps I just didn't think I'd live long enough to see it. When I enlisted, I ran away from my past with no thought for the future. Could I instead run away to the future with no thought for the past?

I'm saved from having to answer when my chit buzzes, a general announcement that has everyone glancing down at their chit hands.

"It's Estes. We've received a transmission from R&D," Songbird says, her quiet tones carrying the hush you only hear when one speaks of the dead. But then, we all know what an update from R&D means. An updated casualty list.

"I wonder how the other teams are faring," RC says after a moment.

I grimace, easily translating *How are the other teams faring?* to *How many of the other teams are still alive?*

Not that I haven't wondered the same thing myself countless times. Per the plan, all of the carriers are required to maintain a complete communications blackout with each other. That way if one group is somehow exposed by the enemy, the rest of us won't be taken down with them. A logical move, though it doesn't make the not knowing any easier. We exchange reports with R&D from time to time, so we're not totally in the dark, but they're few and far between. Still, any time I let my mind go to Ty or Zephyr or any of the others, I don't know what to think. Do I look forward to reuniting with them back at R&D? Or do I mourn for people already weeks dead?

"One way to find out," I answer at last.

Forks go down and plates are pushed back as everyone uplinks to the casualty lists, silently scanning the newest additions to the ranks of the IIA and KIA. Though I tell myself I'm not looking for anyone in particular, I keep my eyes sharp for a few specific names.

Zephyr. Chen. Ty.

I breathe a sigh of relief as I see that none of my old Delta mates are on the lists. In fact, most of the names are those of the rookies we recruited specifically for the Archangel mission, people I only knew by name or didn't know at all. However, there is one name that makes me do a double take:

Tech Specialist Ky Annah. IIA, SIS.

I bow my head as I read the listing for the former Gamma Team specialist. Infected In Action, Spectre-Induced Suicide. Though it's a common enough entry to find on a casualty list, it's still hard to see.

"Annah's spaced it?" 'Vange breathes. "I wouldn't have expected it. Not like *that*."

Songbird shakes her head sadly. "She was a good soldier, but her heart wasn't really in it. Not after NE-2 went."

I frown. "NE-2?"

"Annah was engaged to an engineer from H10," Songbird explains at my confused question. "He worked up on the Orbitals a lot as part of the WMGD project. He was on OP NE-2 when it blew. Annah was pretty devastated. I don't think she ever really got over it."

An image of Annah hunched over a table sobbing the day the OP blew flashes through my mind, and I slowly nod. I'd been surprised to see such an emotional response from the laidback specialist; now it makes perfect sense. And that's not the only thing it explains. If Annah's fiancé was indeed killed by the saboteur's work up on OP NE-2, it can only mean one thing.

Annah wasn't the saboteur.

Though I can't rule out the possibility that her engagement and subsequent devastation were some sort of elaborate ruse to hide her involvement, something tells me it wasn't so. A hunch, a gut feeling— I can't really explain it. All I know is that everything about Songbird's story rings true.

Songbird scans the list once more. "Looks like Brownlee didn't make it either."

"Shame. He was a good guy, always had a kind word for everyone. I'd hate to be the one who had to tell his wife."

"No kidding. At least Lopez and Samara are still alive and kicking."

"Not Lopez. She was on the previous list we got."

"Was she really? Damn."

My eyes flick across the table to where Songbird and RC commiserate across the casualty list in low voices, and a sinking feeling blooms in the pit of my stomach. With Annah out of the running, there are only three suspects left. Which means that the saboteur is most likely one of the two people sitting across from me at this very moment.

34

SEVENTY-FOUR DAYS after leaving R&D, we drop into the Rhyska System, a medium-sized star system ablaze with luminous gas giants that spiral and swirl like brilliant jewels around a single sun.

As usual, I awake the moment we drop from jump, nudged into consciousness by the internal loosening sensation that always comes when we transition back into normal space. I lie on my bunk, eyes open and staring sightlessly through the dark. There's a heaviness in my chest; in my shoulders, my lungs. It presses down on me like an invisible weight, and though I should rise, for once I can't seem to make myself get up.

It's my chit that finally forces me into action, buzzing through my palm however many minutes later with the sharp, pulsating vibrations that signal a link from Major Estes. I check the message with a flick of my index finger, watching as the subject line, text only, spools across my palm.

Mission Timetable—Rhyska System.

Our schedule and roster assignments for the day. I should go through it right away so I can plan for the day ahead. It's what I usually do as soon as I get the timetable. Instead, I de-ac my chit and close my eyes. Fifteen minutes later, I get a call from Songbird.

"Have you looked at today's schedule yet?"

"Nope."

I hang up before she can ask anything else so completely oxygen-deprived. De-acking my chit again, I turn over onto my side and face the wall. It doesn't help. If anything, the heaviness only feels more crushing, not less. Another fifteen minutes pass. My chit buzzes again.

"What do you want, 'Vange?"

"I'm down in the armory with the rest of the team, prepping for the day's ops."

"So?"

'Vange hesitates, some completely uncharacteristic grain of common sense keeping him from simply blurting out, *Where in the fraggin' hell are you?* At last, he says, *"We're about to start suit checks and Psi-Lac refills. You want me to go ahead and do yours along with mine?"*

'Vange, of all people, offering to pick up my slack? Yeah, if that isn't a wake-up call, I don't know what is.

Wake-up call or not, I continue to lie unmoving in my bunk for another several seconds. Finally I reply, "No, I'll do it. Just continue on with the weapons checks once you've done the refills, and I'll be there in ten."

"Acknowledged, TL. Evangeline out."

I cut the link and check the time. 0523. No wonder both Songbird and 'Vange have been on my case; normally I'd have been down in the armory almost a full hour ago. Rolling to the edge of the bunk, I force myself to swing my legs over the side and get up.

Ten minutes later, I stride into the armory located on the lower starboard deck of the *Infinity*. My teeth are fuzzy, and I'm only halfway through a rat-bar that looks like rubber and tastes worse, but I'm here. The room is abuzz with specialists from Gamma and Delta, everyone checking their equipment and gearing up for the ops to come. Going to my gear locker, I swipe my chit to open it and begin doing the same.

"You're looking remarkably pretty this morning," Songbird comments from the gear locker to my right. "Don't you think Sorenson looks really pretty this morning, 'Vange?"

"Hell, yeah!" 'Vange agrees as he slides up on my other side. "That sparkle in his eyes, the rosy glow in his cheeks. I wonder what the hell his secret is. You think he fragged a vacuum sprite or something?"

"Nah," puts in Songbird. "I think it must be all that beauty sleep he got this morning while the rest of us were in here busting our butts."

Snickers break out across the armory, and I shake my head as everyone has a good laugh at my expense. "Frag you," I tell them once the chuckles have died down.

"Yeah, right back at you," 'Vange smirks.

Pulling out my EVA suit, I start checking it for any breaks or weaknesses in the seals. From the corner of my eye, I catch Songbird and 'Vange exchanging a covert look, and I suddenly realize: *They were covering for me.* Making a joke out of my lateness, as though I'd simply overslept or forgotten to set an alarm, rather than let the specialists think something might be wrong with their Team Leader. Yet despite their outward show, they were worried about me. I have a feeling that if I'd stalled any longer, the two of them would have marched into my quarters, dumped a bucket of ice water over my head, and hauled me bodily out of bed.

Strangely enough, the thought makes me feel a little better.

Our mission in the Rhyska System is like all of our other ops, but with one crucial difference. The planetary net around our primary target, a terrestrial planet called Rhyskara, is down. How it happened, nobody knows. Though we commed the OP crews repeatedly, we got no response. Some sort of large-scale malfunction, too big for the skeleton crews to fix in time, would be the most likely explanation.

Either that or somebody did it deliberately. Not that anyone really wants to dwell on that possibility much.

Though the net has been down for weeks from the looks of it, we go into stealth mode anyway, and the bridge crew is put on twenty-four hour alert in case we come under ambush. While that makes for long shifts for the naval crew, it's even worse for the teams. Instead of the five platforms we were expecting, we've now got a round robin on our hands. A tall order, especially now that we're so understaffed. Our only consolation is that at least this is our last system. Once we finish Rhyska, we're done.

Then it's all up to the Archangel.

———

We start with the primary OP and work our way around the network, the two teams alternating Inside and Outside Ops as usual. For a round robin, it's less demanding than I would have expected. Most of the platforms are completely deserted—no squatters, no ghouls, no humans. It's as though everyone just picked up and fled when the net fell, friend and foe alike, leaving only emptiness behind.

I lead my team through one such platform, launcher readied and stun pistol within easy reach. Our steps echo loudly off the silent walls, a hollow counterpart to our filtered breathing as we walk slowly down the abandoned concourse. The air tastes of dust and the flickering lights cry of loneliness, but of the enemy, there is no sign. Raisman and Kagawa cover the doors, and I stand guard over Jethro while he uploads the software. My nostrils continually twitch as I scent for ghouls, but the familiar sour-and-sweet reek never comes, not even when the task is finally completed and we make our way back to the outer hatch. It's strange walking through a platform from end to end without smelling a single whiff of the enemy odor that's become so familiar to me.

We find out what happened to the net on our fifth platform. With no one to guard against and nothing to do but wait around until Jeth finishes with the upload, Raisman starts tapping around in the database.

"You realize that's only a surveillance console," Jethro tells her as he leans against the main command console.

"Exactly. With nothing to do all day but guard one quarantined planet, they must have some killer holo games." Raisman types a few more things in. "Wait, what do we have here?"

Footage springs up from the console, showing an image of the planet below, its dull olive exterior covered by a brilliant blue light—

the planetary net. The timestamp in the lower corner indicates a date almost a five-square ago. Raisman flips through various scenes, all showing some section or other of the net. She suddenly stops, winds the footage back, and points. As I watch, *something* flies through the lowest layer of the net, sliding straight through the latticework like a perfectly shot bullet. *What the . . . ?*

Blazing furls explode through the net as the device goes up in a fiery blast. For a moment, all I see is orange and blue, the incendiary clouds puffing through the electric blue lines of the net as though they aren't even there. Then suddenly the blue winks out, like power going out in a city, spreading out from the epicenter of the blast in every direction.

"There!" Raisman freezes the holo and points to something barely visible at the edge of the frame. A silver shield generator. "The blast took out a whole section of shield generators, which somehow caused a chain reaction through the rest of the network. That's what knocked down the net."

"Don't they have safeguards against that sort of thing?" I ask with a frown.

Raisman shakes her head. "I don't know how they managed it. Do you know the sort of timing and precision that would have been required to get that thing through the net?"

"Difficult?"

"Like a one-in-a-billion shot. Even then, the other generators should have compensated for the ones that were destroyed."

"Should have?"

Raisman shrugs. "Even the best shields will fail if you take out the right generators."

I frown, not liking the answer at all. Billion-to-one shot it might be, but I can't help wondering: *If they got through this net, what other nets might they be able to get through?*

"Got it!" Jethro calls from the next console. "Upload is completed and initialized."

We pack it in, jogging back through the OP, hopping a shuttle, and heading for our next target. Before long, we're coming up on the next platform, where we'll get the outside work started while Song-bird's team finishes up on the previous platform. As we disembark on the hull with our gas canisters, Raisman's words continue to echo through my mind, and no matter how hard I try, I can't get them out of my head.

Even the best shields will fail if you take out the right generators.

————

Our luck runs out on the second-to-last platform. After fourteen Ops that are either deserted or merely ghoul-infested, we finally find out what happened to the military detachment left to oversee the planet.

"It's a trap! Fall back! Fall back to the Control Room now!"

Songbird's voice screams over the com, calling her team back to her as the enemy converges on them from every direction. Footsteps pound in the background, interspersed with shouts and calls, the whoosh of launchers and the whine of stun pistols; while on my face shield, force fences light up my vision until everything before me is washed in the fatal tint of crimson.

From my perch on the underside of the platform, I hover in space over the central shield generator, welder clutched in my right hand while I wait, helpless to do anything but listen as my teammates fight for their lives.

"Lyons, Devereaux—stay tight on the starboard door. Gemma and Ali, you stay on port. Everyone else, group around RC. Whatever happens, whatever comes through those doors, you protect him until he can get that software uploaded!"

A chorus of affirmatives rings out over Gamma Team's channel, cut by the sound of more shots. Over at the next shield generator dish, 'Vange turns his head in my direction. *"TL?"* he asks softly through our private channel. Around us, the rest of our team works on, blissfully ignorant of the carnage just above our heads as they go about their modifications, coms set solely for Delta Team's channel.

I shake my head minutely at him. "You know our orders: Outside team stays outside. Besides, even if we left now, we'd never get there in time. All we can do now is get our work done, and pray to God they get theirs done."

And hope that the enemy doesn't decide to come out for us once they're done with Gamma.

I bend my head to my task once again, gritting my teeth as I weld the new power stabilizer to the dish while I continue listening to the firefight above. In addition to the familiar whooshes and whines, an electric crackle I know all too well sizzles across the com: decimators. From a distance, our armor can handle those high-energy bolts, but up close . . . Archer's neck, charred and black, flashes into my mind, and I mutter a silent prayer to myself.

"TL, they're coming around for another pass! I don't thin—"

A loud crackle, followed on its heels by a high-pitched shriek. On the left-hand side of my shield, a life sign blinks out.

Songbird swears as a couple of stun bolts ring out. *"Erisi! Any luck with those doors?"*

"They've locked 'em open somehow, TL. I can't get 'em shut!"

"Acknowledged! Slide up to help Lyons on starboard."

De-acking the welder, I tug on the new stabilizer to ensure it's secure. My hand shakes within my gauntlet, hidden by the thick fabric though I swear I can feel the tremble all the way up my arm and down my spine. I force myself to keep it together, calling out to my team over Delta's channel for a status update even as two more of Gamma's life signs blink out in a single instant.

"Team Leader . . ." 'Vange's voice audibly quivers, but I have no answer for his plea. I don't even have an answer for my own plea, scratching deep at my heart like a dog at the door begging to be let out.

"We can't hold much longer! RC, ETA!"

"I don't know, I—"

"Port team is down! I repeat, port te—"

Another life sign goes out in a blink of light. Footsteps rain against the decking amidst a flurry of shots, both sides, followed by the solid thunk of bodies colliding. Panting grunts and cracking bones; the snap of a neck and the rip of a combat knife across an exposed throat. I don't need the visuals. Not when the sounds run through my ears like blood.

The stabilizer comes on with a low whine, vibrating lightly through my hands as I adjust the settings and check the power levels.

"We're not going to make it. There's just too many of them!"

Three fast clangs, like that of a head being bashed against a wall, and another life sign drops off the board.

Passing my scanner over the dish, I run a quick diagnostic to verify that all my modifications were integrated into the generator correctly.

A stun bolt whizzes through my ear, followed by the clatter of a weapon skidding across the floor and the wet spatter of blood. Only two life signs remain now, their signatures glowing vulnerable and alone across my visor.

"Almost there, TL. Just a little longer."

"RC, how I—"

Songbird's voice cuts off, sliced away by the crack of a decimator sizzling across the com. A loud thump resounds in my ears a split second later—the thump of a body hitting the floor—and I don't have to check the life signs on my shield to know:

Songbird is dead.

"Infinity, this is RC! The upload is complete! Repeat, the upload i—"

The final voice of Gamma disappears from the universe forever in a fiery crackle. Numbly, I deactivate their channel on my com. It feels unfair that I should be crouched here alive while they're dead, but I know, as every soldier does, that fair never has anything to do with it. In the end, all I can do—all any of us can do—is honor their memory and continue on.

With that in mind, I raise my hand in silent salute. Then, sitting back on my haunches, I stare out into the endless well of space where, shrouded deep within its very soundlessness, I observe a moment of silence for my fallen comrades.

————

It's only later, as I'm racking my gear in the armory after returning to the *Infinity*, that it suddenly occurs to me: With Songbird and RC gone, there's only one person from my list of suspects left.

Ty.

And she's a million light-years away.

35 THE SHUTTLE LIFTS OFF from the platform, accelerating from standstill to hard thrust within seconds. I slump back in my seat, hardly able to believe it. After eleven weeks, eighty-six operations, and seventeen casualties, we've done it. We've finished our last OP.

The mission is *over.*

Nervous excitement fills the cabin, the specialists glancing back and forth at each other, their faces brimming with relief and exhaustion, disbelief and triumph. However, no one celebrates. Not yet. Not until we all pass through the psy check. Not until we know if we all made it.

We debark at Docking Ring 2B, where PsySergeant Han Di awaits us with a security detail as usual. I want to believe with all my heart that none of my people are infected, that we all came out whole, but when you run the Inside mission, all bets are off. All it takes is a few ghouls waiting in the airlock, and you're infected without realizing it before the op even begins.

Though it's my prerogative as Team Leader to be checked first, I cede the position to my ATL. 'Vange acknowledges the favor with a nod of his head before undergoing the psychic scan. He passes with flying colors, after which I signal the psysergeant to move on to the rest of my team. I know all too well the nail-biting agony of those minutes when you wait to find out whether you're infected or whole, whether you'll be heading back to your bunk for a well deserved rest or to a holding cell en route to a quarantine colony. Though I can't do anything about all of the hardships my team has suffered, the exhaustion or the casualties, I can spare them these few minutes at least.

The last specialist passes the check and exits the ring, leaving just me, the psysergeant, and the security detail. I take a breath and try to ignore the pounding of my heart. Though I've been through this so many times it's become routine, this time feels different. As though every op I've been on since this mission began all comes down to this one check. And in a way, it does. My one comfort is that whatever happens to me, at least I know my team is going home. Squaring my jaw, I offer my hand to the psysergeant.

As usual, I can't even tell Han Di's in my mind, his touch light and as noninvasive as possible as he probes for the telltale signs that one of the enemy has taken root in my mind. When he finally releases my hand, I lift my chin and meet his eyes, determined that whatever he says, I'll reply with dignity.

"Team Leader," he begins, a grave expression in his eyes as he shakes his head. "I'm so sorry . . ."

My heart sinks at the declaration, and I bow my head to hide my disappointment.

". . . but you're not getting out of the war this easily. For now, you're going to have to keep fighting with the rest of us."

Wait, what?! My gaze pops up, head shaking in confusion, and Han Di suddenly breaks into a huge grin. The security detail begins chuckling, obvious mirth on their faces as they stare at my gape-mouthed expression, and that's when it finally sinks in.

I'm okay.

"Son of a . . . ! I can't *believe* you made me think I was—!" I stop, chuckles of relief issuing out of my mouth now that I can appreciate the joke a little more.

Han Di gives me a good-natured slap on the back. "Congratulations, Team Leader."

I nod in acceptance and make my way out of the docking ring, ready for nothing more than a meal and bed. My mouth drops open as I emerge onto the main docking deck to find myself surrounded.

I stop, head twisting frantically back and forth as I survey the situation. I'm standing in a small circle of space with my team, surrounded on three sides by people packed shoulder to shoulder, all staring straight at me. I goggle at them all, uncertain what to make of the tableau before me. It looks like everyone on the ship has turned out, all crowded in a huge semicircle around me and my team, who look just as confused as I am. For a long minute, the deck is so quiet you could hear a chit drop. Then the silence breaks, and they're all clapping and cheering.

My mouth falls open in total shock. Everyone on the *Infinity*, from the pilots and shuttle crews to the equipment techs and navy personnel, all the way up to Major Estes herself, is here. Triumph shines in their eyes, along with joy and pride, and I finally understand. They all turned out for *us*. To be here in our moment of victory, applauding our skills and recognizing our sacrifices, sharing our pain and celebrating our successes.

My throat chokes up at the unexpected outpouring, and I'm suddenly overcome with how grateful I am to them. To the pilots and shuttle crews, who constantly risked infection by flying us in and out, and the equipment techs, who made sure our gear never faltered. To the support staff, who always kept our clothes clean and bellies full, and the navy personnel, who worked double shifts to keep the mission on schedule. How strange that *they* should be applauding *me* when it's *I* who should be applauding *them*.

After a minute, the crowd quiets, clearly expecting me to speak. I clear my throat, struggling to find the words, but all that comes out is:

"Thank you."

Two words, so completely inadequate to describe how I feel. For the first time since enlisting, I find myself wishing I were something more than a simple soldier. That I were the sort of lofty person capable of meeting an occasion like this with elegant speeches and fancy words.

However, as I look around at all the joyous faces, it occurs to me that maybe I don't need to be anything more than what I am. Because for all my deficiencies, somehow they seem to understand anyway.

———

We jump from the system within the hour, beginning the two-week journey that will take us back to R&D. Deployment Day is only fifteen days away now—just enough time to make it back as long as we don't experience any unexpected delays. Not that anyone expects to. We're too well armed to invite attack even if we were to stumble across a ship of squatters, and with all the brand new tech installed in the ship, a breakdown is unlikely.

I spend the majority of the first week sleeping. After the long days and short nights we were continually subjected to during the mission, I'm exhausted. Physically, mentally, emotionally. Though we fulfilled our mission, the casualties were high. Too high. I see the faces of the dead—Archer and RC and Songbird—like ghosts in my mind, and a sort of numbness fills my heart. It's as though my mind knows they're gone, but my heart can't quite process it. Perhaps it's for the best, a little respite while my heart catches up to where my mind has already trodden.

A respite from the grief of losing my team, perhaps, but not from losing *her*.

Today I sit at the viewport on the back deck of the *Infinity* and stare out at the stars. They wink and shimmer against the black of space, an endless sea of lamps to hold away the dark. A field of lights shining forever, never to be doused.

When I was young, my mother once told me that each star was a soul, a departed spirit that rose into the sky to watch over us forever. We'd sat out on the porch at our old house on Aurora, and I'd asked her what made them shine so bright. She'd simply smiled that beautiful smile of hers and said:

"Love, of course. Love is what shines through the dark when all else seems lost. So if you're ever missing someone you've loved and lost, simply look up and there you'll find them, burning high above your head in the night sky."

"But there are so many stars. How will I know which one is them?"

"Look for the one that's shining only for you. That twinkles just a little bit more, burns just a little bit hotter, for you. Find the star

that brightens under your gaze, made brilliant by your love, and you'll know—that's the one."

It was only a story, a fairytale to tell young children who lie awake, afraid of the dark, and yet every time I look out into space— *really* look—I find myself looking for *her*. For the star that shines only for me.

Lia.

After a week in transit, we're stopping over at Hera Station for a quick refueling before finishing the trip home. As usual, I have no assignments or duties now that my part of the mission is complete. Just a day of rest and relaxation before jumping again. By all rights it should be an easy day, but of all the days of this mission, all the days since coming to R&D, this one is the hardest. It hangs over my head like a cloud, a day I can't shake or put aside no matter how hard I try.

The second anniversary of Lia's death.

I peer out into the dark divide just beyond the viewport—a *real* viewport, not just a digitized frame. If there were ever a day I could look out into the stars and find Lia twinkling back at me, this would be the day, but just like every other time I've looked, I find nothing. Nothing but luminescent balls of gas burning light-years away, soul-less and untouchable.

The doors to the deck slide open, and Jethro, Raisman, and a few others come in. They brandish some new holo game, along with an invitation to join them, but I tell them no, not today. I have other things on my mind and other aches in my heart, ones that can't be resolved by playing games or laughing with comrades. So I go back to my room, swiping my chit hand across the pad and walking in, but I can't seem to get past the door. Lia's ghost is here, nervously scrambling for her shoes as she explains:

"I had to make sure you were sat, right?"

How many times I've wished I could walk into my room the way I did that night over two years ago only to find Lia there, having waited all night for me to come back. Waited for no other reason than to make sure *I* was okay. How many times I've wished she were here, and I could tell her, *"No, I'm not satisfactory. I'm not okay. Because without you here, nothing is right."*

Only the strange thing is: I'm not sure it's true anymore.

My breath quickens at the thought, as though the idea of not need-ing Lia anymore is a sacrilege, a crime of the heart that can never be excused let alone forgiven. I thought I'd never be able to accept her death—her suicide borne in patriotism, her silent truths never told. How could I say goodbye when I felt only a rage that couldn't be sat-isfied and an emptiness that couldn't be filled? So I used to think, but time, or perhaps experience, has dimmed the pain—the emptiness filled with new loyalties, allegiances worth dying for—and the anger transformed into a drive to do something greater, just as Lia once did.

The sorrow is still there, and her memory hasn't vanished, but her ghost no longer haunts me the way it once did, the cloying odor of her presence softened to a hint of lilac scenting the air. I miss her; I love her; I mourn her. But I can go on without her. I *have* gone on without her. Despite desire or design, despite any conscious decision on my part, I've forged a new life, one tempered by losses but still one worth living. I've put aside the emptiness and found new meaning. The one thing I haven't done is say goodbye.

Though we're not stopping long enough to grant shore leave to the specialists, as Team Leader I can leave the ship at will. After passing through a quick psy check, I stride out across the platform, marveling at the food vendors and the game kiosks and the scrolling ads along the walls. After spending the past weeks on OPs laden with ghouls and squatters, it's strange to be on one filled with just . . . people.

Despite the crowded conditions, I don't have any problems navi-gating the mob, and it's only after an older man in a worn shipsuit backs away after bumping me with a hasty, "My apologies, sir," that I realize it's because people are making room for me. Moving back and giving way for me like they did for Angelou all those months ago on Kittridge Promenade.

I accept the man's apology with a bemused nod, wondering if it's simply the uniform, with its crisp black folds and authoritative gold insignia, that inspires this strange deference or if it's something alto-gether more intrinsically *me*, these people seeing in me the same thing the people of Kittridge saw in Angelou.

Me, like Angelou? I laugh away the idea with a shake of my head. We're as different as space and atmosphere; Angelou the vacuum, remote and brilliant and deadly, his frost-blue eyes piercing the dark like distant stars, while I'm just one of a billion other breaths we take in every day and forget the moment we let it go.

Halfway down the second promenade, I find what I'm looking for: a hydroponics vendor specializing in flowering plants. I ask for a dozen roses, sealed for travel, not even blinking when I see the astronomical cost. The vendor eyes me up and down as she wraps up the flowers, no doubt seeing a soldier on leave buying roses for a wife or girlfriend.

"Flowers for a special someone? How lovely," she adds at my gruff nod. A sad smile tinges her lips. "It's always hard to be the one who's left behind."

"Yes," I agree softly. "It is."

Back on the ship, I put on my mission suit and, flowers in hand, slip out through the upper hatch. I mag my boots and hook myself onto one of the stay-beams, crouching down on the roof of the ship with the ease of long training. Except for a spacer doing EVA work at a distant berth, I'm completely alone out here. Alone but for a galaxy of stars above my head and the weight of a ship beneath my feet. With a silent prayer, I carefully unseal my package.

The roses freeze the second they touch vacuum, any lingering life in those blood-red blooms instantly leaching away in the bitter cold. Yet even dead, they still hold a brittle beauty, their petals frozen in a fleeting moment of eternal youth.

"All she thought about in the end was you. 'Tell Michael: If I could have stayed, I would have.' That's what she said."

I brush my fingers over a single rose, remembering another flower not unlike this. A few petals break off at my touch, drifting weightlessly up from my fingers. I don't try to stop them, but simply watch them float away, like crimson butterflies through the night.

If I could have stayed, I would have.

"I know," I tell her softly.

And for the first time, maybe I really do know.

Reeling back my arm, I cast the bouquet into the vacuum. It bursts apart like a firework, scarlet petals scattering in every direction as they fly out into the void. I magnify my lenses and watch until every last rose petal has fluttered out of sight, swallowed up within the magnificence of the stars and the darkness of space.

Her life, her love; so brilliant they shine through the dark like guiding stars that show you the way and are never lost.

She has no grave. No monument to visit nor stone to mark her passing. But perhaps one day, thousands, even millions of years from now, one of those petals will wash up on the shores of New Sol, borne across the universe by some fey combination of luck and circumstance. And on that day, one especially bright star will look down on that petal and shine brighter than she ever has—a radiant star that shines forever and never dies.

───────

Hours later, I lay in bed as the clock rises on midnight, and my eyes snap open. *She never called,* I suddenly realize. It was the anniversary of Lia's death, and Teal never called.

Something lurches in my chest at the thought of letting Lia's anniversary go by with nothing from Teal to mark it, and then I'm activating my chit before I've consciously decided to do so.

Though we're coms-off for this mission and I can't link her directly, I open a new hmail. My chit stares at me like some sort of evil eye, menacing and cold. I take a deep breath and start to speak . . . but just like before, the words don't come, frozen within my throat no matter how much I might will them to thaw. Seconds pass, one piling atop the next, and still all I can do is stare silently into thin air, mute and alone. At last, I give up.

Dropping my hand, I delete the hmail and de-ac my chit.

36

OURS IS THE LAST SHIP to arrive back at R&D, returning to the station only a day before the Archangel is set to go live. As I step inside its crystalline walls for the first time in weeks, I feel a curious sense of homecoming. Instead of returning to H5 straightaway, I walk the outer corridor of the Central Habitat, looking out over the mists as they creep and drift in billows of pink and gold, lavender and white. It's early morning, and Demeter's light is just beginning to dawn over the quiet halls. The trickle of the waterfalls sings in my ears, and from time to time my hand strays across the wall beside me, knuckles sliding across glassy smoothness or softly caressing the petals of a flowering plant.

I've missed this place, I realize with a jolt. The habitats, the halls, the drifting mists. The crystalline light as it bends and refracts in wild rainbows through the carved panes. Even the unshakeable presence of the Spectres, so close and yet so far, their invisible forms essential within the kaleidoscopic vision of R&D. Against all expectation, in the months I've spent here, this station in the sky has somehow become *home* more than any place I've been since New Sol blew.

My mind goes to the Archangel, with its network of platforms and ships spread out across the Expanse. In less than twenty-four hours, it will strike down our enemies with its sword of light, rippling across planets and stations, colonies and asteroids, until every last ghoul has disappeared, banished to hell or wherever Specs go when they perish. When that happens, what will become of me? Of all of R&D? With the enemy vanquished, they might very well decide our talents could be put to better use elsewhere, the scientists sent off to work on other projects and the testers shipped back to the Navy or Guard, or wherever else they came from. Of course I'll go wherever they send me. I'm a soldier. It's who I am. Still, the thought of leaving this place for good fills me with a sorrow too deep to articulate.

Back in H5, I take care of some small homecoming chores, stashing my gear away and filing my report on our last mission. By the time I'm done, the station is stirring, waking from its drifting slumber in an ever-increasing rustle of movement and sound. I wander the corridors of H5 and H7, looking for familiar faces. The halls are notably empty, the number of those infected or killed higher than I care to count, though I do find testers in small clumps here and there, in the barracks, the lounge, the training rooms. All people I recognize, but none that I know particularly well. The specialists come to attention when I pass through, nodding in deferent, if informal, acknowledgement of my presence.

At 0900 on the dot, I report in to the Division Commander's office, only to be told I have no assigned duties until further notice. With our work essentially done, there's nothing to do now but wait for the Archangel. Though the news isn't exactly a surprise, I can't help feeling a certain dread, like they've already decided to cut us all loose and just haven't told us yet. The idea of spending my last few days waiting to be let go turns my stomach.

"Commander, please. There must be something that needs doing."

"Is the word 'relax' in no one's vocabulary?" Asriel snorts. I raise an eyebrow as if to say, *You would know.* With a roll of his eyes, he relents. "All right, Sorenson. Ty's taking a team down to Javeyn to collect some old testing equipment. If she gives the go-ahead, you can join them. Dismissed."

Ty. So she *did* make it back. My eyes light up, lips curling into an involuntary smile at the news that one of my old Delta mates made it. Then my shoulders tighten, tension instantly knotting down my spine as I remember: Hers was the last name on my list. Joy wars with despair, and for a brief moment I wish she'd never come back at all. That she'd simply died out there in the black and I could rest easy knowing the saboteur was safely dead. Only I can't. Whether she's guilty or not, I have to face her.

With a nod to Asriel, I set out to find Ty. Rather than simply link her, I use my locator to track her down in the armory. She's gearing up for the mission when I arrive, along with a team of six others. I don't immediately announce myself but just stand there, watching her. She looks like the same old Ty, but . . . graver, perhaps. Like she's lived a lot more life since I last saw her, and all that life has finally started taking its toll. As, too, it has on me. A whole host of emotions rise up in me—happiness, anger, sorrow, confusion. She's a teammate I trusted with my life; could she really be the saboteur who's been stalking me these long months?

Ty turns then, wheeling around to speak to one of her subordinates, and her eyes alight on me. Her sudden grin is a punch to the stomach. Despite my reservations, I can't help returning her hearty hug and accompanying backslap with a couple of my own.

"Sorenson! Didn't think you were going to make it back."

"Just put thrusters down this morning. Got room for one more?"

"You bet. And look! Now that we're on the verge of wiping out the ghouls, they've come out with another round of ghoul suits. Clearly they didn't have much to do while we were all away implementing the Archangel tech."

I check my locker, and sure enough, I've got one too. I roll my eyes, half in exasperation, half in amusement. "Oh, joy."

We gear up and drop into Javeyn's atmosphere within the hour. Though I try to act like nothing's wrong, my feet flutter in my boots, anxiety building with each passing minute. Ty glances at me curiously, but if she suspects anything's wrong, she doesn't remark on it. At last our pilot puts us down just outside a city in a very familiar-looking field dotted with metallic cylinders in every direction.

Ty pulls a meter-long cylinder from the ground with a grin. "Remember these?"

"The sound amplifiers?" I laugh, forgetting for a moment that Ty might very well be a saboteur and I should be arresting her, not joking with her. "How could I forget? One blast on those things, and every ghoul in the sector came running."

Per Ty's instruction, we split off in teams of two, taking roamers in every direction to collect the amplifiers. I drive and Ty gathers, scanning her chit hand across each sound amplifier before she stows it in the back to mark its collection. In between amplifiers, we coast along in the roamer, sometimes talking, sometimes in silence. Now that I've got her alone, I have no idea what to say.

"The habitats seem pretty empty."

She tilts her head in acknowledgement. "We took some losses. Zephyr, Annah—"

"Archer, Songbird, RC." I pause. "Anyone left?"

"I saw Chen poking her head into the mess not too long ago, and of course Asriel's still DC."

I nod, gaze falling to her arms where they emerge from the rolled-up sleeves of her tunic. The thick red slash for Zel is still there, just below her elbow, now joined by several newer ones in varying thicknesses, black and red. A quiet hymn to our fallen comrades. I feel a strange lurch in my stomach as I realize that if I hadn't come back, there would have been yet another one on her arm for me.

"Look, Ty—" I start to say, unable to keep silent any longer.

"It's going to rain," she says at the exact same time.

"What?"

She pats her right leg. "It's going to rain. Ever since I broke it, I can always tell."

I frown. "When did you break your leg? On the Archangel mission?"

"No, I broke it in a training op a few weeks before we left. I almost didn't make it on the mission at all. As it was, they wouldn't let me out of the infirmary for, like, a two-square." She casts me a sidelong look and adds sarcastically, "Thanks for visiting me in the medcenter, by the way."

My heart quickens as the implications of her words sink in. I try to remember if I saw her at all during those final weeks before the launch, but I can't recall. Of course, it was such a hectic time, I barely saw anyone who wasn't on my own team. "Two weeks? And they didn't let you out of the infirmary at all?"

"Nope. It was boring as slag, too." She activates her chit, thumbing through her holo archive until she finally stops on a single recording. "See?"

I stare at the holo in amazement. The setting is clearly the infirmary, and the star is Ty herself, waving, smiling, and making faces at her chit lens. She sweeps her hand down, moving the image over her hospital gown until her legs come into view. Her right leg is immobilized in a quick-heal cast, the large casing connected with an array of wires and tubes to a huge machine nearby. *"Two more days to go before this sucker is healed,"* her voice narrates from the recording. *"Can I make it without dying of boredom?"* My eyes go to the date stamp on the bottom of the holo.

It's the night before the energy converter arrived on base.

My mouth drops open as the truth hits me right between the eyes. There's no possible way she could've left the infirmary, let alone gotten to the energy converter, not with her leg imprisoned in the quick-heal cast like that. She's not the saboteur.

Relief flows through me at the realization. Relief, and consternation. If it wasn't her, who was it? RC? Songbird? Someone else who was removed from the list by dint of death or infection? I suppose it'll have to be enough to know that the threat is gone, whoever it might have been.

Heart lighter now that I've cleared Ty and closed my investigation for good, the rest of the collection goes without incident. If any squatters have managed to breed any ghouls since we last fired the Archangel, they aren't within range. The only hiccup comes when we meet up with the others to find one of the amplifiers is missing. Ty checks the original deployment data and suddenly laughs.

"Ha! That's why it's not here. It's the one we lost on the original testing mission. With Zel." A note of wistfulness enters her voice.

"That was months ago; it could be anywhere by now. Can we track it?"

She shakes her head. "I'm not sure. We'd have to check with Dr. Rahman. At any rate, we don't have time to track it down now. Asriel wants everyone back on the station before the big to-do tonight. We'll have to come back for it."

We load up and bug out, putting boots back on the station within the hour. The amplifiers get crated up and stored against the north wall in Habitat 8—a lengthy task even with grav sleds to handle the weighty bins—then everyone's dismissed to clean up and eat. As we step into the Central Habitat, I'm immediately hit by how packed the halls are. R&D personnel of all stamps jam the outer corridor, a bounce in their steps and a lilt in their voices as they chatter in an excited flurry.

I press myself against the wall to make way for a pair of elderly scientists passing by. "What's with everyone?"

"Haven't you heard? Oh, that's right. You just got back this morning." Ty shrugs. "They're going to fire the Archangel."

"Now?"

"Just over Prism. They're going to link all the planetary OPs together and eliminate the enemy down below—or at least, what's left of them—in one fell swoop. It's a final test before the full deployment tomorrow. Everyone's gathering in the Atrium to watch." She checks her timekeeper. "If we go now, I bet we can snag seats before they're all taken."

I shrug. It's not like I have anything better to do.

We're settling down on a couch near the east wall of the Atrium when I suddenly recall the final chip I found in my helmet all those weeks ago. Cloistered away on the *Infinity*, I'd been unable to run the number through the R&D database and had subsequently forgotten about it.

My mood darkens as I think of the chip. By all rights, I should simply toss it and forget I ever found it. After all, with everyone on my list of suspects either dead or eliminated, the threat should be moot. Only what if the saboteur, whoever it was, laid one last trap before leaving R&D? Just because the saboteur is gone doesn't mean the trap won't spring. I should at least check the number.

"Hey, Ty, I'm going to—" A good excuse suddenly failing me, I wave a hand vaguely in the other direction. "Be right back."

I beat a hasty retreat before she can quiz me on my sudden desertion. Jogging across the crowded floor, my eyes light on a set of hygiene units nearby. Rather than go all the way back to my quarters, I shut myself into the nearest unit. Lights spring on as I enter, bathing the cubicle in a soft glow. Through the wall, I can hear the excited din from the Atrium as everyone waits for the final Archangel test to begin, but I ignore it, intent on putting this wild goose chase to rest once and for all. Activating my chit, I locate the chip number and enter it into the inventory database.

Error: No Match Found

Though I should have come to expect the unexpected by now, shock still fills me at the result. A bad feeling creeps into the pit of my stomach. The game has changed once again, but I have no idea why or how. With nothing else to do, I start running the number through every database I can think of, hitting "search" again and again. On my ninth trial, I find a match. The chip's number is for a *shipping manifest*. Specifically, a manifest for a shipment of items originally brought on base months ago.

I frown in confusion, unsure why the saboteur would suddenly change tack so oddly. Through the wall, the noise of the crowd has dimmed, replaced by a single amplified voice, though I can't make out what it's saying. Probably someone announcing the upcoming test. I ignore it, scrolling through the manifest as I search for . . . I'm uncertain what. Halfway down, I stop. There, in the middle of the list, is the serial number and description for the blown ignition regulator from the *SkyRunner*.

I suck in a breath. A chip number from a custom helmet connecting back to an ignition regulator destroyed long before the helmet was even made? Connections are being made between present, past, and future, and I suddenly have the feeling I'm on the cusp of something important. I force myself to think about the situation logically. After giving me seven serial numbers, why did the saboteur suddenly switch to the number of a shipping manifest?

Because it's not about the items themselves, but how they were shipped.

Once again, my eyes slide over the manifest, but instead of looking at the items this time, I examine the details of the shipment itself. Shuttle name, shipment date, invoice number, origin site, and—

Shuttle crew.

Something kicks low and hard in my stomach. All this time, I'd assumed the sabotage was done on base, which never quite added up because the various items were stored and installed in such disparate locations. With Angelou's tight security procedures, no single person would have been able to access them all. But what if the saboteur didn't do their work on base but completed it before the equipment ever arrived?

Pulling up the shipment database, I enter the serial numbers from every chip I found and hit search. Twenty-nine documents come up, including both original shipment and transfer manifests. I set my chit to scan each document for the crew manifest, looking for the one name associated with every single piece of sabotaged equipment I've found. My foot taps nervously on the floor as I wait, the quick strikes of my boot loud in the sudden silence—they must be about to fire the Archangel over Prism. When the results finally come, my mouth drops open.

Every single piece on my list was originally brought into R&D by the *same pilot*.

And there's the connection. After all these months of searching, I've got it: The identity of the saboteur who would do anything, hurt anybody, if it meant stopping the Archangel. I'd crossed her off my list after the converter incident because she didn't have access to H8, but then, why would she need habitat access when the equipment was sitting right there on the ship with her hours before arriving at R&D?

Cheers break out on the other side of the wall, hurrahs and claps and joyous shouts. They spill out of the central chamber and fill the hygiene unit, their hopeful tones brimming on all sides of me, while all I can do is slump on the toilet and stare at that one name in utter disbelief.

The name of our saboteur is Pilot Commander Sarai Chen.

Onboard Orbital Platform N
Command Platform for Prism's Orbital Network

THE DOCTOR STOOD ON THE OBSERVATION DECK, looking down at the swirling pastel world below as the countdown steadily played out. Silently, he counted along with it, letting the numbers slide through his mind like silk, their sweet anticipation a scientific seduction.

Though he knew what to expect, he couldn't help catching his breath as the countdown ran out and the combined force of sixteen OPs shot down through the void, enveloping the planet in a ball of light. Even after the energy had dissipated into the pastel mists, still the palest aura of silver rippled around the planet's form like a halo glowing delicately against the black void of space.

The Doctor smiled slightly at the observation. Halo, indeed. The Archangel was truly well named.

His smile faded as his eyes flicked to the test data running over the wall beside him. Everything had gone exactly as it should have— the OPs firing in exact unison, all perfectly positioned to blanket the planet in an even glaze of energy—with the results of the data only confirming what they'd worked for months to achieve.

The Archangel was ready.

In less than twenty-four hours, their day would finally come. The Archangel would fire once again, not just on Prism but across every planet and station in the Expanse; and in the silver halo of its light, this defensive, one-sided war would turn on its head in an instant, with the human race no longer the hunted but the hunter. Everything—every trial, every observation, every piece of data—told him so, and yet . . .

And yet.

Despite all logic and science, fact and reason, even faith itself, he was afraid. Dread twisted through his gut like the biblical serpent, its cold whisper threatening everything he held dear, and no assurances he might tender himself could shake it. They were still in the game. Maybe not for long, but for the next eighteen hours, the enemy still held a hand in this deadly war.

They still had their final card to play.

The Doctor had no idea what card it might be. All he knew was that somehow, some way, the enemy would make their move. Mindless eaters, merciless conquerors. For so long, he'd bought the same rhetoric as everyone else in the Expanse, never believing them anything more than simply predators. Intelligent, wily predators, but predators nonetheless. Yet as they got closer and closer to the day of reckoning, somehow all of the unanswered questions gathered over the previous months only gnawed at him more, not less, like a puzzle left unfinished because no one had the fortitude of mind to work it patiently to its conclusion.

Seo Pak. Nguyen. The false R&D. The enemy's change in tactics and their inexplicable adaptations. The takedown of the planetary nets and the sharp uptick in the infection rate. For months, every sign had told him the enemy was on the move. That they were abandoning their simple planet-by-planet strategy and gearing up for a new offensive, a massive assault the likes of which no one had ever seen before. Yet he sensed there was something more at play than a simple military strike. There were just too many inexplicable outliers—odd happenings and tactics that made no sense, one-offs of no real consequence that when strung together created a series of events that defied coherent explanation. Regardless of what the others thought, he couldn't help feeling they were indicative of something much more, of some greater purpose to this war than he'd ever suspected.

"And just what is it you think it all means?" the Admiral asked,

raising her eyebrow in obvious skepticism. "What is it you think the enemy is doing?"

The Doctor strolled along the windows of the observation deck, hands clasped behind his back as he considered the Admiral's question. Prism glowed just below him, and though he was too far away to see it, he could still envision every drift, every swirl, every dance of her heavenly mists. He gazed down at the planet for a long time, mind deep in thought, and when his answer finally came, it carried a damning finality that not even the Admiral could refute.

"I believe they're playing a game much greater than we could ever imagine, one that neither you, nor I, nor any other human in the entire universe is qualified to comprehend.

"And whatever their final intentions, if they win the day, if they succeed in this battle and we fail, there won't be anything in the universe we can do to stop them."

PHASE FOUR

37 DEPLOYMENT DAY DAWNS BRIGHT and full of promise. The anticipatory air of the day before has sharpened during the night, honed only keener by the successful final test of the Archangel. It whips through the halls like a spring zephyr carrying the thrill of summer while still retaining the icy edge of winter.

Though I rise early, the rest of the station appears to have had the same idea, for the halls are already filled with people chattering excitedly about what's to come. Their enthusiasm is a living thing, twining about everyone like the plants that wrap these crystalline walls, lush and life-giving. Everyone except for me, that is. Dread lies heavily in my gut, and I can't help remembering another day like this, a day more than two years ago that began with anticipation and ended in despair. Lia died that day, went up in a blaze of light for the whole universe to see, and there was nothing I could do to stop it. But today is not that day, and I'm not that naïve boy anymore. If I want this day to have a different ending, I have to make it happen. Whatever it takes.

"Whatever it takes" equating to breaking into Chen's quarters, in this case.

I stand in the middle of her chamber and cast my eyes over the place, a twin to my own quarters with its bunk, closet, storage locker, and desk. A door on one wall leads to a tiny hygiene unit just beyond. The place is spare, regulation-neat, and I'm not sure what I really expect to find here. A pile of chips engraved with serial numbers? Another laser cutter? Or better yet, a signed note saying, "I'm the traitor."

I shake my head in despair. I emerged from the hygiene unit last night only to get immediately waylaid for a last-minute assignment in H8 with the inventory personnel. By the time I made it back to the barracks, it was barely a minute before curfew—too late to follow up on my surprising lead.

I sigh as I look around Chen's room. Finding her name on the manifest last night only complicated things more, not less. Once again, I've found plenty in the way of clues but little in the way of hard evidence. All I really have on Chen is a bunch of serial numbers for a few "defective" items that all happened to be piloted in by her. Even I can see that my evidence is circumstantial at best. Certainly not enough to warrant anything more than a cursory investigation at this point, even if I did bring it to Asriel.

It's strange. While all the clues point directly to Chen, she's the last person I would have fingered as the saboteur. She's been through the psy checks with me far too many times to be a squatter, and if she has any personal motivation, I haven't seen signs of it. Of course, she's so quiet I've seen little of her personality at all. Who knows what she might be hiding beneath that inscrutable exterior?

If only there were more time! I could turn this whole thing over to the top brass for future investigation, like I *should* have done so many times before, and be done with this whole thing. Now it's too late. The Archangel is due to fire in a matter of hours. If Chen really is the saboteur, she's going to make her play today. For all I know, she's already made it. Which means I have to act, *now*, before it's too late. Hence my breaking into her quarters using the laser cutter I originally found planted in my locker, a little piece of irony that's not lost on me. I need hard evidence, and I need it fast.

Trying not to feel like a criminal, I get to work, stripping down the bunk and going through the closet. Checking the desk and forcibly popping the storage locker with my combat knife. Opening up the air vents and knocking on the walls and floor in search of hidden compartments. Despite my best efforts, I turn up nothing out of the ordinary. Uniforms, gear, a password-protected tip-pad that I don't even bother trying to crack. My efforts end in the hygiene unit, where aside from some basic linens, toiletries, and a few a bottles of makeup, I don't find anything.

Discouraged, I lean on the sink and try to think through my next step. Not only have I not found any evidence to tie Chen to the sabotage, I've probably earned myself a permanent demotion to scut once they find out I illegally searched a Pilot Commander's personal quarters. With my luck, I'll be taking out garbage for the rest of my life . . . assuming the saboteur hasn't killed us all by the end of the day.

Garbage. It occurs to me that while I went through Chen's trash bin in the main room, I neglected to go through the one in the hygiene unit. Not expecting to find anything but determined to be thorough, I sift carefully through the bin. Used tissues, old packaging, and those disposable towelettes girls use to remove makeup, along with a couple of empty bottles of concealer. Like I thought—nothing. I thrust the bin aside, ready to get out of here, when something occurs to me. Pulling the empty bottles out of the trash, I open the cabinet again. Three more bottles of concealer rest on the top shelf.

Five bottles of concealer? I rummage through the cabinet some more, but I don't find any other makeup. No lip stuff or eye crap or any of the other goop girls like to rub all over their faces. Though I don't know much about this kind of stuff, I did share a room with my teenaged sister for three years. Long enough to know that five bottles of concealer is a lot. Did she simply stock up before coming to R&D, or does she have something to hide?

I think back over my time with Chen, from our initial meeting on Kittridge Promenade to our impromptu piloting lesson and the crazy mission on Nomia that almost left us all stranded. *Nomia.* A conversation during a g-ball game shortly after the mission comes to mind, and with it, the question I put to Ty:

"No, seriously. Why don't you like Chen?"

"Let's just say we have . . . philosophical differences."

Philosophical differences.

The answer was so vague, I didn't really mark it at the time. I'd figured it was just man troubles or whatever it is women usually fight about. Now I can't help thinking I gravely underestimated that statement. The question is: What exactly did Ty mean by that? If only I'd followed up on it! Forced Ty to explain herself more fully to me rather than letting it go.

Once again, I flip through my experiences with Chen in my mind: out piloting lesson, our mission on Nomia, Kittridge—

Kittridge. The space station Angelou and I stopped at during our initial flight to Prism. The station where we dumped our original flight team because Chen was already waiting there to take us the rest of the way. I remember our time on the station, how our journey to Chen's docking bay took us straight past one singularly vocal Spectre Priest . . .

Slag! I drop the bottles, only one thought in mind. *I have to find Chen.*

Before it's too late.

———

"Control, this is Pilot Commander Chen in the *SunStreamer* requesting clearance for take-off, per scheduled maintenance run 875. Please respond."

White noise hisses over the com. "SunStreamer, *this is Control. Permission for take-off granted. Have a nice flight, Commander.*"

"Acknowledged. *SunStreamer* out."

The com snaps off, followed soon after by the sound of thrusters firing. From the storage locker just outside the cockpit, I stand with my ear to the door, listening to the vibrant hum of the engines as the ship lifts off. My heart beats in a crisp staccato, pulsing in my chest, my head, my palms where they wrap around the cold barrel of the decimator. A decimator—exactly like a stun pistol except for one key difference.

A decimator can kill.

The minutes unspool as I stand with my hand to the door, waiting for the gap between us and the station to widen and our signature to disappear off Control's sensors. Through the crack in the door, I can hear Chen dictating her mission report into her chit as she takes the ship through some basic maneuvers. The maintenance department installed new jets in the forward thrusters, and per regulations, Chen is doing a live test run before the ship is cleared for regular use. A task that could easily have waited until after the Archangel deployment, so I can only assume she's as bored as the rest of us. That or she wanted to get her hands on a ship for some purpose of her own.

At the fifteen minute mark, I decide the wait is over. Slipping from the storage locker, I stalk softly into the cockpit. My boots ring lightly against the decking, but the thrum of the engines along with Chen's voice, recording her report, easily cover my passage. I'm only a couple of steps away when she finally becomes aware of my presence, turning with a jolt only to find the barrel of my pistol centimeters from her head. She freezes, eyes widening as she takes in me and the gun.

"Hands off the control panel," I command. "Switch us to autopilot. Verbally."

After a short hesitation, she does as I say, eyes never leaving me even when I march her away from the controls and over to the other end of the cockpit. She starts to speak. "Sorenson, what—"

"Push up your sleeves." The smooth, unblemished skin of her wrists comes into view, and I toss her the packet of towelettes I found in her cabinet. "Clean your wrists."

"This is rid—"

I give a little flick of the decimator. *"Now."*

Another pause, then slowly she begins wiping her left wrist. I hold my breath, suddenly convinced my theory was wrong—

Then the concealer comes off, and I'm staring at the tattoo of a dark rainbow twined about an eight-pointed star. The same symbol I saw on the wrist of that priest all those months ago when I passed through Kittridge Promenade with Angelou on my way to R&D. Chen was waiting there to pilot us through the final leg of the journey, and just like that priest I saw, she bears the same mark.

The mark of the Order of the Spectre.

It all fits. Not just the makeup bottles, but other things. The way she always keeps her sleeves buttoned even when it's hot, her reluctance to speak of her past. Those missing months between her departure from the Golden Aces and her arrival at R&D. No doubt she was with the OS during that time, making plans. Now I just have to find out what those plans are.

For a long time, we merely stare at each other. At last she asks, "How did you know?"

"Let's just say I finally put all the pieces together."

Another pause, then we both burst out at once:

"Tell me what you did to sabotage the Archangel!"

"That mission was classified! How could you have possibly found out?"

We both stop. And again:

"Sabotage?"

"Mission?" I frown, confused. What mission is she talking about? Chen starts to move, and I quickly whip my decimator back into her face. "No! Stop trying to confuse things. I know you planted the laser cutter on me, and I know you're the one who's been sabotaging the equipment on base! Now I want to know what you've done to the Archangel, and I want to know n—"

The floor leaps up beneath my feet as the ship lurches hard to starboard. I catapult across the cockpit, thrown to the floor by the force of the motion, Chen right behind me. The decimator flies from my hand, bouncing off the far wall and falling to the floor, and I slide after it. I reach out my hand, scrambling for the pistol, when suddenly the ship rocks hard the other way.

Back I go, thrown in the opposite direction by a second lurch, this time from the port bow. My hands scrabble for purchase, but all they meet is air. Air, and smooth hard floor as I hit the ground once more. I slide into the opposite wall, hitting the surface with a loud whack. I grab onto a chair leg, struggling to find my feet, when the ship suddenly levels. I start to stand—

Only to find a decimator barrel centimeters from my face.

Chen stands over me, eyes hard as tritanium. "Never attack a pilot on her own ship," she states matter-of-factly. Her ten pilot's chits gleam silver in the cabin lights, and I inwardly groan as I realize she retained her connection to the ship this entire time, autopilot notwithstanding. The decimator wavers in my face, and I brace myself for the coming shot.

Click.

Chen ejects the energy cartridge in one quick motion, dropping it to the floor in front of her. Before I can react, her boot comes down, crushing it to bits in a single stomp. She tosses the now-useless deci-mator across the cockpit, though she continues to hold up her left hand, palm out and chits gleaming, the message clear. *The ship is the only weapon she needs.*

"Now, you want to tell me what the hell is going on?" she de-mands. "How did you know about my infiltration work for MI?"

"Infiltration work?" I blurt out. I stare at the broken decimator cartridge in disbelief, wondering in what universe a traitor and sab-oteur willingly disarms herself. For all her anger, Chen has a *what-the-hell* expression on her face, and I suddenly can't help thinking I made a big mistake. I cock my head at her. "Wait, you work for Military Intelligence?"

Now she frowns. "You didn't know? You knew about the tattoo. Why—" Realization dawns on her face. "Wait, you thought I was a member of the OS?"

She takes my dumb look as an affirmation. Activating her chit, she pulls up a holo profile of herself. A badge, I realize after a second. Golden flecks flicker through the profile, a holographic watermark that's almost impossible to fake, and if this is a forgery, it's a damn good one.

"You're MI?" I repeat again, my brain still stuck on that one in-surmountable fact. For months I've been tracking down the saboteur, the traitor who's been leaving defective equipment with these strange chips in their wake, and now that I've finally tracked her down, she's Military Intelligence?

"Retired," she says shortly, de-acking the badge. "I left when I came to R&D. Now it's your turn. What the hell is going on? Why'd you jump me, and what's all this about sabotage?"

I hesitate, but my eyes go to that destroyed decimator again. She had every reason to harm me—kill me, even if just in self-defense—but she didn't, instead disabling the weapon before anyone could get hurt. What kind of a saboteur does that? When I found the makeup bottles, I assumed she'd left the Aces to join the OS—it would cer-tainly explain the strange time gap between her tour in the Aces and her arrival at R&D. But couldn't a stint in MI explain it just as easily?

My confused brain is on overload, and I don't know what to think anymore. However, the undeniable fact is that something strange is going on, and clamming up isn't going to get me any answers. So after another a long hesitation, I do as she asks, starting all the way back with the laser cutter, then working my way through the defective equipment, the chips, and how they eventually led me to the shipment numbers.

To her.

She glares at me. "So I brought in a few shipments that contained defective equipment? That's awfully circumstantial evidence, considering how few pilots we have on base."

"I thought the same, until I figured out about the tattoo—"

"The tattoo!" she huffs. Her mouth twists into a grimace at the mention, but a reluctant understanding enters her eyes all the same. "I guess I can see how that might have looked rather damning."

I shouldn't trust her. All the evidence led me straight to her, and I have no reason to believe what she's said isn't a clever lie. Yet everything about her strikes me as genuine, from the exasperation in her voice when I mentioned the tattoo to the deep pain in her eyes when she spoke of MI. Either she's telling the truth or she's one hell of an actress.

"It's like—" I stop, uncertain whether I should continue.

"It's like?"

"It's just that something about this whole thing has been off from the beginning. Except for the OP blowing, none of the defective items really did that much damage or seriously threatened to derail the Archangel. Some of the items weren't even tampered with at all. It's like whoever planted the chips had some other motive besides sabotage, like they were trying to lead me to something. Or someone."

Chen raises a doubtful eyebrow. "And that someone was me?" A speculative gleam lights her eyes. "Wait a second. Let me see those shipment numbers."

I hesitate, still not entirely sure I trust her, and finally link her the info. She scans it quickly, pulling up the corresponding manifests and flipping through them with practiced ease. What she's looking for, I have no idea, but judging by the way her eyebrows suddenly shoot up, she's clearly found it. She nods at me. "Look at this."

She enlarges the last manifest, highlighting a single line with a stroke of her index finger.

Pickup Origin: Military Depot S6-4112

I frown at the words. "I don't understand. What's the significance?"

"You were looking for a common denominator? Every single item on your list came from this same military depot."

"Is that significant?"

"According to our records, out of eighty-seven shipments we've received in the past year, we only received eight shipments from this particular depot—"

"—and seven of those eight contained items on my list," I finish with a low whistle, finally seeing what she's getting at. "That does seem like more than a coincidence, but if that's true, someone at that depot is either a squatter or a traitor."

"And not just anybody, but someone very high up," Chen puts in. "Do you know what the security on an S6 Depot is like? It's worse than R&D, yet out of eight shipments, our saboteur managed to hit seven. For someone to deliberately slip us doctored equipment so consistently over such a long period, they'd have to have some real clout."

We both stew over that tidbit for a moment, neither of us liking that idea at all. Then again, I point out to myself, maybe it's all bullslag. Maybe Chen's just trying to cover her tracks by throwing another suspect at me, one eminently reasonable but completely out of my capacity to verify or confirm. I regard her from the corner of my eye, trying to decide if she's on the level, when something she said suddenly sinks in.

"What if they didn't miss?" At Chen's confused look, I explain. "You said that out of the eight shipments this depot sent, they managed to hit seven. What if they didn't miss the eighth shipment at all? What if *I'm* the one who missed it?"

Even as the lights go on in Chen's eyes, I'm pulling up the manifests, searching until I find the one in question. I'm expecting it to be a recent shipment, perhaps one that came when I was out on the Archangel mission, but it turns out to be the oldest shipment of the lot, arriving approximately a year ago. No wonder I missed it. I wasn't even on R&D yet. My first instinct is to dismiss it out of hand—how could someone target me if I wasn't even here yet?—when I remember the chip from the generator dish and how it referenced a stabilizer that didn't arrive on the station until weeks later.

That disturbing recollection in mind, I scroll down the manifest until I find the cargo list, and I immediately groan. There must be at least a hundred items on there. Assuming someone did slip something in there, how would I even find it without a serial number to guide me? I glance at the list anyway, hoping something might stand out. I'm three quarters of the way through when something finally catches my eye—an item called a data relay conduit. However, it's not the name that catches my eye but the multi-part serial number, which is noticeably longer than any other on the page. A seven-part serial number, to be exact. Hmm . . .

Pulling up my list of numbers, it doesn't take long to confirm my suspicion. Each section of the number for the data relay conduit corresponds to the first three digits from one of the chips.

Any lingering doubts I might have had vanish as I stare at the number. This is where the saboteur has been leading me all these months. To a data relay conduit delivered nearly a year ago. Even Chen seems impressed by the evidence, despite her late entry into this saga.

She shakes her head. "When you first started babbling about saboteurs and chips and scavenger hunts, I thought you were lunar, but this—"

"We have to get back," I interrupt. "I have to find this conduit *now*, before the Archangel fires. The power relay knocked out life support, and the dish blew up an entire OP. Who knows what this conduit could do? For all we know, it could destroy the entire Archangel system."

"One problem." Chen nods to the part information, which she pulled up on her chit. "The conduit's no longer on the station. According to the records, it was transferred to a facility off-base shortly after it arrived at R&D."

"Not on the station? Then where is it?"

"It's on the planet. In the main relay station down on Prism."

"Prism?" My heart sinks at the answer. With the offensive set to deploy in less than three hours, no one's allowed to go planetside. In the time it would take us to return to the station, debark, locate Asriel, and convince him to take my case to Angelou, it will be too late.

That's assuming I can convince Asriel of anything. With my history of lying and telling stories, I don't exactly have the strongest case here.

I groan in frustration. After months of following this strange trail, I'm only a step away from finding the answers I seek. To hit a dead end when I'm this close . . .

"So if they didn't open the net for us, is there any way to get through?"

"Nope," says Herrera, at the exact same time Chen says, "Maybe."

The memory hits me like a bolt from the black, and suddenly I know without a doubt that Chen is innocent. The clues *did* lead me straight to her, but not because she was the saboteur. No, they led me to Pilot Commander Sarai Chen because in all of R&D, *she* is the only person who can get me through that net.

———

Pink mists furl up around the viewports as the shuttle comes to a stop just above the blazing latticework of the net. Strapped into the copilot's seat, I check my restraints for the fourth time and tell myself I'm not making a huge mistake. From the seat beside me, Chen raises an eyebrow.

"Are you sure you want to do this?"

I swallow hard, a strange mix of terror and elation running through me. Elation at finally reaching the bottom of the rabbit hole; terror at what I might find. For all I know, this is a trap, and I'm walking straight into it. But trap or not, I have to find out what's down there. I have to find out where this trail leads, for my own sanity, if nothing else.

I nod once. "It's not what I want to do; it's what I have to do."

Chen regards me for a long moment. What she's thinking, I don't know, but something tells me this is her destiny as much as mine. As though fate has been propelling her to this moment as surely as it's been propelling me, though I can't even begin to guess why. Turning away once again, she finally nods. "Okay."

With the necessary question asked and answered, Chen gets to work, her hands a blur as she switches the ship over to manual control. Holo panels vanish and new ones pop up, dials enlarging while others shrink. The holographic control matrix disappears altogether, a puzzling move until I catch sight of the ten glowing chits in her hands, one at the base of each finger, and realize the wireless uplink between her pilots' chits and the ship are the true source of her control. Clearly the holographic yoke is a visual aid only, one she has no desire to use.

After a few more minutes of adjustments, she sits back in her chair, scanning the panel one last time before nodding in satisfaction. She makes a couple of quick motions with her thumb, and on the digitized viewscreen I see the corona surrounding the ship wink out.

Our shields are offline.

A tendril of fear whips through me as I comprehend just how vulnerable we are without our shields. If I'm wrong about Chen or if she's not as good a pilot as I hope she is . . .

An image of the ship being sliced to ribbons by those fast-moving bands of light flashes into my head, and I force back a shudder. As if guessing the direction of my thoughts, Chen frowns. "Second thoughts?"

I shake my head hard. "Not for a minute."

She smiles faintly at that, as if recognizing my trepidation because her own is mirrored in my eyes. Turning back to the control panel, she slowly curves her hands into position, fingers wavering almost imperceptibly, as if feeling for something invisible right beneath her fingertips. Below us, the net spreads out in an ocean of fire, the fast-moving bands rippling like blue flame within the glowing pool. I hold my breath, eyes glued to Chen's hands as I wait for the inevitable drop.

I'm flung back into my seat as we take off with a jolt of acceleration, skimming across the surface of the net like a stone skipping across a pond. We're so close I can practically feel the ripple and burn of energy just below us, but instead of dropping, the nose of the ship lifts, the thrust only increasing as we curve upward in a steep arc. I squeeze the armrests, stomach in my throat as we soar higher and higher. At the apex of our ascent, the ship flips over in a gut-wrenching loop-de-loop.

Then, like a great bird of prey soaring high in the sky, we tuck in our wings and dive.

38

FACE-FIRST, we hurtle toward the net at the speed of insanity. As the solid blue surface rises up to meet us, I realize I've made a terrible mistake. Squeezing my fists tight, I brace myself for impact, but at the last instant the energy bands shift apart. Blue lightning crackles over the viewports on all sides as we shoot through the triangular opening a heartbeat before it closes again.

Blue lights up the cockpit as the net swallows us whole. I barely have time to think, *We made it*, before the next layer is upon us. Just like the first time, the bands slide apart a moment before we reach them. Even before we're through, Chen hits the brakes, reverse thrusters screaming as they try to check our angled descent. I slam into the left side of my seat, *hard*, as she whips us around in the opposite direction, like a roamer skidding crazily around a sharp curve.

We slide through the third layer by the skin of our teeth, the bands so close I can feel their power vibrating through my chest and thrumming in my ears. A burst of thrusters, and then I'm slamming into the right side of my seat as we slew back the other way in our quest for the next opening. The view is dizzying, bright bands of energy weaving in and out and around each other in a flickering blur, gaps opening and closing so fast I can barely track them as we continue our headlong descent through the net. Electricity ripples through the air, filling the cockpit in nigh-visible waves, shifting and shimmering like liquid glass along the edges of my vision. I squeeze my hands tight and tell myself to breathe as back and forth we go, snaking crazily along a serpentine road only Chen can see.

I dare a glance at my pilot. She sits bolt upright in her seat, body tense and jaw taut, the minute flexings of her fingers speaking of an exacting control almost out of human range. Awe fills me as I watch her fly. She moves as though she's part of the ship, rolling when it rolls and swaying when it sways, breathing with each curve and thrust of its motion. Her head shifts slightly toward me, and a shiver runs down my spine as I catch sight of her eyes.

They're *glowing*.

Even though I know it's just the pilot lenses, enhanced to allow her to navigate, the sight still makes me shiver. What does she see in those shining depths? A glimpse of heaven, luminous and bright? Or the depths of hell, alight with cerulean fire?

We skim through another gap, skidding around the inner edge a hairsbreadth from disaster, and then it appears. Peeking through the latticework in glimpses of gold and lavender—clear, glorious sky.

My gut clenches, every muscle in my body tightening as we zoom closer and closer to that final latticework. *Just one more.* One more and we're home free. My lips move in silent prayer, the words a terse counterpoint to the hum of the net in my ears. *Please, please, please.* The blue light intensifies, punching like a fist into the cockpit as we rush in an unstoppable tread straight into—

The bands slip open, and we soar through the gap with textbook form. Shields go up a second later, followed by the silvering of the cabin lights that indicates stealth mode. Chen lets out a high laugh, the sound halfway between a crow of joy and a cry of relief, and despite her confident piloting, I get the feeling she was just as terrified as I was. She buries her face in her hands, draining off the worst of her adrenaline with long breaths in and out, before finally slumping back into her seat and engaging the autopilot with a wave of her hand. I completely understand the feeling. Though I know the worst is over, it still takes a few minutes before I can bring myself to release the armrests from the death grip I've got on them.

For several minutes we drift, unspeaking, as the ship takes us down toward our target destination. I watch the endless skies sail by through the viewports, thinking as my heart rate slowly drops back to normal. Now that we're through the net, that sense of destiny is back, stronger than ever before, and I can't help wondering about this woman whose lot's been cast in with mine though I know so little of her.

"You told me once you'd been recruited by Angelou," I say. "That he was the one who brought you to R&D. What happened? How did you go from being an elite pilot to a testing grunt at some base in the mists?"

Chen continues staring through the viewport, not turning, not acknowledging me in any way. Seconds pass, stretching into minutes, and I'm convinced she's not going to answer, when—

"It was back toward the beginning of the war, when the Order of the Spectre was just hitting its stride. MI was looking for pilots to infiltrate a key OS cell, and they came to the Golden Aces because, well, we were the best. The OS was looking for pilots, you see. People who could break quarantine lines and bring their people to 'enlightenment.'" Her voice twists with derision on that last word.

"At first the mission went well. MI gave me an ironclad cover, and the OS accepted me without ever suspecting what I was. When it became clear my skills were far greater than those of any of the other pilots they'd managed to recruit, I moved up quickly through the ranks, getting the tattoo and finally breaking into the inner circle. I continued to report back to MI whenever I could. They were sure the OS was planning something big, and they were right. Turned out the OS had secured four freight carriers, large enough to fit over ten thousand people all told, along with the codes for the planetary net around Atropos. The plan was simple. Jump into the system, drop the net, and take our followers down to the ghoul-ridden planet below so they could find enlightenment. After which we would break up and spread across the Expanse, bringing the infection with us wherever we went."

My stomach twists, gut churning as I recognize this story from countless news feeds. I want Chen to stop . . . and I want her to go on.

"I leaked the news to MI as soon as I could, and together we came up with a plan to stop them. It was stunningly simple. We jumped into the system as planned, dropped the net, and then halfway through, I gave the signal. MI sprung the trap, reactivating the outer layers of the net and effectively caging us all inside. It seemed like the plan had gone perfectly. All that was left was to wait until the military came and rounded us all up."

"What happened?" I venture after a minute, already knowing the outcome but not why it came to pass.

"One of the other pilots panicked. Afraid of being caught, he decided to make a break for it. Dropped his shields, aimed for one of the holes in the bottom layer, and—" She breaks off, only a ragged breath frosting the silence, and quietly finishes, "The debris from when it struck the net hit two of the other ships, ripped straight through their bellies and gutted them open to the sky. Mine was the only ship that survived."

Mine was the only ship that survived. Such a matter-of-fact statement, and yet its very simplicity speaks to its innate horror more than any detailed explanation she might have provided.

"The funny thing is I don't think he ever would have tried it if I hadn't told him my theory about navigating through the net's holes." Chen shakes her head, and I can almost see the regrets turning in her eyes. "They held me in MI for weeks afterwards, running me through endless interviews and debriefings—trying to decide if I was to blame, I suppose. I didn't think they'd ever let me out of there. Then one day Dr. Angelou walked into the interrogation room. Forty-eight hours later, I was en route to R&D."

I nod, easily able to guess from my own experiences how that might have gone. My eyes fall on her tattoo, to the star with its loathsome rainbow, and I jerk my head in its direction. "Why didn't you ever get it removed?"

She arches an eyebrow. "Walk into a doctor's office with *this* on me? With sentiment against the OS running so high after the 'accident,' who knows what would've happened? It's not like I had the clearance to tell them why I had it. I guess it just seemed easier to hide it, and . . ."

"And?"

"It felt wrong to remove it," she finally admits. "Like I was trying to wipe the past away, pretend it never happened and that those people never died. As much as I wanted to, I couldn't do it. Although maybe I should have anyway. Ty accidentally saw it once and has disliked me ever since. Not that I blame her, considering."

She shakes her head, not needing to finish. I sneak a look at Chen where she leans back in her chair. With her lenses de-acked and face unguarded, she looks sad. As though grief is etched into her very makeup now, her every moment pervaded by a quiet sorrow so deep and pure it can never be sullied. How could I have worked with her all this time and never seen it? That the sorrow she carries in her is no different than the one I carry in me.

"How do you do it?" I suddenly ask.

She glances over at me, and the mask slides back on, sorrow replaced with ordinary curiosity in a heartbeat. "What?"

"That," I say with a jerk of my head toward her blank face, so easily masked within a single instant. "After everything that happened—MI, your mission, the casualties—how do you just lock it all inside like that? Go on as though nothing happened?"

Chen blinks, startled by the question, but her lips purse in thought, and at last she says, "Some burdens you never put down. You just find an easier way to carry them."

Lia, gone. Aurora infected, and New Sol blown to smithereens. Tabs, Zel, Herrera, RC, Archer, Songbird. Even my parents, both out in the far reaches of space, possibly never to be seen again. No matter how many ways I add it up, the weight is always the same, the burden always just as heavy.

I let out a quiet sigh. "What if you can't? What if it's still too heavy?"

"Then you find someone to carry it with you."

Teal.

My sister's face flashes into my mind, and somehow the idea of talking to her, of seeing her face again after all these months, doesn't seem so terrible anymore. I touch my chit where it peers out from the specially designed hole in my gauntlet. One link is all it would take.

I smile faintly. Assuming I had the courage to face her wrath after ignoring her all this time.

We're directly over the city when Chen de-acs the autopilot and flies us the rest of the way. She sets us down lightly on the northeast corner of the relay station, powers down the shuttle, and turns to me with an expectant look, as if to say, *It's your show.*

I nod at her. "According to the records, the part we're looking for is in a console on the 101st floor."

"Let's go."

Even though it's not an official mission, we gear up as if it's one anyway, pulling on helmets, holstering weapons, and adjusting gauntlets. Knowing I was facing a potential saboteur and wanting to be prepared for anything, I wore my usual mission gear, but Chen has only a regular flightsuit. Still she makes do, augmenting her simple jumpsuit with some spare gear and weaponry from the ship's armory. Even though the planet was cleared last night, we both grab our launchers. With a million squatters still living in the city below, that's over a thousand new ghouls bred every *hour*. My new "ghoul suit" notwithstanding, there's no sense taking any chances.

As we step out of the shuttle onto the roof, I check the time. A few minutes past ten hundred. That gives us a little less than two hours to find the device, figure out what it's for, and get back to the station before the Archangel goes live. Painfully aware of how little margin for error that gives us, I jog swiftly to the entrance, Chen right on my heels. Luckily, my security clearance as Team Leader is high enough to gain access. We slip inside and head directly for the stairwell.

It's strange coming back to this place after so long, everything familiar and yet not. Lights automatically turn on at our passage, the white capsules disconcerting after the golden light of morning, while the soft flow of air whispers from the ducts above. Cold air; silent, but blessedly odorless as it frosts over my nose and cheeks. Without the presence of the others, this place is different. Not simply an abandoned building, but a tomb now, infused with an emptiness only found in the grave. Only the quiet hum of a far-off generator offers any company within these silent halls.

We hit the first landing and head down another flight, senses alert for any sign of danger. Our boots ring against the metallic floor, unusually loud without the typical background noises to temper the sound. I strain my ears for anything that might not belong, but all I hear is the thudding of my heart, beating a rapid counterpoint to our steady treads as we twist and turn through the stairwell into the heart of the station.

The 101st floor is similar to the floor where I worked on my last mission here, a large room subdivided by dozens of machines and consoles quietly humming away. Though the dust-resistant equipment is clean enough, the whole floor has the abandoned feel of a place that *should* be dusty, if only the automated cleaners weren't so efficient. Shaking off the chill that shivers through me, I pull up the floor plan for the room and search for the Primary Information Array, which is where the records say the part was originally installed. It doesn't take long to find.

The array rests on a huge circular platform, almost like a dais, set into the middle of the room. At its center is a thick crystalline column rising to the ceiling, while around the outer perimeter of the platform sits a flat holo table, donut-shaped and held together by four towers rising from the platform at equidistant intervals. They angle upward until they all meet and conjoin with the central column shortly before disappearing into the ceiling. Indicator lights in green and blue glow steadily along the gleaming towers, and the entire central column glows an unearthly silver. A soft purring comes from within the towers.

"That's intense," Chen comments with a low whistle.

I dumbly nod, unable to take my eyes off the machine before me. Between the gleaming towers and the glowing column, the array is beautiful, almost a work of art, and yet the longer I stare at it, the more I feel this impending sense of doom. Will I take this thing apart only to find another chip with a random serial number on it, just another clue in an endless wild goose chase that may or may not mean anything? Or have I finally reached the end of the line? There's only one way to find out.

For the next hour we labor on the array. According to the manifest, the item we're looking for is called a data relay conduit, a long cylindrical device that runs all the way up the middle of the central column. Though I have the schematics and the basic conduit location, actually reaching it without breaking or deactivating anything else proves to be a trickier proposition. For that matter, I'm not even sure where in the conduit the saboteur's tampering might be. Uncovering the bottom half won't do us much good if their handiwork is in the upper section.

Doubts notwithstanding, we keep at it until we've finally uncovered enough of the conduit to remove a section of the carapace midway up the cylinder. As I unseal the seams and carefully pull off the cover, any worries I might have had about chips and wild goose chases vanish in an instant.

Weaving in, around, and all through the guts of the conduit is a *bomb.*

———

"It's not a bomb. At least, not any bomb I've ever seen," Chen adds, carefully withdrawing her hands from the pulsing white filaments.

"Then what is it?"

She shakes her head. "I don't know, but whatever it is, it definitely doesn't belong here."

That's the understatement of the day. Anyone looking at the creeping mass of metallic fibers wrapping the crystalline components would immediately know it for the abomination it is. They twine through the guts of the conduit like the tendrils of a parasite, capturing it tight in a stranglehold of pulsating grotesqueries that flicker in tainted shadows across the pristine crystal.

Chen gingerly examines the filaments some more, slender fingers prodding, lifting, and pulling, careful not to disconnect or otherwise disturb the strange arrangement. "No, definitely not an explosive," she repeats with a shake of her head. She pulls back a bunch of filaments, pointing to multiple spots where the fibers actually plug into the conduit. "Look at this. These aren't just wrapped around the conduit; they're actually integrated into its workings."

"You mean like some sort of bug or spy device?"

She shrugs. "Possibly."

"Okay, but why would someone want to spy on the relay station? It doesn't contain any tactical data about the war. It's just scientific readings drawn from the planet itself."

"Everyone on Prism's a squatter," Chen points out, "so assuming someone local installed the device, this has to be the work of the enemy. Perhaps they simply wanted to keep tabs on our progress, to see how close we were to creating a working weapons prototype."

"Maybe," I agree, but the idea still doesn't feel right to me somehow. While Chen's theory makes sense on the surface, it doesn't explain the trail of clues leading me here. Why would the enemy go through such lengths to tip their hand to me? Especially this late in the game. With the Archangel set to fire in a little over an hour, it hardly matters now.

Activating my chit, I pull up my schematics for the station and examine them. As the main relay station on Prism, it not only gathers data on a regular basis with its own sensors, but also archives all the testing information from the rest of the planet before sending it up to R&D. The Primary Information Array appears to be the second to last stop in the process, where the information is copied to the archive and then immediately sent to the antenna for transmission.

Chen suddenly lets out a whistle. "What do we have here?"

I lean in, peering over her shoulder as she pulls back some fibers to reveal a silver box no larger than my hand. A row of blinking lights confirms it's active, and a clear panel reveals some sort of control chip inside. Judging by the dozens of filaments protruding from the box, this is the source of our electronic parasite.

"Is that a miniature transceiver?" I ask, recalling something similar I saw in training several months ago.

"Looks like it."

"Then it is a spy device, transmitting information to an outside recipient."

"Either that or someone outside is transmitting information to *it*."

Everything inside of me goes cold, something about the suggestion feeling terribly right in the same way the thought of a spy device felt wrong. I leap to the holo table, activating the crystalline surface using the manual controls. Tapping on the table, I search through the database, issuing commands through trial and error until at last the main page of the archives hovers over the table in front of me. I frown at the page, uncertain what I'm even looking for, let alone how to find it.

Knowing Chen's done more missions in the relay station than I have, I ask, "Is there a way to compare data from the Sent Files and Archived Files to see if anything differs between them?"

After a moment Chen nods, her fingers flying over the table as she types in several commands. "There! I've set the console to scan both sets of data and highlight in yellow any files that contain discrepancies. It may take a few min—"

Yellow highlights burst to life, marking file after file even as the list continues to scroll over the table before us. My jaw drops. There must be hundreds—no, make that *thousands*—of files marked, at least two-thirds in all just based on a quick visual estimate. They range from as recent as yesterday to almost a year old.

I pull up a few files, blinking helplessly as vast arrays of numbers spool out before me. While a few columns have labels I recognize— *Air Pressure, Temperature, Test Number, Location*—on the whole, these arrays make zero sense to me. From her wide-eyed expression, Chen's as lost as I am. I'm scrolling through the information, looking for anything that might clue me in, when a file with a holo recording attachment catches my attention. The timestamp shows it's from last night, around the time they did the final planet-wide eradication of the ghouls on Prism.

I frown, wondering why the archived holo would be any different from the one transmitted up to R&D. Queuing up both versions of the recording, I stand back and watch with Chen as the two clips roll simultaneously side by side.

Two cities appear in the air before us. Or rather, two recordings of the same city—every detail down to the last sidewalk tile is identical. While I don't recognize the city itself, it looks akin to others I've seen on Prism, with the same crystalline mineral worked into the architecture and the same pastel skies. From the pattern of light, it appears to be early evening, Demeter still up and shining while Persephone has already gone to bed. For a long minute, nothing happens. Then it comes, silvery and bright, lancing down through the pale evening to light the streets with a metallic sheen.

The Archangel.

I glance between the two holos, but so far everything remains identical. The angel's rays lie across the two cities for a handful of heartbeats, their beams momentarily at rest before diffusing away into the evening light. I continue to watch the feed until the detector lights come on a minute later, white and harsh compared to their silvery predecessor, and—

My throat closes up, lungs choking on their own oxygen. In the sent file, everything looks normal—the white light, the empty space— but in the *archived* file . . .

The ghouls are still there.

It's undeniable, those rainbow-black shapes arcing through the air, visible for those short moments while the lights burn around them, never fading, never disappearing, never *dying*. I gape at Chen, looking to her for explanation while she looks to me for the same thing. Without saying a word, we queue up the feed for another city, then another and another, comparing sent and archived footage for a dozen or more places. The results are the same in every holo. Total annihilation in the sent files, ghouls aplenty in the archived ones. The realization hits me like a physical blow, all the wind knocked out of me in an instant as I recognize the truth.

The Archangel *doesn't work*.

"How is this possible?" Chen gasps, her incredulous question breaking the silence. "We tested and tested the Archangel! Have they found some way to survive it?"

Perhaps. Or more likely, I realize with a sinking feeling in my gut, *it never worked at all.*

My eyes fall on the device, still tucked away in the back of the console. If I had any doubt that the enemy is behind all this, it's gone now. The doctored footage confirms it. I shake my head, the pieces finally coming together in my head. "They were feeding us false data. That's what this device does. It hijacks the outgoing feed, allowing the squatters to replace sensitive information before it goes up to R&D. Don't you see? The enemy didn't learn how to survive the Archangel; it never worked in the first place! They only tricked us into believing it did by doctoring the data."

"That makes perfect sense except for one thing: *Us*," Chen points out. "I smelled it with my own nose when the Archangel fired and the ghouls disappeared. More than once!"

"I did too," I admit with a shake of my head. "Look, I have no idea how they managed to do that. Maybe they found a way to get out of range, or they learned a new way to disguise their scent. I don't know! All I know is that the only thing that matters now is getting this information back to the station before—"

"They fire the Archangel," Chen finishes.

I go back to the console and activate my chit again. If we're going to bring this to Angelou, we have to have proof. I'm about to start downloading the data when Chen stops me with a hand on my wrist. Using the very tip of her combat knife, she carefully inserts it into the silver box we found and presses down on a tiny catch just inside. I hear a soft click, and then the blinking chip at the heart of the transceiver ejects neatly from its casing.

Chen smiles at me sadly. "Faster this way."

I nod in response, pocketing the chip safely away in my belt pouch. "Let's go."

Quickly, we close up the panel and shut off the consoles, returning the room to its original state within minutes. As we take the stairs two at a time, it suddenly occurs to me to wonder: *Why now?* The small amount of data I saw indicated that the saboteur had been doctoring test results for months before I ever came on station. Why is it only recently they started simulating a false positive?

No time to think the question through, I burst out of the roof access a step ahead of Chen. Our shuttle awaits on the far side, and I barely have time to think, *I hope the ghouls haven't found our shuttle while we were gone,* before a loud scrape catches my attention.

I whirl around to find a man kneeling at a control panel on the base of the antenna, a toolkit at his side. Even without seeing his face, I can tell he isn't one of ours. Not with those clothes. He can only be one of the locals, a squatter, though how and why he got up here is a mystery. Perhaps he's the one who originally installed the transceiver? Instinct takes over, and I go for the stunner on my hip, my boot scraping across the roof as I pivot and take aim.

The squatter jerks around just as my finger squeezes the trigger. My heart freezes, eyes widening in horror as my shot takes him straight through the eye. Like a recurring nightmare never quite shaken, I can only watch as his body drops, killed instantly by a one-in-a-million shot . . .

. . . and a shiver of ghouls burst from his head.

39

SOUR-AND-SWEET explodes in my nose, so intense tears form in my eyes. I don't wait for them to clear but let my launcher rip, sending blast after blast toward that eye-watering cloud. Beside me Chen is doing the same, the rip of her aero-launcher resounding through the cool morning air. I throw my back against hers, and she immediately catches on, turning with me as we try to carve out an impenetrable bubble of gas around us. The odor is so thick it's impossible to tell where exactly the enemy is, let alone how many there are. All I know is that everywhere I turn, all my light sight shows is *black*.

"Sorenson, grenade!"

I blink, brain momentarily stymied by the pressure before suddenly catching on. Shifting my launcher to one hand, I reach for my belt.

Light bursts in every direction as the grenade hits the ground a meter from my feet. My lenses darken, automatically compensating for the sudden brightness, and that's when I see them fully. Roiling black rainbows frothing through the air around us, held back mere meters by a cloud of gas that is already starting to dissipate.

"Vaccin' hell! There must be thousands!"

Chen blasts off another round with her launcher. "Where did they all come from?!"

"The squatter," I answer grimly, ejecting a spent cartridge and locking in the next. "They came out of that squatter."

"How is that possible?"

"I don't know, but we have to get out of here!"

We spin in another circle, pumping another layer into our protective shield. The ghouls writhe and twist just outside the edges of the cloud, their menacing shapes flickering in and out of the light. My nose is on overload, the sharp scent of sour-and-sweet burning a hole straight through my nostrils and into my brain. Pain splits my head, and blood pours from my nostrils in coppery rivulets over my lips and tongue. I spit once, twice, trying to get the blood out of my mouth, but I don't dare take a hand off my launcher to wipe it away.

I hear a click as Chen finishes another cartridge, then—"Last clip!"

"Me, too!" I yell thirty seconds later. Despite our best efforts, we're losing ground. A soft breeze has blown up from the east, and our carefully constructed shield is starting to slowly blow apart. The black shapes are closing in now, inching in with every ebb of the shield.

"We have to run! Carve out a passage toward the shuttle and go. It's our only chance!"

A pause. "On three?"

"Agreed! One."

Still strafing the mob, we spin toward the northeast.

"Two."

We bring our launchers up together.

"Three!"

Click.

Our ammo runs out a second too soon, Chen's launcher making a last-ditch effort before shutting down while mine simply clicks on an empty cartridge. The sudden silence is a death knell, cut only by the hissing of two injectors as we each shoot ourselves up with our one dose of Psi-Lac.

"Chen," I start to say, knowing only that I owe her some sort of apology for dragging her into this, but having no idea what the words should be. I clear my throat and try again. "Chen, I—"

Before I can finish speaking, the soft breeze suddenly whips up into a hard gust, scoring across our shield like a million tiny daggers. Our remaining shelter falls apart in a single instant, dispersed by an icy wind that knows no mercy, and then a thousand black shapes come rushing through the space—

—straight into Chen.

I gasp and stumble back as the sour-and-sweet stench disappears in a heartbeat, masked within the shelter of a single body. Comprehension explodes in me as I realize what they've done. The ghouls didn't *die* that first time we shot the Archangel down upon them.

They *hid*.

Like a single light bulb blinking on in a dark room, everything is illuminated at once. The Spectres were *playing* us all along! That transceiver wasn't simply there to stall us or throw us off the track. They were feeding us false data for one reason, and one reason alone: Because they *wanted* us to create the Archangel! They wanted us to create a weapon of mass destruction, and once we'd made it to their specifications, they all hid, sliding inside the minds of the squatters around them so that all traces of their presence were gone. And we, tricked into believing the Archangel worked, installed the weapon on *every OP across the Expanse!* What the weapon is really meant to do, I have no idea. All I know is:

We're only minutes away from firing it.

"Michael."

I look at Chen, heart in my throat, though she seems oddly composed. "I don't understand. Why did they take you and not me?"

A slight smile tugs at her lips as she taps gently on the arm of my suit. "Guess they finally got those darn suits right. It's just a shame I'm not wearing mine."

The ghoul-proof suits! Guilt rockets through me as I stare at her plain black flight suit. I close my eyes, an icy chill settling down deep into my bones. "What have I *done*?" I whisper.

"You discovered the Archangel doesn't work!" Chen's voice snaps me back to reality. "Don't you see? You were *right*, Michael. Not about me, but everything else. Now you have to get back up there and warn the others before they fire that weapon!"

"But—"

"Now! Before this Psi-Lac wears off and I try to stop you."

She's right. I have to go, and I have to go now. Nodding, I take a step away, and then another, unwilling to simply leave her but knowing I have no other choice. I'm halfway to the shuttle when her voice rings out through the clear pastel sky.

"Hey, Sorenson! *Pro libertate* . . . ?"

I stop and look back at her where she stands, proud and unyielding under the noonday sun, and finish, *"Pro vita."*

She nods once, and then in one smooth motion, she lifts her stunner and shoots herself in the head. I watch her body crumple to the ground, hitting the roof with a loud thud, and then I'm running as hard as I can for the shuttle.

─────

My hands are shaking so hard I can barely buckle myself into the pilot's seat. Luckily, the autopilot works through voice commands, shooting me up into the clouds before I've even finished locking the restraints. I check the timekeeper in the arm of my suit. Forty-five minutes until the Archangel is due to deploy. With the trip up to the station only taking a matter of minutes, I should still have plenty of time to make it up there and find Angelou before the fireworks start. But despite that knowledge, I can't help drumming my fingers rapidly across the arm of my chair, every voice in my head shouting, *Hurry, hurry!*

Before long, the clouds part and the planetary net appears above me, glowing blue and bright within the drifting mists. Knowing there's no way I could navigate through the net the way Chen did, I activate the com for the nearest AP. There's a long pause as the officer on duty keys in my request, then finally he comes back, a strange catch in his voice.

"Team Leader, you're not on my list of approved arrivals. In fact, there's no record of you even taking a shuttle off the station."

My heart sinks as I take in his words. Because I hijacked the shuttle and left without permission, I'm not cleared to return. I was so worried about getting off the station, it never occurred to me I might not be able to come back. *Slag! Slag, slag, slag!*

I try to stay calm as I reply, "That's correct, Lieutenant. I had to leave under . . . *unusual* circumstances. I'll be happy to explain once I'm back on the station, if you'll just drop the net and let me up. I can give you my personal authorization code."

Quickly, I rattle it off, but the lieutenant isn't giving a centimeter. *"I'm sorry, Team Leader, but I can't let you on without official authorization. There are all sorts of security protocols that must be followed in a case like this. I'll have to link this in to my CO and let her take it from here."*

Panic starts fluttering through me at his pronouncement. "How long do you think that will take?"

"I don't know, Team Leader. Thirty minutes? An hour? It's a busy day, and she's much in demand elsewhere."

An hour! But that will be too late. I argue with the officer, but in vain. He won't listen to my explanations, won't let me through the net, won't even connect me directly to his CO or anyone else on base. He probably thinks I'm a spy—or worse, a squatter.

I throw off my harness and pace frantically around the cockpit. If there was ever a case of being so close and yet so far, this is it. Maybe if I went back for Chen? Except that even if she weren't infected with a few thousand ghouls, she's currently lying stunned on the roof of the relay station. I'm close enough I could probably reach someone in R&D directly, but even assuming the AP didn't block my transmission, who could I link that would be able to help me? My fellow testers don't have the authority to authorize any sort of shuttle clearance, and even the Division Commander would have to check with Angelou first.

Angelou!

My mind goes back to my recruitment, to that initial trip to R&D on the Colt Crawler. Angelou occasionally used me as a gofer on the trip, linking me with basic fetch-and-carry requests. A boring job, but it wasn't like I'd had anything better to do. Now I'm grateful for it. Because of that boring job, I have his private link number. Assuming he hasn't changed it, that is.

With a silent prayer, I activate my chit and flip through my link log, scrolling back through the months until I find the last time Angelou linked me. His number is encoded to prevent me from seeing it or transferring it to anyone else, but as far as I know, there's nothing to stop me from simply hitting "Re-link." I thumb the command, holding my breath as I wait to see if it'll work.

A second later, the link is dialing.

I cross my fingers, hoping against hope that Angelou will be curious enough to actually answer my link instead of simply blocking it. Vacuum knows he wouldn't have any problem hanging up on me, assuming he didn't already block me the minute we arrived on R&D all those months ago. But my wish comes true when, a moment later, the dialing pulse stops and Angelou's cadaverous voice filters through my chit.

"You'd better have a damn good reason for linking me like this, Sorenson."

I grin, the stern response no less than what I'd expect. I explain my situation with the net well enough, but when I get to the Archangel, my tongue gets tangled up and my brain can't seem to find the right way to explain. In the background, I can hear Angelou muttering quietly to someone outside the link, and I sense that he's fast losing patience with my inane babble.

"Please, sir," I finally say when it becomes clear he's not following my convoluted story about chips and saboteurs and transceivers. "Just let me back onto the station and hear me out. Then if you don't like what you hear, you can bust me down to scut or throw me out an airlock or whatever you see fit to do."

He snorts, apparently amused by the vision of him throwing me out an airlock, and says, *"Hold on."*

A minute later, the net opens.

"You'll find me in Habitat 8," comes Angelou's voice through the link again. *"Don't keep me waiting."* Then he cuts the com.

I land in the nearest hangar, pass the required psy check, and am on a tender back to the main station so fast I can only imagine what Angelou said to the lieutenant. An officer trails me to H8, no doubt to make sure I actually go there, where I find that Angelou has already cleared me for access. With a nod to the officer, I step inside.

Now that the mission's over, Habitat 8 feels like a ghost town. The crates of old testing equipment and racks of spare uniforms and parts are still there, but without the excess mission clutter piled around the habitat, it feels surprisingly empty. I spot Ty and a few of her special-ists inventorying equipment from one of the racks—probably more make-work she begged from Asriel—as well as assorted military per-sonnel scattered here and there. Angelou stands in the middle of the open space, speaking in a low voice with an inventory technician while consulting something on his tip-pad. When he spies me, he dismisses the technician with a wave of his hand.

"Well?" Angelou says, the one word dripping with impatience.

I take a deep breath, summoning up my courage. "Sir, it's about the Archangel. Over the past few months, I've been noticing some strange—"

"Sir?" a voice interrupts from my left.

An officer approaches, the patch on his uniform marking him as the one in charge of the Maintenance and Repair Personnel. He snaps to attention under Angelou's gaze.

"Yes, Captain?" Angelou asks, already losing interest in my story.

"Sir, per your orders, we ran another scan of the interstellar com-munications array. All diagnostics have checked out. We did find a missing cell on the aft antenna during our manual inspection of the array—probably blown out during the last big storm. However, as we have several redundant cells, it shouldn't affect operations in any way."

"No, but have a team replace it anyway," Angelou orders. "There's no point in implementing the Archangel across the Expanse if we can't tell it what to do when the time comes."

"Yes, sir. A repair team is already on it, and the new cell should be in place within the next five minutes."

"Good. Link me as soon as it's complete."

He dismisses the officer and returns his gaze to me. I struggle to retrieve my earlier train of thought.

"Sir, I've been down to the relay station on Prism, and I've uncov-ered some alarming—"

Angelou's chit hand snaps open, his eyes going to his palm even as his other hand bids me to wait. With a muttered, "One second," he strides several steps away, already subvocalizing into his chit in re-sponse to whatever link he just received.

I let out a huff of frustration, foot tapping impatiently as I wait for

Angelou to finish his call. Anxiety is eating away at me, and though I know the Archangel won't fire without Angelou, still my tension mounts with every second that passes. Across the way, the doctor is speaking rapidly into his chit, and I strain my ears in his direction on the off chance that I might catch some of his conversation, but I hear nothing. At least, nothing from Angelou's quarter. Now that I'm listening, I *do* sense something. There's a strange vibration, a sort of buzzing in my ear, like a sound I can almost hear but not quite. I turn my head left and then right, trying to pinpoint the source of the noise.

"Hey, Sorenson!" It's Ty, wandering over from the other side of the habitat. "What are you doing here? Asriel send you down to help?"

"I have to speak with Dr. Angelou," I answer absentmindedly, still focused on trying to locate the disturbance. If anything, it's only getting stronger, trickling through my ear canal like a rash, itchy and coarse. I push past Ty, taking a few tentative steps toward the north wall, and stop.

Ty frowns. "What?"

"Do you hear that?"

"Hear wh—" She stops, cocking her head to one side. "What is that?"

I shrug in answer. Whatever it is, she's not the only one hearing it. Scattered people around the habitat have stopped what they're doing, faces turning and foreheads wrinkling as they search for the disturbance. Even Angelou seems to have taken notice, his chit hand lowering as he scans the habitat.

The buzzing increases, razing through my ears almost painfully, and I press my palms against my ears to ward off the sensation. There's something vaguely familiar about the feeling. A low vibration rumbling in counterpoint to something much higher, so piercingly high it transcends my own capacity to actually hear it, so that I'm not sure if it's really there at all or if I'm just imagining it.

My common sense catches up with my train of thought, and I roll my eyes. *Deficient!* Of course I'm imagining it; I can't hear something past my range of hearing.

But I can remember *it.*

"The amplifiers!"

My eyes zero in on that mountain of bins we brought back on

board only yesterday, now stacked neatly against the north wall among some other crates, and then I'm running for the wall. I drop to my knees by the nearest bin, fumbling for the lid while Ty goes for the one next to it. Dread is seething in my gut, all my instincts screaming that something is very wrong, though I don't know what. At last, the catches release, and I fling open the top of the crate.

Blue light spills from the bin, the brilliant illumination splashing ominously over the crystalline walls even as the piercing sensation intensifies and the vibrations increase.

"What the *hell*?"

Every single amplifier is glowing with blue fire, the vertical lights up each cylinder nearly burning my eyes with their brightness. I throw open another bin and then another, while beside me Ty does the same. More blue splashes across the walls, licking across the surrounding crates like cerulean flame. I grab the nearest amplifier, huffing a little as I take the full weight in my arms. Quickly, I thumb the off switch on the control panel. Nothing happens.

"It's not turning off!"

"Neither is mine!"

The pressure in my ears is building, the pulsing sharp enough now it's starting to hurt. I throw my free hand over one ear, but it doesn't help. The sensation is like a tuning fork being shoved directly through my eardrum. A rumbling vibration thrums through the soles of my boots.

"I don't get it!" Ty says, throwing down the first amplifier and trying another, to no avail. "These were all powered off when we stowed them. How did they all suddenly turn on?"

"What was it Dr. Rahman told us?" I say. "That when networked together, one amplifier could serve as a remote control for the rest?"

Our eyes meet, and sudden understanding hits us both at once. "The missing amplifier!"

"Someone on Javeyn must have picked it up!"

And on quarantined Javeyn, that *someone* could only have been a squatter. Only what purpose would they have in turning on some old testing equipment that didn't even work the way it was supposed to anyway?

I flick my gaze over the crystalline walls around us, the glassy surfaces shining with a brilliant pearl-blue sheen. Reaching out, I rest a hand on the nearest surface. Vibrations shudder up through my hand and down my arm, buzzing through my skin and making all the hairs on my arm stand up. I have a sudden flashback to our original mission, to that moment near the end when Ty unzipped her jacket to find her necklace shattered across her chest.

Her *crystal* necklace.

Crystalline walls.

My eyes widen as the sudden implications sink in. *Oh, God!* If one amplifier could shatter a little necklace, what could *five hundred* amplifiers do?

Even as I ask myself the question, I'm dropping the amplifier in my hand and yelling to Ty, "We have to get out of here *now*!"

We leave the bins and take off. Ty is screaming to the others—*Get out! Get out!*—while I go directly for Angelou, grabbing his arm and urging him toward the door. He twists and turns in my grasp, trying to pinpoint the danger, but I refuse to let him stop. The whole habitat is shaking now, the vibrations cutting through the air in nigh-visible waves that seem to warp and weave reality itself, and I know however much time we have, it can't be long. The others sense it too, footsteps pounding past us as everyone runs for the door, propelled by their own fear as much as Ty's calls.

I pick up the pace, terrified of getting left behind in the great exodus. Something pops in my left ear, and then blood is dripping across my ear canal in a warm trickle. Still the thrumming drills deep into my head like an awl while lower down vibrations shoot up my legs, their violent waves strong enough to visibly rumble through the floors and up the walls. More footsteps run up behind me, and suddenly the weight on my shoulders lessens as Ty appears beneath Angelou's other arm. She gives me a hard nod, and together we haul ass for the door. Angelou's feet drag across the floor, not quite able to match our rhythm, but I pay them no mind, intent only on reaching safety.

CRACK!

We're halfway there when the wall directly above the amplifier bins splits apart. Cold air rushes in through the fissure, whipping around us in a frozen wind that whistles across the crystal with unearthly fury.

CRACK!

A second crevice erupts off the first, adding its own high-pitched howl to the earsplitting tones already shrieking through the habitat. My pounding head pounds harder, bludgeoned by the sounds, but I push on, racing against the fissures that continue to split and form through the walls in every direction.

CRACK! CRACK, CRACK!

Everything is shaking—walls, floors, boxes, racks—so hard we can barely keep on our feet. A giant fracture explodes in the floor beneath the bins, snaking out across the crystalline surface beneath us. The whole floor seems to leap up beneath our feet, throwing us into the air with a hard jerk. We all go down, plummeting to our knees with a hard crunch. Angelou cries out in pain, but Ty and I are already up, hauling him back to his feet and lunging for the door. We're almost there now, the exit only meters away.

CRACKCRACKCRACKCRACKCRACK!

We throw ourselves at the door, shoving our hands at the access panel before stumbling into the security airlock beyond. I could almost scream in frustration as we're forced to wait for the system to confirm our bio-signatures—*Come on, come on!*—then finally we're out of the vestibule and running through the walkway toward the station. Even in the passage I can feel the vibrations, shaking faster and faster as the sound continues to rise in search of that perfect meld of volume and pitch . . .

CREEE-AAAAAC-KKKKAA-SHOOM!

Like a soprano breaking a glass with a single high note, H8 blows apart in a fury of sound. Ty hits the deck and I follow, throwing Angelou to the floor and flinging myself over him just as a hail of crystalline shards squeal through the walkway with deadly precision. Pain blossoms across my back as fragments pour over us in a rain of daggers, sinking into my buttocks, my legs, my back, everywhere! The floor bucks, shudders running violently through the walkway as the stabilizers try desperately to compensate for the unexpected loss of H8. I dig my boots into the floor, hands scrabbling for purchase as the passageway judders up and down in sharp jerks. Wind is whipping through the jagged hole behind us, its frenzied voice rising higher and higher as it bounces along the crystalline halls, and I suddenly know:

This walkway is not going to last much longer.

Crystalline shards bite into my palms as I propel myself to my feet with a hard shove. The floor seesaws madly beneath my boots, tossing me back to one knee before I finally manage to find my footing. Bracing myself against the wall, I shove a hand under Angelou's armpit and haul him up from the floor, while on his other side Ty staggers dazedly to her feet. Shrapnel falls from her back in a shower of glass, tinkling across the floor in musical counterpoint to the brutal crunch beneath our boots. The tunnel bucks again, the walkway plunging up and then down, throwing us into the air for one heart-stopping second before slamming back into our feet with a spine-numbing thud. The floor is shivering so hard that it feels like it might tear apart any second. I glance at the others, eyes meeting as our minds meld in an instant of perfect accord.

As one, we begin to *run.*

Crunch, crunch, crunch, crunch! Our steps plow through the shrapnel in brutish harmony. Voices shout encouragement, barely audible over the chaos, and I look up to see a bunch of soldiers at the other end of the walkway, holding the doors open with their bodies while they wave us on. Energized by the sight, I surge through the churning tunnel, my feet finding a rhythm to the pitches and rolls almost without thought. We're nearly there when the jagged remains of H8 let out a mighty groan. I dare a glance over my shoulder just in time to see the back end of the walkway shear off with a mighty *crack!*

The station pitches back on its axis, unprepared for the sudden loss, and we all go flying down the walkway and into the arms of the waiting soldiers. My legs buckle under the impact, but it doesn't matter. Hands grab my uniform, and then the three of us are being yanked through the vestibule and into the station.

I clutch the wall with relief, heart pulsing a million beats a minute as I stare out through the viewports. The walkway is just a jagged tunnel, bitten off at the end where H8 used to be, and the energy shield is completely off. The shield generators must have been blown out of the grid by the shockwave, I realize, remembering that long ago storm I witnessed. The Rhyska mission flits across my mind, Raisman's words almost a taunt now: *Even the best shields will fail if you take out the right generators.*

My gaze moves on to the next habitat. H7 is still there, but now it sports a gaping hole in its side, like a stab wound, the long wall ripped open by flying debris. As I watch, a huge chunk of the wall collapses, breaking off and tumbling out the side through the mists below. The station yaws again, accompanied by the low moan of the stabilizers as they fight to keep us balanced and aloft. Angelou is activating his chit, pulling up some sort of program even as he fires off question after question to the baffled officer beside him, but somehow I know this battle will be decided long before the doctor can do anything. Heart in my throat, I clutch the arm of a bench and wait for the outcome of R&D's final stand. It's not long in coming.

All the lights wink out at once, a strange half-light falling across the station with only the sun-drenched crystal to light our way. The moaning cuts off, its voice swallowed up in a single instant, and with it goes the ever-present hum of the station machinery. Terror fills my heart as a deep-seated silence descends over the halls. I glance around wildly, reaching out for the comfort of another human being. My horrified gaze meets Angelou's as, for a brief second, we hang motionless in the air—

Then the whole station starts to *fall*.

40

WE PLUMMET THROUGH THE MISTS, nothing to check our plunge now that the energy shield is gone. Screams cry out through the corridors, underscored by loud cracks that thunder through the glassy halls as more habitats shear off, their delicate walkways unable to handle the stress. The station yaws with each loss, pitching this way and that, its living cargo along with it, thrown off balance by its constantly changing form.

I cling to a bench along the outer wall for dear life, face pressed to the viewport. My stomach is in my throat, my heart thumping so fast it's fit to burst. Mists and rain fly past the windows, the thick vapors, once a veil of solidity, now proving themselves to be completely insubstantial in the wake of our fall. They fly out in an aura around us like the Red Sea parting to admit our passage, and through the swirling violets and dissipating pinks, I see a brilliant shimmer of electric blue.

The planetary net.

It zooms up from below, the faint network of beams shining brighter with each passing second. My heart clenches in my chest. Even if the net weren't constantly in motion, it still wouldn't contain a hole anywhere near large enough to admit the station. And with the energy shield offline, blown apart by the explosion of H8, there's absolutely nothing in the universe that can protect us. Terror grips me at the sight of my imminent death, every muscle in my body frozen in fear though inside my mind is screaming in panic.

By some twist of fate, the shattered remains of Habitat 7 hit the latticework first. Blue bursts across my vision, refracted in every direction by a thousand panes of cut crystal exploding in a cacophony of high-pitched chimes under the noonday suns. Crystalline shards fly everywhere, hurled indiscriminately every which way as the deadly slivers slip through the net's holes with surprising stealth. Orange explosions blossom amidst the blue—shield generators hit by debris— and the Central Habitat lurches, spun off-kilter by the whistling shrapnel pattering across our hull. Still the net comes, rushing up at us in a wave of orange-marbled blue, its brilliant light bursting across the wall before me—

—only to wink out moments before we fall through.

Burning generators rain from the sky on either side of us, their smoking carcasses twisted around blackened crystal, and then we're through the field and hurtling down through the atmosphere below. But the net's fortuitous destruction will only delay our doom, not stop it. At this height and speed, we'll be killed on impact!

Still clutching the bench, I turn my face away from the viewports, unable to watch anymore. Across the corridor, Ty's wedged herself into an alcove between a couple of potted plants, Angelou clutched tight in her arms. We're the only three left, I see, everyone else scattered through the halls by the habitat's violent pitching and rolling. A man lies nearby, his head smashed open against the far wall, and it's all I can do not to be sick. Stifling the urge, I focus on Ty and Angelou. Her mouth is set and determined, muscles standing out against the folds of her uniform, but I recognize that look on her face. The sort of look that says she'll die before she lets Angelou go, and as for Angelou . . . I'd expect the doctor to be terror-stricken, frozen with fear, but instead he's got his chit activated, fingers frantically working over the holo hovering above his hand.

It's station control, I realize, recognizing the layout at last.

My hands squeeze the bench leg, white-knuckling as I watch him work. Angelou is muttering to himself, swiping the holo this way and that, making connections with one finger while severing them with the next. Red and gold lights go off and on across the holo as he attempts to bypass broken relays and smashed stabilizers, connecting functioning equipment with new power sources and cutting out the damaged parts that are stopping up the network. Brute concentration shapes his face, a maniacal sort of determination shining in his frost-blue eyes, and my heart swells with a strange sort of pride. This is the man who built R&D.

And this is the man who will save it.

We continue plummeting, not pitching so much anymore as simply falling, and I dare another peek through the viewport. The ground is in sight now, still far off in the distance but looming closer with every second. Despite all hope, fear washes over me, cold tendrils sweeping down my spine like some sort of parasite, creeping through my veins and turning me to ice from the inside out. Time seems to stand still, everything around me reduced to the simplest of sensations: the tang of blood in my mouth, my aching arms around the bench. The cold surety of my death. Tears prick my eyes, and I realize I'm not ready to go. Still, I grit my teeth anyway, determined to die like a soldier.

"Yes!"

The lights go on as the station machinery whirs back to life. The station jerks up as a giant energy net springs from the Central Habitat, like a giant parachute, arresting its fall. I fly up and back down, backside slamming against the floor hard enough to rattle my teeth. We're still falling, but much slower now, the massive energy net creating enough drag to cut some of the fatal momentum. A warm thrumming fills my legs as a multitude of propulsion units turn on, slowing us even more. The question is, will it be enough? I close my eyes, bracing for the inevitable impact.

Dirt flies up as we hit the ground hard, skidding across the land in a blaze of rocks and earth. The impact radiates all the way up my spine, knocking my head back against the wall. Stars burst in my eyes, and everything momentarily goes black.

Consciousness comes back in a head-splitting rush. I blink several times, pain stabbing through my head as I try to bring my vision back into focus. Everything's a blur, a meaningless collage of shadows and light. Panic cuts through me at the unaccustomed blindness, and I rub my eyes in an attempt to clear them. At last the blurriness starts to fade, vague shadows resolving into familiar shapes and colors. Cracked halls and dirt-covered viewports; broken crystal and torn plants; Ty's large form slumped against the opposite wall, Angelou still clutched in her arms.

Reassured by my renewed vision, I close my eyes and gingerly rest my head against the wall. The station is eerily quiet; no voices, no screams, not even a peep of machinery now that we've crash-landed across the planet. Only silence.

For a long time, I just sit there, blinking back tears of pain as I try to decide if it's worth getting up. It's the cries that decide me, the soft whimpers and groans and moans that begin filtering through the station that make me get slowly, achingly to my feet. My head swims, probably from the hard knock I took when we landed, and I lean against the wall and wait for it to pass. Pain radiates through every part of my body, from the bruises upon impact to the shards of station still in my back, but it's a bearable pain. It's the pain of being *alive*.

To my utter relief, Ty and Angelou stir soon after. Judging from their groans, they hurt as much as I do, but they make it to their feet with a little help. Ty and I exchange a look, not sure where to start.

"The Atrium," Angelou says, answering our unspoken question with surprising strength. "That's where everyone was gathered to watch the Archangel deploy. That's where they'll be."

I nod, grateful for the leadership. Together, the three of us carefully pick a path through the rubble, wending our way around broken benches and shattered crystal. We pause outside an office long enough for Angelou to kneel beside a fallen officer and take her pulse, but after a moment he only shakes his head. He doesn't bother with the other two people we pass. It's clear to all of us that they're dead.

We reach the Atrium to find the place in shambles. People sprawled over the floors and tables, intermixed with splintered furniture and plant detritus. The tables, at least, were bolted down, but I can only wince as I imagine how many people must have gotten hit by flying chairs and other debris. Despite their rough ride, people are already getting up, limping around as they attend to their fallen comrades. Miraculously enough, while injuries are high, the death toll seems low, almost everyone moving in some form or other, if only to moan in pain.

"We should find a med-kit," I say before realizing how utterly ridiculous that sounds.

A snort comes from Ty, followed immediately by a little whimper of pain. I totally know the feeling.

"Maybe not," I amend, recognizing that even if we had a first aid kit in the Atrium, it would be almost impossible to find in the chaos.

"We can still check on the survivors," Ty points out, "and maybe if we're lucky, we'll run into a med-kit out there."

Suiting action to words, she hobbles toward the person nearest her, a middle-aged engineer in a blood-streaked silver coat. He's conscious, though clearly in a lot of pain. Ty checks his pulse, speaking to him in a quiet tone as she holds his wrist. I'm about to follow her into the crowd when Angelou sags beside me. Alarmed, I make a grab for him, catching him before he can plummet to the ground and supporting him with one aching arm. Eyeing the battered room, I try to locate somewhere safe I can set him down. I'm about to lead him to a nearby couch that's still miraculously upright when the sound of running footsteps catches my attention.

What the . . . ?

I barely have time to wonder who could possibly have the energy to run anywhere at this point when a woman rushes in from the corridor behind me. A woman with hair as black as ink. My mouth falls open.

"Chen."

She turns and looks at me, concern etched across her face. Then all the detector lights go on at once as three thousand ghouls take flight from her head.

———

Lights flash, pouring over the room in streams of white, illuminating the enemy strike with perfect precision. Angelou is the first to go, doomed by his own proximity to our former pilot, and Ty follows shortly after, head jerking up in mute shock just in time to see the ghoul that claims her before it disappears inside her head. Shaken from my initial stupor, I start to go for my launcher. Only the cartridges are spent, used up on the roof of the relay station, and for the second time today I find I'm completely helpless.

Dropping my hand, all I can do is stand there in mute horror as ghoul after ghoul flutters from Chen's head, rainbow-black shapes that roil in the light as they sweep through R&D possessing military and civilians alike. They rise up into the air, swarming in shivers so thick they blot out the light, only to drop like bats into the defenseless population below. Screams peal out as people try to fight them, twisting away, running, batting at the shapes with flailing arms, but it's no use. The enemy can't be fought this way, our corporeal defenses meaningless to a species that has no form.

Heart pounding, I watch them whirl around my head, certain that any moment one will come for me, dive through the chaos to bring my life as I know it to a close. But none of them ever do. Just like on the rooftop of the relay station when they all went for Chen and not me, it's like I'm completely invisible, no more host material than some inanimate object like a table or chair. But then, I'm the one person in R&D currently wearing a ghoul-proof suit.

Which means *I'm* the only one who can *do* anything.

The knowledge jerks me from my inaction. Grabbing an injector of Psi-Lac from Angelou's own belt, I dose him up with a quick *hiss*, holding him still when he would've jerked from my grasp.

"Come on!"

Dumping the vial, I hustle him out the door. Together we weave through a maze of corridors and debris, leaving behind the crushed remains of the Atrium, though its blazing lights and terrified cries still follow us no matter how far we go. A gaping hole in the outer corridor affords us escape, ushering us out of the white-drenched halls and into the yellow light of day. I stop, blinking against the sunlight as I try to gather my bearings.

We've crash-landed just outside a city. A very familiar city, I realize after a moment, the same one where I left Chen. I can tell by the tall figure of the relay station off in the distance. She must not have had much charge left in her stun pistol when she shot herself, to wake up so soon. Not that knowing where we are gives me any clue where to go. Instead, I simply drag Angelou as far from the fallen sky station as I can, terrified of what that army of squatters inside might do as their Spectres take control. However, with our injuries, it's clear we won't get far.

Minutes later, we collapse in the shelter of some nearby trees, their draping branches affording us at least a little shelter from the outside world. Enough so that any casual onlookers from the habitat or the city won't notice us, I hope. Now that my initial adrenaline is subsiding, I'm having trouble thinking. Grief and terror send shudders through my body, and even my hands can't seem to stop shaking. I bury my head in my arms, my only thoughts now: *Where do we go, what do we do?*

Hands grasp my arm and pull it away from my face. I barely have time to register the injector before the needle plunges into my arm, a vial of Spec 1280 loaded up in its chamber. My blood pours into the vial, the thick fluid turning the clear substance crimson. Withdrawing the vial, Angelou shakes it up, staring intently as the two substances continue to mix, until at last the contents turn clear again.

Uninfected.

Though the news comes as no surprise to me, Angelou breathes a visible sigh of relief. Dropping the injector, he grabs my hand and wirelessly syncs to my chit, data flying through the uplink in a blur of information too quick for me to read.

I squint at the data stream. "What is this?"

He looks up, frost eyes almost white beneath the noonday sun, and I can't help shivering under the intensity of his gaze. His answer, when it comes, only sends more of a chill through me.

"The Archangel."

I shake my head, unable to accept the answer though the proof is flying through the air before me. "Doctor—"

"We don't have much time," he says, cutting me off. "With everyone else gone, all of our hopes are in your hands now. I'm linking you everything. Access codes, locations, everything you need to operate the Archangel."

"You don't understand—"

"There's a secondary control center, created in case something were to happen to the one on R&D. You have to get there as soon as possible. I have a ship hidden down here on Prism in case of emergencies—

the *Eos*. The authorization codes and location are here as well," he says with a nod to my newly uploaded chit, rising to his feet and hauling me along with him.

"Doctor!"

He stops, whether because of my tone or simply because he's finished the upload, I'm not sure. For once, his eyes don't hold sarcasm or superiority or even brisk matter-of-factness. They hold hope.

I swallow once, twice, pushing past the awful lump forming in my throat. "Doctor, it doesn't work," I finally choke out.

He shakes his head, not understanding. I open my mouth again, and suddenly the whole story comes pouring out.

"The Archangel doesn't kill ghouls; it never did! That's what I was coming to H8 to tell you. The enemy implanted a transceiver in the relay station to hijack the signal being sent up to R&D. Don't you see? They've been feeding us false data all along, getting us to create . . . I'm not sure exactly. A weapon of their own design, I suppose. And when we finally created it, they tricked us into thinking we'd found our ghoul-killer, hiding inside the squatters' heads so we couldn't pick them up with lights or force fences, not even with scent. I wish with all my heart that it worked, but it doesn't. I—I'm sorry. I'm so, so sorry."

Angelou is staring at me in horror, shaking his head as if unable to believe what I've just told him. Fumbling in my pocket, I pull out the chip we took from the relay station's transmitter array, passing it silently into the doctor's numb hands. For a moment, all he can do is turn it over and over between his fingers, as if scared to actually access it. Finally, he uplinks it to his chit, sharp eyes quickly finding the evidence Chen and I uncovered at the relay station. I hold my breath, wondering what he'll do.

Disbelief morphs to rage in an instant. His jaw clenches and his nostrils flare, anger washing over his features in a dark rush while spots of color mottle his pale cheeks. Pure, unadulterated fury lances from his eyes, and I involuntarily take a step back.

"That relay station was *secure*!" he snarls. "There's no way a squatter could've gotten in there, not without help. Who? I want to know *who* did this! Who betrayed us all by helping them?"

He starts poring over the chit again, fingers moving in a blur as he searches for something known only to him. All of a sudden he stops, a single clearance code hanging in the air before him. A strangled cry leaches from his lips, all color draining from his face in an instant. He clutches his chest, and I know in that moment that if someone had shot him clean through the heart with a laser pistol, they couldn't have killed him more thoroughly. Then he does something I would never have expected in a million years.

He sinks to his knees, puts his head in his hands, and cries.

———

I sit under a tree, numb to my very soul, and wait for Angelou.

He got up a little while ago, red-eyed and strangely calm, muttering something about sending a link. I wondered how he'd do it, with R&D smashed to crystalline pieces across the planet's shores, until I realized the APs surrounding the station were still intact, or intact enough. As long as his chit is powerful enough to reach those Atmospheric Platforms—or his chit's fitted with a sat-link—he can use their interstellar broadcasting equipment to send a link anywhere.

Whatever the message was, he's heading back in my direction now, apparently finished with his link. A minor relief to me, as squatters have already started to surround the wreckage. Though they haven't spotted us yet—unsurprising since there's another, much larger, distraction at hand—I know our luck won't hold out forever.

"Sorenson."

I look up at Angelou's voice.

"You have to get out of here, tell them what happened. Go see Colonel Mittag at Military Intelligence Headquarters on Yratia. Tell him I sent you." He links me the name and coordinates.

"Sir, aren't you coming with me?"

"It's too late for me."

"Surely you have some pharmaceutical reserves on your ship? If we dosed you regularly with Psi-Lac and Spectra—"

"And what? Go to a squatter colony? Live out the rest of my life as a slave to these creatures?" Contempt drips through his voice at the idea, and not for the first time I can't help thinking I've vastly misjudged him. Saw an untouchable demigod when there was only a man. As if reading my thoughts, his voice softens. "Besides, there's one more thing I have yet to do here."

The blade appears from his tunic as if by magic. I barely have time to think, *Angelou carries a knife?* before he's grabbing my wrist. Pain stabs through my arm as he digs the blade deep into my flesh. I let out a surprised yelp, wondering if his Psi-Lac has finally worn off, when the blade reemerges.

With my coma capsule.

He tosses it to the ground, grinding it into the dirt with a single twist of his heel. My eyes widen in horror as I realize what he's about to do. He raises his hand, and I grab his wrist, shaking my head.

"No. Sir, no! Please, you can't!"

"They know too much. We all know too much. Look!" He nods to the sky, where a ship is already sailing upwards, free and clear through the gaping hole in the planetary net. "The net is gone; there are no blocks to interstellar travel. Already squatters are starting to make a break for it. Regular squatters are bad enough, but the people of R&D aren't regular squatters. There's no telling what kind of damage they could do, what sort of classified intel they could give away before the military gets here to quarantine this place. The damage to the war effort could be *immeasurable*. Unless somebody stops them first."

My mouth goes dry, lips trembling as I consider his words. Every cell in my body revolts at what he's proposing, and yet I know he's right. These are civilian and military personnel working at the most classified base in the Expanse. The information Angelou himself knows would probably be enough to lose this war for us, if it got into the wrong hands, and how could it not with the planetary net open and squatters already converging upon the wreck? I want to protest, to say there must be another way . . .

Only there isn't.

I look down at the gaping hole in my wrist, then to the tiny bump in Angelou's. He signed on for this—the same as I did, the same as everyone else did—and if I were one of those squatters back in that broken station, I know what I'd choose.

Tears brimming in my eyes, I drop his wrist.

Angelou stares at his coma capsule for a long moment, face

ineffably sad as he intones softly, " 'I have fought a good fight, I have finished my course, I have kept the faith.' " He lifts his head then and smiles at me, a rare, genuine smile that brims with humanity from the inside out. "Win this war for us, Sorenson."

He pulls up the command with a few flicks of his finger, raises his hand, and at the last moment stops. He leans forward, eyes intent. "Don't tell *anyone* you have the Archangel. Tell everyone I died, and the Archangel with me."

I frown. "Not even the colonel?"

"Not even the colonel. If you tell him—if you tell *anyone*—it will get back to *her*."

Her? I start to ask him who he means when suddenly his wrist flicks. His body seizes up, face twisting in a rictus of pain as the coma capsule does its work, stripping away the higher functions of his brain and motor cortex until he crumples, a near-lifeless husk, to the ground.

Off in the distance, cries rise up from the wreck, the salvagers undoubtedly seeing the same thing I just saw. Pain lances through my chest like a sucker punch straight to the heart. I try not to think of all the people in that station, all surviving a terrible fall only to ultimately endure a worse one as Angelou activated every coma capsule on that broken base at once. I try not to think of Ty and Chen, Asriel and 'Vange. Preston, Inoue, and Jacobi. My precious Delta Team, and all the other teams. Civilians, military, and PsyCorp. People I lived and worked with, people I called my friends. People I called my family. I try not to think of them.

I fail.

The last thing I see before I turn around and flee are Angelou's frost-blue eyes, staring sightlessly up into the pastel pink skies, never to view the mists of his sky home again.

Onboard the *CES Retribution*
Flagship of the First Admiral of the Celestial Fleet

SHE WAS IN THE SHOWER *when the link arrived, buzzing sharply through her hand with a sting bordering on painful. The Admiral cut off the pulse with a quick flick of her finger. Whatever it was he had to say to her, it could wait.*

Twenty minutes later, fully groomed and dressed, she reactivated her chit. A curious chill fell across her shoulders as his face sprang up from her palm. His usually composed features were livid, frost eyes burning and spots of color dappling his cheeks.

"How could you?!"

Rage suffused his voice, of a kind she had not seen on him in nearly fifteen years, not since the day they argued and henceforth became the Doctor and the Admiral.

"Did you think I didn't know what you were up to? That I didn't know about your precious little Helios Project? I may not have known the details, but I knew enough. Enough to know that whatever it was could only be of the basest nature, in violation of all morality, all ethics, and even God himself! But I did not interfere. I left you to your pursuits, though perhaps I should not have, and this is how you repay me?! By throwing us to the enemy? By helping the very creatures that would destroy us for eternity?!"

He leaned in, eyes piercing through the holo like knives, and whispered, "I know it was you. I know it was you who sold us out. And what is it you've learned, Icaria? What is it that makes you so secure you would destroy humanity's best hope for survival?"

Though she'd long since schooled herself never to let emotional reactions dictate her outward appearance, she flinched at the sound of her name, given so long ago and yet left unused for years. No matter that it was a recorded holo and not a live feed; the word still reverberated down to the pit of her stomach, shoved deep like a dagger by the one person in the universe with the power to wield it.

He shook his head, the rage in his eyes transforming into a bleak despair. "How could I have failed you so miserably? Led you astray when all I wanted to do was teach you? If I could do it all again, I would not know what to do differently. I would not know how to avoid this terrible pass."

"No, I don't suppose you would," she intoned quietly.

"So all I will say is this: I don't know what you believe you've accomplished, but I do know you will regret it. And while I won't be the one here to mete out whatever justice you've earned for yourself, I swear to God you will rue the day you betrayed me and wish with all your heart that you had taken a different course."

His gaze bore into her for a few more seconds, and then the holo ended, freezing on the very last frame. His jaw was set with fury, his mouth twisted with contempt, and yet his eyes held more than mere rage. Beneath the anguish and confusion, the sorrow and the wrath. Beneath a well of betrayal years in the making now finally come to fruition.

They held love.

For a long time she simply sat there, staring at the final image of that message, body frozen and face a mask. All but for her eyes, which pored over every last detail of his aged face and never wavered. When at last she hit "Re-link," the message that came up told her everything.

Error: No Receiver Found

Not disabled, not deactivated. Not "unable to establish a connection" or "interference glitch." None of the usual messages one received in the event of a transmission error or an interstellar network malfunction. Not even the sort of message one saw if a user's chit had been completely damaged or destroyed.

No Receiver Found.

It was the sort of message you got only if the user's chit had been completely wiped, erased so thoroughly that even the most extensive search would find no trace of its existence, as though the user had never even existed at all. The end result of an all-consuming liquidation program that burned through the filaments of your chit and left nothing alive. The kind that, in high-level officials like the Doctor, automatically activated in one circumstance.

The user's death.

A vibration in her palm signaled an incoming link from the Retribution's captain. Leaving the Doctor's holo hanging over the palm of her hand, the Admiral put the call on audio-only.

"Admiral, I'd like to request your presence on the bridge immediately. We're receiving some incoming information I think you'll want to see."

"I'm occupied," she answered shortly.

A thick silence hung across the link. "We've received reports regarding our bases on Voce Bella, Ka Mala, and Jyara Prime. More reports are coming in as we speak, all from key military bases, supply depots, and manufacturing facilities solely responsible for creating and supplying the weaponry and tech used in the war."

"And?"

"They're all gone. Every last one of them has been destroyed."

She blinked, the news surprising and yet somehow not. "I'll be there momentarily."

De-acking the link, she took one final moment to drink in the Doctor's face before he, too, disappeared into the palm of her hand. Then, with nothing else to be done, she carefully finished her morning ritual, tucking her blouse in just so and slicking every single loose tendril of hair back with hairspray. The last thing she did was push up her sleeve to reveal a tattoo lased neatly over her right wrist.

A tattoo of a dark rainbow twined about an eight-pointed star.

Picking up a vial of liquid bandage, she began spraying the substance over the tattooed skin, watching as the clear liquid automatically colored to match her natural skin tone. She continued to spray until the mark had completely vanished, hidden beneath a flesh-like coating indistinguishable from her real skin. Then, buttoning her coat, she left the room.

41

CRYSTALLINE LIGHT SHINES DOWN *around me, refracting across the empty halls like a scattering of diamonds. I run through the outer corridor of the Central Habitat, launcher in hand as I search frantically for the others. Outside the mists drift and swirl as ever, but inside all is silent. All is still. My voice echoes off the walls as I call for them once, twice, three times. Where are they? I have to find them, I have to warn them!*

A noise behind me makes me stop. Chen is there, inky hair caught up in a neat bun as usual. I spin in a circle, and suddenly everyone is back. Ty, Archer, RC. Zephyr, Asriel, and Evangeline. Songbird and Kagawa; Raisman and Herrera. Inoue with his trembling courage, and Angelou. Always Angelou, standing there amidst the others, his frost-blue eyes glittering strangely in the pale light. He holds up his chit hand.

"No!"

Then everyone drops to the floor at once. I fall to my knees by the nearest victim. It's Zel, her bright ponytail spreading in red-gold strands across the floor. I grab her, shake her, scream her name, but nothing I do makes any difference. She's gone. Staggering to my feet, I stumble through the maze of bodies, unable to escape the sea of faces, when something catches my foot and I go sprawling. I lift my-self up only to see Angelou again—lying on the floor, staring up at me with sightless blue eyes, condemned forever to look and look but never see. I reach my hand out to close them, and suddenly they snap to life, icy gaze fastening over my own, merciless and all-knowing.

"Win this war for us, Sorenson," he whispers.

I lurch back with a cry. Turn around to flee, but the bodies are everywhere now, hemming me in, trapping me here with their blank faces and dead eyes. In desperation, I turn to the observation ports.

The pastel mists are gone, and in their place are ghouls. Millions upon millions of ghouls, pushing at the crystalline walls of the sta-tion, trying to get in, their forms so tightly packed all I can see are black rainbows roiling against the glass. I whip my launcher up, frantically pointing it this way and that as they lunge against the walls again and again. The whole station shudders, and a crack ap-pears, snaking like a fault line through the delicate crystal. I hold my breath, eyes fixed on that single fissure—

Then suddenly the walls around me shatter, and we're falling. Falling and falling, and I don't think we'll ever stop . . .

I come awake with a gasp. Pain knifes through my back as I jerk into a sitting position, but I ignore it, gaze already sweeping the dimly lit room for my launcher and pistol as I struggle out of bed.

Bunk, storage closet, desk. Plain metallic walls gleaming softly under the yellow emergency lights. I have to take it all in twice, eyes coming back around for another pass, before it sinks in: I'm not on the station anymore. It was just a dream.

Except that it wasn't.

Slumping down onto the bed, I rub my eyes and check the time. 0350. That's almost four hours before the nightmares woke me this time. I suppose I should be grateful to get even that much sleep, but all I feel is exhausted. The sort of all-consuming exhaustion that bores deep down into your very soul and can't be extinguished no matter how much you sleep. Assuming you can sleep at all.

Padding into the adjoining hygiene unit, I go through the usual motions, drifting from toilet to sink to shower in a half-aware haze. The water is hot, but everything inside me is numb, has been ever since I bugged out on Angelou's ship I-don't-even-know-how-many days ago, leaving the remains of my entire world literally shattered across the ground. The failure of the Archangel, the station's fall, those final moments when Angelou released the coma capsules; it's all locked away inside, knotted deep within my gut like a festering sore that's painless now but will be agony once it bursts. Unlike my physical body, which is agony *now*.

The rinse cycle finishes and the disinfectant spray comes on, razing my back like a hundred tiny lasers. I brace myself against the wall, gritting my teeth through the pain as the spray does its work, sighing with relief when it finally ends. A small sliver of crystal drops from my shoulder as I step out of the shower, just one of a couple hundred still lodged in my back, buttocks, and legs. Thank God for my armor, or the crystalline shrapnel that nailed me when H8 blew would probably have killed me outright. I pulled what pieces I could reach, but the rest will have to wait until I reach the MI base and can receive proper medical care. Until then, all I can do is run the disinfectant spray to keep the infection at bay and endure the pain. According to the ship's computer, I've still got nine days to go. At least Angelou's ship has a good supply of painkillers laid by in its infirmary.

I get dressed and take a few, chugging them down with a glass of water as I check my heading in the tiny cockpit. So far, so good. Everything about this ship is sleek and state-of-the-art, including a fly/nav system that basically pilots itself. All I had to do was feed in the base coordinates and let the ship do the rest. Which means I don't have to worry about crashing the thing but also means I have nothing to do.

Nothing to do but lick my wounds and think, that is. Nothing to do but remember.

I squeeze my eyes shut. If I let the memories in, they'll never let me go. To distract myself, I start cleaning up the place. Pak wrappers, dirty dishes, soiled clothes. In the six days I've been onboard, I haven't exactly been the most considerate houseguest. No doubt Angelou would be appalled if he could see what I've done to his precious ship.

If he were still alive to see it.

I start in the galley, throwing away wrappers and putting dishes in the sanitizer, then move on to the bedroom to make the bunk, tucking in the corners tight and smoothing the blankets until it would pass any Celestial Guard inspection. My last stop is the hygiene unit, where I start by turning on the self-cleaning jets in the shower, then throw the loose toiletries in the drawer. My R&D mission uniform is crumpled up on the floor where I left it the first day I came aboard. Crystalline shards still cling to the back, sharp and deadly. I carefully brush them into the recycler, fold up the uniform, and stop. Slowly I reopen it, heart thudding as I stare at the black fabric.

The suit is ruined beyond repair, the back completely torn open by flying shrapnel. I finger the pattern of holes across the back. The layer that held the ghoul-repellant gases has been slashed open in several places. By the time the station hit the ground, all of the air would have long since seeped away. Which means I had no more protection from the enemy when Chen walked in with a head full of ghouls than anyone else did.

They let me go.

My knees give out, and I sink to the floor, head shaking in denial. No, it can't be! Maybe there weren't enough ghouls for everyone, or maybe they just overlooked me for some reason. Only I remember that awful moment when Chen walked in, how Angelou and Ty—the two people closest to me—were the first to go. Everyone else in the vicinity was taken within moments after they went.

Everyone except *me*.

The question is: Why? What reason could the enemy possibly have for sparing me? Out of nowhere, my mind suddenly flashes to that final data chip I pulled out of my helmet. The custom-made helmet created specifically for *me*.

No, it can't be!

I shake my head, refusing to believe there could be any connection, but even I can't deny the similarities inherent in the two situations. The Spectres singled me out, spared me on not one, but two occasions—on top of the relay station with Chen, and then only minutes later in the fallen Atrium. The same way the saboteur singled me out personally on two occasions, first planting the laser cutter in my personal locker and then later the chip in my custom-made helmet.

The laser cutter. Everything goes back to that, I suddenly realize.

It was the first clue in a trail of bread crumbs leading me straight down to the relay station where I found that transceiver and learned the truth about the Archangel. Only if Chen's theory was right, there never *was* a saboteur on R&D. But how could a saboteur at one of our military depots have possibly managed to plant a laser cutter in my locker? I think back to the night I found the cutter. How I was fumbling in the dark for clean clothes only to have the laser cutter tumble out . . . from my *Celestial Guard mission uniform.*

My eyes widen in shock. All this time, I figured the cutter had been planted in my locker—that's why I assumed someone in the Testing Division was to blame—but what if the cutter wasn't planted in my locker at all, but in my *Guard uniform?* Slipped into one of my side pockets, perhaps, without me noticing? It would have been easy enough to plant in the midst of a crowd, and the cutter is certainly light enough that I might not have noticed, especially if it happened shortly before I retired my Guard uniform for good. It would even explain why Asriel found no evidence of tampering with my locker when I first brought him the cutter. I rack my brain, trying to remember the last time I wore my CG mission uniform. The answer comes like a bolt out of the black.

I last wore it during the evacuation of ScyLab 185g, less than twenty-four hours before I was recruited by Dr. Daedalus Angelou.

My mind flashes through everything that's happened since that day, since the day the Specs invaded a seemingly insignificant ScyLab and in doing so threw me straight into the path of Daedalus Angelou. I recall my last conversation with Gran, only hours before I left for R&D, and those final words she spoke to me.

Don't forget who the real enemy is.

The *real* enemy. Stars burst in my brain at those words, and it suddenly occurs to me—the common denominator? It isn't a human. It's the *enemy.*

Spectres on ScyLab 185g where the laser cutter could have been easily planted on me.

Spectres on Military Depot S6-4112 using chips to lead me to the truth of the Archangel.

Spectres on the Prism relay station using our own data to create a weapon of their design.

Spectres stealing the lost amplifier and using it to blow R&D from the sky.

Spectres ready to infect everyone the instant we hit the ground.

Ready to infect everyone except *me*, that is. They let me go and took everyone else, so that when Angelou needed someone to give the Archangel to, *I* was the only one left.

My gaze flicks to my hand, to the chit buried deep in my palm, now the only living key left to the magnificent Archangel, and a chill runs down my spine.

They designed a weapon, tricked us into implementing it across the Expanse, and then minutes before it was set to fire, they threw the station down from the sky in a blaze of sound. And when the dust cleared, everyone was dead, and it was me *who walked away with the Archangel squarely in the palm of my hand.*

My hands start to shake. The sheer magnitude of what I'm contemplating is staggering. More than staggering, it's *terrifying*. For months now, I've felt like I was being personally manipulated, led by some unknown entity for purposes I couldn't begin to guess. A feeling that was only confirmed when I found the serial number from the energy converter's chip stamped on my helmet. I followed the trail, this intricately choreographed path weeks, even months in the making, from the planting of the cutter to my recruitment into R&D, my discovery about the Archangel to the destruction of R&D, and for what?

All so I could walk away with the Archangel in the palm of my hand.

Everything inside me goes cold. Objections immediately spring to mind—I'm just an ordinary soldier. I'm no one. Why give it to me when there were a thousand more qualified people available? For that matter, why not simply let Angelou fire the weapon and be done with it?

It's all in the timing. They literally took R&D down minutes before the Archangel was set to fire. So they wanted us to create the Archangel and implement it, but not fire it? Or at least, not fire it *yet*. What they're waiting for is a mystery I can't answer. I only know that somehow, irrevocably, *I've* been made a part of it.

Fear trickles through me, cold and raw, and suddenly it's all too much. I have so many questions begging to be answered, but there's no one to answer them. How could the enemy manage to pull off such an incredible chain of events, and why? What purpose could this terrible strike possibly hold? And even more importantly: Is this the end of their plan . . . or only the beginning? All this time, we've presumed to know our enemy. To know how they think and where they'll strike and what they want, and yet the truth is that we know *nothing*. If there's anything I've learned from the Fall of R&D, it's that the enemy clearly has abilities and motives beyond our knowledge, perhaps even beyond our capacity to understand. An old saying of Gran's pops into my mind: *You need all the pieces to put the puzzle together.* Suddenly I feel like I'm trying to do a thousand-piece puzzle with only fifty pieces in hand.

My lungs seize and my brain freezes, smothered by all the pain of the past days and the weight of these new ideas. My mind is spinning in circles, struggling to find something, just *one thing* I can be sure of, but it's like the ground is caving in beneath my feet, dropping away around me before I can find any footing. Then a single thought crystallizes in my brain.

I have to talk to Teal.

The urge to see my little sister is a sucker punch to the gut, hard and fast. That knot tied deep down inside of me is unraveling, the threads spooling out of control in every direction, and suddenly I need nothing more than to tell Teal *everything*. About the station's fall, the failure of the Archangel, my terrible suspicion I've been played by the enemy. But most of all, I need to tell her about the end. About that awful moment when I let go of Angelou's hand, knowing what he would do, knowing that everyone would die . . . and I let it go anyway.

The same way she knew Lia would die if she got off that train . . . and she let her go anyway.

"You knew *what she was going to do! How could you've ever let her go?"*

"I let her go because I knew *what she was going to do."*

I close my eyes, heart sinking as I remember all those times Teal tried to explain it to me. But I'd never understood. Until today.

I activate my chit, fingers fumbling as I uplink with the ship's com system and dial. I have to see Teal. If anyone can unravel this mess, Teal can. My brilliant little sister with her ability to put things together and see the far-reaching ramifications of events long before anyone else can. *She'll* know what this all means. She'll know what to do.

Endless minutes pass as I wait for the link to connect. I anxiously pace the room, impatience mounting with every step I take, until at last a message flashes up.

Error: Unable to Establish a Connection

Disappointment washes over me, the desperate urge to see my sister only intensified now that I've failed. I set my chit to keep linking until it connects, but it's no use. I get the same message no matter what I do. After five hours, I collapse on the floor with a bitter laugh, the irony of the situation not lost on me. For months I've had chance after chance to talk to Teal and always refused, and now that I actually *do* want to see her, I can't get through. Maybe there's no justice in this twisted universe, but apparently it *does* have a sense of humor.

De-acking my chit, I slump against the wall with a sigh. "Where *are* you, Teal?"

But just like every other time I've asked, there's no one here to answer my call.

42

"WE'RE CALLING THEM HITCHERS."

The clipped tones echo through the interrogation room, chilling the air like an early spring frost. I blink at the unexpected declaration, gaze fixed on my fingers where they brush lightly over the hard metal surface of the interview table, and finally rouse enough to ask, "What?"

"Hitchers," he repeats, "because they can 'hitch' a ride in a squatter's head for temporary lengths of time. All the freedom of a ghoul combined with the subterfuge of a squatter. It's really quite brilliant."

Brilliant. As though the mass infection and subsequent loss of three thousand people is a tactical maneuver to be marveled at and not a deep-abiding tragedy to be mourned.

I slowly lift my head, the cold admiration in his voice enough to shake me from my stupor, and meet the colonel's gaze. His eyes are that of an interrogator's, emotionless and cold. Everything in this room is cold. From the cold metal of the chair seeping through my trousers to the cold tabletop beneath my fingers to the cold air blowing down my collar from the vent above. I was numb when I first walked into this room, but after five days with Mittag, I'm downright frigid.

"Not to worry," he adds, misinterpreting my silence. "From what we've been able to gather, ghouls can only hitch with someone who already carries a squatter. We believe it's the presence of the squatter that allows the ghoul to hitch without actually bonding to the host themselves, thereby allowing them to leave at will even if the host is still living. We've had our suspicions for some time, but were never able to confirm them until now."

Suspicions. I resist the urge to laugh. Secrets, is what he really means, though whether those secrets could have saved us or not, God only knows. *Tell me, Colonel, how many lives is one secret worth?*

The thought runs through my mind, though not my mouth. Instead, my eyes stray to the metal cuffs lying empty on the tabletop before me. I may not be sleeping in a cell or chained to this table, and this may not be officially labeled an interrogation, but that doesn't mean I'm not on trial all the same. The sort of trial where my fate won't be decided by a jury of peers, but by the determination of one or two men; where a sentence of "guilty" won't result in a court martial but brain-draining by PsyCorp or banishment down a dark hole.

The sort of trial where my very life hangs in the balance.

And so I've sat in this cold room with this cold man for five days running, telling my story again and again as I wait for them to decide if *I* am responsible for the Fall of R&D.

As if reading my mind, Mittag's lips curl into a half smile. "My apologies for the interruption. Please continue with your account."

I blink a couple of times, trying to recall where I was when Mittag interrupted with his remark about hitchers, and shake my head. "There isn't much more to tell. After the hitchers took everyone in the habitat, I tried to get Angelou out, but it was too late. He'd already been infected. He gave me directions to his hidden ship and instructed me to come here, to you. As the flight recorder in the ship can attest, I came straight here."

"Without even stopping for medical care, no less, despite the seriousness of your injuries."

"My injuries, while painful, weren't life-threatening, and I felt the information I carried was too important to be delayed."

"A most commendable attitude. Exactly what I would expect from someone personally recruited by Daedalus Angelou." Mittag leans back in his chair, an appraising gleam in his eye. "And it didn't seem strange to you that the hitchers took everyone in R&D *except* you?"

My breath hitches slightly in my chest, but I force myself to answer normally. "As I said before, the scientists at R&D had developed a ghoul-proof suit—"

"Ah, yes. The suit. Which you no longer have."

"I'm sorry, sir. Because of the injuries to my back, the only way I could get the suit off was to cut it off. Since the suit was clearly destroyed beyond repair, I saw no reason to keep it and recycled it."

Mittag nods, but doesn't answer. I mentally hold my breath as he flicks an appraising gaze over me. For the most part, I've told him the absolute truth from beginning to end, recounting the way I was recruited into R&D and all the big events that eventually followed afterward, up through the fall of the station and the devastation of the coma capsules. I handed over the transceiver chip on the very first day of my arrival, explaining its origin and including Angelou's belief that we were betrayed by a regular human, though I didn't know who. The one thing I haven't told him is my terrible suspicion that I, personally, was being manipulated by the enemy. Because there's no way I can explain that without telling him *why* I was being manipulated by the enemy.

Don't tell anyone *you have the Archangel. Not even the colonel. If you tell him—if you tell* anyone—*it will get back to* her.

Angelou's voice whispers in my head, and I secretly touch my middle finger to my chit. Though physically no different, my chit is a lead weight in my palm, the Archangel's presence a metaphysical burden so heavy I can hardly bear it. More than anything, I just want to be rid of the whole thing. All it would take is a few words in Mittag's ear. A few words, and he'd have the Archangel and anything else Angelou might have stuck in there out of my palm for good. But every time I open my mouth to tell him, I remember the way Angelou looked when he pulled up that clearance code and discovered he'd been betrayed. How he clutched his chest and cried out as though his very heart had been cleaved in two. And though I have no more idea who this "*her*" is than I did before, still I know:

Dead or alive, I can't betray him.

So I continue to lie, day in and day out, or at least hide the truth. Does Mittag suspect I'm holding something back? I don't think so, or he would have had me subjected to a chit scalping and deep psychic scan already. Both of which would be highly illegal and a violation of my human rights, but somehow I don't think MI stands on legalities much. In fact, I have the strange suspicion that only Angelou's name has kept me from both so far. Even gone, his name still carries great power. But Angelou's name notwithstanding, if I give Mittag *one* reason . . .

But I don't, though I bleed inside with every moment I'm forced to recount, answering Mittag's questions one at a time, my responses always consistent, always the same.

We're circling back around to the sound amplifiers when the colonel receives a link, eyes flicking over the text pooling across his palm. Though his outward demeanor doesn't change, something in his sudden stillness tells me this isn't an ordinary link. My suspicion is confirmed when he signs off and stands, our interview clearly over. I start to rise, but he waves me back to my seat.

"You're about to have a very distinguished visitor." He regards me for a long moment, cold eyes unreadable, then suddenly leans in and whispers, "Fail this interview, and there is no one in this universe who can save you."

I go cold at the colonel's words, the already frosty air freezing to ice around me. Dumbstruck, all I can do is watch as he swiftly pivots around and leaves the room, one thought on my mind.

Who does even the Head of Interrogation fear?

Then the door opens, and in she walks.

At first glance, she seems like any other officer of the fleet I might meet, middle-aged and dressed in the immaculate black-and-golds of the CE Navy. Her hair is a light blond, her height nothing remarkable. I search her collar for insignia, some sort of identifier, and my eyes widen. They made us memorize the insignia in basic—along with the name that goes with it—but I never thought I'd actually see it in person. First Intergalactic Admiral of the Fleet.

I am in the presence of the highest ranked military personage in the entire Expanse.

I jackrabbit to my feet, the salute coming without thought as she advances on me like a predator that never misses its prey. Her cheek is carved from contempt, her jaw formed without mercy; the tilt of her chin is arrogance incarnate. I picture those long fingers, like a spider's legs skittering across its webs, and I inwardly shudder.

The Admiral halts a scant meter away, her hair glowing like ice over a pond beneath the bright ceiling lights. I plumb my memory for her name, but I can't seem to recall it. Ever so slightly she tilts her head up, surveying me. The light falls over her face, illuminating her eyes with pale fire, and my heart drops out of my chest.

Her eyes are *blue*. Not just any blue, but the pale blue of a morning frost gilding across a dying grass. A shade I last saw exactly twenty-four days ago, staring sightlessly up at a pastel sky amidst a sea of shattered crystal, never to close again.

Oh my God.

And suddenly I know beyond a doubt exactly who this woman is. I know whose clearance code Angelou found when he searched through that transceiver chip, and I know why her betrayal cut him to his very core. The name I was searching for comes back in a rush.

First Intergalactic Admiral of the Fleet Icaria Avery Angelou.

The woman Angelou warned me about with his dying breath is his *daughter*.

————

We face each other across the interrogation room, the frost-eyed admiral and I. She speaks without preamble.

"You recognize me." Not a question.

"Yes." I hesitate for the barest heartbeat. "You have your father's eyes."

A beat passes. I've surprised her, though I'm not sure what makes me think so; her expression never changes.

The Admiral acknowledges the observation with a slight dip of her chin, and I'm suddenly reminded of an old adage I heard as a child: *Where souls are kindred, the eyes always breed true.*

For my sake, I can only hope that's right.

"It seems you did know the doctor," the Admiral continues smoothly, those frost-blue eyes, so uncannily like Angelou's, sweeping over me like a hawk eyeing a mouse. "At least a little."

"Join Division 7, and you'll be one of the few who helps determine if we win this war."

"It's all right to be angry with the dead."

"Win this war for us, Sorenson."

His frost-blue eyes staring sightlessly up at the pastel skies, never to see his sky home again.

A lump forms in my throat at the memories, and it takes all of my strength to reply evenly, "You could say that."

"I could, but I'm more interested in hearing what *you* have to say. While I have no doubt the colonel has been unerringly accurate in his reports, I imagine they hardly do your story justice."

Justice! My hands clench beneath the table, fisting in the legs of my trousers as I struggle to keep my anger from showing. This woman singlehandedly threw R&D to the enemy, and she would speak to me of *justice*?!

The numbing shock I felt upon meeting her, upon realizing who she was, is finally wearing off, replaced by a loathing so acute it burns like an ember deep in my gut. The blood of three thousand people runs red across her hands, and yet there she stands, hands folded unconcernedly over the back of a chair as though those three thousand lives are nothing more than an entertaining story to be told!

I stare at the cold-eyed woman before me, a strange cocktail of fear and loathing sloshing in my gut. My hands itch for action, but aside from a quick flare of the nostrils—a movement that could easily be attributed to the habitual ghoul-sniffing adopted over time by all servicemen—I manage to keep my response to a deferent nod. "Of course I would be honored to tell the First Admiral everything she wishes to know."

At her command, I launch into my account, careful to keep my story strictly in line with what I've told Mittag. No doubt she's watched every account of the events I've given since arriving on base. If even a single detail changes in this version, she'll know. The Admiral listens silently, nothing in her demeanor to give away what she might be thinking, until I get to the part about the relay station.

She pulls something from her pocket. "Is this the transceiver chip you found?"

My mouth goes dry as I behold the device in her hands. *The transceiver chip.* Comprehension hits me in a flash, and I could hit myself for being so deficient as to turn over the chip. Didn't Angelou tell me that anything I passed on would eventually make its way back to her?

Now, because of me, the one and only piece of evidence implicating her in the fall of R&D is wrapped up neatly in the palm of her hand.

Disgust fills me as I realize she's going to get away with *everything*—the tampering of the relay station, the fall of R&D, the deaths of every single one of those three thousand people on base—and the worst part of all is that there's nothing, *not a damn thing in the universe*, I can do about it.

I swallow once. "Yes, that's it."

"So what can you tell me about this chip?"

"Sir?"

"Surely you must have examined it to determine its function. What have you learned about it?"

Her blue eyes bore into mine with the intensity of a laser, and I suddenly realize: *She's testing me.* She knows the transceiver chip implicates her, but she has no idea if *I* know that.

My mind races back over my past week with Mittag, but to my relief, my memory quickly absolves me of all guilt in that area. After all, I had no idea who *"her"* was until the Admiral strode into the room sporting Angelou's eyes. *If she believes for even one second that I know what's on that chip . . .*

I give an apologetic shake of my head. "I'm afraid I don't really know anything about it. I'm just a soldier; this technology is beyond me. Chen and I only figured out what it did by checking the station archive. Dr. Angelou examined the transceiver chip briefly, but," I shrug with deliberate helplessness, "he didn't share his findings."

Something flashes in the Admiral's eyes, so quick I wouldn't have caught it if I weren't looking directly at her, and I inwardly snort. If anyone is conversant with Angelou's constant paranoia, it would be his daughter.

The Admiral grills me about the chip for several more minutes, dancing around but never quite touching on the real question of *who* was behind the device. What she makes of my answers, I have no idea, but at long last she breaks off her line of questioning and waves at me to continue my original account. I breeze through the rest of it as quickly as I can, gritting my teeth as I choke out those final events with the Fall, the mass infection, and Angelou's coma capsules, ending with my flight off Prism.

Story complete, my voice lapses into silence. After only a few hours with the Admiral, I'm wrung out, mentally and physically. Sweat coats my skin beneath my uniform, the wet drops only amplifying the chill in the room, and it's all I can do to keep from outright shivering. My muscles ache with the poisonous combination of cold and tension, and even my feelings for the Admiral have cooled, the fear and hatred solidifying into a hard knot in my stomach, like dry ice, burning and freezing at the same time. Immersed in misery, I sit and wait for the Admiral's next salvo. When it comes, it's like the final strike that takes down my shields.

"You were with him when he died, the Doctor."

Despite my better intentions, I bow my head. "Yes."

"Did he say anything in his last moments?" she says at last, as though it doesn't really matter if he did or not. Linking her hands behind her back, she strolls casually to the viewport, digitized to show a view of space though I suspect it's merely a one-way wall.

My chest tightens as I stare at her retreating back. There's something so *Angelou* in her deliberate carelessness, in the way she tilts her head and walks a room and clasps her hands, that I could almost forget who and what she is.

Murderer. Traitor. Collaborator.

Almost. Except that when I look into her eyes, I can't help but see the difference. For within the doctor's eyes had lain a softened brilliance that spoke of a deep-abiding humanity that welled up from within his very soul and could never be corrupted; whereas in the Admiral's eyes, all I see is a biting frost that goes on and on and never thaws.

"Say anything?" I repeat, momentarily at a loss for words.

Don't tell anyone you have the Archangel. Not even the colonel. If you tell him—if you tell anyone—it will get back to her.

I hesitate, uncertain of my answer. The knot in my stomach intensifies, burning both hotter and colder, and I realize: *I want to* hurt *her*. More than anything, I want to tell her the truth, the whole truth and nothing else. How he warned me against her with his dying breath, spitting out her pronoun like a curse, every fiber of his being focused only on hiding the truth from her eyes!

I inhale sharply, ready to tell her all, then—"He asked me to lead us to victory," I finally say. " 'Win this war for us, Sorenson.' Those were his dying words."

"I see."

Then without another word, she turns and walks out of the room.

I sit unmoving at the table, alone but for those two words hanging crisp and quiet in the chill air. I lied. Not out of mercy or some sort of misbegotten pity, but because the truth would have been a death sentence. Yet as I sit here contemplating her final words, somehow I can't help feeling that the lie hurt far worse than the truth ever could have.

43

I LET OUT A YELP as the bandages are ripped off my back in one fell swoop. The nurse attending me clucks sympathetically as she throws the old dressings—along with half the hair off my back—into the recycler.

"You did say 'fast,'" she points out with irritating condescension.

I grunt, not deigning to dignify that completely true assertion with a response. She merely laughs and begins dissolving the suture ointment off my back.

It's been over a week since my interview with the Admiral, and judging by the fact that I haven't been locked in a hole or brain-drained by PsyCorp, I can only assume I passed the interview. In the intervening time, I've had a few more sessions with Mittag, but they're less detailed, less intense, more like he's going through the motions than really grilling me for information. He even mentioned something about possibly having me reassigned, which I take for a good sign. Whatever conclusion the top brass has come to, apparently I'm not being held responsible.

The nurse continues her task, patiently spreading the cool solvent over each scar, then dabbing the suture away as it dissolves. Despite the persisting sting, her touch is soothing, the matter-of-fact ministrations a strange sort of comfort after the past few weeks. Against my will, my eyes start to prickle, even this indifferent comfort enough to make the inner pain flare up all over again.

I carried the shards of Sky Station Epsilon-065 around in my back for nineteen days after The Fall, unable to pull them out myself or obtain proper medical assistance during my flight from Prism. Once I arrived here, it took over three hours for the doctors to pull every last piece of shrapnel from my legs, back, and buttocks. I refused any anesthetic, passed out from the pain after the first half hour, and spent the final two and a half hours in blissful unconsciousness, only waking as they were rubbing in the suture oil that would slowly stitch up my wounds from the inside out. Or at least that's what they told me. Despite their promise, everything inside me still bleeds, and I don't think any amount of suture cream in the universe could ever staunch the flow.

Some burdens you never put down. You just find an easier way to carry them.

Chen's words echo in my head, a gift I don't deserve, though I keep it anyway. Her face flashes into my mind, and I wonder what will happen to her. Will the squatters down on Prism take care of her, tending to her empty body along with the rest of our people? Or will they simply leave them all to rot beneath the pastel mists and golden suns? I'll probably never know.

"All done," the nurse says with a final swipe. "Unfortunately, there is a bit of ointment left in your upper back where the suture cream fused with some of the deeper cuts. If we'd been able to get to them sooner, we might have prevented it—"

"It's fine," I interrupt. "Can I have my clothes back?"

As she goes to get them, I walk to the full-length mirror at the other end of the exam room. Turning my back to it, I awkwardly glance over my shoulder. The silvery ointment has fused into a feathered pattern over the mocha skin of my shoulder blades and upper back.

"My goodness! I didn't see it before, but that scar pattern almost looks like wings."

I flinch as if struck, grabbing my clothes from her hands and quickly pulling on my shirt. My gear is on and I'm heading for the door in under a minute. As I reach the exit, I pause for the barest moment.

"Only ghouls can fly."

Any response she might have made is swallowed up in the whoosh of the door behind me.

————

Back in the room I've been assigned to while on base, I activate my chit, hand practically shaking with anxiety as I cue up the link. In my weeks aboard Angelou's ship, I was never able to clear up the communications issue, whatever it might have been, and once I arrived here I was immediately put under a com blackout for security purposes. No links in, no links out. It was only as of this morning that the blackout was finally lifted. I can finally link my family to let them know I'm okay.

I can finally link Teal.

My foot twitches in my boot as I uplink to the interstellar array on base and wait for them to put the call through. While I'm forbidden to speak of classified matters—basically anything that's happened since I arrived on R&D—I'll take anything I can get, even if it's just a chance to hear her voice again. To tell her I'm sorry. That as angry as I was, as betrayed as I felt all those months, I still missed her.

That as much as I hated her, I never stopped loving her.

My chit beeps, three high-pitched pulses, and I frown as I read the message spooling over my hand.

Error: Unable to Establish a Connection

What the hell? It's the exact same message I received when trying to link her from Angelou's ship.

My heart lurches, fueled by an uneasiness some four weeks in the making. Could there be some sort of security field around the base, keeping anyone without special authorization from linking out? As an experiment, I try linking Gran. Over the past several weeks, she's left me half a dozen messages to call her, but between my issues with the ship's communications and my com blackout here I haven't had a chance to contact her. I uplink with the station's interstellar com system, then listen as the line rings, only now thinking to check the time. It's the middle of the night on New Sol. Damn! My timing's off, as usual. Still, at least I get a holo recording rather than an error message. I watch the recorded message hovering above my hand, and my anxiety turns to full-blown dread.

For a moment, I can't figure out what to do. Then with a shake of my head, I pull up the base directory and start hunting for Mittag's link number. Enough is enough. I've spent twelve days answering his endless questions again and again. The least he can do is help me make one link.

I try calling him first, then when he doesn't answer, search for his chit signature on the base map. He's in the Command Section, an area I'm definitely not cleared to enter. So I go to the next best place: the corridor leading to his quarters. He has to sleep sometime, right?

Five hours later, his lean form rounds the corner. He frowns when he catches sight of me, clearly not crazy about seeing me unless it's on the other end of an interrogation table. When I ask him about the com system, he shakes his head.

"I cleared you for interstellar communication myself," Mittag says. "If you can't get through, it would have to be some sort of technical issue on the receiving end. Most likely a temporary phenomenon, like solar flares or atmospheric interference. I'm sure it will be cleared up in due time if you keep trying periodically."

His words make perfect sense, but when I think of all those times I tried to link Teal from space, somehow the explanation doesn't add up.

"Please, sir," I beg as he starts to push past me. "I tried for days to make a connection before I even arrived here. I just—" My voice catches, and I cough once to clear it. "I just want to make one call."

The colonel sighs, but he finally relents. "All right, I'll see what I can find out." Activating his chit, he asks, "Name, planet, and link number?"

"Teal Sorenson, link number 098-A34-013-K112. Planet: Iolanthe."

The Colonel starts keying in the information, stopping when I say the planet name. "Iolanthe. You're sure she's there? Not home for a visit or on summer break?"

"Yes, sir. My parents both serve in the fleet, and my grandmother would have sent me an hmail if she'd gone home. Is there a problem?"

Mittag slowly de-acs his chit. A chill runs through me as I take in the look on his face. It's the look officers wear in one situation, and one situation alone: When they go to inform a family that their kin in the service has fallen. I shake my head, not wanting to hear, but he speaks anyway.

"I'm sorry, Team Leader. Iolanthe was hit by a mass ghoul invasion almost four weeks ago. By the time the fleet arrived, it was already too late. Iolanthe is under full planetary quarantine. There were no successful evacuees."

He briefly puts a hand on my shoulder, turns, and walks away. I stand stock still in the corridor, unable to do anything but listen as his words reverberate in my head.

Mass ghoul invasion.

Full planetary quarantine.

No successful evacuees.

I shake my head, unwilling to believe what I've just heard, but Mittag's cold tone left no room for doubt. And though he never came out and said it, still his meaning tolls as clearly as the wind whistling across the crystalline walls of R&D.

My sister is gone.

Something inside me ruptures, every loss, every pain, every trauma splintering through me in a rush of agony, and just like that, my final hope shatters, littered in shards at my feet as surely as R&D lies shattered across Prism while the bodies of those I love die a slow death inside.

Iolanthe
Four Weeks Earlier

SIRENS SPLIT THE AIR, WAILING through the dorm in a torrent of sound. I lurch to my feet, driven from sleep by a primal reaction kindled deep within my gut. Off-balance, I grab for the desk, steadying myself as I try to shake off the fog enough to identify the threat.

Depressurization? Fire? Core breach? My sleep-fogged brain scrambles for an explanation from out of the myriad drills I've been forced to undergo over my lifetime even as it quickly rejects them all.

"What's going on?!"

Divya's panicked voice cuts through the darkness, barely audible over the pounding of the alarms. I'm just about to tell her I have no idea when my palm vibrates. A holo surges up from my chit, shining brightly within the darkened room, and my heart stops.

Ghouls.

I stare at the force fence grid above my hand in disbelief. The outer fences along the eastern edge of the town are lit up like an asteroid field, red dots glowing menacingly around the blue-white structures of the spaceport.

My jaw drops. Impossible! Eight hundred and fifty thousand to one, and they choose the *one?* I shake my head, refusing to accept the evidence in front of my eyes. *Maybe it's just a few stray ghouls that somehow managed to stow away on a cargo freighter . . .*

But even as I think it, three more fences go up in scarlet, and I know: This is not a few along for a ride. This is a full-scale *invasion*.

Any vestige of sleepiness evaporates, driven from my system by a jolt of adrenaline straight to the heart. Steel hardens in my veins, and in an instant I'm up and moving, yelling at Divya to get up—*we've got ghouls!*—even as I lace on my boots and reach for the backpack in my closet. The sirens are loud enough to make my ears bleed, but I resist the urge to cover them so that I can grab the sniffer from my pack and pop it into my nose. My nostrils flare, revolting against the alien feel of cold, hard metal, but I ignore it, pushing it in tighter, making sure it's secure. I glance at the clock: 3:27 a.m. The ghouls couldn't have picked a better time to invade if they'd tried.

I pull up the town's force fence grid again and study it, checking the tripped fences for timestamps, calculating the shiver's speed and trajectory. Everything on the eastern edge is lit red. As I watch, fences start lighting up on the northern end of town as well. So they're sweeping in from the north and east. Good. With the school situated on the west edge, that gives me time. Not a lot of time, but enough.

I hope.

I minimize the grid but don't turn it off, letting it pool in a small circle of light across my palm. Pulling on my jacket and hat, I spare a quick glance at my roommate. She's huddled in the corner of her bed, clutching the sheet and whimpering like a malfunctioning clone-bot. I roll my eyes and dismiss her, already marking her as infected, dead, or both.

"Teal?" she chokes out as I reach the door, and I reluctantly pause.

"Ghouls, Divya!" I yell at her whimpering figure. "Move fast or die slow!"

"What do—" she starts to say, then the door shuts behind me and I'm gone.

Out in the halls it's pandemonium. Doors opening and closing; students stumbling out of their rooms half asleep, a few dressed but most not; scared voices mingling with pulsing alarms and panicked footsteps. A couple of staff members try to impose some sense of order on the rabble, calling for students to quiet down, to dress and line up in two rows as if this is some sort of deffin' fire drill!

My lip curls at the sight of them. Ghoul bait, all of them. By the time they're ready to move, it will be too late.

I shoulder my bag and push through the mob. An RA yells at me to stop, to line up, but I ignore her. There's a stairwell through the door at the end of the hallway that will give me a straight shot out of the building. From there, it's a short jog to the southwest academy gate, and from there the auxiliary spaceport. I don't know how many crafts they have available, but when the first ships take off, I intend to be on one. *Run or die.* With ghouls, there is no other option.

Two meters from the end of the hall, a door flies open in front of me. I jump back to avoid being smacked, surprise stinging me when the Queen Bitch herself appears.

"Move it, Djen!" Vida is yelling back into the room. "If you're not ready in ten seconds, I'm leaving you!"

She turns and almost runs into me, stopping short and backpedaling at the last second. For a moment, we eye each other, both of us not only dressed, but dressed to go outside. A messenger bag is slung over her shoulder, and in her nostrils I catch the dull gleam of a sniffer. I give her a grudging nod, my respect for her going up the smallest notch at the evidence of her quick thinking. After a heartbeat, Vida returns the gesture, apparently seeing in me the same thing she sees in herself.

A survivor.

"You have a plan?" she asks curtly, all past animosity temporarily shelved in the face of a greater threat.

A feral smile curls around my lips. For the first time since I was exiled to this misbegotten school on the edge of galaxy, I do have a plan. Not just a plan, but a purpose. I nod, eyes hard and heart harder.

"First, we run. Then, we *fight*."

ACKNOWLEDGMENTS

I would like to extend a sincere thank you to all the people who helped take *Archangel* from my mind to the shelf. My professional colleagues who have and continue to make this series possible: Betsy Wollheim, Matt Bialer, and the team at DAW Books. The intrepid readers who have provided much-appreciated critiques and support: Christine Berman, Joyce Alton, Carla Rehse, Diana Robicheaux, and Michelle Hauck. Last, but never least, my family: Douglas Fortune, Sharon Fortune, and Wendy Fortune. Your support and suggestions mean the universe to me.